SECRET BLOODLINES

Book I, The Hollywood Years

By June Latimer Jackson

This is a novel based on some true facts. All resemblance to persons living or dead is purely coincidental.

ISBN: 0-75963-089-5

This book is printed on acid free paper.

1stBooks - rev. 8/16/01

Acknowledgements

Arthur and Margie Elkins, my benefactors and loyal friends who believed in me.

Ruth Jean Cole, patron of the arts and literary endeavor.

Cheryl Jones Latimer, my supportive daughter, with weekly encouragement.

Tammie Hope, dear granddaughter, studying to be a doctor, emails me weekly encouragement.

Daryl Jones, grandson, law school student who encourages me.

Robert Brott, Esq., my faithful and loyal attorney.

Reda Schlossberg, who years ago one winter in Arizona told me, "You will write a best seller." This was when we stayed at her home for two weeks.

Honorable William and Helen Fall, both deceased, distant cousins from North Yorkshire Moors. Bill, an author himself, said in 1985 on my last visit, "Keep working on your books." He knew the struggles of writers everywhere.

Christina Jones Wright, my very supportive daughter. Always there for me.

Paul Lippman, my long-suffering editor.

Jean Greene, who typed my tapes and lived my story with me.

Therese Ann Hiester, writers' assistant and computer operator.

Julie A. McCarter Brock, computer technician.

Gladys Tabor, famous author who years ago encouraged me to write.

Gertrude Foster, also famous author who believed in me.

Beatrix Potter, my mentor in spirit.

Dr. Mark Elliott, Dr. Changxin Li and Dr. C. R. Charles.

Steve M. Cole, Computer Engineer and great technical advisor.

Elaine and Larry Failing and Family, so helpful, so kind.

The following people were invaluable technical advisors and loyal supporters:

Dr. Freddie Bass, Jeff Brake, Jim Brake, Gloria Burke, Mary Jo Cole, Suzanne Cole, Margaret Comfort, Carl Deal, William Greenleaf, David Lawson, Bill Mueller, Laura Jo Mueller, Jocasta Murray, Betty Myers, Amy Sue Rabb, Craig Schwabe, Sheila Schwabe, Carla Whitehead, Patty Yurgaites and Keifer Yurgaites, Mary, our Postmaster, Bud Palin, Photographer.

Table of Contents

Table of Illustrations

Prologue

1300 - 1919 A.D.

It was on a Tuesday just after the highest sun of the noon hour when Earl Edward S. Worthington rode along the rocky path on his Shire. He was close now, and knew he should make his home in northern England before sunset. The huge war-horse picked its way along the path with heavily feathered legs that now swung forward toward a destination it knew so well. The Earl had liked the horse ever since he had inherited it as part of his father's estate two years earlier. He had a fondness for this noble bay stallion with a marking shaped like a white spear point down the center of its face. The Earl put a steel clad hand on the withers and gave his trusty animal a couple of well-deserved pats. This was instantly answered with a surprisingly soft nicker from the great horse.

The armor the Earl was wearing was cumbersome but necessary in this time of tension in that part of the realm, due to the revolts in Scotland.

His mind wandered as he thought of his son, who was to marry in two days. The dowry had been impressive and it cemented an important alliance. His son's new father-in-law would now add his strength to the defense of the northern border. He was pleased with himself and wondered what their children might be like. Would they have a son to carry on the Worthington name? Would this grandson also be a nobleman and warrior, as he was? In another generation would a Worthington still be a hereditary ruler of the country?

On a Tuesday, sixteen Worthington family generations later, an event would come to pass along the shore of the Detroit River in the United States of America. Near this surging mass where it is quickened by a lake in a great chain of flowing blue liquid, the same sun that warmed the Earl on that cool fall day would set again over seven hundred years hence. The virgin White Pine that grew along the water's edge during the Earl's life time would be but a memory then, and in their place the large metropolis of Detroit would have been built.

The Earl Edward on his way to the wedding party could never have guessed that a direct descendant of his, Winston Chandler Worthington, would attend a party of his own in a place called Detroit, thus setting into motion a chain of events that would create a secret bloodline. The fabric of this bloodline also would be woven from the fortunes of another family whose shield would bear a gold cross on a crimson background, the crest of Latimer. This dynasty would start building a castle in another part of England in 1300 AD, when the Earl's first grandson was to be four years old.

Hence, the Latimer dynasty continued.

Figure 1 Alsace Lorraine, France, 1890

I - Mister X

"In The Beginning"

1919

My name is Lily. My story begins with an episode in my Mother Florence's life which explains the circumstances that gave me impetus to write *Secret Bloodlines.* It all started one Tuesday afternoon, two decades into the twentieth century when Florence's family received an engraved invitation to a very exclusive party in Detroit.

Florence's only brother, Robert Edward Jackson, was an automotive engineer with fresh ideas for automobile design, whom Henry Ford had hired away from a large Canadian firm. Robert wanted to show his family the exciting world of the Detroit automakers of 1919.

A banquet and ball was being sponsored by these automakers at the prominent Book Cadillac Hotel. Robert and his wife, Osa, were invited, as were his sisters, Florence and Grace, and their mother, Harriett Latimer-Jackson.

Winston Chandler Worthington was their host, and during the evening Chandler talked to both Robert and his family about his life in the auto industry, mainly about how Robert had helped design wheels for some of his vehicles. Neither Florence, Grace nor Harriett had realized just how important Robert was in the auto industry.

Chandler could not help but notice Harriett's youngest daughter, Florence, with her strawberry blonde curls cascading below her shoulders and framing a face of profound innocence. Chandler guessed she was about eighteen years old. This brought back memories of his youth and a longing to be younger. Chandler started a conversation with Florence which lasted through the remainder of dinner.

Shortly after dinner the men retired to the smoking room for cigars and brandy. Harriett, Grace, Florence and Osa then went to the powder room, where Florence found herself among women of high society discussing social topics and Paris fashions. She was mesmerized by the elegance surrounding her and their host Chandler, a strikingly handsome man. A few minutes later they headed to their reserved table by the main ballroom. As they approached the table, Robert was talking to Chandler and Grace's husband, Stanley Gilbert. The musicians were softly tuning their instruments, focusing their attention on the director.

Chandler asked Harriett if he might dance with Florence. Florence was quietly elated when her mother gave her approval. When the music began, it was announced there would be two consecutive waltzes, the Blue Danube and the Emperor Waltz. Grace had started dancing with Stanley. Robert and Osa joined them on the dance floor. Florence blushed vividly when Chandler took her hand and led her to the dance floor.

The waltz was the only dance step Florence knew. Her brother had taught her at a church party just a month before. Almost everything Florence experienced that night was a first. It was an adventure wrapped in splendor. As they danced under the massive crystal chandeliers sparkling overhead, Florence feeling the firm hand of Chandler around her waist, decided she wanted to live her entire life with the rich. The opulence of the ballroom, the gorgeous gowns and beautiful jewelry made Florence feel this was what she had been waiting for all her life. Her face flushed pink as Chandler held her tightly to his body while dancing.

The ball had ended far too soon for Florence, but later, as she was getting into Robert's car, Chandler called out, "I'll be in touch with you in a few days."

Chandler, true to his word, contacted Florence a few days later, and they started seeing each other intermittently, because Chandler was not always in Detroit where Florence was training to be a Red Cross Nurse. Robert said Chandler had business elsewhere. Throughout that spring and summer, Chandler would take Florence and Grace on trips, also Mother Harriett when she was able. One time they boarded a yacht going out on the Detroit River, and on their way back Chandler said he wanted to take Florence to Windsor, Canada. He promised her another ball, just as beautiful as where they had first met.

Chandler was generous and seemed to genuinely love the family. Of course, since he was so much older than either Florence or Grace, no one thought anything about this handsome middle age gentleman taking out these young ladies.

A few times Grace and her mother were unable to go with Florence and Chandler, so to keep from disappointing Florence, Harriett allowed her to go with Chandler unattended. By this time Florence felt very close to Chandler. He was, after all, a wealthy gentleman from a fine family. Unfortunately, Florence was unaware that Chandler was fifty-two years old and twice divorced.

Robert, Harriett's only son, had become the head of their household when his father died in 1904 from peritonitis following an appendectomy. At only fourteen, he helped his mother run their general store in Toronto. Later they moved to St. Catherine's where they opened another general store. All these years he had shielded his mother and sisters and was ever watchful over Florence. But he trusted Chandler, his good friend.

Florence began working at the Women's Lying-in Hospital in Detroit, a hospital generally for mothers giving birth. Through 1919 there were extra duties added due to the soldiers who had been seriously injured by mustard gas in World War I.

Seeing Chandler was the one thing in Florence's life that truly made her happy, and Grace began to suspect that Florence was feeling a little too close to Chandler. So she said to Florence one evening, "Really, dear, you should look for someone more your own age."

Mother Harriett agreed.

"But I can talk to him," Florence replied. "He understands me."

Later that same evening Robert and Osa came over and along with Grace's husband Stanley, the five of them decided that the relationship between Florence and Chandler had grown too serious. However, when they confronted Florence with their fears, Florence could not understand why they were so worried. Robert then began to feel a little foolish and decided to drop the matter.

Several weeks had passed and no one had heard from Chandler, so Florence grew quietly concerned. Robert felt a little perturbed. After all, Chandler was his closest friend.

Still later, poor Florence, the beautiful idealistic girl who was staying with her mother, found herself in a profound state of fright and confusion — she believed she was pregnant. What was she to do? In those days, one had to go to a doctor for the old-fashioned rabbit test for pregnancy, and the taboos of 1919 were like another world compared to today. So she sobbed in her room, afraid to tell anyone. Days passed into weeks, and she alternated between living at Mother Harriett's in Saint Catherines, Ontario, Canada, and Robert or Grace's home in Detroit.

Finally one weekend they were all at Mother Harriett's, where the Latimer-Jacksons and Gilberts had a big dinner. After dinner Florence wasn't feeling so well and excused herself to go to her room. After clearing the table, her sister noticed Florence still hadn't come out, and this was completely unlike her. While she hated to do dishes, she still helped.

Finishing dishes, Grace walked into Florence's bedroom, where she found her crying. In hushed tones, Florence divulged her secret. She was afraid she was pregnant. Upon hearing this, Grace was in a state of shock! Such a disgrace as this had never happened in their family.

Still, she grabbed her sister, hugged her and said, "Oh, no, you must be wrong. We'll go to Uncle Robert."

Uncle Robert, the brother of their late father, Walter Jackson, was a physician.

Grace added, "We'll call him, and we have to talk this over with Stanley, too. He'll know what to do. How can we ever tell Robert? He's the one who introduced you to Chandler."

They continued lying on the bed, whispering, in an effort to find a way out.

Finally, tapping on the bedroom door, Stanley asked, "Is Florence better? Come on out and join the family at the radio. We finally got it to work. I put some copper wire over to the window. And later Mother is going to play the piano. She has the new sheet music, you know."

"We'll be out soon," Grace replied. They opened the door after Florence tried to fix her face, combed her hair and put a little rouge on her cheeks.

The minute Harriett saw her daughter, she said, "What's wrong, are you ill?"

As she walked into the kitchen Florence said, "I think something I ate disagreed with me. I'd better take some baking soda and water. I have terrible heartburn."

This was a Friday night and they were all staying over for the weekend.

The next morning, Grace told her husband the terrible news, and Stanley said, "I'll handle it. I'll talk to Robert outside."

He said that they were going to do some work for Mother in the yard. The men were outside; and in the meantime, no one else knew of this except Florence and Grace, who were in the dining room drinking tea and peeking out the window while all of this was occurring.

Mother Harriett Latimer was knitting one of the Afghans she made every year for someone, and her hands moved quickly as she asked, "Why is everyone so quiet?"

It was difficult for Florence and Grace, but they did discuss other things, like what flowers she planned to cover up that winter, because summer was fading fast.

About this time, Robert and William Stanley headed for the house, walking briskly through into the living room, where Robert announced, "We all have to have a family talk. Would everyone please come into the parlor."

Figure 2 Me and my wonderful Steiff bear, 1925

The parlor was for baptisms, showing off a new baby, a funeral, or some serious family discussion. This qualified as the latter, in no small way. The women followed the men, walking right past the dusty pipe organ without even noticing it, an otherwise unheard of action on their part.

They moved into this musty room and sat down somberly, all except Robert, who said, "We have a serious family crisis."

Florence bent forward on her chair and was sobbing.

Robert walked over, put his arm around her and said, "It's all right."

Harriett looked up and asked, "What is this? What is wrong, Robert?"

"Florence has been wronged," he answered bluntly.

Harriett's eyes grew wide, she looked very serious and frightened.

"What do you mean, *wronged?*"

Then she turned to Florence.

"What is it, child?"

In a tearful voice Florence said, "I know I did a terrible thing, and I've gone to the priest."

She clutched her rosary. "I've said all my Hail Mary's, and I can't say it, Mother, but I, I'm in trouble."

The women quickly retired to the bedroom. The men huddled, looking out the window, each wondering what his next move would be to save Florence.

Mother Harriett sobbed and cried, as they all did together. Now sixty-five and widowed when Florence was only five years old, she found herself with a nineteen-year-old daughter carrying an illegitimate child.

Several hours passed before Harriett rejoined the family. Then she said, "I haven't raised my children this way, I must have done something wrong. This is a terrible scandal against our family. We're Latimers, we're Jacksons!"

Mother Harriett Latimer was a direct descendent with a title in the Latimer line from North Yorkshire, England. The Latimer name was Norman (LeLatimer), originally from France, but their ancestors were Ladies and Barons in England, too. Mister Jackson had woolen mills in Doncaster, England, and lace mills in Belfast, Ireland. This was not just *any* family, this was a family of breeding and honor, who were very loyal to each other. This particular tragedy, however, began to tear at the threads that had bonded them.

After discussing this, the family decided to call Chandler. Robert located him and brought Stanley with him to an arranged meeting in a restaurant. It must have been a very strained meeting for both Chandler and Robert, but Chandler talked to them and apologized. He said he had never meant for any of this to happen, but that he dearly loved Florence and would be willing to "post bans" with the local priest in Canada, registering intent to marry. He said he would have a problem with his family, as they wanted him to marry someone closer to his own age, but he would try and convince them.

As Chandler started to leave, he said to Stanley, "Would you excuse Robert and me for a minute?"

They walked some distance to the door, then Chandler turned, with his back to Stanley, and handed Robert an envelope. "I hope this will help — please give this to Florence," he said.

Robert slipped the envelope into his inner coat pocket. Chandler then turned and walked away. Robert felt numb as he walked slowly back to the table. Stanley studied his stern face, then said, "I honestly don't think Chandler gives a damn about the situation."

Robert hadn't sat down and didn't answer. He just stared off across the restaurant, seeming not to hear Stanley.

Finally he said, "Chandler said he might be able to post bans for marriage in Canada."

"I sincerely hope he meant that, Robert."

Robert took out the envelope Chandler had given him for Florence, and opened it as Stanley watched. Inside were ten fifty-dollar bills.

Robert and Stanley returned to Mother Harriett's home, where Robert told Florence and the family about the meeting with Chandler. Florence was excited when she heard what Chandler had said about posting marriage bans. The rest of the family did not feel as excited. They felt Chandler suddenly seemed to not be the trustworthy friend they had believed him to be.

Robert gave Florence the envelope with the money, and Florence said, "See, Robert, he must love me!"

The next day Florence went down-town and bought herself a little marriage booklet. She slept with it under her pillow every night, dreaming of the time when Chandler would come after her.

It never happened. Florence had to stay with her mother in Canada, and she helped run the store until it became too obvious that she was pregnant. In those days, this was a terrible disgrace. For months she prayed that her knight, Chandler, would reappear. He did not. He became an unspoken reference in the extended family except for the synonym, "Mister X."

Florence and Mother Harriett then visited Grace and Stanley in Detroit, and they felt that she should move back to Detroit. They believed the medical care in the hospital where she had been working was better.

Grace planned the trip to Detroit. She and Osa wanted to buy a few things to help Florence move into a home they had leased on Pasadena Avenue. Mother Harriett moved in with her.

Fire broke out, and it must have been fairly late because Florence was in her nightdress when smoke was discovered. It would appear that the fire, smoke and commotion so frightened Florence that they had to rush her to the Women's

Lying-in Hospital (This is Hutzel Hospital now, a teaching hospital and part of Wayne State University in Detroit). It was there that Florence went into labor.

Figure 2A Lily on her first Birthday

Figure 3 Mystery man holding me.

II - LILY

junio de 1920

I, Lily, was born to Florence on June 6, 1920, in the very hospital where Florence had been capped as a Red Cross nurse.

They said I was a very tiny baby. I was told later by Aunt Grace that while pregnant, Florence refused to eat big meals. She did eat a lot of fruit. She figured if she didn't eat as much she wouldn't get fat. But it wasn't fat that made her abdomen big.

Aunt Grace said, "Thank heavens, though, she loved corn bread, potatoes and poached eggs."

She had stopped eating all sweets, even her favorite chocolate covered cherries and maple nut fudge.

She was now in a hospital with this wee infant that weighed two pounds, thirteen ounces and would be in the hospital nursery four weeks because she was so small. In 1920 they didn't have all the modern equipment for saving an infant of that size. I believe God wanted me to live, because there was a mission He wanted me to carry out. Aunt Grace said that the nurses and doctors said I was the smallest baby to survive in their hospital.

Doctor Lincoln, the delivering physician, had gone back home to fix up a small wooden apple crate, and he put me inside of this on a folded horse blanket covered with a flannel cloth. Around the top edges of this box were light bulbs which gave out warmth for this make-shift incubator. I believe that this is why I have always hated hot weather and bright light. Doctor Lincoln made this little contraption in which I stayed fourteen days, Grace would recall.

Florence's breast milk was put into a little bottle, but I became allergic to her milk, so Doctor Lincoln created a formula of goat's milk, water and, I understand, a drop of brandy and honey. Well, what concoction indeed! They fed me this mixture with an eyedropper. Doctor Lincoln said I was actually too small and not strong enough to suck on the breast. I really have a debt of gratitude owed to Dr. Lincoln.

Aunt Grace also said that Dr. Lincoln was very proud of my survival. He told her that any infant who would fight this hard to live, yet enter the world without a father surely deserved every chance she could get; and goat's milk was one of the best foods. He based this opinion on the fact that he raised goats, drank goat's milk himself and gave some to his juvenile patients with Rickets, in which he noted improvement.

I saw and talked with Doctor Lincoln at age fifteen when Mother Clara took me up to show me off to him. He seemed happy to see me, but after asking me what my hobbies were, my school grades, and did I go to church, he asked me to leave the room while he talked to my mother. I have often wondered why he would need to talk to her in private, but in those days you didn't question your parents.

Now known as Hutzel Hospital, this hospital has a picture of me with a teacup on my head, according to Aunt Grace. The hospital is supposed to have a cigar box some of the nurses padded, in which I was photographed. This was supposed to have been placed in the archives of the Women's Lying-in Hospital and I have desperately tried to get a copy of that picture.

During a telephone call I placed from California a few years ago asking about this photograph, they transferred my call to the hospital security division, then put me on hold so long that I finally had to hang up. In July of 1996, my physician, Reed K. Freidinger, sent a letter to Hutzel Hospital asking for information. They requested that I give my mother's name at the time of birth, plus a copy of my birth certificate. We complied with their request and sent a copy of the original birth certificate. In August, Hutzel Hospital sent me a letter saying, "We no longer have medical records that date back to 1920."

I called and wrote the Editorial Office of the Detroit News in August telling them I had a newsworthy question. The question was, "What happened to the hospital records of the smallest baby to survive at Hutzel Hospital (Women's Lying-in Hospital) in 1920?" As of this writing, I have heard nothing from anyone.

Aunt Grace said that when Florence came home from the hospital, it was difficult for her because of how society viewed illegitimate births in those days. There was so much of a stigma connected with unwed mothers. Her friends no longer talked to her and when they saw her walking down a sidewalk they would cross the street to avoid her. Often she would cry and wonder why nothing was ever heard from Chandler. She had been so sure that Chandler was going to marry her. Grace said Florence felt so ashamed she rarely spoke to anyone anymore. After eight weeks, Grace said, carrying me around on a pillow and hand feeding me with an eyedropper, plus all of the tension she felt, was too much for her.

They found a family willing to take me in — the lady's name was Lottie. My Uncle Robert and Grandmother Harriett Latimer paid the cost. Lottie continued to feed me with an eyedropper for several weeks. Lottie had six children who would push me in a baby buggy, back and forth, to keep me from crying. During one visit from Grandmother Harriett and Aunt Grace, they witnessed these children violently pushing my buggy and they became fearful, so then decided to find a better home for me.

Not too much time passed before one of the nurses in the hospital heard about a lady who had lost her baby. In fact, there were two women who had this tragedy occur that same week. Grace and Florence went to see if one of these two ladies, Gusty or Clara, would be able to care for a very small infant. Gusty declined, but Clara said she would love to.

Arrangements were made and Clara agreed that this baby could stay temporarily with her. This was an agreement between Florence and Clara. In time Florence divulged to Clara some of her dreams and family secrets, saying she was waiting to see if Chandler would come back.

After much waiting and several different meetings in Canada between Chandler, Stanley, Grace, Florence and Clara, with young Lily in tow, it finally was obvious there would never be a marriage between Chandler and Florence. He had already married someone else, a rich Southern widow. Money married money.

"As time went by, Clara became extremely attached to you," Grace continued. "She asked Florence to consider letting her and her husband, Walter, adopt you. Florence talked to her family, and they were totally against the adoption. But Florence said, 'Well, I don't care! That's what I'm going to do!'"

Florence had changed a great deal after meeting Chandler. She had become headstrong, opinionated and determined that she would lead an unburdened and hopefully affluent life. I remember Grace and Stanley telling me, "Florence always did what she wanted."

They arranged for the adoption to occur soon. Florence was eager for this to happen, as she had met a wonderful man named Roy Levant from a good family. She said that the fact he had a very lovely home on the water didn't hurt anything either. Roy had asked Florence to marry him, but Roy's mother was not in favor of this wedding. She said she did not want her son to marry a woman with a "bastard child" Her added remark was, "A child like that is nothing but a bad seed!"

Roy talked to Florence and Clara and they all conspired to solve this big problem. Florence and Roy became engaged upon the condition that I would be adopted, Grace learned later. Walter and Clara adopted me in 1923. In 1924, Florence and Roy were married.

In the adoption, Walter and Clara changed my first name to Lily, which terribly upset the family, excluding Florence. I think, to get the adoption through, Florence would have done almost anything.

I remember vividly that until I was eight, we had many secret meetings with "Santa", or as they also called him, "Mister X". I later learned that Mister X was indeed Chandler Worthington, who arranged clandestine meetings over the years.

Sometimes they would meet at the Prince Albert Hotel in Windsor, Canada; and it was really fun for me, because, as I got older, I realized that every time we went to a hotel to visit Mister X, I would receive presents and clothes galore. This gentleman we called Mister X was very kind to me. I have many happy memories of him. I recall, on one occasion, we were on our way all dressed up and I was wearing a beautiful bonnet. My mother, Clara, put Vaseline on my patent leather shoes and polished them to a high gloss. She said, "You have to look your best and you have to act your best so Mister X will give you more presents."

Growing up, I knew Clara as my mother. I was told that Florence and Grace were my aunts and that Harriett was "one of my grandmothers." Years would pass before I learned the whole truth.

Once we were on our way to Windsor, Canada, via a large ferryboat and stayed overnight. I was about five years old and remember holding on to a railing. There was a strong wind blowing in my face and I remember seeing white caps on the water. Aunt Florence, Mother Clara and I always went on those trips. We stayed at a big hotel. I remember the dining room where we had lunch and dinner. There were high booths of walnut, with highly ornate carvings. I ran my fingers over the handcarved wood in the booths and remember the feeling that those high-backed booths were our secret hideaway. I was brought up with Damask tablecloths, good silver and fine china dishes. I have always appreciated these things because they always reminded me of my father.

I recall other times at a table with beautiful silver and china. The waiters wore snow white cloth napkins over one of their wrists and everything looked so elegant to me as a child. I was happy there during those visits because whenever we met Mister X he always gave me presents. He made sure he ordered me the food that we both liked. I knew that I liked him, but I also knew that he liked me, too. He was kind to me and he was fun to be with because he would do things like fold my napkin to make a crown and put it on my head.

I remember when he did this one time, he said, "I knew you were a princess."

I know I always ate well, and I remember the mashed potatoes and gravy. I have loved them ever since. One thing that was strange was whenever I was at home and not meeting with Mister X, I was the last consideration. I was told to be seen and not heard. But when we would go on these meetings with Mister X, I was encouraged to be the center of attention. I knew Mister X was treating me as a loved member of the family. Once a child has been introduced to an admiring and loving acceptance, it remains in his or her memory forever. My greatest desire, as a child, was to have Mister X pay attention to me, and, should I add, never, ever leave ...

When we had these meetings, my mother and Aunt Florence would have me sit next to him so I would be close during the dinner. On one of these occasions, it had been raining. I don't remember where we had been, but I was in his arms when we entered the hotel lobby. I remember touching the collar on his coat. It was fur, and to this day, I can still feel those soft hairs of his fur collar against my hand. Whenever I touch anything with fur, I think of Mister X that day, and the many other times at the Prince Albert Hotel. It's interesting how these connections have stayed with me all those years. Just like when I eat Brussels sprouts, or lamb chops, I think of him, as well as his softly patting my back when he would carry me.

One time he ordered froglegs for dinner. My mother and Aunt Florence ordered chicken. As he was eating the froglegs, he leaned over and said to me, "Lily, do you think you might like to taste the froglegs?"

"Oh, I think I could do that. What do they taste like?"

"Like your chicken," he replied.

"Well, then, I'd like very much to try a bite."

He watched me take a bite and then he asked me if I liked it.

"Yes, I do, it's like chicken." He smiled. "I knew you would like froglegs, because you are so much like me." He winked.

I always loved mashed potatoes and gravy, which apparently was his favorite, too, because he had double helpings. He always used his spoon to make two depressions in the middle of the mashed potatoes, then filled these with gravy. To this day, I make the same little holes in the middle filled with gravy, just like he did on my plate that night in the Prince Albert Hotel. On every trip I was given beautifully wrapped boxes containing elegant hats with long satin ribbons, a beautiful fur coat on more than one occasion, fur muffs, fur and silk hats, and many other presents. I would lay them on the floor, tear the tissue paper and dance around full of happiness.

This feeling of joy, the knowledge that I felt secure that the world around me was right, was not primarily because it was pleasurable, but because I have seldom experienced this feeling of safety that I did when near Mister X.

On one occasion the dining room seemed very secluded because it was a private room. The French doors were closed, separating us from the main dining room. I remember the man with the napkin over his arm closing the double doors so we had this part all to ourselves. I put the fur coat on, held my muff and danced around this dining room. Mister X gave me beautiful presents. One time there was a funny little fur covered toy monkey. He looked like the monkeys that used to sit on the organ grinder's shoulder in Detroit. He had a cute little red hat that looked like the bellboy's hat at the Prince Albert. I had him for years.

I always got jewelry. I had so many shoes from these visits that Mother had a special shelf built into my closet.

But this time, I think the most memorable thing was the froglegs, and his fixing my mashed potatoes like he did, and Brussels sprouts he'd feed me from a toothpick. A youngster remembers the special little things that are done.

He asked, "How do you like Brussels sprouts?"

"It tastes like cabbage."

He said, "Yes, it does, and it's good for you."

Imagine a little girl liking Brussels sprouts! I remember that my earliest recollection of the Prince Albert Hotel was when I was about five. I remembered Mother and Aunt Florence telling me over and over, years later, all these stories, but after age eight I don't remember seeing Mister X ever again. I used to cry and ask why we didn't go to the Prince Albert to see Mister X anymore. Even as a child, I knew that he had made the effort to come to see me for years. Then he stopped, with never a word. Several times I had asked Aunt Florence and Mother Clara why we never saw Mister X any longer. Finally, after many years had passed, Florence said Mister X had died in an automobile accident when I was nine years old.

A few years later Aunt Grace told me a little more about Mister X and his friendship with the family. She said that we did not have the kind of wealth that he had, but she said that she was happy that I had a chance in life, that I lived. That's the best gift of all. Many years would pass before I learned Mister X's identity and the fact that he was my father.

Fixing his little girl's mashed potatoes in a special way, just because he couldn't resist it, was love. I knew I felt love in that instant. Winston Chandler Worthington showed me, in many ways, that he loved me. A child knows. Unfortunately, a child knows if they are not loved, too.

It was only just after my mother, Florence, took ill and passed away that Aunt Grace sat down and told me the whole truth about my real father. I was sure of his actual name when Florence once wrote in a letter to me: "Winston Chandler Worthington, I don't ever want to hear his name again!" I was threatened repeatedly by "Aunt" Florence, that if I searched for my real father, I would be cut out of her will, and she made good on that threat.

It was in the early 1970's that a letter about Winston Chandler Worthington was sent to Col. James and Ruth McNevin, who were friends of mine. They called me to come over and get the letter, which was in response to their letter to Florence, as I had asked them to write.

Florence finally wrote, "Yes, Lily, Mister X was your father. He was Winston Chandler Worthington."

Whenever we would mention Mister X, or Chandler, Florence would become very angry. There was a lot of bitterness felt about this subject in our family. The solidarity of our extended family started to crack when blood relatives were not allowed to adopt me. It was always a forbidden subject, and getting any information out of any of the family members was like cracking a bank's safe.

After my mother died, I got the rest of the documents that prove who I am. I received this, along with a few trinkets, but Florence made sure the bulk of her estate went to Cousin Norman and Uncle Roy's family.

God had to have a reason for me to survive. Maybe it was only my will to live, maybe God had a plan for this child that so many people deserted and didn't want. Possibly there was a plan, after all? You see, we're all here for a reason and I know what mine is. Mine is to make people happy, if I can.

Mister X gave me a baby coat of rabbit fur with tiny little ermine tails around the collar. I only have the ermine tails of the bunny coat left. Time is a destroyer, but not entirely successful! I still have the seal muff and wonderful memories.

I have often wondered what it would have been like to have been the legitimate daughter of Winston Chandler Worthington instead of the illegitimate daughter. Now at seventy-eight years of age, the fact I never met my half brothers and sisters hurts me deeply. Yet, some of them are alive today. They would be close to my age. Aunt Grace said he had a child soon after he was married.

There is nothing I want that they have. I just want them to recognize me for who I am. I want the story told for the simple reason that I think most children who are adopted have the right to know, if they wish to know. If families were to pull together, working instead to raise babies, praying for strength rather than separating the child from its bloodlines, maybe I have accomplished something. I strongly believe that we are what our genes are, and that these are our personal road map through life. Our genes determine our behavior, our physical makeup, as well as, to an extent, our psychological self. Of course, a loving home and caring parents add to this. But knowledge of the source of these genes should not be denied a child.

I have been a staunch genealogist most of my life. I began to take a strong interest in genealogy when I was in my twenties. I started remembering innuendoes, or seemingly insignificant remarks, while listening to my relatives. My Uncle, Harry Baines, who was in the British intelligence, said that he did the same thing years ago. He said that many little pieces that, by themselves don't look like anything, often form a picture when combined. It's taken many years to get the facts.

Until I was eighteen I didn't learn of my adoption. I really didn't know too much then about my own father, only his name, and my childhood memories. I remember his face, because I saw him from the time I was a toddler until I was eight years old.

Those are small things, but they are things that remind me of my father. I think his eyes were brown, because I know that they were darker than mine were. Mine are green, and my mother's were blue.

I remember him saying, "You're as pretty as your mother."

That's the only thing I ever remember him saying about Florence. Mother Clara, who adopted me when I was three, was always with us, and sometimes Grace. Robert was never at any of these gatherings. I suppose Robert always had a feeling of guilt, and terrible disappointment in Chandler, and blamed himself for my mother getting in trouble.

I only remember the good about my father. He was always nice, he had big strong hands, and I remember he squeezed my hand when I put my new gloves on that he gave me. He said, "Now you really *are* a princess."

So, there was something loving and kind in this man whom everybody seemed to hate because he abandoned me. But he had family commitments from a very wealthy family, who certainly were not a bit interested in having him marry a little nobody Red Cross nurse from Canada. Little did they know, however, that this Red Cross nurse's ancestors were very rich and powerful people!

Figure 4 Me in buggy

Figure 5 Me with Great Uncle Jack's farm wagon, Sebewaing, Michigan, about 1926.

III - Hubbard Lake

1925-1927

The family was planning a trip to see the land that Grandpa bought in Hubbard Lake, Michigan, from Mister McCoy. Grandpa was planning to sell some as waterfront lots, build a cottage, and later a lodge called Tanglewood. Mister McCoy arranged to have a cabin built using Grandpa and Richard's ideas. The cabin would sleep six.

We all gathered at Grandma and Grandpa's house to hear the letter from Mister McCoy. The kitchen had a hand pump on the sink, and we'd use kerosene lamps until the electricity came into that area. The letter went on to say it had a new outhouse, not far from the cabin, a "three-holer," the words "three-holer" underlined.

Immediately plans were made to go there, but Uncle Richard had a photo shoot to do, so he followed the next day. He was a professional photographer, and a tool and die designer for Packard, Ford and General Motors.

There were suitcases all over the place. Richard was trying to figure out where to put them.

Richard said, "We can't use the Sunday car." (This is what we affectionately called our 1924 Packard). "We'll definitely have to use the big car."

This was a boxy 1919 Dodge with quite a bit of room inside and could have many items strapped on the outside such as the ten-gallon water bag Uncle Richard hung there. Grandma Weigmann said it looked terrible. The old Dodge had a jump seat behind the driver's seat. The back seat had heavy velvet loops to hang on to. I have a cute picture they took of me, framed by those big headlights of the Dodge.

Figure 6 Uncle Richard driving 1916 car, wearing goggles.

It really looked to me like we were going on a long expedition. Many suitcases went inside, with two under my feet. Then there were three atop the car roof and two in the trunk behind the rear spare tire.

Richard said, "Goodbye," and we were all ready to go. Nuzzie, our chauffeur who came over from Germany with Grandpa, drove, with Grandpa next to him. Mother, Grandma and I were in the back. Grandpa was wearing leggings and hiking boots and had a walking stick leaning against his seat; he looked like Teddy Roosevelt when he went into the wilds.

Then off the clan went to the newly discovered lake in the North Michigan woods. We did stay a night at Aunt Anna's in Sebewaing. Great Aunt Anna served wonderful food, and big fresh-picked wild blueberry, elderberry and apple pies.

I enjoyed visiting Aunt Anna's sugar beet farm, where they also grew vegetables and many fruit trees. They had horses named Nancy and Jack, a cow named Betty, and fifty chickens I loved.

Arriving at the farm, we got our things into our rooms; and, of course, a big meal was fixed. They went out, killed chickens, plucked them, washed them at the spring and brought them in to be introduced to Aunt Katy's and Aunt Anna's secret recipe. Let me tell you, that fried chicken was cause to smack your lips! Of course, they used lard to fry in — they rendered fat from their own hogs. I'm sure there was lots of cholesterol in that chicken, but those people lived to be in their eighties and nineties.

We ate this wonderful country dinner of creamed cauliflower, big slices of beefsteak tomatoes, mashed potatoes, chicken and gravy. They thought nothing of making four cakes and four pies. I helped mix the piecrust, Mother rolled it out, and Grandma and Aunt Katy filled it with fresh sliced apples. They put cinnamon, sugar and streusel on top, and we made four big coffeecakes, as well. They used wood-fired ovens to bake them all. Everything smelled and tasted so good no one minded the work.

The other great thing about the farm, was when you went upstairs to your bedroom at night there were puffy, fluffy feather ticks on those big beds. When you laid on a feather tick it was like lying on a cloud, it was so soft and cozy. The patchwork quilts were all hand made and soft, too. The pillows were made of goose down from their own geese.

As we got ready for bed, the sun was nearly hidden behind the big barn. Grandma said it was sleepy time, also time to say my prayers. I loved the tick-tock of the wind up metal alarm clock on the dresser. It was the only sound in an otherwise quiet room and it put me right to sleep — with a little help from the mantle clock as it chimed.

A rooster would crow in the evening and in the morning, too early! Grandma had said to me before we left Detroit, it was always peaceful at the farm. It was long ago, but I remember every bit of it. I wish everyone could enjoy mornings and nights like that forever!

In the morning the sun was up like a big orange pumpkin and roosters were crowing. Grandma was telling us to hurry up. We got into our robes and hurried downstairs to the outhouse. That icy water from the kitchen hand pump would wake you up if you weren't already. Then it was back to our rooms to dress. Upstairs everybody had a big basin, a pitcher of water, wash cloths and soap in their rooms. After dressing, I heard Aunt Anna calling us for breakfast.

Grandma said, "Hurry up, hurry up, I've got to make pancakes."

Back down we ran to the breakfast table, which I'm telling you was just as wonderful as the evening table. What pancakes they were! Besides buttermilk pancakes, they had potato pancakes, eggs of every description and apple fritters. Those potato pancakes were the ones I liked. There were thick slices of bacon from their own smokehouse and ham that you could cut with fork and butter fried fresh caught fish! This was *living*. But, of course, I *loved* food.

The women all made beautiful aprons. I still have the apron Mother put on that day to help.

While they were mixing the pancake batter, Aunt Anna said, "Lily, we need more eggs. Take this basket out to the hen house. Get all the eggs you can find in the nests. If you don't see enough, you may have to push a hen over and get a newly laid egg. But ... she may peck you, so be careful."

'Well, who's afraid of a chicken!' I thought.

Away I went scampering out to the hen house, and I had gathered eight eggs but was sure I needed more. I saw a hen sitting there, and I thought, 'She doesn't need all her eggs.' I pushed her over a little and grabbed an egg as her peck missed. I told her, "We only need one more for breakfast and then you can keep the rest of them."

As I put the egg in the basket, I noticed it was almost hot.

I ran as fast as I could to get back to the kitchen; and as I flew through the screen door, I exclaimed, "Aunt Anna, hurry, quick!"

She said, "What is it, child?"

"You don't have to cook this egg," I replied. "Feel it, it's already hot."

As I brought the basket into the kitchen and sat it down, everybody started to laugh. I truly believed the egg was cooked because it was so warm. Everybody told that story for years.

They decided to stay one more day, and I thought, 'One more day of eating like this, fine! I want to stay!'

Later we got ready for another night's sleep, and the next morning they decided we should leave no later than seven. By then Richard had caught up with us in his own car. Aunt Anna loaded the car with a basket of eggs, half a ham and baked chickens all wrapped up. Fresh butter had been put in separate crocks in the cold springhouse water the night before, with plates over them. They put those in Richard's car in a big box covered with newspapers to keep them cool.

So we took Highway 23 to Hubbard Lake, driving along Lake Huron toward East Tawas, Greenbush, Black River and almost to Alpena.

Grandma's cousin, whose name was Mulerwise, lived near there. They owned a general store and a bakery. We stopped in to see the family, talk and stay overnight. Our families showed respect for one another and a togetherness that taught self-esteem and understanding.

The following morning we had another memorable breakfast with the Mulerwises, then Grandma said, "Breakfast is over so we better get started. We're planning on spending two weeks at the new cabin." Everyone hugged and promised to come back.

We had brought two extra butter crocks, which we left full of butter; and we also left some big brown eggs. Grandpa had brought them some Saunders candy from Detroit, yum! We went into their bakery, got whatever baked goods we wanted and back into the car we went.

Mother and Nuzzie took turns driving. My mother was a brave driver. I always called her Amelia Earhart on wheels. She was fearless! Nuzzie was a little worried, because the road became less and less the closer you got to the lake until it became the dirt trail that was left after the forest was logged at the turn of the century. At times water was up to the center of the wheels, but Mother was undeterred, pressing on with single-minded determination. In some places streams were running rampant across the road. Grandpa got in front of the car and ran his walking stick over the surface of the submerged road to look for holes which Mother couldn't see. She crept along in first gear behind her tester. He'd lift the stick and yell to her that she could make it through. When Grandpa got tired, Nuzzie would perform the changing of the hydro guard.

After about an hour we finally came to Hubbard Lake, where Mister McCoy was waving a flag. He smiled and said, "Welcome to Hubbard Lake!"

We pulled up our two-car caravan at the second cottage on the lake and stopped.

Grandpa had bought thirty acres.

Looking at the cabin, Grandma said, "That's it?"

"It's brand new," Grandpa replied, "Look at the pitch of the roof. Look at the new outhouse. A *real* three-holer!"

Richard got out of his car, and we followed. Everyone was walking into the cabin with eggs, ham, crocks of butter, suitcases and patchwork quilts.

I could hear the waves as they gently lapped the shoreline. The sand squishing up between my toes was heavenly.

Mother yelled, “Put your shoes on and get back here!”

I thought, ‘Who wants to wear shoes while walking along a sandy beach?’

They had an icebox, but the secret ingredient, ice, no one had remembered. Some of the crocks were taken to the spring gushing up beside the cabin.

Indians were working nearby making new roads, and Grandpa said, “Oh, the Indians are here.”

Mister McCoy said, “Yes, I told them what you were going to pay to clear the roads.” Grandpa was going to subdivide. The workers had their wives and children with them, and they were looking at me.

I said, “Grandpa, could I go play with the children?”

“Why, yes,” he replied.

Grandmother Weigmann immediately said, “She shouldn’t be playing with the Indians.”

“Why not?” he said. “They’re working for me and their children are very nice, well mannered, too. Besides, I don’t talk about it much, but we have a lot in common.”

Grandma gave him a strange look, but he went right on talking. “Hunny, these are Indians of the great Chippewa Nation. They were here long before we were.”

I walked slowly toward them, and Grandpa went over to talk to the men. One of the men nodded to one of the women. Pretty soon she brought a little brother and sister over, and I was introduced to Little Jay and Mary.

We were at Hubbard Lake ten glorious days. I think Grandma Weigmann couldn’t handle much more, but there were many return trips.

The Indian children brought birch bark. They softened it in the spring, then showed me how to make a water dipper. Grandma almost had a heart attack when she saw me with a little penknife the children let me use. Later, they taught me how to make miniature birch bark canoes, the edges whipped with sweet grass.

Grandma decided to take me by the hand to the three-holed outhouse. There was a little one for children, a medium for ladies and a big one for men. It reminded me of *Goldielocks and the Three Bears*, but that’s where the comparison ended.

Grandma said, “You wait for me,” then she lifted her long skirt and tiptoed in. She was a petite woman who attempted to be very proper. All of a sudden I heard a shriek.

Grandma screamed, “Snake, snake!” as a garter snake slithered out under the door.

Grandma hadn’t noticed me as she ran past with her skirt hiked to her waist, screaming, “Snake!”

Besides, I did need to go, so I sat on that smallest hole with tears of laughter in my eyes. I looked around for toilet paper, but there was only the old Sears catalogue. I remembered Mother Clara had told me, "The dull pages, not the shiny ones."

When I got out, I cleaned my hands on the dewy grass and walked back to the cabin.

Grandpa asked me why I didn't follow Grandma, and I said, "Because I had to go, and the snake went away."

For breakfast we had fresh caught perch, sautéed in butter. And Grandpa made bean hole beans.*

The first night, Grandpa, Nuzzie and Uncle Richard pitched tents, roasting homemade Mullerweise wieners over the fire. Later all bedded down for the night. It was quiet, except for a Great Horned Owl hooting over and over.

Suddenly there was a shrill scream. It was Grandma, and Richard almost knocked his tent down getting out. Grandma was standing on her cot, looking down and yelling, "A *mouse*!"

The whole camp was up. I caught it in a small box with Uncle Richard's help. Then I stood there and giggled, because Grandpa was wearing his striped pajamas. I had never seen him in his striped pajamas before.

The next day Grandpa and Nuzzie bought mousetraps. Grandma was afraid of animals and afraid of catching a cold. The country was not her forte.

The rest of the days were spent swimming, investigating God's handiwork, gathering wild berries and making three sizes of small birch bark canoes. I learned a lot from my Chippewa friends. They appreciated the forests and the beautiful birch trees, as I did, and I loved my Chippewa friends.

---

*Grandpa's Old Fashioned Baked Beans in Appendix.

Figure 7 Uncle Richard loved cars!

IV - The Coal Bin

1927 - 1932

Mother Clara would lock me in the basement coal bin when she thought I had disobeyed. This coal bin was almost below the dining room area. I would listen to the clock chime on the mantle, so I knew what time it was. I guess that's why I like clocks so much. It must have been because that chiming clock kept me company. I'd mark the time with coal on the wood slats of the walls. I had a big old tiger cat that would sit by the slat door while I'd push three fingers through to pet him. His name was Ben.

The cat's name actually was taken from Ben Hur, my foster-dad's favorite book which I started to read at age 9. Ben didn't leave me except to snoop around in hopes of finding a mouse or to be able to lick an empty can cover from the malt Dad used to make his home brew. In fact, I used to lick Dad's malt measuring spoon and give the jar lid to Ben.

V - Mrs. Van De Zant

1930

Most teachers in elementary school slapped or ruler-whacked my left hand to make me use the right one. (I am left-handed and write with my left now in spite of their efforts.) The Italian piano teacher used to hit me on the knuckles when I didn't play my scales properly. It seemed I was always getting ruler slaps on my hands.

But Mrs. Van De Zant was the only teacher who didn't hit my left hand. I'd write short stories and poems for her. She looked at them and often asked if she could keep some.

She always said to me, "Dear Lily, no matter how much they hit you on your left hand, that is the hand with which God told you to write." She was the only teacher who felt that way. She always encouraged me, often saying, "One day some of your writings will be in a book that you wrote."

I thought this was a remarkable thing to say, both because it was a prediction and because it showed such faith in a young girl. Maybe Mrs. Van De Zant was right. If only every student today could have a teacher like Mrs. Van De Zant.

VI - Grandma Harriet Latimer

1930

Figure 8 Grandma Harriett Latimer - from France to England to Canada, a titled lady with a heart of gold.

Figure 9 Old Dodge, Hubbard Lake, Michigan, 1926.

It left a very heavy weight on my heart when my Grandma Harriet Ann Latimer-Jackson passed away. It was near Thanksgiving when I visited Aunt Florence's house where Grandma lived.

Grandma was eighty when she passed away. It was amazing, but she never had so much as a line on her face. Her hair was white as Easter Lilies in the bright sun. Her clear hazel eyes never dulled with age, and she thought and acted much younger than her years. She could tell stories of her youth in Europe for hours. "Her mind is so sharp and clear," everyone said.

I spent many vacations with her and would sleep with her in her feather tick bed. This one particular time Grandma got sick. Doctor Lincoln came to the house; and after examining Grandma he told Aunt Florence to take her to the hospital.

As Grandma was leaving she hugged me and said, "Remember, Lily, you are a "Latimer." That's one of your distant ancestors. You are a famous Latimer. You be a good girl, mind everyone and do as they say. Remember, darling, I love you!"

"I will always love you," I said, clinging tight to her. I kept saying, "Grandma, I can take care of you. I'll take care of you. I'm going to be the greatest doctor in the world."

She smiled and said, "I know you will." This conversation caused me to seriously think of becoming a doctor. I kissed her goodbye.

After Grandma was driven to the hospital I was taken back home. There I took my doll buggy and went up and down the street. We had a lot of birds falling out of the oak and maple trees around the houses and I would pick them up and try to save them.

A neighbor, a French woman, Jean, had a cat that was sick. She said to me, "Do you think you could help my cat?" Her cat had hurt its paw. I told her I thought it was broken. I said, "Sure, I can fix it." So I took her kitty over to our garage. We were the second house from hers. In this garage I had opened what I thought was a "hospital". I borrowed all the gauze, alcohol, iodine and other medicine I could find in the medicine cabinet. I even had Mercurochrome and peroxide — that's what they used back then. The cat's paw looked odd and moved in unusual ways and felt different from the other paw.

So I went in the kitchen and took a lot of matches. I knew they would punish me if they found out. Later, they did. I broke all the heads off and just used the sticks. I marched myself out to my make-shift hospital and laid the cat in my doll buggy. Using white tape and the match sticks, I made a splint. I remember very clearly — I took four match-sticks with some cotton underneath and wrapped the paw with tape. Of course, she hopped with a stiff leg. I don't know if I did it right, but about a month later the splint was taken off and that cat was walking on her foot.

I somehow had this ability to treat sick animals. Maybe it goes back to my Great Uncle Robert Jackson who was the doctor in our family. Maybe that had a genetic bearing on my abilities. I really did want to become a physician. But when I got out of high school my family thought it was so silly. "A woman wants to become a doctor?" they would exclaim. "Nobody wants a woman doctor, " they said. So, since that was pooh-poohed away, I told them my second choice, which was research.

Grandma passed away the sixteenth of December, 1930, and I still miss her.

Grandma respected her daughter's requests, but could not understand some of her decisions. Grandma wanted to teach me French. Once at the dinner table Grandma placed her hand on the table and said, "Lily, this table is really 'la tableau' in French. I want to teach you French."

"Aunt" Florence was coming through the swinging door from the kitchen with a gravy boat in her hand, and she asked, "Why are you teaching her that awful old language? She's American!"

Florence was sometimes very unkind, a hard and driven woman to the end.

But Grandma had encouraged my wish to someday attend medical school and was always supportive. She believed in me. She was one of the few people in my life who really loved me.

VII - Uncle Al

1930 - 1931

When I was ten Uncle Al lived with us to save money. Due to the Depression he had fallen on hard times. Great Uncle George and he owned and operated a shingling company. They also worked for a coal company to raise money for the truck they needed.

Uncle Al was my stepfather's brother. He and Uncle George were living in two dormer rooms upstairs. It was a bit crowded in the house, but I enjoyed their company because they had such great tales to tell about the Great War (World War I). I listened over and over about the intrigue and planning for spy operations, and their various escapes.

Uncle Albert was a radio telegrapher and operator. His nickname was Sparky. He enjoyed every minute of this rather dangerous job. He said it was like running from danger while your safety was in your mental cunning. He liked this because he said it was like a game of hide-and-seek when he was a child, but for real in the grown-up world.

In our basement there was a pool table, ping-pong table and slot machines, bought from the Harmony Club. Sometimes Dad would play for money downstairs.

Uncle Al also had a telegrapher's key in the basement. We set up a small radio hookup. He taught me International Morse Code from an old book and how to use the key. I wanted to be a licensed radio operator like my uncle.

He told stories of hiding during the Great War (as World War I was called then). He carried the heavy radio equipment to a location, buried it, then sneaked back into a French town. He would later get the equipment and report the position, strength and rate of advance of the Germans. I would listen to this, enthralled. We had put old maps up on thc wall that were used to give topographical and geographical significance to his stories.

Figure 10 Uncle Al, 'Sparky', World War I radio man.

At ten I became very interested in maps and the history of the world. I can thank Uncle Albert for this. For greater authenticity, he even put his uniform on and I dragged him all over the neighborhood so I could show the other kids my real war hero uncle.

A lady Mother knew asked Mother to ask Dad to help her get a job at Michigan Bell Telephone Company as he was Chief Accountant with his own office. She figured he'd get her a job and he did. This lady, Ada, had six children from a couple of marriages to support. Mother gave her clothes and food, and Ada paid her back by telling tea-leaf fortunes for her friends in our house. A couple of Saturdays a month I looked forward to these influential ladies coming. This meant the best bone china, teapot, linen and silver. She would tell our fortunes after all the nobility, as she put it, had left. Even Uncle Al would have his fortune read. This is the way I learned how to tell tea fortunes.

One day she said to my mother, "Lily's as good at reading tea leaves as I am; we ought to put her to work."

This became a standing joke at our house: that if Dad ever lost his job, Lily would read tea leaves with Ada and we'd all get rich. Little did anybody know that in some ways, this actually would happen.

Uncle Al had several girlfriends he wanted to impress and would have me read their tea fortunes. This surprised them, because so many turned out to be true.

One Friday night, I was setting the table for morning and a severe storm was coming. I wasn't too happy with the thunder and lightening. Mother used to say that if it thundered badly, "It's because Lily did something wrong."

Uncle Al announced he was going out with his friend, Buddy, to the beer garden. Dad declined because he had to get up early in the morning for golf.

Suddenly I had a bad feeling inside and a headache, too. Something said, "Stop him!"

I said, "Uncle Al, don't go out. You're going to get in trouble."

"Oh, no, I've lived through a war, I won't have any trouble. I know how to handle myself."

Buddy came with his new car, which they wanted to show off to the girls.

I said at the table that night, "Mother, I just don't know if I should set five places tonight."

I hesitated in finishing the place settings, and Mother said, "What are you waiting for?"

"Mother, there won't be five of us here for breakfast tomorrow!"

"Would you stop this. You're trying to be a fortune teller again. I'm going to tell Ada what you're doing!"

"No, I've got a bad feeling. He shouldn't have left."

"Set the table, then get ready and go to bed! No more of this thinking you're a famous fortune teller!" she ordered.

It was near midnight. I was supposed to be asleep. I heard the phone ring. I jumped out of bed and went to listen at the keyhole.

I heard my mother say, "What?"

I opened the door and rushed down the hall to hear my mother exclaiming, over the phone, "It can't be! Oh, no! Oh, God!"

I knew it was about Uncle Al. I ran to the phone. In the 1930's, phones were black and stood up like a candle. I tried to grab the narrow bell-shaped receiver.

Mother said, "Stop it, stop it, Lily. It's the police department. Go get Walter!"

"Daddy! Daddy! Quick, something's happened to Uncle Albert!" I yelled, running into the room.

He grabbed a robe and was still tying it as he ran down the hall to the phone. He heard the police reconfirm that Uncle Al had been killed in a car wreck.

Before I fell asleep that night, I sneaked down in the dark to get a flashlight in the kitchen. I crept downstairs to the basement. He had screwed down the key so I couldn't get that, but I grabbed the codebook and quietly went back to my room. I tried to study the code with the flashlight, but the batteries were weak.

With tears streaming down my face, I prayed to God, "Please bring Uncle Al back to life. If you can't, keep him in heaven, because he has never done a bad thing in his life. Just because he went with Buddy to the beer garden to show off the new car to the girls, it wasn't Uncle Al's fault. He was just trying to be a friend to Buddy."

Some years ago, my mother and I were going through an old trunk and she said, "I suppose you would like this picture of Uncle Al in his World War I uniform and his World War I 'shell casing' table lamps."

"Of course I would."

I remembered this story when I saw his old picture in the corner of the living room as I was dusting. And of course, the lamp he made from a shell casing he brought home. This story is dedicated to all the members of our old radio club to whom he was teaching code and all the other old "Sparkies" world wide.

Later, after the funeral, our club held a military ceremony in the empty storage shed we had designated as the Allied Command. I gave a farewell speech to the men and women of the armed forces and my school pals. Between sentences, not even the sound of a gliding butterfly was heard. We all loved Uncle Al for sharing his life with us. Of course, he had taught me even more than Morse Code. He taught me, "There's always a turn in the road, and the road never stops. No matter what happens in life, remember there is always another corner to turn." He said he learned that when hiding from the Germans. He said a dead end street or a building that looked like he couldn't enter or exit never blocked him.

"That's what you have to remember in life, Lily," he had told me. I always have.

Uncle Al was in his late thirties when he got killed, but I don't think that he's really gone. Anybody who could send messages with a telegrapher's key like he did has to be somewhere. I'm sure he's helping God in heaven.

VIII - Exiled

1932

It was in the early fall. Mother Clara came running through the house screaming, totally hysterical. I didn't know what had happened to cause this, but Mother Clara was very excitable and often got this way. I really didn't know whether it was something serious or just one of her "normal tantrums", as Daddy called them.

As she came running up the basement stairs, she kept screaming, "Run to Davis', run to Davis'!"

Many times there were arguments I could hear between her and Daddy, and then I would be shoved down into the coal bin. Sometimes she would give me a piece of bread and butter, then push me down the stairs. If I was lucky, there was peanut butter and jelly on it.

We lived in a beautiful area of Oakman Boulevard that was quite peaceful and almost rural compared to Detroit itself.

This one time I remember running to the basement door. I still heard her horrible scream. She was yelling, "Go over to Mrs. Davis', run to Davis'!"

I ran back to my bedroom, not knowing why she wanted me to run to Mrs. Davis. I tore into my bedroom and closed the door. As I did this I heard some more arguing, and finally my door was pushed open. My dad stood there with a hatchet in his hand. Suddenly he was heading for me, and the only thing I could think of was to head for the window. It was already half open. I pushed it up, kicked the screen out and jumped. Of course I was young and thin, and if you think you can, you can do most anything. I flew through the window, ran across the yard and I remember jumping over the fence.

I ran as fast as I could to the rear door of Mrs. Davis' porch, screaming, "Mrs. Davis, help, Mrs. Davis!"

Figure 11 My cat, my friend, Ben

Well, she could see out the window by her sink that I was in some kind of trouble. My mother kept screaming, "Get her in, lock the door."

I ran through the kitchen door of Mrs. Davis' house. Her husband, who was working in the basement tying fishing flies, came running up the steps as she was fiddling with that knob to push the door shut and get it locked. It was turmoil, believe me.

He kept asking, "What's wrong, what's wrong?"

I said, "I don't know, I don't know what happened. All I know is that my dad has a hatchet and he's going to kill me. I know he's going to kill me!"

Mister Davis was a big strong, handsome man of about forty. He liked to hunt and fish — a real outdoorsman. My dad was about the same age, but I figured that if I was to be safe, I sure would be in their house. Mrs. Davis tried to quiet me down.

I was crying and I remember that she guided me into the living room, sat me in a big chair and said, "Now you stay right there."

She pulled the shades down and the curtains shut over the window so it became quite dark in the house and nobody could see us through the window.

She said, "Now stay right there. I'll get you some cocoa and something to eat, I'll do something — this is terrible!"

I was crying as we talked, Mrs. Davis trying to calm me down and herself, too! There was pounding on the doors. Apparently Walter was running around to the front and the back door of their house and my mother was running after him.

It was about this time that Mother called out in a loud voice, "Call Lorene." Apparently Mrs. Davis had all the phone numbers of the family and she did call. All I know is that Uncle Ernie and Uncle Carl came over. I could hear Mother screaming, "He has those terrible headaches again!"

As far as I could figure out later, the whole thing stemmed from something I must have done to his dill pickles. I had taken a dill pickle out of the jar in the refrigerator and apparently I had not tightened the cap enough. I later figured out that's what it must have been. Mother said it was something about his dill pickle jar falling. I don't think it broke, but it was just that some of it spilled. I didn't realize exactly what had happened, but I found out many days and even years later, as the story was retold. Evidently Mother was trying to defend me and get me out of the house. I stayed for several hours at Mrs. Davis' house and then Uncle Richard came over in his car with Grandma and Grandpa, while Dad was taken over to some local hospital. I don't know where they treated him or exactly what happened. I was told later that he did go back to work, but he arranged to have the time missed as sick days off. He never missed a day of work, just two days of sick leave in forty-two years. I think in his entire life he never missed any work until this incident. He was the only Michigan Bell Telephone employee of forty-two years who only missed a couple of days of work — on sick leave.

Later that week I was driven somewhere in a car. Aunt Florence and Uncle Roy met us at Grandma and Grandpa's house before we all drove to Marine City. Mr. Nussbaum, our chauffeur, driving us in the big Packard.

I didn't know when we got there that I would not be going home for some years. I would be in a strange bed, I wouldn't have my doll, bear, dog or my Nancy Drew books — nothing. I wouldn't even know where my dog had gone. I wouldn't have my clothes, and all I had was the shirt on my back! When we got to this house in Marine City, it was shabby and it didn't look like anything where I was used to living.

I asked, "Grandpa, are we taking clothes to the poor again?"

Whenever I outgrew clothes, we would drive to different families all over Detroit and Hamtramack with them like the food we gave away. I thought Marine City must just be another place for leaving clothing or blankets for children in need. This definitely looked like a poor neighborhood, and I thought we must be going there to give my clothes away.

Grandpa didn't say anything, so I asked Mother and Grandma both, "Are we bringing clothes to these people?"

Finally Grandpa said, "No, my dear, we have to find a nice kind person to take care of you for a month or so until we can get Daddy all well again."

So we walked up on the front porch steps. They sagged a little as we stepped on them. I thought to myself, 'I don't want to live here.'

The lady who opened the door was plump, had bright red lipstick, long earrings and henna-dyed hair.

I took one look at her and I thought, 'That's not who I want to live with!'

Mother pushed me through the door. I saw Mister Nussbaum get out of the car with a suitcase with Grandpa and Grandma following him. Nussie looked sad and so did Grandpa. I turned to Grandpa, "Grandpa, I don't want to stay here. Can't we just go back and I can live with you and Grandma?"

Grandpa answered, "Well, maybe, yes; but right now we have to keep you here for a week or two. We're going to work something out. You just give us a little time to work this all out."

Well, this week or two turned into three weeks and I had to enroll in school. The woman absolutely was just as bad as I thought she would be. I knew after I was there twenty-four hours that I had to run away. I could not stand this. I guess it was some of the worst weeks of my life, and there had been many others. When I walked to school it was bitter cold with an almost continuous icy wind blowing off of the St. Clair River from Canada. Believe me, if you want to be cold, I always said to myself, this is the place to go.

What was just as bad were the rooms that the two other girls and I slept in upstairs. Another girl slept downstairs, as did the lady, herself. The rooms we had were small and kind of a dormer room almost like an attic with a narrow staircase coming down to the main floor. Apparently she was some kind of a foster mother, but I really didn't know what that meant in those days. There was a double bed, a cot and room for three of us to sleep. I had to share the bed with another girl, and a bigger girl slept on a cot.

When we woke up in the morning, I just couldn't believe my situation. There was a chair where we had hung our clothes. I had washed my socks by hand before putting them there, so I would have clean ones to put on the next day. They were stiff in the morning, frozen solid! That's how cold that room was. We had to come downstairs to use the bathroom which had a big old dirty iron bathtub with claw-type feet. There was a ring that never came out of the tub no matter how much it was scrubbed.

I was really afraid of everything in the house, because it was so dirty and such unusual living conditions from what I had been accustomed. I knew I had to make my plan to escape. Every day I thought about a way to get out and how I would do it. I planned for weeks, putting together a plan to leave for good. I think the thing that set me off the most is a delicate subject. I was twelve and I had already had my first period. My mother had always supplied me with the proper things girls needed. Of course, in those days, that was for me, Kotex, which is the only thing they had, as I recall. So when another period occurred, I went downstairs to the lady and asked her where the box of Kotex was.

The lady looked at me strangely.

"Here, my dear, you don't use Kotex."

So I asked, "But, why?"

My mother had told me before she left that anything I needed was paid for and she'd given the lady money for extra supplies.

She said, "Follow me."

She took me to a back washroom that was a part of the laundry room. Hanging on a wooden rack to dry was a bunch of rags. There was an old flannel sheet rolled up in the corner. She said, "You just tear off pieces of this sheet and make your own pads. When you're through using them, wash them in the bathtub and hang them on this wooden hanger until they dry."

Well, I just couldn't believe this!

I told her, "But I don't want to. I want what Mother always gives me. I want my Kotex."

"When you're with me, you'll do it this way!" she said.

That night was when I made up my mind that there was no way I could continue living there.

I kept thinking, 'I will talk to these girls, and I must find out what's downtown. Maybe I can buy them an ice cream cone and I can find out what the town looks like.'

I knew there had to be a cafe downtown because I heard the girls talk about hamburgers. If I got a letter from home, as I was supposed to from time to time, there would be three or four dimes, or sometimes, from Grandpa, two quarters.

I thought, 'I'll pool all this money together. I'll take the girls for an ice cream cone, figure out what's going on in that town in the process and where the highways are.'

This was it. I had made up my mind. The last card I got there had been five dimes besides two quarters from Grandpa. I told the girls if they would show me where this cafe or the ice cream place was, I would buy us all a sundae.

They were so excited.

One of the girls, whose name was Julia, said, "You're going to get us a sundae?"

I said, "Yes, my grandfather told me to in his letter."

Grandpa had said, "Get the girls a sundae and one for yourself," so they took me right after school to where the ice cream shop and cafe was. It was really a truck stop on the corner of Highway 29.

When I got home that night I further planned my escape. I had to figure out what I'd have to take, which I reasoned should be a minimum. I decided I'd put double clothes on my body, two shirts, two skirts and two underpants. I had a coat, purse, a cap, a tam-a-shanter, on my head and also my schoolbooks to take with me in the morning. I also had a big ugly-looking portfolio into which I put my books.

In the morning I carried two books and stuffed some other things in that portfolio and closed it. I walked to school as usual with the girls. I went into the school and stayed in the class until lunchtime. Then I told my teacher, and later the school nurse, I wasn't feeling very well and that I might have to go home. I told the nurse it was my period time; I had a bad headache and was very sick.

After I had sat in her office telling her how I felt, she asked me to lie on the cot for ten minutes. She came back when the time was up and talked to me. I told her it was a little worse.

She said, "Maybe you should go home and get some hot soup."

That's when I got my chance to leave. I left the school about ten minutes before the bell rang and had a head start to get on my way before anyone knew which direction I was going. When the bell rang, it made more confusion because there were kids piling out all over the place. I continued to walk briskly behind the school and kept walking east and south to get to the road where I knew the cafe was. I walked into the cafe like I was looking for someone, but I was really snooping around. I walked into the restroom, checked my face and hair and put on earrings. The rich smell of plumeria increased as I redid my "Tangee" lipstick. I walked out to a truck driver whom I had seen in the parking lot next to the driveway, and —

"You wouldn't be going to Detroit, would you?" I asked.

He gave me a quizzical look. "Well, yes ... yes, I am going to Detroit."

"Well," I said, "I've lost my money. I left my purse in the bathroom when I redid my lipstick and no one can find it. I'm in terrible trouble! I have to get to Detroit. My grandparents are waiting for me."

I guess I must have fooled him, age wise, because the earrings and lipstick might have made me look a little older. He didn't seem to be bothered by my asking and he said, "That's terrible. If I can help, I'll take you down. I'm leaving in about thirty minutes. If you want to hop up in the truck cab, you can."

He got out and walked around the truck looking at tires. Then he came back and said, "Why don't you call them?"

I said, "They're not home in the daytime. My grandpa's a chef and he's out and my grandma's got a doctor appointment, so she isn't in, either."

"Oh," he said, "What part of Detroit are you going to?"

I said, "Dexter Boulevard and Joy Road, or Grand River, any of that area would be fine."

He said, "I go right down Grand River and I'll pass Joy Road, not Dexter. Would that be close enough?"

"Oh, that's wonderful. You could just drop me off on the corner of Joy Road, that's great."

He stopped one time to fill his thermos jug at a cafe and I ran in to use the bathroom. He brought back the thermos jug and he had bought two candy bars. They were Clark Bars, my favorite.

"Would you like a Clark Bar?" he asked.

I said, "Oh, thank you very much. This is the kind my mother always gets me."

We talked quite a bit about my family, my grandfather and Sanders hot fudge topping. I told him how Grandpa helped develop the product, baked for the company, and all the things he did. I told him about the Woodward Avenue store and all the pictures I had that my Uncle took of the store way back in the 1920's.

He said he used to go to the Woodward Avenue store all the time to get a hot fudge sundae and we really had a good conversation all the way down.

He pulled up and dropped me off at Joy Road and Grand River on the right side of the street. We both said goodbye and I crossed at the light. He even waited there 'till he saw I was safely on the other side of the street before he started to pull out again. I remember waving goodbye and thinking what a nice man he was. He was a perfect gentleman and he tried nothing funny.

I had started to think, as I crossed with the light, 'What am I going to do next?'

It was getting dark; and I had to get to my grandparent's home, which was still quite a hike. I had to figure out the most important thing: what was I going to say when I got there?

'What are they going to do to me?' I wondered.

I decided I'd go to the back garden gate of the alley to approach our house when I got there, so I started taking side roads and alley roads all the way there. I figured the least conspicuous I could be the better, because now it was after six at night. Young girls then weren't usually on the street that late walking in a business section or on a main highway. I kept zigzagging all the way down and finally got to the alley behind my grandparents' home. I opened the garden gate to the rear and went along the side of the garage. This is where the staircase was that led up to Mister Nussbaum's apartment above the garage. I figured if I went to talk to Mister Nussbaum, and Grandma and Grandpa hadn't seen me yet, that I could maybe lay some kind of a plan that might allow me to stay. I thought that possibly Nussie would be on my side, too. I knew my grandfather would be.

He had known my grandfather and they had come from Europe together many years earlier. I know they had a lot of heartbreak in their lives. Nussie said he nearly got killed in a skirmish in the German military in 1890. He was getting old, too, as was Grandpa. Mister Nussbaum seemed to me like someone I could trust. I sneaked into the garage and tried to listen to see if I heard anything. Then I walked up the outside staircase toward Nussie's room and knocked on the door. He was in his little apartment. He opened the door and was startled to see me.

He said, "*Oy vey*! Lily! What are you doing here? Come in! Does Grandpa know you're here?"

"No," I said, "No one does; I just arrived."

"Well, how did you get here?" he asked.

"Oh," I said, "Some people drove me. They were coming to Detroit anyway."

"Oh," he said, "You should have called us. I'd have gotten you, wherever you were coming from. Did you walk far?"

"Oh, no, just from Grand River."

"Grand River!" he exclaimed.

"Yes," I answered.

"Oh, I better call your grandpa."

"No," I said, "Just one minute, Nussie, I want to talk to you first. Nussie, the lady I stay with, where you took my little suitcase in, was very mean to me. I can't tell you all the bad things that happened, but I can tell you they were awful. She had a man who lived next door to her and would come over lots of times for dinner. They said things that were bad and there were a lot of other things going on in their bedroom that we girls could hear and didn't like. It was very embarrassing. Once or twice, when she was out somewhere to the store, he would come over alone and help himself to whatever was in the refrigerator. If we girls were coming around the corner, or would happen to get trapped by the doorway, it was time to run, because he always tried to push his body against ours! We used to be so afraid of him that we would lock ourselves in the bathroom. It was the only room that had a lock. I just knew that I couldn't stay! I couldn't stay anymore! There were a couple of other things, too, then I knew I just had to go. There was no use calling Mother, or Aunt Florence, because I knew they would never let me come to their house. I figured the only thing I could do is tell Grandpa and you and Grandma all that had happened."

"Well," he said, "Why didn't you call that lady, whoever she was, that recommended this lady that boarded children? Didn't you have her name?"

"Well, no, I really don't," I replied. "I think I know it, but I'm not sure. I only know there was a card exchanged, but my mother took the card. I know that I just had to come home. I can't live there anymore, Nussie."

He said, "I think you should be home, too. I really never thought you should have been in that place. I'll walk you over to the house."

He led me a little ways from the garage and to the rear of the house where the back door was. We walked up the steps to the kitchen and through to the sunroom, but there wasn't anyone there. We came back toward the basement steps and listened. We heard a noise in the kitchen and Nussie said, "Grandpa's in the basement."

I said, "Oh, what will I tell him?"

"Never mind, let me talk," he advised.

We walked down the stairs and there was Grandpa. Nussie walked in first.

He said, "I've got a surprise for you." Grandpa looked up.

He was cooking something. Grandpa had his own kitchen in the finished basement where he pre-tested candy and pastry for his restaurant as well as for Sanders.

As we entered, I could see the sugar bubbling and I knew he was making some kind of candy. I thought Grandpa would faint. Nussie told Grandpa how I had left the boarding house.

Grandpa said, "I'll turn this off, the candy doesn't count! Come, come, let's go upstairs. Nussie, take her up to the guest room. I'm coming straight up! Forget the candy, we'll do it later. Grandma is with Richard, to the eye doctor. That's why there is no one upstairs."

We all came upstairs where Grandma had her kitchen. Then Grandpa said, "Now we have to make a plan. Oh, when Clara and Florence hear of this, there'll be trouble. You know how Grandma is. She gets just as nervous as Clara does. Where will we put you? What will we do? She will take you away, for sure. Walter is still too sick and I'm sure he'll try to kill you again. It's that pain in his head. He's on new medicine, though."

I turned to Grandpa and I said, "But Grandpa, why can't I live with you? Why can't I live in the attic? I won't be any trouble at all. I'll stay in the attic. It's a cute little room and there's a sewing room and a storeroom next to it. I'd be fine up there. I only have to come downstairs to use the bathroom and to eat, and I don't even eat much. Look, it won't cost you as much as they're paying, a dollar and a quarter a day over there. All this money for boarding out could be saved. I know mother always gives them extra money to get me things that I never receive, too."

Grandpa said, "I am going to lay a plan. The sewing room is a good idea, if I can just get Grandma and Richard to go along with me. Right now I think you should go hide in the guest room."

I thought I heard a car engine as I walked toward the guestroom.

Grandpa turned quickly and said, "Quick get in there. I'll try and bring you something to eat a little later. Go in there, quick, quick, hide! Nussie, back me up in what I say."

"I will," Nussie replied.

As I said, both of the men were from Munich and had been through quite a bit in their lifetime. So they had a strong bond, even though there were several years between their ages. I was terrified. I didn't have my clothes, only what was on my back, and I was getting hungry. The books had been getting heavy, and I put the book bag down on the floor. I sat in the room on the edge of the bed wondering if some of my stuffed animals that I had collected were up in the attic. I had my teddy bear from Germany which Grandpa gave me, that I had missed so much. I knew I had the big lop-eared rabbit upstairs. He was my good luck rabbit that I put on my bed when visiting here, and the bear, too. And then some of my Nancy Drew Mystery books were up there. I wished I could have them to read again. Books were always my friends. But I didn't dare open the door.

I heard Grandpa talking, then I heard the other voices. A little later I heard someone coming down the steps toward the door. The door opened and it was Grandpa. He had apparently gone up in the attic, because he sneaked into the room quickly and handed me my stuffed rabbit. Yes, even at twelve years of age I loved my stuffed animals.

He said, "I'll be back. Keep your rabbit there, talk with him, and don't come out until I tap on the door with five little taps." Then I heard voices again and I heard the car door slam. I heard Uncle Richard's voice, and I was terrified they were going to send me away again.

'They may even put me in jail for running away,' I was thinking. 'This is a terrible thing, but Grandpa won't let them hurt me, I know that much. Wait 'till they hear what this lady did to us girls. How she treated us and how mean she was.'

Then I heard Richard say, "What?" in a loud voice!

Then they were arguing in German that changed back into English from time to time. Then Richard said, "She can't stay here! We can't take care of the kid — Ma's too old!"

There was a lot of excitement. I heard Grandma saying something. I heard the five little quick taps on the door, and in came Grandpa, Grandma and Richard.

I threw my arms around Grandpa, Grandma and Richard all at once and said, "Don't let them send me away, I can't live with that lady."

Grandma said, "We'll keep you for a few days, but we're going to have to talk this all over with Clara and Florence."

I figured at least I was safe for a while, and actually I was there three days. Grandpa made a big chicken dinner with mashed potatoes and gravy. Oh, yes! It was so good! I couldn't even force myself to eat some of the food at the foster home, it tasted so awful. In fact, I don't even think some of it was safe to eat because of how she let it lie around the kitchen unrefrigerated.

I went down to the basement kitchen and helped Grandpa finish the candy recipe, which was a magnificent toffee that we ate later that night. The next day we experimented with some more pralines in a thick candy topping similar to toffee, but a little bit more firm. The pralines were rolled into that shape like the toffee had been. This had chocolate and three different kinds of chopped nuts. I learned so much from Grandpa about cooking, baking and candy making.

The third day Aunt Florence came and she was furious. So did Clara, and it was hard to tell which one was more angry. I had never seen them so mad before, and that is saying a lot, because they both had been angry with me more times than there were hairs on my head. I was terrified and shaking inside.

Aunt Florence said, "How dare you run away after we paid all this money to have you kept there! That just shows how ungrateful you are!" She kept turning to Clara as we all moved into the hall.

Then she said, "You see what I mean! Do you understand now? You might have known it! She's just like you-know-who, and can't be trusted either!"

I wondered, 'Who was "you-know-who"?'

I tried to go on explaining, but of course in front of the men I couldn't say everything.

Grandpa then said, "Just a minute, she has to talk to you women alone. Clara," he said, "Florence, Hannah, you talk to her alone."

I had done a little explaining to Grandpa, but not too graphic. Well, Grandma Hannah Weigmann, Aunt Florence, Mother and I went back into the bedroom and the door was closed. I explained what the neighbor did, or tried to do, pushing up against us girls. I also told them about what the lady said to me about the Kotex, how terrible the place was and how serious the deficiencies were.

I sat sobbing and wailing, "I can't stay there anymore. Grandma, I thought that I could stay at your house, maybe in the attic."

As I looked up, I saw Grandma Weigmann's face was very pale white, and she was shaking, so we had to sit her down in a chair. In the time frame of my explanation, this was an extremely shocking story about an almost forbidden subject. Most women in society wouldn't even talk about such topics. There wasn't any television; you didn't hear this type of thing in movies, plays or over the radio. This was such a repugnant story for Grandma that we thought she was going to faint. Florence's face turned beet red and Clara looked the other way from me.

I knew, even at my age, that they had allowed this to happen to me. None of them seemed to want me. But, sin by omission is still a sin, and I said this to them many times years later.

The plan was that I would have to wait three or four days and could stay at Grandma and Grandpa's until they found another home. They did find a place west of Detroit, toward Redford. These people were quite nice and they lived in a very nice two-story home. I didn't want to be there, of course; I wanted to be home, but this was far better, to say the least, than the place in Marine City. Their dad was a tool and die engineer in one of the motor factories. He was well built and looked a little like a football player. They had beautiful furniture, nice food, good table manners and I really felt more at home there than I had anywhere up until then. And the mother of the family was a wonderful cook.

I shared a bedroom for the first week with their daughter and then moved into another room. I think the daughter's name was Catherine. She was very courteous, polite, and a good student. If I remember correctly, the last name of the family was Lingman.

They had two sons, both in college. The Lingman's sons were really sharp, intelligent young men. I'm sure they were going places and probably did very well in their lifetimes. Their mother was a rather tall woman, usually had a smiling face and loved to bake. She made scrumptious dinners, and on Fridays she made lemon pie. I would say that she could have been Norwegian or Danish.

The family had sufficient money and I can't imagine why they bothered boarding me at eight dollars a week. As she had said, maybe it was just to have a companion for their daughter.

I remember the rate for my keep was raised about two months later to ten dollars a week. I often wondered at the time if it were because I sometimes asked for second helpings when they had mashed potatoes and gravy! They were very good to me. I got a big kick out of one thing that's continued through my life. Every time we walked home from school for lunch, which we did daily during the week, Mrs. Lingman always had Franco American spaghetti or Campbell's tomato soup with croutons. That was a definite standby. We usually had that with a glass of milk, and sometimes a peanut butter and jelly sandwich. And raisin oatmeal cookies. Today, every time I open a can of Franco American spaghetti or Campbell's tomato soup, I think of the Lingman household. Well, from 1932 through 1935 that was the standard fare for lunch after school. Breakfast was usually Quaker oatmeal, Kelloggs corn flakes or Post shredded wheat. It was ten times better than what I got in Marine City, that's for sure. Of course, there were no more of the terrible experiences that I suffered in Marine City, either.

While I stayed with these people, Aunt Florence would drive to see me about every two to three months and Mother Clara would come about every two weeks. She would sometimes come by auto or streetcar. We would go up to a restaurant that was called the WigWam for lunch or dinner. It had a real Indian teepee shape for an entrance and Indian decor inside. I loved that restaurant. That was the only time I saw any of my family and I was quite sad about it all. Christmases were very blue. I sure wasn't happy, because of being homesick, but I was happy with the way I was treated by the Lingmans.

After about a year and a half, Mother said that Walter was feeling much better. They had given him some medication to calm him down and to keep him from worrying. You see, he was worried about getting sick because he was afraid he could lose his pension. He was an executive in the accounting department of Michigan Bell. It was sad, too because years later I learned that when he did die, due to a stroke, after working there forty-two years, he had lost his pension. They did give him some company stock, I remember, but I know my mother was very upset about the pension. Well, at any rate, that was really their main worry, it seemed. I was, I guess, among other things, considered an unwanted catalyst for his and Mother's temper tantrums. But I also felt Daddy was ill.

Finally, with Walter's improved health, although he still had hypertension, I was allowed to go home. I couldn't wait to get there. I can't explain my desire to return, as they weren't always that good to me, but it was just the only thing I knew as home. Also, I got to see more often the only one left that I'd call my inspiration, and who I knew loved me: Grandpa Weigmann. Dear Grandma Latimer had died a few years before.

"Well, we will see how things work out," Mother Clara said.

I don't ever remember anything that I did that was really all that wrong. I really wasn't a bad girl, in that sense. There were no drugs in the schools in those days, I didn't drink and I didn't run around with boys. I just didn't know what it was, but I just could not live up to their expectations. I still feel the guilt and yet don't know what I did. As far as my girlfriends, Dorothy Leeke, Virginia Finn and Katherine Leonard were concerned, the only thing we ever did that would be considered real bad was roller skating on the street at night in front of the house. We would do this up and down the road in front of our house.

When we moved to a different address on Oakman Boulevard, we would go to family picnics at Uncle Carl and Aunt Lorene's. I can't imagine I ever did anything wrong there, except I always wanted to play their baby grand piano. I did learn long ago, not to touch the organ or the harp because those were things they didn't want anyone to touch. But they didn't mind my practicing on the piano. That family was so musical and so in tune with life. What I admired about Aunt Lorene and her mother, Mrs. Marlis, was that they were very loving toward each other, and of course, she had her children quite a bit later in life; I'd guess about age thirty. But, thank God, they were blessed with the children they so dearly wanted. I remember baby-sitting one of them. I'm trying to think which one it was. All I had to do was sit there and feed him something if he got hungry. It was on a Christmas and I helped trim their Christmas Tree, which was gigantic. They were the kind of togetherness family that I guess all of us would love to have. Uncle Carl was so kind to Aunt Lorene, and she was kind toward him. The children received lots of love from both of the parents and their grandma who lived with them. They had security; they had a lot of things I really missed.

Mrs. Marlis, herself, was quite a cultured, well-educated woman and certainly a wonderful person. She taught me how to crochet, bake bread and how to make the best biscuits in the whole wide world, next to Grandpa's. We always had them in the summer with strawberry shortcake. I swear, those biscuits of hers raised four inches tall! I still make her biscuits and I think of her every time I do. That is where we would often go, and that's where so many of my happy moments were spent.

I am sure that Clara unwittingly took me to where I experienced love; and therefore she did me a great favor, of which I think they were not aware. There were certain other times, though, when I was away from home that I wasn't so happy. One such time was when they had a large picnic with all the Bund members. That's when the Germans sat at one table; and I was seated at a card table by myself, under a tree, but about five feet away from the long tables. I never could figure out why, and I asked one time because there were children at the long tables.

I asked, "Why can't I sit at the long tables that were put together, and why do I have to sit alone?" It wasn't just Mother Clara who explained this; there was a German gentleman who spoke with a very heavy accent, who turned to me and said, "It's because you're not a German."

I couldn't figure out why I wasn't a German. If this was my Aunt, my Uncle, my niece and Nephews, how could that be? I just didn't get it. My mother and dad were there; this was before I knew I was adopted. I heard the words "Bund membership" and I had no idea what that was. I guess this was about 1932 through 1936. My age was between twelve and almost sixteen; and I had some knowledge of the world, but I had no idea what a Bund was in 1932 and 1933. I had no idea who Hitler was until 1936 to 1938, but by then I was beginning to figure it out, by age fifteen or sixteen.

Figure 12 Adolph Hitler, about 1939, the danger cloud over Europe begins!

The Bund was established in Detroit and Uncle Carl was the Treasurer of the "Harmony Club." The Bund had their meetings there in another room. Sometimes they would take me, but would make me sit outside while they went into a large hall. They closed the doors where they showed newsreels of German propaganda about Hitler on a regular movie screen. I know, because I peeked. I was listening to Hitler's speeches, and while I didn't understand the language I got some of the gist of what they believed from their treatment of me. Lots of times, though, when I began to ask questions, I was put in another room with the younger children. Any small child and up to my age of fifteen, were put in there. Those over fifteen were allowed to go sit with their elders. They were later called in English, the "Hitler Youths." I met some pretty influential German people at these meetings. I heard some of the speeches because part of the time when they kept me in that little room with the other children, I would hold my ear to the crack of the big sliding doors to hear a little bit of what was going on.

So, when I was at the family picnic and was ostracized, and they said it was because I wasn't a German, then I began to figure some of it out. I still didn't know that I was adopted and I still couldn't understand why they didn't think I was good enough to sit at their table. I just figured I wasn't good enough to be a German, whatever that meant. I just figured it was something I did that was wrong. What I did learn later was that I was English, Irish and French, Latimers being originally Norman from Alsace Lorraine, plus a little Hungarian.

I do want to emphasize, though, that Uncle Carl and Aunt Lorene were very good parents and very loving to their children. I don't think they realized at first what they were getting into, being around Bund members. I believe it was 1937 when Uncle Carl, or Cully as they called him, got a different job and quit working for Bund via managing the club. Uncle Carl was no longer working for the Harmony Club. Perhaps they realized that they were getting in too deep, or they were getting into an organization that was dangerous for them. Maybe they realized that the beliefs of Hitler were not compatible with theirs.

Then at my grandparents I heard a man with a nice voice on the radio, his name was Bob Trout, tell about what the Bund was in America. I began to understand. I loved Bob Trout's voice. "I'd like to talk on the radio like that," I told Grandpa as we sat there together, listening. Years later, I did this in Arizona.

I always loved Aunt Lorene; she was so beautiful. She had the same colored hair and curls that later I learned my own real mother had years before, beautiful strawberry blonde hair. I didn't get to know her children, which would have been my cousins, hardly at all. I had only seen them a few times, partly because I was placed in different boarding homes, family farms and Campfire Girls in the summer.

It was too bad, but I had the same treatment by all my adoptive family, both mothers, including my own blood relative, Uncle Robert, who I knew cared about me in some ways. Apparently his wife didn't want his children to know who I was. I didn't get to really meet either of Uncle Robert's boys. I only met one at "Aunt " Florence's funeral, years later. I was so appalled, because he didn't know who I was! My very own cousin!

I remember he leaned over toward me and said, "How do you know so much about my family?"

I kept saying, "But I'm a Latimer like you, a Jackson like you!"

I turned to Aunt Alice, Aunt Grace and his mother, Osa, at the table where we were eating in the church after the funeral, and I said, "He doesn't know who I am?"

They didn't respond. Aunt Grace and Osa both told me that they would talk to me later and that they would also explain this to him. As the hearse was leaving for the cemetery, Aunt Osa introduced me to my cousin and I shook his hand. My daughter Carolyn and I got into our car to go to the cemetery. My "Aunt" Florence's secrets were slowly being revealed! Still, it was the emptiest feeling in my heart, that Uncle Robert and his wife did not tell their children that I was their blood cousin!

IX - Who Am I?

1938

I was the daughter of Clara Wagner, and just eighteen years old. The words "Happy Birthday!" were ringing in my ears, but I was sobbing. I was lying on my bed with Clarice, my bed doll, that Grandmother had bought in Paris, and my dog, Heather.

I had tear-filled eyes.

I said, "Lily, no; Grace, no; Lily Wagner, no! Who am I?"

I could not believe what the last hour had brought into my once somewhat happy young life. Now my mind was spinning in confusion.

'My name is not Lily? My mother is my stepmother? My aunt is my mother? My name is really Grace Lucille, not Lily Lucille? If Clara Wagner is not my mother, and Walter Wagner is not my father, what is my last name? Who am I, really? How could my mother, Clara Wagner, do this to me? Why was she trying to say Aunt Florence was my mother?'

I really was too young even at eighteen and inexperienced at life to completely understand. Facts about who my natural father was appeared wrapped in mystery!

My happy eighteenth birthday party had culminated in my being summoned to a private conference in my bedroom with my mother and Aunt Florence. In this closed meeting they had been stiff, strained, and their voices and manners terse.

Mother Clara broke the heavy silence by saying, "You are old enough to know some things we kept from you until you turned eighteen."

Aunt Florence sat there in frozen silence.

Clara then said, "Aunt Florence is really your mother."

I sat there in a confused, wide-eyed daze. It appeared to me that my mother had disowned me. She said my aunt was my mother!

I was looking at a new person whom I had always called my Aunt Florence. She stared back at me, then down at the floor, looking extremely uncomfortable.

I stared at both of them and said, "Mother?"

They both stared at me and said nothing.

My mind racing, I thought, 'What do they mean by this? My name is not Lily?' How often does anyone speak the word "mother" in questioning uncertainty? It's a cry for comfort, a call for help and a request for understanding. 'My name is really "Grace Lucille"? Why don't they say something? My mother is not my mother? My aunt is my mother?'

This was the night of my birthday and graduation party. The rest of the family had left except Grandpa and Grandma Weigmann, Uncle Richard and Uncle Roy, Florence's husband (who I thought was my uncle). They were all still in the living room as we came out of the bedroom.

My mother said, "Stop this crying! Lily, we promised to tell you together now. You've got to thank everyone for your gifts and say goodnight."

I tried not to show my emotions as I said goodnight to my guests and hugged everyone goodbye.

I thought, 'What was I supposed to call Mother Clara? How could she now not be my mother?'

When I went to bed that night I just said, "Good night, Mother."

Mother said, "We'll talk more tomorrow."

Figure 13 1938 graduation card.

My dad never said a word. Everybody seemed to be nervous and very hush-hush as they left. I remember lying on that beautiful honey maple Jenny Lind bed, one of my birthday presents that matched a rocker, cricket table and vanity with a bench.

I cried myself to sleep, still not knowing why Clara and Walter Wagner were not my parents, while my aunt was my mother and Uncle Roy was my stepfather. When I woke up the next morning, I was almost afraid to leave my room. 'What do I say to her?' I wondered.

Dad had left for work, so the only one I had to confront was Mother Clara. I went out in the kitchen.

"Why don't you make yourself some French toast. That always calms you down when you are unhappy."

"I'm unhappy because I'm not your daughter anymore."

"You *are* my daughter. You're my foster child and Florence is your mother, the one who gave birth to you."

"Well, why did you wait until my eighteenth birthday to tell me?"

Mother Clara didn't answer. In those days they didn't use the words "birth mother." It didn't ring clear in my mind. To this day, I still wonder why they waited until my combination birthday-graduation party to announce this. What hurt was I did not know the truth sooner. All my life I thought I was part of them. I saw in my mind the obvious truth that, not just Mother Clara and Florence knew this secret, but the whole extended family. For the first time I didn't feel whole. There was the knowledge that half of myself was an unknown. After the revelation, I wondered how far my parental roots extended. In what country did my real father's family originate? Did he think of me? Did I have brothers and sisters? What school did he attend? Did he like the water, swimming and boats like I did? And dogs and cows like the ones I loved at Aunt Anna's?

The heart-breaking story told me on my eighteenth birthday left me with an unquenchable thirst for information. It is the single-most important reason for my lifetime interest in genealogy and history. Yet, to this day, in my mid-seventies, I still hurt and my mind yet begs the answer to: "Why wasn't I wanted?" As a young lady I wasn't allowed to attend school functions — never dances — unless Mother accompanied me. I was never allowed to wear silk stockings (nylon didn't exist then), only Lisle, a rayon cotton mix. Mother said, "Lisle stockings are more ladylike."

I remember something she said when I was fifteen minutes late getting home from Dorothy Leek's (at 7:15 PM!) and they banished me to sit on the back porch. It was shocking because I now understood those words (which they had often uttered when angry with me) in a new way. I remember the words Mother said in anger, "Go back where you came from!" It meant, "Go back to Winston

Chandler Worthington," but I thought it must have been, "Go back to Aunt Florence."

As I continued to think about this, it meant that my Grandpa Weigmann, whom I dearly loved, wasn't my grandpa.

'They can't take Grandpa away!'

I thought, 'Maybe that's what they meant that time they had the Bund picnic and said, "You're not German." But if my aunt was my mother, who was my father? What was he like? What was his name? What is my real name?'

It was like my father and mother died; and for months, even years after that, I was in mourning. Later I was told my real father died in an auto accident! I felt my world, as I knew it, had been turned upside down. I needed more facts. I hadn't even thought to ask for a birth certificate. They said his name was Worthington, that some of his family were down Easterner Yankees with family in Canada and Massachusetts. I felt so alone!

I thought, 'I have to go talk to Grandpa. He'd understand me. So would Nuzzie. Grandpa and Nuzzie are the ones I can talk to.'

When Mother went shopping, I called and Grandpa answered.

I said, "When will you be alone in the house, or could you and Nuzzie meet me at Sanders? I need to talk to you."

Figure 14 Grandpa, a great man, a great chef, a friend.

Figure 15 Sanders Store, Woodward Avenue, Detroit, 1925

"I think I should come pick you up."

"No, I'll meet you. I want our meeting to be a secret."

"I understand. You go to Sanders, Oakland and Grand River."

"Okay," I said. "I'll be there in about thirty minutes."

I walked quickly toward Sanders. I saw the car come up and park. Grandpa and I ordered our hot fudge sundaes for free because Grandpa had an interest in the store. We were eating this wonderful French vanilla ice cream, smothered with magnificent hot fudge topping.

"Grandpa, I don't know who I am anymore, but I love you and I don't want you not to be my grandpa anymore. You're my best friend."

"Nein, *nein,* you will always be my granddaughter. You're my little '*totskala*.' You're my only granddaughter; you're the only grandchild that I have. Do you think I would ever give you away? You'll always be my granddaughter, Lily."

"That's another thing that worries me. My name is supposed to be Grace Lucille, not Lily Lucille."

Grandpa said, "You'll always be Lily Flower to me," and he gave me a big hug. Afterwards we went to the car, and he said, "Nuzzie, let's drive over to the new development of houses."

Grandpa was one of the first to build California style houses in our area. He built over sixty houses in Dearborn. Even as a child, I would look at the blueprints with him. He was curious to see if the buildings were on schedule.

Talking to me as Nuzzie drove, he said, "Just remember what I told you. Nothing can ever take you away from your grandpa. I'm sorry you had to find out that way, and on your birthday, terrible! *Gott im Himmel!* Is there something you need? What about a new hat? We can go to Hudson's."

"No."

"Wouldn't you like some new clothes?"

"No, I really don't want anything. I just wanted to be sure you were still my grandpa."

He gave me another big hug. "Remember what I told you whenever we went up to the farm or Hubbard Lake? I told you to look up at those great oak trees and giant pine trees. What did I say?"

"You told me you would be in every leaf of every tree," I replied. "And every acorn and every wild rose bud. Whenever I have trouble, I'm supposed to look at the trees and know you'll be near me."

I still do it to this day. I often think of Grandpa as I walk the farm paths looking at the stately maples. He was such a noble and wise man. I was so lucky to have someone so pure of heart, so honorable. Like Grandma Latimer Jackson, these people were traditionalists; they epitomized honor, trust and love.

X - Meeting John Moran Severette

"Now, the Story Really Begins"

agosto de 1938 a enero de 1939

"*Cherie, je t'aime mon petit chou*!" (My sweet, I love you, my darling!) said John. His French was flawless.

Life's memories are like ragged cliffs, a pounding sea, a blowing wet wind in your face, or wriggling your toes in the sand. They are a song that stays with you all your life, such as "I'm in the Mood for Love." It's sweet, yet vibrant like "The Warsaw Concerto," thunder and lightening like the code "..._" — awakening memories that are stirring within.

At the age of eighteen I wanted to go to Wayne State University. I wanted to be a doctor.

Mother Clara replied, "But, Lily, you have to start earning a living. Beauty School is a real opportunity!"

I thought a minute, then said, "I could make a better living as a doctor and help people."

"We can't waste money. It doesn't do girls any good to get a fancy education. You only need to know how to cook, clean and change diapers."

The argument was settled. I was marched off to this beauty school. I didn't like it either, but I always loved to put on makeup, even nail polish on my dog's nails.

My teachers liked me. They said I had a dramatic flair for design in hairstyles.

This is where I met John Moran Severette, my first love. This is where "*Je t'aime, Cherie*" began. He was three years older than I was, with wavy red hair and gorgeous blue eyes.

His mother owned a large beauty salon in Detroit. She was an expert in wigs and hair design. I always admired her. She and her family were from the Normandy area of France. This is the same area my Grandmother Harriet Ann Agnes Latimer was from, as well as Alsace. My mother, though North Yorkshire English, was French and Irish, just as John was! John was sent to beauty school, even though he was already a student at Depaul University. Mrs. Severette wanted him to carry on the business if she couldn't. He had planned to return to college after beauty school.

My mother and father were with me when we met. After signing me up at the Detroit Beauty College, we walked out into the hall, where John was talking with some students.

He looked toward me, saying, "I'm John; are you a new student?"

"Yes, I'm Lily."

"Do you live nearby?"

"No, Oakman Boulevard."

He said, "We're neighbors. I live two blocks off Oakman."

Dad then said, "You will have to come over, John. We're having a big picnic on Labor Day."

John said, "If I can get away, I'll be over, and thank you."

Sure enough, guess who showed up at our house. The wavy red-headed young man, John! The picnic was in full swing with several of our family attending in the back yard. Everybody contributed to the picnic in potluck fashion, along with Hattie, Grandma and Mother's cook, showing her southern skills with barbecued beef ribs, so deliciously luscious. I've never tasted any better anywhere. Grandpa was in seventh heaven as was Nussie — he loved to eat and cook like Grandpa.*

---

*Recipe for Hattie's Barbecue Sauce with Grandpa & Nussie's special additives, see Appendix.

Figure 16 Me, age 18, hours before beauty contest, my hair still in pincurls!

After six weeks at beauty school I was permitted to work on the public. People were already asking for me, special. The head of the school would compliment me, writing glowing notes to my mother, but I longed to study medicine.

"Mother," I said, "Maybe I could own my own beauty salon, then make money for medical school."

"All you think of is business or medicine!" she said, disgusted.

Five weeks later, the school had a big hairstyle show at the Book Cadillac Hotel. Helene Curtis, a prominent beauty product manufacturer, sponsored it.

I will never forget the gorgeous dress I wore of baby blue satin, its flowing princess lines touching the floor. I don't think Daddy knew how much Mother spent at Hudson's. My long hair was finger wave set with tiers of sausage curls hanging down the back. The attraction was the precision finger wave as my hair was in waves to shoulders and tiers of curls below.

We walked around the dance floor of this beautiful ballroom while numerous camera lights flashed from the beauty magazine photographers. I was third runner up. I received a makeup kit and a coupon for a screen test at MGM in Hollywood. John attended with my parents.

John and I became very close friends. We talked about our likes and dislikes. He wanted to be a doctor, as I did, but decided to be a pharmacist instead.

By the time Thanksgiving came we knew we were in love. My family was strict and never allowed us to be alone, except to walk to the movies and back. And they timed us, knowing when the movie started and ended and allowing forty-five minutes walk each way. Near Thanksgiving Mother asked John to come over for her yummy marshmallow melts.*

My dad asked him if he wanted to hear the Burns and Allen radio show. John did, and we gathered around the "Big Majestic" radio. I had seen pictures of George Burns and Gracy Allen in magazines. I could almost see them while I listened.

John was sitting next to me. He kept patting me on the knee when no one was looking. Then he motioned towards the porch. I knew we couldn't leave while the radio show was on. I put my finger up to say "Wait." We waited for the show to end.

Then I said to Mother, "Can we go on the porch?"

She replied, "Just raise the shades so I can see you."

I lifted the three ivory colored fringe-bottomed shades. Donning our coats, we walked outside to the porch swing.

After we sat down, John moved very close, looking into my eyes, and said, "I love you, *mon petit chou*."

---

*Recipe for Mother Clara's Marshmallow Melts in back Appendix.

I thought I would die! I had dreamed about love. I wanted him near me, but how?

He said again, "Cherie, I really love you! *Je t'aime, Cherie*!" I've never met anyone who thinks like me the way you do, and we both should be doctors. Maybe if we work on it we can, and I have a plan."

I asked, "How?"

He said, "The way things are developing overseas, with the Germans invading Poland, France and Great Britain will be next. I plan to enlist in the Navy. I was told I could get a commission as an officer. If we were married, our futures would be secured. I'm guaranteed my Navy training for medical school. If there is a war, I'd work for my medical degree as a pharmacist afterwards. I could then help you through medical school!"

This sounded wonderful!

He said, "I want this to be our secret engagement. I'm going to ask your parents if we can get married at Christmas."

"I don't think they'd agree, John," though my heart was beating so fast. "Engaged!" I whispered. "Oh, John!" Our eyes met, but all we could do was hold hands as he handed me his class key from DePaul University. I didn't really know the full significance of what it meant when taking it, but I almost cried. He brushed my cheek with his lips, making sure my folks didn't see. We couldn't even hug, my parents ever watchful.

I whispered, "I know I love you, John, I do!"

But we could only hold hands.

"I promise you, Lily, we will be together always, *mon Cherie*," he said, speaking his fluent French, which he started speaking as a child before he spoke English.

The weeks passed quickly, John visiting our home several days a week. He even played ping-pong with Dad in our basement playroom. We played a foursome with Uncle Ernie and me a few times.

John arrived on Christmas Day with three presents. He greeted my parents, giving Mother a box of candy and Dad a box of cigars. Then he handed me my present. We stood by the lighted Christmas tree as I opened the box, which held a gold watch with two diamonds.

"Oh, it's so lovely!" I exclaimed.

Facing me, he pulled a small box out of his suit coat pocket, then turned toward my parents, and said, "Mister and Mrs. Wagner, I would like to ask for your daughter's hand in marriage."

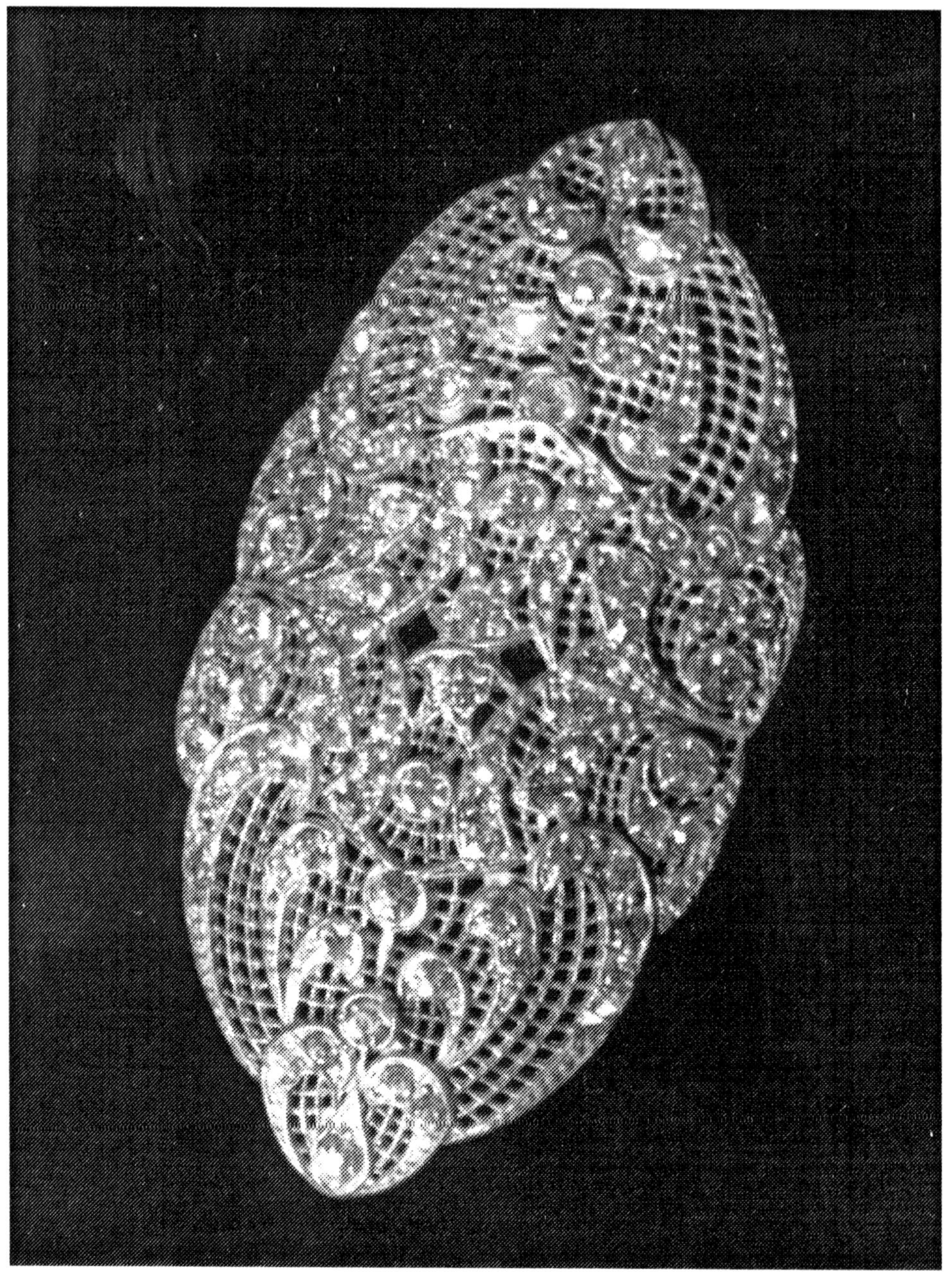

Figure 17 Diamond brooch that was my mother's, given to me at age 18.

It was as though a thunderbolt hit the house. My dad's face turned beet red and my mother jumped up, "Oh, no, no, she can't be married! She has to finish beauty school!"

John said, "Please, Mrs. Wagner, you haven't heard what I have to say. I'm going in the Navy. I have two years of Pharmacy College; I can transfer toward a medical degree through the Navy. Then Lily can join me. I'll be an officer; I can support Lily. I love her and Lily loves me."

John opened the box and showed them a ring with three sparkling diamonds, then handed it to me!

Loudly protesting, Mother said, "No, no, later John, maybe in a year."

Standing up, they both said family members would be coming over soon. John certainly got the message. We walked to the door. I just tried to hug him without being too explicit about it. How do you hug someone and not hug him? I just gave him a hug around the shoulders, he did the same. Our eyes met and we both knew what we were thinking. Neither of us had been dissuaded, in the least. I was not allowed to accept the engagement ring, but they did allow me to keep the watch.

I think they wondered, "When did they ever find time to find out they were in love?" In my family, a young couple was watched and hardly got to hold hands, let alone do any heavy petting. There weren't any chances to do that unless you were sitting in the back row of a movie theatre, and then just kiss. You just obeyed, not that you wouldn't hope otherwise. But the discipline was firm in my parents' house.

Usually, the closest we could get together was walking in the rain or snowstorm, arm in arm. I remember he had a tan Khaki trench coat and I had a beautiful black Karakul fur coat trimmed in sealskin with matching muff. We sang songs as we walked the two miles each way to the movies. Some of the songs were "It Had to be You," my favorite, "Good Night Sweet Heart," "You're the Cream In My Coffee" and Cole Porter's "You Do Something To Me."

A romance had been under way, and it was fostered by both of us. Just being in the same room when our hands touched, it was like a spark of lightning. I would see him walking very fast, crossing the road, corner to corner, so he could get to our front porch steps quicker. I would feel my heart pounding and goose bumps on my arms. The anticipation of waiting to see John always turned minutes into hours. I felt like I was charged with a special magic energy, meant just for me. When our hands touched, our bodies demanded more, but these desires had to be suppressed.

The extent of my sex education could be summed up by: "It's the birds and the bees, and you will find out when you get married." My girlfriends, Virginia Finn, Dorothy Leeke and Jane Leonard were told this, too.

Janet, a new neighbor, said her father had never seen her mother totally bare! She walked into the bathroom while her mother was in the tub and asked her mother what her father thought about the birthmark on her hip. Her mother told her she didn't know; he had never seen it!

John and I were allowed to go into the basement to play ping-pong. I am quite sure someone upstairs was listening to make sure there were no lengthy gaps in the pings! Sometimes my Uncle Ernie would come down on some excuse to get a couple of bottles of Dad's home brew locked in the fruit cellar. We were rarely left alone. The few times we were close enough to hug and talk was during lunch hours at the beauty school. During these times we sat on the back steps of the beauty school. It was maybe five to fifteen minutes that we met there each day. We discussed our future, the kind of house, even the furnishings.

John said, "Your kitchen will be all-electric. I am going to get you an electric mixer, refrigerator, washer and dryer, too."

Bendix had just come out with them. My mother had the first Sears Cold Spot refrigerator and Bendix washer-dryer pair on the block.

One Sunday John had borrowed the family car to pick me up for church. After we got in the car to go home, John reached in the back for a package. He handed it to me, and when I opened it up there was a beautiful blue satin little Chinese brocade jacket top and pant bottom for a baby.

John said, "This will be for our baby someday when we have one."

He told me his father had sent it to his mother while he was in the Navy in World War I, for John when he was several months old. The ship was torpedoed, even though the surrender had already been signed. A German submarine, running under radio silence, didn't know. His father went down with many of the crew. I felt so sad as I handed his precious keepsake back.

We had all kinds of plans of being the best doctors. We also liked inventing creams in my mother's kitchen. He used my mother's Universal mixer to make them. Into the mixer John would pour mineral oil with melted bees' wax, adding glycerin, almond oil and drops of rose oil; half of one batch had a drop of peppermint oil. We presented this to my mother and dad as our first historic cream.

Four days before New Years, John called; and he said, "My family has extra tickets to the New Years Ball at the Book Cadillac. Would you like to go?"

"Oh, of course, yes, yes."

John came to the house and asked permission. My parents checked with his, and permission was given. His parents let him use their car. They were going also, but with other relatives. I wore that gorgeous blue satin dress again with

Mother's diamond necklace, beautiful matching earrings and my Christmas watch.

It was my first ball. As we left, my father and mother said to be home by one. "And, we'll wait up for you."

It was a beautiful ballroom with crystal chandeliers surrounding the entire ballroom and dining room.

John was just old enough to drink, but did not. We had a wonderful dinner, but we really enjoyed the dessert cart. We picked their famous Napoleon pastries with layers of *pate a choux* (puff paste like cream puff shells) filled with custard, strawberries, whipped cream, chocolate glaze, and topped with more whipped cream and a Maraschino cherry. This was *ecstasy.* Later, dinner coffee and mints were served as we talked, looking deep into each other's eyes. The orchestra changed from soft dinner music and began to play the magnificent big band music. A wonderful melody we loved to dance to was "Dancing Cheek to Cheek" by Irving Berlin. John and I danced the night away. And now he could hold me close. For the first time I could put my head on his shoulder. We still watched cautiously because his parents were on the dance floor at times.

As balloons fell from the ceiling, amid strains of "Auld Lang Syne," we had our first real kiss. The lights dimmed, brightened, then the midnight hour had arrived! I felt like Cinderella. I'd have to go home soon. John brought me home dutifully at 1:01 A.M. The lights were on in the house and the porch light on. Mother and Dad were waiting, saying "Happy New Year". Saying "goodnight" quickly, John left.

A week later on the school's back stairs, John held my hand as he told me his plan. He had talked to a Navy recruiter. John said he was coming over after dinner. That evening John told my parents he was enlisting in the Navy and was waiting to see where he'd be assigned. He again asked that they allow us to be married, once he was officially accepted. They said I was too young to be married, regardless. They were not going to give their permission. John and I talked to them that week, to the point of bitter crying and tears.

This was before we were officially involved in World War II. All of us who lived through this era knew something was going to happen soon to cause our country to be in the war. We would definitely have to help England. Poland already was a victim of Hitler's desire for power. War was in the newspapers, on newsreels at the movies; and the radio was on for hours, in case there was late breaking news. Dad also listened to his short-wave radio and would let me listen. It was a sober time. Everyone was tense but secure in the knowledge that whatever Americans had to do, we would accomplish it. Some in Europe felt this was the bravado of a young country still wet behind the ears. But we really knew that whatever task was demanded, we would succeed! It was an exciting time in our lives. The bonding of Americans was like the love of a mother and her newborn.

During the last weeks of beauty school we used to harmonize on the back steps. One of the songs was, "I'd Be Lost Without You," and I still sing this song. Another of my favorites was "It Had to be You." That kept my spirits up long weeks and months later. Gus Kahn wrote the lyrics, and the music was by Isham Jones; I'm a music lover. These words are for everyone who's a lover: "It had to be you, I wandered around, and finally found, somebody who, could make me be true ..."*

The seriousness of getting into the Navy, planning careers, a wedding in the backdrop of these tumultuous times, added to the urgency of our actions. Decisions had to be made quicker. War seemed imminent. The next day John and I, sitting on the back fire stairs, were intently studying a book of maps.

"I could be gone six, eight weeks, but I've got a plan that will work."

As John studied the map of Texas, he pointed to El Paso.

"I met a fellow at the Navy recruiting station, and I told him of our dilemma. He told me he married his girlfriend in Mexico, right out of El Paso, and is taking her to the submarine base in Connecticut."

I said, "They'll marry us? Without Mother's permission?"

"Yes, anybody can get married. How much money do you have?"

"I guess, about forty dollars." That was a fortune to me.

He said, I can raise thirty or forty dollars, and I want you to leave for El Paso when I give you the word. You will have enough money for three days. I will write to the main post office, or meet you in El Paso. Lily, we're going to be married in Mexico!"

We were hugging each other, relishing our plan.

The excitement boiled. I met him on the back steps again.

It was finally arranged I was to meet John at the *Greyhound Bus Station* in two days. Everything happened so fast. I packed my black patent leather hatbox. I took my tote-like bag to school earlier and put it in my locker. I said to Mother that we were designing hairstyles. I brought home my wig case and took the wig form out. In it I put the book of poems by Longfellow Mother had given me and my Grandma Latimer's beautiful billowing peach taffeta negligee that was from 1900, still perfect and very precious.

I thought, 'I'll wear that on my wedding night.' I wouldn't have a wedding gown, but took my lovely blue satin formal. I also took makeup, three changes of clothes, my Bible, some pictures and my teddy bear. The teddy bear always reminded me of Grandpa who gave him to me so many years before.

I wore my fur coat and cap, the muff attached to my belt, and away I went to school. I had written my parents a note telling them I loved them and was

---

*By permission from the music company for use of these lyrics.

leaving because I wanted to marry John and I wanted to be a doctor, but they wouldn't let me do either one. I said I would phone them as soon as I could. I went to school that day. I went through all the classes 'till lunchtime. Then I took my things out of my locker and walked down the back staircase where we had been planning our future, kissing and singing our songs. Going through my mind with each step on those metal stairs was the realization that I would probably never see this meeting place again.

I thought, 'He promised his mother that he would watch her beauty shop for her tomorrow, but at any time John could be called to report for duty.' He had enlisted in the Navy. 'He told me that he would be at the bus station and I am going,' I assured myself.

I took a cab to the bus station (it cost me a whole fifty cents), and bought my ticket for El Paso, Texas. John was there. It was very emotional. We hugged and we cried. He had this wonderful solid muscular body like a football player has. He had big shoulders and his bright wavy red hair to accent those beautiful blue eyes.

John made me repeat this: I was to check the post office every day until the letter or John came. He or the letter had to be there in three days. That's all the money I would have for a hotel and meals.

John drew me close as the last "All-aboard!" was called.

He said, "I love you, *mon cherie* Lily! Just three days," he added, holding up three fingers, "And then no one can keep us apart."

I was the last person to board the bus.

"Oh, I love you, too!" I said, as I held up three fingers through the window of the bus. And I blew John a kiss through the window as the bus pulled out. We both waved until the bus turned the corner. I had an empty feeling in my chest, but I was so sure that no one could keep us apart.

John had given me a box of chocolates and a rose. This was a joyous time. I was on a bus, leaving to be married in Mexico.

Figure 18 Dancing Cheek to Cheek - danced to this with John Severette

98
IT HAD TO BE YOU
Words by Gus Kahn Music by Isham Jones
Moderate swing
Why do I do just as you say, why must I just give you your way,
Seems like dreams like I always had, could be, should be making me glad.
Why do I sigh, why don't I try to forget?
Why am I blue? It's up to you to explain.
It must have
I'm thinking

Figure 19 It Had To Be You - our song

Words by Gus Kahn, Music by Isham Jones, © 1924 (renewed) Warner Brothers, Inc., Rights for the Extended Renewal Term in the U.S.A. controlled by Gilbert Keyes Music and Bantam Music Publishing Co., and administered by The Songwriters Guild of America, World Rights outside the U.S.A. controlled by Warner Brothers, Inc., All Rights Reserved, Reprinted by Permission of Warner Brothers Publications, U.S. Inc.

Figure 20 You're the Cream in My Coffee - We sang this over and over.

XI - El Paso

1939

The trip on the bus was like on most buses, but in those days the buses and the bus stations were much cleaner. The diners and the country cooking was good. Travelling cross-country really was fun. I enjoyed seeing the people, differences in specialty foods of the area and even their voices, a little drawl, a slight twang, as we were in the South and West. I had seen Mexican people only a couple of times in Michigan. And I contemplated this most momentous trip in my life (or so I thought), my thoughts of John and our soon to be wedding.

Entering El Paso, Texas, there were Mexicans and real cowboys with big Stetson Hats, like in the movies! I had arrived at last! I had to get my hatbox, the wig box and all the rest of my things that I had to carry.

I carried my coat as it was much warmer than Michigan. I went to the ticket lady's booth and asked her where I could go to get a reasonable room.

"There's a nice little hotel around the corner, down the street a block, on the right," she said pointing. "It's an apartment hotel where a lot of women do stay. If you go there, tell them that Ledy at the bus station sent you. You can rent a storage locker for your things and get them later."

I said, "Oh, thank you, Ledy. I'll do that." It turned out to be only a dollar.

I entered the lobby of the three-story red brick building.

"Ledy sent me, and I need a room for maybe two, or three days," I told the woman at the desk.

As I checked in I was confident and very excited. I had a chance to eat a tamale at the last dinner stop, and I thought they were out of this world! So I asked the hotel clerk, "Is there a place where you can get those wonderful tamales?"

"Yes, right here behind the hotel, just a little ways," she answered, motioning with her hand.

Then she told me how to get to the post office. It was too late. I'd have to wait until tomorrow. I went to the restaurant, and I'll never forget those tamales and the enchilada! To this day, I could eat Mexican food morning, noon and night. Returning to my room, I showered and got into my pajamas. The room was cozy with a big lounge chair in the corner, even some magazines on the end table.

"I'd better get to bed early," I thought. Crawling under the covers, I suddenly felt a sense of accomplishment.

The anticipation was starting to steadily build. I was sure John knew I was in El Paso by then, and I finally fell asleep.

I rushed to the post office the next morning. I was too excited to eat breakfast. I couldn't wait to get there. I went to the General Delivery window and asked if there was a letter for me.

The man came back saying, "No, there's not a letter."

I was pretty dumbfounded. "Well, it's supposed to be there. Would you look again, please?"

He did, and he came back with a slight frown. "Where would it be coming from?"

"I think it's Connecticut, but it might have been Michigan."

"No, nothing," he said. "Is he in the Service?"

"Yes, the Navy," I said.

"Oh, well, I'm sorry; but we get more mail at 1 PM, so check a couple of times a day."

"Oh, I will."

I left thinking, 'I wonder if they eat tamales for breakfast?'

I looked across the street, and there was a Woolworth's. It had a big cup of coffee painted on the front window with "DONUTS 5 cents" painted underneath.

I thought, 'That's it, I'll go get a cup of coffee, a donut and buy a newspaper.'

I ate my donut and drank the coffee as I read the paper. I kept thinking about how soon John's letter would arrive.

After I looked the paper over, I walked around to see what El Paso was like.

They had all kinds of little shops and wonderful Mexican goods. The colorful shawls intrigued me and also the beautiful creative pottery, colorful hand embroidered blouses, silver and copper bracelets and silver and turquoise jewelry. I bought a pair of silver and turquoise earrings. I think they were a dollar, which was a real expense for me. I wanted to look gorgeous, and they hung longer than any earrings I'd ever owned. You didn't see that kind of jewelry very much in Michigan in those days, and I wanted to surprise John. I was at the post office before five once again.

The man said, "Sorry, there's no mail." I was really sad; and he said, "Oh, I wouldn't worry. If he's in the Navy, you know; it could have been delayed."

The next day came, and I had to pay for the three days at the hotel. There was no letter when the post office opened and no telegram. I didn't know what to do. I walked back to my room; it was my last night. If I paid another day there, I wouldn't have enough for a bus trip anywhere.

I thought, 'I'll read the paper some more.'

I saw pawn shop ads. I was getting scared. One pawnship said, "Open 24 Hours," and another place said, "Call Anytime Up Till Midnight," and another ad said, "Jitney Travel $13 Los Angeles."

I thought, 'Well, okay,' so I walked to the pawnshop.

It was a well-lit city, and it wasn't that late. The man at the pawnshop offered me five dollars for my watch. I was near penniless, but I wouldn't take the money.

I went back to the room saying to myself, 'Now let me see that paper again.'

There was the jewelry store and it was open until nine p.m. I walked back downtown.

I went in and said to the man behind the counter, "I have to get to Hollywood."

You know that's the first thing I thought of when I saw that Jitney ad for $13. I thought, 'I may have to do that. I could take advantage of that coupon I have and get a screen test. I could transfer my mail to the main post office in Los Angeles or Hollywood. This is what I'll do. I can't stay here.'

There was no way to call John. I didn't know how to call a submarine base and I had no number. I just counted on the letter or the telegram.

I sold the watch to the jeweler for $25.00. I know John paid much more. I was sad, but I had to do it. With what little I had and that twenty-five dollars, I called that Jitney number before midnight. The man said he'd pick me up at the hotel. He was leaving at 5:00 a.m.

He said, "You've got to be ready outside about a quarter to five."

I was standing in the lobby with my baggage at 4:30 a.m. and the jitney pulled up. The driver saw me come through the swinging door. I didn't even know what a jitney was at the time. I paid him the thirteen dollars and the fifty cents extra to pick me up. The entire back end of this vehicle had double seats that were facing each other; and then this little seat, called the jump seat, that pulled out behind the driver's seat.

He said, "Here, kid, you can take the jump seat."

He put my baggage on top of the vehicle where there was a metal railing. He was nice enough to tie a blanket over my things. The hatbox was shiny patent leather; and the wig case was red snakeskin, very beautiful. I got in and discovered that the seat was less comfortable than it looked.

I was the only woman in a vehicle full of men, and those men didn't look clean or happy. They smelled of raw garlic and alcohol on that warm breezeless early morning. I was not comfortable at all. I thought of it as a big extended car. The driver, on the other hand, had put on a generous amount of lotion that mixed with his beer breath, producing a sickly sweet stench. When he let out the clutch the vehicle lumbered on its way west.

There was an early rain as the sun rose into a pink sky, an omen promising good fortune. I was still so sure of myself, even though I knew something had happened to John. I knew I was going to make it, and I was going to find him. We were going to get married in Mexico. I knew Mexico joined California; and Tiajuana, Mexico, was on the USA border just below San Diego, California. That's where I'd go to marry John.

So the trip was a little rough, but I didn't care because I had a mission. I was going to do it, and somehow I would find John. The jitney plugged along.

The driver said, "We'll be arriving late. Maybe 1 a.m. We'll be driving all day and night until we get there, then I'll let you off by the Los Angeles train depot."

I thought, 'Okay, I'll go inside the train depot and get directions for a hotel for one night or sleep in the depot overnight. I'll comb my hair in the bathroom, get a newspaper and figure out where I'm going. Pennies count now.' I'd go to Hollywood and the post office. I had put in the change of address in the El Paso post office.

Well, the jitney made it, and I went inside the train depot.

They had lockers in the train station you could rent for twelve hours for twenty-five cents. I put two dimes and a nickel in and shoved the luggage in, along with my hat and muff. Then I went to the bathroom, put cold water on my face, redid my makeup and combed my hair. I bought a newspaper and ordered coffee right there in the waiting room where they had a quick service stand. I went over and asked a ticket man, when his aisle was empty, if there was a decent motel where a lady would be safe.

He said, "There is, but it's not right around here."

It was already late, but I wasn't that tired. I decided that I would just sit there reading the newspaper and snooze with my head on my coat as long as I could. I had this faith. I knew it was doubtful for a forwarded letter to get there that soon, but when morning came, the same ritual was repeated, splashing water on my face, combing my hair and the rest so I'd look human again.

I put another quarter in the locker and went to the post office. I talked to the postman at the window and told him my story of how I was looking for either a telegram or a letter, General Delivery. He went back, looked and returned saying, "No, there's no letter, but you can check later."

I said, "I don't know if I'm going to be here."

"Where will you be?" he asked.

I said, "I'm going to Hollywood." I don't know why I said that. I said, "Do you have a post office near MGM or Paramount Studios?"

"Yes, Ma'am."

"If I'm not back in two days, anything coming here for me, you could send there?"

"Okay," he said. "Here, take this card. Fill it out now. I'll send anything that's here, there."

I thought, "I covered all of my tracks. It's a last resort. I'll write John at the beauty school and his mother's home."

On the outskirts of Hollywood there were lots of apartments and rooms to rent. I had to have a place just for the night at that point, so I finally found a very small rooming house and rented a room for four dollars, seventy five cents a night. After putting my things in the room, I went down the hall to shower. On the way back, the landlady met me.

She asked, "Do you have a radio?"

"No."

"I have an extra one. You can borrow it. You look so lonely. It's my son's. He's in the service."

"I'll take good care of it and return it when I leave," I replied.

I got another newspaper, listened to the radio and tried to read the paper, but my mind kept thinking of John.

I wondered, 'Where is he? What is he doing? He must have known that I had reached El Paso.'

I had put the change of address in, I'd checked the mail and would do it again. I was sitting and thinking of the song on the radio called "All of Me." It was so beautiful. It meant that all of me was yours.

I thought, 'If things had turned out differently I probably would have been with John now, singing this song or "Dancing in the Dark" and "Embraceable You" or gliding across a dance floor.' These songs are precious — to one's heart a dream to dance to.

These songs were especially sad in a way, because many of the ones I heard were the songs that John and I had listened to, sung together and danced to. Tears started streaming down my face.

XII - Baba

1939

I found a newspaper ad that read, "Lady will share apartment at Green Gables apartments," which was close to Paramount Studios. I was barely knocking on the door when three girls opened it and one grabbed me when I said I had fifteen dollars! I was going to sleep in the Murphy bed they showed me.

After taking the money, the redhead said, "You sleep on the couch. We're professional dancers and need a good mattress. You're not a dancer yet."

I said, "I can dance, but I'm not a professional like you are."

She said, "Stick with us, honey, we'll show you the ropes. What do you know?"

"A little tap and soft shoe. I had lessons at the Riviera Theatre. Dorothy Leek and I would go on Saturdays. I paid ten cents to have my tap lessons on the stage before the movies started."

They looked at each other. "Oh, well, that may help," the tall red-head said, demonstrating her dance ability with a high kick. "I'll teach you, but for now you do the housework around here!"

There were five of us girls in a one-bedroom apartment of the Green Gables. Needless to say, I only stayed with these girls a short while. I had just arrived in Los Angeles; and when I called Central Casting, there were no jobs. I started looking at help wanted ads. I had just given up an opportunity to go with Howard Hughes and two other dancers to Las Vegas, but I knew I was there to get into the movies, not only be a dancer. I knew of "the other" that often went along with those trips to Las Vegas with men one didn't know and wanted no part of that! It was imperative that I find work. However, I really wanted to get into the movies. I kept thinking, 'Maybe John could see a movie I was in and find me.' That day's ad said, "Dancers needed."

With what I had learned at the Riviera, I thought, 'I might just as well try it.' So I walked to the nearby corner and took a bus.

Getting off the bus, I didn't know the area of the job address. I saw this building; and it didn't look at all like I expected, especially the marquee, "Dancing Girls." It was a burlesque! 'Oh, no, is this where the job is? It's not open,' I told myself.

It was still very early. At any rate, I walked in. Inside the back stage door there was an old gentleman sitting. He waved me toward an office. The door was open. A sort of a comfortably round, but very beautiful older woman sat behind the desk.

The pink lampshade on her desk let off a soft glow that gave her a quality of the surreal. She reminded me of a faded English Rose, yet there was a quality that made her look young. There was an inner youth, like this person had never aged. There was a radiance that emanated from beneath what I experienced with my eyes. I could not explain this.

Strangely she seemed like someone I'd met long ago. Looking back, she must have been about sixty. She motioned to me and stood up from behind the desk, saying, "Come in, dear, come in."

I walked in, almost hesitantly. I'd never been in a burlesque theatre before.

"I'm Baba," she said. Then she looked me over a little bit. Her eyes were sharp with experience. There was authority in her voice, yet gentleness. "I guess you're here looking for a dancer's job?"

"Yes, but I've never danced in a place like this."

She laughed softly and said to me, "Turn around."

I turned around.

She said, "Turn around again, then sit down."

"How long have you been in Hollywood?"

"About two months." I sure stretched the truth here.

"Have you ever done any stripping?"

I almost died in my tracks. I sat straight up in my chair and held my legs tight together while my hands grasped my purse. I looked at her and said, "No, and I'm not going to. I came in here because I can dance. I'm not a stripper."

Well, she just laughed, then said, "You know there's nothing really wrong in stripping, but we do have some intermission acts where you might be able to do a little dance. How old are you? You look terribly young. We couldn't have you here if you're not over eighteen."

"Well, of course. I'm nineteen." (I wasn't.)

She said, "You know, I've been in this business a long time. I used to be an actress and a dancer. Actually, I'm from Europe. Now I find myself at this kind of desk, in this kind of a building." With that, she pulled a drawer open and out came a bottle of vodka and a glass.

She said, "Do you want a drink?"

"No, I don't drink."

"Imagine that, you don't drink!"

She was smoking a cigarette, drinking her vodka; and I was watching her face. She had been very beautiful once, that was obvious. She had an accent, perhaps Polish, I thought. She was well dressed in a fine black suit with a lovely teal-color crepe blouse. Her clothes looked expensive. Her hair was reddish with specks of gray. I always thought of her as Baba Rose. Everybody called her Baba. In spite of the fact that I was shocked at the kind of place I was in, I still had a comfortable feeling around her.

She sent me out into a makeup room next to the costumes. It certainly was nothing like Paramount or MGM studios. This was rough, cold and impersonal with a lot of mirrors and lights. The costumes hung loosely on long, uncovered pipe racks.

She followed me in and said, "Let me see your face."

She got some makeup brushes and makeup. Apparently, she knew how to do that, too.

She said, "All right, try this costume on."

It was a short costume with black satin pants, a tuxedo white front and all black vest, bow tie, high hat, heels and tights.

She said, "Let me see what you can do."

I did a time step and soft-shoe, and she liked it. She said, "You're cute enough, you're young enough. The men just might throw money at you. You're not hired. I'm going to see what you do on the stage between acts. Those guys are so hungry, you're liable to make enough money, honey, that I won't have to pay you. You know they'll throw money at you."

"Well," I said, "nobody will hurt me?"

"Oh, no, we have bouncers," she said.

Baba also began talking to me a little about her own self. She said she had taught Carmen Miranda how to walk with her high hat. She called it a "fruit basket on her head." Baba had taken some acting and drama lessons from Phyllis Lawton. She called herself a drama coach. She had learned a lot from Ellinore Glenn and somebody by the name of Zilona or Silona. I looked at her eyes and thought, "She's a lot kinder than she might have appeared."

Finally she said, "Kid, are you hungry?"

"Well, I haven't eaten since last night."

"You haven't eaten since last night? Oh, come on, kid. We're not open here yet, you know. If you want, come with me; and we'll go have lunch. The other girls will be here in a while. The show will be on, but I want to introduce you to some people. We want to see how you act, what you do. Maybe we'll put you on Saturday."

She mentioned the Trocadero and asked, "Have you ever been to the Ambassador Hotel?"

I said, "Sure, I was a coat attendant at the Ambassador and worked as a cigarette girl at the Trocadero."

"That's where we're going, honey, to the Ambassador."

We went out the back door. The old man was still sitting there and tipped his hat as we walked by.

"I don't have that much money to eat there," I said, very worried.

"Honey, this treat's on me. I think you need somebody to watch over you."

I'll never forget what we had to eat because I have loved shrimp all my life and seldom could afford it. Just like lamb chops and frog-legs. We had a wonderful luncheon. Yes, shrimp!

She said, "The first thing you have to do is eat right, honey, if you want to look good on stage. You don't need pastries and a lot of fatty foods. You need fish, fruit and vegetables."

She was really ahead of her time. The Ambassador Hotel to me was *glamour*. Our wonderful lunch began with a shrimp cocktail. The shrimp looked as long as my biggest finger. I was just elated and, of course, excited, because looking around the room, I saw all these beautiful people. Soon people were coming over toward her. At the time, I didn't know who they were, but one of the persons approaching our table was Wally Westmore. He was a makeup artist, one of the well-known Westmores; and he worked mainly with Paramount. I almost fainted dead away, because one person who walked over to the table was Caesar Romero. I'd seen him in movies. I never thought I'd see him in person.

I was shaking and was about ready to stand up when he approached the table, but that wasn't what I was supposed to do. Baba just put her hand on my shoulder and said, "I want you to meet my next star."

He just laughed and asked, "Where?"

She said, "I'm going to make this kid famous."

"Good Luck," Mr. Romero said as he walked away.

Baba asked, "What name are you using?"

I told her that my name was Lily Wagner, but I should change my name because it was too much like a famous star.

She looked at me and asked, "What name do you like?"

I said, "I like Judy, but that would be too much like Judy Garland. I've been thinking of a new name."

"What is it?"

"Judyenne."

"That's it, we'll call you Judyenne."

The people at the burlesque were very nice to me. I was really the youngest one there. Looking back, everybody was trying to protect me. I was still a "green" young kid. Maybe that was why they liked me so much. I was not intimidating. I was somebody they could baby — they did, and they started calling me "Baby."

During our lunch Baba was questioning me and said, "I suppose you're from Ohio and want to become a famous movie star?"

"I lived near Ohio, and yes, I'd like to be a movie star."

"Why?"

"Well, I suppose, because I have to be successful. Then maybe somebody will pay attention to me."

"I couldn't imagine why anyone would not pay attention to *you*, dear. You're a very beautiful girl. So many girls come to Hollywood and they get into all kinds of trouble. I would hate to see that happen to you, because you're just different. Have you done any acting?"

"I was in several high school plays and was picked as an extra. I did a cattle call. It was in a western. When I called Central again, they said that there would be a part for a girl with long hair. Since I have long hair, I got a job on horseback, but I think the scene was cut."

She said, "Tomorrow we'll get started. Where are you staying?"

"At the Green Gables apartments near Paramount."

"How can you afford to stay there?"

"Five of us girls are sharing the one apartment. I only got to stay there because I had $15. When I knocked on the door, the girl that answered was a tall dancer with long legs, running around in the same tights you want me to wear."

Baba laughed. "Well, then, there's five of you in one apartment?"

"Yes, the older girls are dancers. They had to have the bedroom and the Murphy bed, so I sleep on the couch."

The next day, I went back. Baba's door was closed to her office. That's where I was supposed to report, so I tapped on the door.

She said, "Come in. Come on in the dressing room. I want you to put on a costume and the fishnet tights."

"But I don't do that type of work."

"No, no, you're going to be covered up with this adorable costume."

I didn't know what she had in mind, but at least she had a cute costume like for a cigarette girl. The skirt was full like a tutu. There was heavy watered silk taffeta over the tutu-like material.

She said, "Before you do that, put on some body paint." I had never put body paint on, only facial makeup.

She started patting me all over with this big puff after I got my clothes off, except for a bra and panties, then said, "I want you to put on this little black bra, these little G-string pants and then put on your fishnet tights."

The bra was nothing more than a string with two rose buds.

Well, I did that only because she said I would be covered up with this cute little costume. As I was pulling on the costume, I heard a door slam. The next thing I knew there was a strange man staring straight at me.

"So this is Baby?" he questioned.

I didn't know who he was, and I was terrified. I grabbed the little cigarette girl costume with the short frilly bottom and held it up to my waist. He started to laugh.

Baba said, "Yes, she is going to be my new star, and I've named her 'Judyenne.'"

He said, "Just think of me as your daddy. Put on your costume, honey."

I did; and Dimples, our lead dancer, came over and worked on my hair.

About that same time, that man, who was now over in the wings, yelled, "Come out on stage. I just want to see what your stage presence is. Because, if you're not going to make money for us stripping, we're got to have something, honey, that you are going to make money with."

I later learned he was Ivan Kahn, a booking agent. He watched me walk across the stage and down the runways.

"When you bend this way, you wriggle your butt that way," he said, gesturing with his behind.

By this time, he had walked within one foot of me.

"Take your hands, hold them this way," he coaxed with both his hands held up, fingers curving toward his chin and fluttering his eyelashes. "Cock your little head and move your eyes up and down. You're so childlike and innocent looking, this will really go over. I like it! Where's my photographer?"

A photographer walked up and before I knew quite what was happening, he had snapped several pictures of me.

Ivan Kahn said to Baba, "I'll be in touch."

He walked over and tapped me on the shoulder, saying, "Don't worry, Daddy will take care of everything."

Shortly after, Baba said, "Come with me," as we got in her luxurious car with her driver-bouncer, Frank. We drove to Santa Monica to visit her cousin, Madam Zurenski. I understood from Baba that she was a high priced astrologer to the movie stars. There were a lot of very important people in those days who had their palms read, and who had a psychic seer.

I'll never forget meeting her. When we entered the grounds, it was a large house with big blue Hydrangeas all around it. This was a large Spanish style stucco mansion with a two-story red brick and Spanish tile-roofed wing, a wrap-around side porch and French doors. We went through a side door where she apparently had a studio, and Baba called out her name. Behind the French doors, to the left of us, stood a handsome, dark-haired man. I thought he looked like a cross between George Raft and Rudolph Valentino as he walked away.

Baba then said, "I want you to meet my Baby, Judyenne, who I'm going to make a star."

Smiling, Madam Zurenski greeted us.

She laughed and said, "Oh, she always wants to make someone a star. One of these days, she's going to hit it lucky. Maybe it's going to be you."

Madam Zurenski had the sweetest face, like Baba's. She was a little taller, with a kind of a flowing, muumuu-type dress. She was wearing a little turban. I noticed that her hair looked dyed reddish auburn and was rather pretty. She asked us to come out on the patio verandah, where a young girl came out wearing a little maid's uniform and served us tea and cookies.

Baba said, "This kid is living and sleeping on a couch at the Green Gables apartments with a bunch of dancers. She shouldn't be around those hoofers."

Madam Zurenski said, "You're right. I've got lots of room here, so she can stay here. Let's show her the house. Come with me." So Baba and I followed her up the beautiful winding staircase.

There were five bedrooms upstairs. One of the bathrooms upstairs was very large, at least 20 feet wide and had a steam cabinet in it, too. One bedroom had a private bath. There was another wing I never got to see then. Downstairs were two bathrooms plus the servants' quarters. As the maid disappeared through the dining room, I noticed a commercial "Wolf" range through the swinging door to the kitchen. Of course I loved to cook and loved kitchens.

We went upstairs to a little bedroom that had violet flowered curtains and a birdcage.

Madam Zurenski said, "This is my pet bird, Tootsie. You can share the room with Tootsie, if you don't mind."

"Where did it get the name 'Tootsie?'" I asked.

"Oh, from Al Jolson's song," she replied.

I was just thrilled, because this was a beautiful home. This was what I was really used to, so I said, "But I don't know if I can afford the room."

"Is five dollars a week too much?" she asked.

"Oh, I'll take it!" I exclaimed.

Baba said, "You don't have to pay now, you'll be doing your act tomorrow and you'll probably make ten to fifteen dollars when they throw money on the stage."

I thought, 'They're going to throw all that money at me. I can pay five dollars easy.'

Madam Zurenski said, "Oh good, that's settled. We've got lots to do, teaching you how to walk, high kick and many dance routines, and acting — the works! Yes, Baba, you're right, Judyenne has promise."

Well, I was ecstatic! This was the chance of a lifetime. How many people would take that much interest in me?

XIII - Madam Zurenski

1939

It was extremely interesting and exciting at Madam Zurenski's. I saw the famous and some infamous people who came there, as well as backstage at the burlesque house where dear Baba tried her best to make a star out of me.

I couldn't imagine paying only five dollars a week in that gorgeous mansion, meals included!

I had to get my things out of the apartment at the Green Gables; and I didn't know how welcome I would be moving out, so I was hesitant to take the streetcar or bus. I mentioned this to Baba after more dance practice.

"Don't worry," Baba said, "I'll get Frank to take you."

A new man was backstage taking Frank's place, so Frank drove me to the Green Gables. Of course, I feared trouble because they needed my money to get by. I was paid up, though. I walked in and just said, "I'm going to move out."

They had a funny look on their faces. They weren't going to give me my suitcase, nor any of my belongings.

"I have to move," I added.

One of them said, "You have to give us a month's notice."

"You didn't tell me that when I moved in."

Finally, Frank, who was standing behind me and practically filling in the arch of the doorway with his big frame, asked, "Did you hear what the young lady said?" Only it wasn't a question.

Everybody was suddenly quiet.

"Judyenne has to get her belongings!"

Of course they didn't know who Judyenne was. They knew me as Lily, so I explained that this was my new stage name.

One of the girls said, "Well, you owe me a dollar."

I gave her the dollar. The hatbox and other belongings were brought to me. Frank gathered everything as I carried my coat, muff and fur hat. I said goodbye to the girls. I didn't want them mad at me. A couple of the girls followed me outside and watched me get into this beautiful, shining black Packard. It had such class! I just loved the heavy chrome on the front. I felt rather elegant, because Frank opened the back door for me and put in my things. Frank shut the door. Then he walked around, got in the driver's seat; and away we drove. I really did feel like a star as we drove back to Madam Zurenski's.

I began almost a glamorous life for an eighteen-year old kid. I was happy to go to my room and my new friend, Tootsie, the bird. I did wake up a couple of times because of Tootsie making little sounds.

The following day I found out that along with wearing the cigarette girl costume, I would be given candy cigarettes to toss out to the audience as I walked up the runway.

Morning came early; and I was already to leave, not knowing which bus to take. The phone was ringing as I came down the stairs. I didn't know if I was supposed to pick it up or not.

Then I heard Madam Zurenski say, "You can pick it up, Judyenne."

She must have known it was Baba.

Baba said, "Don't take any buses. Carlos is bringing you here," just like she read my mind. "You have to practice for a couple of hours when you get here."

Figure 21 On Location - Yes, Big Al was always watching from a director's chair with his driver near his big black shiny car.

"Oh, Baba, I thank you so much. I was wondering which bus to take."

"No, it's all taken care of; but, breakfast first."

"Oh! All right, I will." I had forgotten about eating; and frankly, I was just too scared. This was my first day on stage! I walked towards the dining room. I didn't see Madam Zurenski or the maid, but I knew Carlos was the Philippine cook and chauffeur for Madam Zurenski and guessed Maria, the maid, was his wife.

Maria came from the kitchen saying, "Your breakfast will be ready in just a few minutes."

I said, "Oh, I can make it myself."

She had a strange look on her face.

"Oh, no, no, we are supposed to make your breakfast. Please, just sit here at the table."

I did and then Carlos came out. He smiled at me and said, "You must eat good. You've lots of work to do today."

I thought to myself, 'This whole household knows what's going on.'

A lady was bringing in big zippered bags full of beautiful clothes. Everybody took their clothes to the cleaners, including their hats, muffs and gloves. She came swishing through the room with packages, bags and other things. I had seen this lady before backstage. She said, "This is your day, Judyenne!"

And I was terrified.

The maid served two poached eggs on wheat toast and orange and pineapple juice mixed.

Baba said, "No bacon, ham or sausage, except on Sunday."

I thought, "If I eat like this, I will lose weight." But at 108 pounds I really didn't want to lose weight.

Madam Zurenski came in, and I started to stand up.

She said, "Sit, sit," and they brought her the same thing. "I want you to learn to eat healthy."

I thought, 'How much do I have to pay for this?' I ate it all, but I waited 'till she finished hers. Then she said, "Carlos is going to take you over to Baba's now; and either Frank, Al, or Carlos will bring you home."

I said, "If I knew the right bus, I could save you the trouble."

"No," she said, "Because you'll be putting in long hours. We want to be sure you get home safe."

So the big day had arrived. I remember eating the eggs and drinking the juice. Oh yes, there was coffee; but she said I must weaken it down with milk, very much like my grandmother used to do. When I was ready to leave, my body was trying to be calm while my mind was racing through an imagined list of problems that I might encounter.

Finally, she put her napkin down, saying, "Well, I think it's time for you to go."

I walked down the side steps where Carlos backed the car up and put me in, though I still wasn't used to people opening doors for me.

So into the car and away we went to Baba's theatre. I was let out at the backstage door of the burlesque house.

As I entered, there was a lot of activity. Two of the dancers, Dimples and Elizabeth, I got to know very well. Dimples became my best friend. Dimples was one of the lead dancers next to Elizabeth. This burlesque theatre was the Cadillac of burley houses. Dimples and Liz were waiting to be chosen to go to Vegas and later they were.

Everybody seemed to be trying to get me ready for something: makeup, costumes and such; but I still had to get used to the G-string and convince myself that I wasn't nude. The other girls practically were. Besides costumes, I had a lot to learn and awfully fast.

Twelve times they made me parade up and down the longest runway which was between the two shorter ones. I had to do it over and over again, because I wouldn't wriggle my fanny like they wanted me to.

The choreographer finally said, "You have to do it right. You have to get them to throw money on the stage!"

The other girls said, "If they don't, then they'll have to pay you. That means you're gonna have to do what we do."

I took it as meaning I would have to do a strip tease.

Well, anyway, I wriggled the right way, and did it enough times that I was getting good at it. One thing I had to do was bend down close to the edge of the runway and flutter my eyelashes as I threw out the candy cigarettes. The house was empty. Except for the people working there, there wasn't anyone out in the audience during practice.

But there was that man I had seen at Madam Zurenski's, the man who looked like Valentino. He was watching me closely. I took him to be a stage director, maybe.

The audience would be very close to me when I tossed the cigarettes out. That was an experience, believe me! Well, the show went on. It wasn't my type of music, certainly not the "Rose Marie" music I really loved. They said I was great. I was terrified. I did what I was told to do, what I had practiced to do. They had spotlights on me and all kinds of colored flashing lights, which I wasn't used to. I was standing at the edge of the runway bending over and leaning forward, not realizing the top of the sheer bodice of this little costume would fall away from me! At that point, all that was covering my breasts was two little rosebuds on the nipples. I wasn't prepared for the patrons' reactions. The men were screaming, and the whistles and catcalls were almost deafening. Money was being thrown all over the stage. One man started to try to climb up on the runway. I had to complete my number until I could exit to the wings. I didn't know at first from the roar whether I was being booed or not.

Anyway, I ran into the wings. Then I came back out, did my little curtsy, turned around, wriggled my rear end and ran back in the wings.

I was happy, believe me, when I got off stage. I didn't pick up any of the money. It was swept up.

I remember that Baba was all excited, saying, "They love you, they love you, they love you! There was thirty-six dollars on the stage."

She said, "I'm going to pay a month at Madam Zurenski's out of this, okay? I'll give you five dollars for yourself."

My rent was paid for the month, I got five dollars and Baba got her share. I was happy over my first appearance. I made it! I was introduced as "Baby Judyenne."

There were calls of, "Bring Baby on, bring Baby back!"

They made me run back out and do my little wriggle. I threw out some more cigarettes and then went back.

The next day I had a new costume. Things were changing, but not accidentally; the skirts were shorter!

The next afternoon and evening show I'll never forget. The costume was white satin and fur, very tight, and my behind had a round bunny tail. The costume plunged nearly to my navel with two round fur bunny tails on my breasts. I had big long bunny ears lined with velvet on a cap. I carried a basket to hold the rabbit feet I threw out in the audience during the bump and grind music. The music was very precise; I could hardly miss a beat. Besides, the audience wouldn't notice, they were too busy watching the action!

There were some rather important people in the audience who later showed up back stage. Baba said they were prominent show people. After the show a very impressive-looking gentleman came towards Baba. He was in his forties with a round, medium build. He was wearing horn-rimmed glasses. He was introduced as Mister Kahn, a talent agent. The thing I remembered most about Mister Kahn was the ring he wore, a huge diamond.

I was then introduced to another gentleman who joined us.

Baba said, "You're very lucky he happened to be passing by. He doesn't usually come to these parts, do you, Frank?" introducing him as "Frank Orsadi"

She told me he had been Mister Louis B. Mayer's bootlegger, and Mister Orsadi lived near Mister Mayer in Santa Monica, "Almost our neighbors!" she added. Another gentleman she introduced me to was Tony Conera, and I didn't know who he was either. Later I learned he had an interest in the "Rex", a gambling ship.

Several days later, Baba wanted Frank to drive me to Perrie's. She wanted me to get Gypsy dance lessons. She said she could refine my tap, which was limited. So off I went and had, I think six or seven lessons. Dimples went with me. She watched, then would have me practice this later backstage.

We did some beautiful Gypsy dances, using several very exquisite veils. Due to special lighting, the near see-through veiling covering us only showed our bodies as shadows. The costumes had continued to shrink until at times I felt I wasn't wearing more than a smile, but always a G-string and a rosette bra.

Madam Maria Auspenskia had a private studio for lessons in drama and in the arts. This was based on her training that she had received in the Moscow Art Theatre. She was a Russian actress who worked in movies here until about 1940. She was quite old then, but she looked kind of elusive, a still-beautiful Greta Garbo type. These were intriguing women, like characters you might meet on the Orient Express. Baba paid for me to go to her drama class. Instructors that she hired taught these, but once in a while Madam Auspenskia came into the school. She was very gracious, petite, and truly a lady. Baba said she had a title. She had a walk, too. It was a little bit sexy, but almost noble. You wanted to stand up when she entered the room. When she spoke, it made chills go up my spine. Of course I had seen her in movies for years. She had those eyes that pierced right through a person when she looked. I determined all that from one meeting, and I was in awe of her. I had seen all her movies and still remember her.

One of the most wonderful things that Baba and Madam Zurenski did for me, besides being like my family, was to take me to all the beautiful night clubs to meet such famous people. I had been to the Trocadero and the Brown Derby, too; the Coconut Grove was a place just full of glamour and people with gorgeous gowns, furs, diamonds and money. It was just unbelievable, the stars who came to our table. One was Jack Carson, who may be remembered for Arsenic and Old Lace. I just loved that picture. He "smuggled" me into a couple of studios so I could watch what was going on and learn more.

I saw Ginger Rogers one time at the Coconut Grove. I never talked to her, since I never got that close; but at least I saw her. Myron Selznick, a relative of the producer, David Selznick, was there one time; and Baba introduced me to an agent by the name of Feldtman.

I wasn't famous, but I just happened to be with people who were.

I remember Baba said, "The most important thing for you to do is be seen."

They dressed me up in a silver lamé dress and high spike heels. It was gorgeous. I could hardly stand to take it off. My hair hung way past my waist.

One night at the Trocadero Baba said, "If we brush your hair too hard, we're going to bruise your bottom!"

She was really proud of me. Baba said, "Everyone looks at you, because you've got the longest natural hair of anybody in this town."

I remember one night when we were in the Ambassador Hotel, I whispered, "Isn't that man over there Wallace Beery?"

"Yes," Baba answered.

I said my Uncle Richard knew him personally. Uncle Richard was a stand-in for Rudolf Valentino in Hollywood during silent pictures. He was also a well-known photographer. He took Mr. Beery's picture in 1926. I have a copy with Mr. Beery's autograph to my uncle. At that time it was back home in my parents' dining room.

Figure 22 Wallace Beery, movie star, 1926

XIV - The Bijou

1939

Dimples was planning to go to Las Vegas, I think for a week or two. Baba was drinking an awful lot more; we all noticed it.

I told her, "You're really still a very beautiful lady, so I don't know why you're drinking so much. People usually drink when they are unhappy."

"How would you know?"

"Well, " I said, "I had a couple of uncles and a dad that drank. Whenever they drank, they told me they were unhappy."

"Kid, it's too late for me."

I told her, "You've taught me a lot. You could open a school and teach dancing or drama. You'd be a great teacher."

Half-smiling she said, "No one has said that to me before."

"Well, I mean it. You've been a good friend to me; and, Baba, I don't want you to get sick. You're like my family."

"Maybe you're right," she said. "I'll make a deal. I'll try to keep a promise to you. I'll slow down on the drinking."

"But, Baba, it's not just a promise to me; you've got to make a promise to yourself."

"Zooks, you're an awfully smart kid," she said. "Now, I've got a surprise for you. A beautiful new costume. You're going to like it, but first we have to do the bunny routine again."

"Tell me about the new costume."

"I'll tell you later after repeating the bunny routine tonight."

"I've already done that twice," I replied.

"This is a little different," she said. "You'll have a similar costume, with a thin sheer skin that you put on over the satin. Then, you peel the sheer skin off, and it will be your coming out of the bunny skin."

"With my skirt?"

"Yes, but shorter. And, you'll throw lollipops at the audience."

But I had a foreboding. I would need both hands to peel myself out.

This time the music was even more pronounced; and I thought the drummer was a lot louder than usual, so I didn't like it. As I peeled off the skin and was backing up the center runway, I was supposed to throw the sheer skin out into the crowd. It came right off; but as I did, the skirt popped off as I bent over. I was on that runway in front of a packed house with a G-string and two bunny tails on my boobs, but the skirt was gone. I grabbed the skirt and held it up in front of me. I ran as fast as I could off the stage as the whistles got louder. I forgot about the lollipops. I only remember running into the wings. Back stage I was really hysterical. I looked at the skirt and Baba came running over.

She said, "It's all right, it's all right, Judyenne; it's just a snap that broke."

They were still screaming out front, so she said, "You'll have to go out."

I said, "I'm not going without my skirt." I called it my tutu skirt. Anyway, we whipped two little ends of it together, and I walked that slinky walk back out like I was supposed to originally. I threw more lollipops, and this time there was even more clapping and cheers. They yelled over and over, "Baby, come back! Baby, come back! Baby, don't cry," because they had heard me crying when I left the stage.

Later as Dimples left by the back stage door, she said, "Honey, if you want that thing to stay up, pin it with a safety pin."

As the days went by, Baba kept drinking heavier and heavier. More and more I went in to see her, and more and more I saw she was getting worse. She had terrible headaches and was nauseated. I kept putting wet washcloths on her head. Finally one day I ran out back and called for Frank. I asked him if he would go to the drug store and get a big heavy rubber ice bag.

He said, "Sure, and we can put ice cubes in it from her refrigerator."

"And, Frank, maybe you should get some milk. I could fix her some hot milk with cinnamon. I'll need the milk, cinnamon, sugar and bread."

He said, "I'll get some; it might help."

Of course, there were pans, a hot plate, toaster, coffee pot and other things in her office. I fixed her hot milk with cinnamon and sugar on toast. Cinnamon helps settle one's stomach. Baba ate the cinnamon milk toast and started to feel a little better, saying, "That tastes really good. I'm not as sick as I was."

I said, "Baba, why don't you come home with me tonight."

She said, "Maybe it would help if I did get away from this place."

She made a phone call, and I left to find Frank. I guess she called Madam Zurenski.

After I got Frank, I came back and refilled the ice bag.

Then we all left the Bijou together in Baba's car, and Frank drove us back to Santa Monica. I mentioned that there was a long wing of the house I had never ever seen. Well, Baba entered that sanctioned wing of the mansion like she owned the place. She said Madam Zurenski was her cousin.

I went upstairs to my room and took care of Tootsie; I covered him up after I cleaned his cage, fed and watered him. It was late. Poor Tootsie didn't live on normal people's hours.

In the morning Baba was up for breakfast, and apparently she had been in the big wing with her cousin.

She was even smiling and said, "You're right, Judyenne, I needed to get away."

We had poached eggs on whole-wheat toast, slices of cantaloupe and honeydew, and little girl's coffee, as I called it.

"This is what you eat every morning?" Baba asked.

Madam Zurenski said, "Yes, and we don't wash it down with vodka, either."

They didn't give her a drink, and I know she was always used to having a drink in the morning. Baba was telling her how good I was and what kind of minor tragedy happened on stage when a snap broke on my skirt. She said she had a big surprise for me at the Western Costume Company. Frank drove us, and when we got there they showed Baba what looked like a very beautiful cardboard cake. This big cardboard cake was being moved to the Bijou.

I asked why, and she said, "Look at all these cute little costumes. You're going to be the one in the middle of this cake and that's your surprise."

The top came up, and the sides opened. There were to be four other girls in there, five all together. The four dancers would wear a G-string and rosebuds. I had much the same as they did, but something new in bathing suits, a stretch lamé like spandex. I would come out of the cake in pink and silver. I was supposed to run around looking like a candle.

That was my surprise, because she was trying to make it up to me for the costume accident. Baba did many wonderful things for me. She was one of the only women who treated me like a real mother, except for Grandma Latimer. Sure, Mother Clara loved me in her way, and maybe Florence did, too; but Baba and Grandma Latimer treated me with respect. She was like a second mother to me, but one who was a caring and unselfish guardian. Baba and I were very close. I really felt we were related. You often develop affection for people you work with in show business.

We did the show exactly as I outlined. It was a real big hit; and what I threw out on the runway were fake candles, actually candy sticks. The thing about the bathing suit I had on was, it shimmered as lamé does and was very tight. I looked like I was nude, but I really wasn't. There were a lot of pictures taken. I heard later that those pictures were taken to Las Vegas.

Back at Madam Zurenski's, Madam Zurenski said, "I've had three phone calls from people in the audience who saw your act and liked it. We've got several invitations. We're taking you to a big party," she added.

"Me?"

"Yes, Baba, myself and Frank are going to take you to a private party. We're going to take the cake, you and the other dancers, too. You will be seen by several agents — important movie VIP's."

Well, that was wonderful news. Good things and bad things have a way of interchanging, though. As we entered the house, that suave-looking Valentino, whose name turned out to be Big Al, was there. He had something to do with the gambling ship and also had Madame Zurenski do his fortunes, I had been told. He was standing there listening while Madam Zurenski was talking. He wasn't moving, just watching me. I think I was afraid of him, but intrigued as well.

XV - Benjamin and Big Al

1939

Our favorite restaurants were the Cantonese Gardens, owned by Harvey Key, and Mister Chang's Cathay Gardens. These owners were friends of Baba. Many times we'd bring Chinese food home in those white buckets with the little wire handles. I always thought it was so funny because the five and dime store sold gold fish in the same containers. I'm glad they didn't have recycling then!

We didn't just go to the Trocadero. These restaurants were very important, not only for their exquisite cuisine, but as a social gathering place for many a struggling extra, as well as dancers, wanting to be seen among the rich and famous. We also loved the little Jewish delicatessen (Oh, how wonderful their food was!), I think on Grover Street.

At the theatre everybody was buzzing and busy. Excitement was in the air. We had been told that we were going to be taking our cake routine to a very special show! Baba wouldn't say where, and Frank wouldn't tell me in the car. Madam Zurenski knew it all, of course, but she wouldn't tell me either.

We practiced on our routines all day, then Baba gathered us backstage to announce that we would be leaving in one hour. Our show will be aboard a big ship!

"A ship?" I asked.

"We are going aboard a big gambling ship, the "Rex". This is a great opportunity for us all," Baba explained.

'There was a lot of trouble with those boats,' I thought. 'The paper said there were several of them off the Santa Monica coast, and the city and federal government and Big Al's people were at some odds.'

I had never been aboard any gambling ship, but actually, it was exciting.

I thought, 'It must be legal because they allow it to operate there.'

Anyway, we were all a-twitter. Many things had to be taken over there. How they got the cardboard cake there, I wasn't sure, but this was a half-size version of the other big one, so not quite as difficult. Dimples said they had barges to do that. Dimples and Elizabeth, our best dancers just back from Las Vegas, and I were the only dancers this time.

We were going with Baba, Madam Zurenski and Frank. Shows went on before and after dinner.

This was a huge ship. The Mafia controlled these ships that steamed at least six and sometimes twelve miles out to sea. We took water taxies out to the ship. The costumes followed on a barge along behind in our wake.

The production number was called "The Naughty Girls Birthday Cake." I thought that was so cute. The venue made the show seem lighthearted, almost comedy-like. On their stage on that glamorous ship it took away the feel of burlesque. This was nearly a full size theatrical stage. They had a troop of their own professional dancers. The atmosphere was high class.

It was all glitter and glamour, the audience a different type of people. They were the "upper crust" the wealthy mingling, you know. This was closer with what I wanted to be identified. We did our naughty girls in the birthday cake routine; and afterwards, we were asked if we would like to join the guests, of all things! We never mixed with the customers at the Bijou. We had brought formals in addition to costumes and makeup cases. Mine was blue and silver with rhinestone shoulder straps, very low cut and quite slinky. I wore spike heels with rhinestones on the heels. I guess we looked like showgirls, and I began to feel like I was a showgirl! I really wasn't, but I was learning fast.

When we joined Baba, Madam Zurenski and Frank at the table we were at the other end from the host. We had to raise our glasses in a toast. It was champagne, so I just took a couple of sips to look like I was drinking.

Yes, and the host was Big Al! Then we were introduced to the birthday boy who turned out to be Tony Conera! I think I mentioned he was backstage a couple of times, as was Big Al. I think he had some monetary interest in the Bijou, but wasn't sure.

Baba thought I was her long lost daughter; and in many ways she was protecting me, while she jet propelled me toward success. I'd have been proud to be her daughter, in spite of her drinking, because she was the sweetest person, and she cared. Considering she had come from Europe not too many years earlier, she knew show business, spoke perfect English and outdid everyone at crossword puzzles. As the waiter took the drink away, I asked for ginger ale. He brought a ginger ale club soda mix with a cherry. Things livened up as the band played popular songs. Oh yes, I was asked to dance with the birthday boy and did, and who cut in? — Big Al!

At dance intermission, Baba whispered we'd be leaving soon. I hated to leave. Among the people who went by our table were Adolphe Menjou and Caesar Romero, both favorites of mine. From where we were I could easily hear dice hitting wood and the roulette wheel's ball rolling around, mixed with shouts of either happiness or pain, depending on "Lady Luck" at that instant.

Baba and I had been seated at the party table of Tony Conera when Baba said she wanted to introduce me to Benjamin Segal. Turning to Mister Conera as we stood, she said, "We'll be leaving soon. We enjoyed your party. Again, happy birthday, and good night."

"Sure, Baba, night. See ya, Judyenne, Frank."

She then took me over to be formally introduced to Mister Benjamin Segal. He had come to the burlesque house a few times. He was sitting, as always, at the corner table, with two huge men seated next to him.

Walking over to him, Baba said, “Benjamin, I want you to meet my protégé, Judyenne. I’m making her into a star, honey! You know Frank.”

Of course, you have to understand the times. There wasn’t TV, and pre-release media blitzes to launch a person’s career. These were entirely different times.

Mister Segal stood up, which Baba later said was very unusual. He shook my hand and looked like he was devouring every part of me with those baby blue eyes of his. He was wearing a light blue hounds tooth jacket with navy blue slacks and a flamboyant pink silk tie with a beautiful diamond stickpin. He was really good looking, but I was frightened of him because I knew who he was. Still I said, “How do you do, Mister Segal.”

As Baba was turning to go, Benjamin said, “You’ll have to call me, Baba. We’ll all have to go to dinner. We’ll have a party or something, won’t we?”

And believe me, I didn’t say a word. I was getting nervous. Now, he took a couple of quick steps toward me. That was when he put his right hand on my left hip and waist. I kind of turned part way to the left, which was a big mistake, because he removed this hand, putting it on my shoulder.

As we said goodbye, his hand dropped down over my breast, giving it a little squeeze, and he asked, “What ya like to eat, honey?”

As he squeezed me closer, he whispered in my ear, “Judyenne, I can do more for you than Baba. I’m a friend of all the studio bosses.”

Baba, seeing this, blurted out, “Shrimp!”

Her exclamation carried the inflection of alarm, like protecting her child. I later had to laugh at how funny that really sounded. As Benjamin let me go, his parting words, “I’ll plan a big party, Baba, for Judyenne,” made me shudder.

Benjamin’s better-known name was “Bugsie Segal”, and he was a real mobster. He was a big tipper; and he threw very expensive parties, like the one on the “Rex”. He didn’t like the name “Bugsie” and you didn’t call him “Bugsie” to his face, probably without consequences.

Baba, Frank and I left on the next water taxi, but I didn’t see the rest of the girls until the next day. Our car was parked where the taxi docked.

Soon we were at the mansion, and Baba did come in. Madame Zurenski said she had a client, so the rest of us went into the huge living room to listen to the radio.

Whenever Baba would stay, the house seemed alive! In addition to being a chauffeur, Frank was a business partner of Baba’s; and they both were very protective of me.

I thought, ‘It was so different to dance at the “Rex” instead of the burley. I have to get away from that place. I’m going to have to dance in a beautiful place like that ship with everybody so well dressed and very formal,' I continued thinking.

I am sure the darkness made it look more glamorous. Later I learned the ship was open all the time and never "went to sleep."

XVI - Alexander

1939

Early the next day I was again at the burley house, and when I approached Baba's door it was ajar.

Going in, Frank said, "Maybe you better go talk to Baba again and make her one of those hot cinnamon milk things."

"Oh sure, I'll fix it. She's sick because she sure drank a lot last night."

"Yes, I know," he agreed somberly. "Judyenne, you may not know this, but she has bleeding ulcers, so someone's got to talk to her. She listens to you."

"Well, she didn't listen to me last night."

"No," he said, "But it's worth a try. I'll get you the ice bag."

Really only half the room was like an office. The other half was like a studio with a couch, large pillows, an end table, a lamp and books. I mentioned the little hot plate earlier, and she had a refrigerator in the office, too. I got the milk, cinnamon and sugar, then made toast. Baba came out of the bathroom, and I asked if I should get her the ice bag.

"Frank's bringing it," she replied.

"Please, Baba, lay down and rest," I begged.

I noticed her ankles were swollen and I thought, 'They shouldn't be swollen like this.' Then I remembered Grandma Latimer Jackson. She had swollen ankles and heart trouble. "Have you been to a doctor lately?" I asked.

"Oh yeah, but none of them know what to do with me."

She ate her hot milk cinnamon toast, and Frank came in with the ice bag.

Baba said, "You don't have to go on today. You made enough money yesterday."

"I didn't make any money yesterday."

"No, no, I've got to give you a cut. I got so much money for bringing you girls on the 'Rex' for the cake dance, so I owe ya."

She pulled out thirty dollars! Some people wouldn't make that much in two or three weeks!

Baba said, "I want to talk to you, but stay with me today. I've been thinking about what you told me about drinking and my ulcers. Anyway, I'm afraid. Frank's taking me to the doctor today, and I'd like you to go with me."

"Oh, sure I'll go with you," I said, "I'll go right in with the doctor, then he won't hurt you — I won't let him."

Baba smiled.

I would protect my dear Baba, who in many ways was not only a good friend, but an aunt, a mother to me; yes, I did love Baba. She was like a mother to me, the one for which I had been longing to have all my life.

Frank finally returned saying, "We have a one o'clock appointment."

I sat there talking to her and refilled her ice bag. I got a folded blanket off the shelf and put it over her.

As I covered her up, she said, "You know, you're so good to me. I would have had a daughter about your age."

"You had a daughter?" I asked.

"Yes, it was a long time ago, and I wasn't married."

This caught me with great surprise. However, Florence hadn't been married either when she had me. It was all the more surprising because having a child out of wedlock wasn't so common then. And if it happened, it was always kept a secret if possible.

"She was a beautiful baby," Baba continued with remorse and sadness in her voice. "But there was nothing I could do; I had to give her up."

I knew Baba was a tough woman, but I also knew that inside that exterior was a deeply compassionate person. Seeing a longing in her eyes when she said what a beautiful baby she was, I wondered if this could possibly be the reason for her drinking.

She said, "I was in the theatre. I was in another country. I just know she must have the same long auburn hair that I did. Most of my family came to America. We left Russia just before the Revolution. I just want you to know that you mean a great deal to me, Judyenne. You have come the closest to what I think she would be like out of all the girls I have met on stage anywhere, and ever since."

This touched me deeply because it was really a compliment, so I said, "Maybe you should try to find her."

"I wouldn't know how. Too many years have gone by. I trust you, Judyenne, and I want the best for you. Somehow I think you were sent to me."

I patted Baba's hand, saying, "I think God sent me to you." Then I thought, 'Well, if it makes Baba happy to think of me like a daughter, it makes me happy, too.'

As Baba rested, I thought I should check the post office. I was still hoping for a letter from John, and still going to the post office with letters to John, in care of his mother. Dimples would address a letter with her name, as did Maria and Elizabeth. They had P.O. Boxes. So he was getting a lot of mail from different girls, but they were my letters inside. I still thought John would find me; and I would look him straight in the face, knowing I did nothing that would make him disappointed in me while I was dancing at the burley. I was a virgin.

Baba got up to change clothes to get ready for her appointment.

We got into the car at about twenty-five minutes to one and left for the doctor's office. I could see that Baba was in pain, but I thought the hot milk was going to help. We arrived and finally Baba was admitted, but the nurse said, "You can wait here."

"No, I'm going with her."

"And I want her in there with me," Baba announced.

I followed them in and listened to what the doctor said. He had x-rays taken. Then he put them up to the light and showed them to her. He told her that her ulcers were serious and said if she kept drinking, she would die. He gave her some medicine and told her to stop drinking and what she had to eat. She didn't like that part, because she really liked fried foods. But worse was "Stop Drinking!"

"Tell Judyenne, and she'll watch over me. She's like my own daughter."

The doctor said to me, "I want complete bed rest and no drinking! If that drinking doesn't stop, her ulcer will rupture and she will bleed to death!"

It scared me something terrible and maybe even Baba. Frank was asked to come in. The doctor repeated the warning. We left, taking the elevator down to ground floor and walked back out to the car. Frank helped me get Baba into the car; then I gave him the prescriptions.

Frank stopped to get the prescriptions filled; and returning, he said, "Baba, do you still want to stop at the theatre?"

"Yes," she answered.

It was hard for her to get out of the car when we got there. She went to her big file cabinet that was locked. Taking a key from her purse, she unlocked the cabinet and pulled something out. By this time it was about four o'clock and I didn't know if I was doing the night show or not. First we had to get her to wherever her home was; I really didn't know where she lived. I always had seen her at Madam Zurenski's or the Bijou.

She said, "I'm going home with you. I think I'll take the bedroom next to yours, and you'll be near me if I get worse. I don't want to be alone."

This made me wonder where Frank stayed. She made a phone call to Madam Zurenski's from her office saying, "Ta Ta, this is Baba. I'm going to stay in the room next to Judyenne tonight. There was a pause, then she said, "Not very good, but I've got medicine and Judyenne's going to look after me."

This other name was not what all people called Madam Zurenski, but people very close to her called this magnificent woman "Ta Ta." I couldn't imagine giving Madame Zurenski a nickname. She was a gracious, slender and handsome woman of great dignity. Many of the powerful people who came to see her at her grand home conveyed this on her.

"I'll be staying for three days, Judyenne, then I'll be fine."

So we left for Madam Zurenski's; and when we got there, she said, "Take the room across the hall." Then she gave me a little bell that I put on the nightstand in Baba's room by her bed.

Frank came up with a glass of warm milk and the medicine; then we got her to bed.

I was sitting in Baba's room after Frank and Madam Zurenski left and I said, almost to myself, "Well, I'd better shower, get dressed and go back to the theatre."

Baba opened her eyes, looked at me and said, "I don't want you to go. Whatever you would have made, I'll just give you twenty dollars instead."

"You don't have to pay me to sit with you, I'll just make it up tomorrow night."

"Judyenne, actually we're just training you. What you're doing is getting experience. You're not costing us anything."

"Well, all the costumes."

"That's *my* investment. I buy lots of costumes. I'm always making deals and I always get one."

It was a phrase she often used.

'She is one smart Russian,' I thought to myself.

The next evening when Baba felt better for a short time, we all made cabbage rolls in the kitchen, taking turns at the stove. Baba and I were helping Carlos and Maria, showing them her Russian cooking. And could she cook! We made Baba sit down, though. Well, the best borsch I ever tasted in my life was made there, too; and it still makes my mouth water.

We stayed longer than three days, Baba realizing she needed a little more time. Frank was in charge of the theatre. About a week later she started feeling much better. Being away from the Bijou probably didn't hurt, either. And she wasn't drinking as much. We only let her have a little Brandy and milk to sip to get to sleep at night. We mixed whatever she did get with milk, and I made some really neat concoctions.

She was bedded down for the evening and seemed happier. I explained to Carlos and Maria how to make the hot milk and cinnamon toast for Baba. I added, "This is what you feed sick people," and Carlos and Maria thought I was cracked; because they had all this great food they had prepared. They didn't cook anything like Madam Zurenski, who was ahead of her time, health-wise, as I said.

"Let's try this first," I suggested. "Cinnamon is good for the stomach." So they did, and I had everybody a believer in that milk toast with sugar and cinnamon on top. Baba did have some mashed potatoes and gravy later the next night. I didn't know if the gravy was so smart.

Baba said, "I liked that milk toast you made, Judyenne, it makes my stomach feel good."

"It's good for the lining of your stomach."

She got through the night and only rang the bell once. After three days she sure looked much better. I went to the theatre and did an afternoon and one night show. Otherwise, I didn't leave the house. I never went there in the mornings any more. I thought we were licking the problem as she was actually getting color in her cheeks. She wanted to go back to the theatre, but we all begged and pleaded for her not to yet. So she waited four more days.

They did eat a large variety of healthy fresh fruit and vegetables and had homemade soups. Madam Zurenski insisted on eating a healthy plate, but Carlos and Maria cooked differently for themselves. The smell of spare ribs drifted upstairs, and Baba knew people downstairs were eating them. It was like trying to keep a bee from a clover field! She insisted she have a couple, but we limited this. "Well, just three and mashed potatoes, OK."

That was how it went with Baba. We returned to work at the theatre again following the fifth day and also went to see the doctor. He took more x-rays that morning. Then he examined her, and the x-ray pictures showed the ulcers were healing. But he didn't want her to go back to work.

She said, "I have to watch the theatre. I have to be there."

He said, "All right, Baba, but I'm against it. How about if you spend just part of the day, and not 'till two in the morning!"

Baba said she wouldn't go in 'till afternoon, anyway, if there wasn't something special going on. That worked out very well for about another three weeks, and we kept her at Madam Zurenski's.

Even living in Madam Zurenski's sumptuous mansion with servants and good food, after three more weeks Baba started getting sick again. It began when I heard her ring her bell from across the hall. Rushing to her room, I saw she wasn't in her bed, then I heard choking sounds coming from the bathroom. I knocked and called, "Baba?"

She opened the door; and the first thing I saw was blood on the sink and on the toilet seat, too.

"I'm throwing up blood! Call Frank, get Frank!"

I half carried her back to bed, grabbed the phone and luckily caught him on the second ring.

"Frank, thank God, get over here! Baba's throwing up blood. Come quick!"

I think he had dropped the phone before I finished, because I heard a crash and the phone went silent.

"It's all right, Baba, Frank's coming."

I rushed to get a wet wash cloth and returned to wipe her face and hands.

I ran down the stairs as fast as I could and hollered, "Maria, Madam Zurenski, Baba's worse!"

They ran upstairs with me. Actually I thought we should go straight to the hospital. Madam Zurenski called the doctor. He decided she'd go to his office at once, so we all got in the car and left.

Baba kept saying, "Judyenne, baby's got to come along." She kept repeating this. She sounded delirious. Frank flew in that big Packard.

I was really too young to know how serious this was, but I sat next to her holding her hand and thinking, 'I can't lose another person I care so much about. We have to save Baba.'

Arriving at the doctor's office we were whisked into Doctor Goldstein's exam room and the nurse looked as worried as we did. More x-rays were taken, and in a few minutes the doctor came back.

"You are just going to have to go into the hospital, Baba," he said. "At least a week."

Oh, no, no, I can't," she protested. "I can't leave the theatre!"

"There's no 'if's' or 'ands' about it," Madam Zurenski said. "I'll take charge if I have to. We'll manage. Frank could run it by himself. It's imperative that you go."

The doctor turned to Madam Zurenski and Baba, then gravely said, "Your life depends on it. You must be in the hospital, Baba. I'm sure Madam Zurenski can handle things for a few weeks. I think a nice rest out on the desert would do you a world of good. How about Palm Springs? But first the hospital. As your doctor, I am *not* asking!"

Madam Zurenski said, "Of course we can take care of things. We're going to have to call Alexander in, though, to help."

I wondered who Alexander was? It turned out to be her brother. Baba was taken to the hospital and I went to see her every day. The only ones allowed to see her were Frank, Madam Zurenski and myself. Later Alexander was included. After a ten-day stay, she did look much better. Once again my heart stopped its racing that seemed to never leave me since that morning in the bathroom. I knew I really would be lost without Baba. Incidentally, Alexander turned out to be devastatingly handsome, but his personality wasn't. They called him "Alexi" most of the time.

On the ninth day, all of us were at the hospital; and Baba was having a fit, talking rather loud to the doctor and Alexander. "It's my business and I'll run it. I have Judyenne and Frank. Judyenne and I can run the place."

I didn't like Alexi. I didn't trust him. I knew that Baba felt this, too. My eyes met Baba's, and instinctively we both knew that Alexi wanted to take over the business. The doctor came in and gave instructions.

Baba spoke up again, "Frank, Judyenne and I can run the place!"

"Absolutely not, for another several months," the doctor ordered. "You are going to take it easy."

"I can't lose my business. I have to be there a couple of hours at least every other day."

"Let us try a couple of more weeks, then see how things progress. And let's see if we can slow your drinking down."

"Well," she huffed, "I think you're overdoing it. There's nothing wrong with a good slug of whiskey in a glass of warm milk. Judyenne puts cinnamon and sugar on top."

When she said, "Judyenne puts cinnamon and sugar on top," the doctor positively cringed; then challenged with, "What good is the cinnamon and sugar if you wreck your stomach with all that alcohol?"

She said, "Because Judyenne says cinnamon heals the stomach."

"Yes," he agreed, "But you ruin it by adding the liquor to it."

"Well, I'll use vodka then," she countered. "That's what I prefer to drink anyway."

"Vodka is even worse!" he practically yelled.

Alexander interjected, "Maybe she could settle for a little glass of wine."

The doctor fairly turned purple with this helpful suggestion, and I could see that Madam Zurenski was getting a little uptight, too. Baba was enjoying every second of it, but I think I was in danger of biting the end of my tongue at that point. Poor Doctor Goldstein had about capitulated in frustration.

It was decided then that she would go back to Madam Zurenski's with me. Getting out of that hospital was step one. And then there was supposed to be two weeks in Palm Springs. Frank would go with us. We both saw a gleam in Alexi's eyes. There was money in the Bijou, and he knew it.

He turned and said, "Judyenne can't go; she's got to work."

Baba said, "She works when I tell her to, not when anybody else does."

There was a little silence for the first time with Alexander, and I could see we were in the hands of a troublemaker. Alexi was coming from the standpoint of aggression, not defense. Madam Zurenski was listening to both sides.

I thought, 'Well, she is very fair. Maybe she just thinks her cousin should retire.' We all ended up at the main house in Santa Monica, and I put Baba on the terrace. I gave her plenty of hot milk, but she wouldn't drink it unless it had cinnamon and sugar in it. I had to laugh. She wasn't really craving alcohol that much. This surprised me. She even cut down on her smoking and was actually trying to do what Doctor Goldstein ordered. Then she started asking me questions about my past.

Days wore on. A couple of times Baba let me go with Alexander to the theatre. This one night I redid the cake number, and Alexi was watching all this with some new ideas.

I put on the tutu with the taffeta cover over the top skirt. Alexander came out and said, "Take the skirt off."

I said, "What?"

"Take the skirt off," he repeated, with more emphasis.

He walked over to me and pulled on it. It snapped like it did the other time. I was standing there, but still had my fish net on. "I don't do that. I'm not a stripper. I'm a dancer."

"Well, then, you don't belong here if you can't do what the other girls do."

I was waiting for my friend Dimples to say something, but nobody said a word. So I looked him straight in the eye, bent over, picked up my skirt and walked back to the dressing room. I marched myself right past the iron racks of costumes, took off my costume and got dressed. I walked outside, crossed to the corner and caught a bus.

I was thinking, 'They can take that job and shove it!' I had heard one of the dancers say it once. Anyway, that's how I felt about it. The bus driver told me what bus to transfer on, and it took me to Palisades Park. I walked to Madam Zurenski's mansion on the ocean. I went in the side entrance, and she met me in front of the main staircase.

"What happened between you and Alexander?"

I thought of Baba being right up the stairs with surprisingly good ears, and I didn't want to upset her. So I said, hesitantly, "What do you mean?"

"I mean you two had words. Why?"

"He ought to be ashamed of himself. He could get in a lot of trouble trying to force me to strip," I replied in lowered tones.

"He did what?"

"He tore off my tutu skirt. Alexi said I'd have to strip, so I left."

"I'm going to make a phone call," Madam Zurenski said, leaving the room.

As I walked upstairs I didn't know if she was going to throw me out or not. By now I had acquired a lot more than a patent leather hatbox, makeup case and coat to move. I went back up to my room, then into Baba's room to see how she was.

One look at my face and she said, "All right, spill it."

"What? Spill *what?*"

"Tell me what's wrong. Judyenne, I read you just like you read me. You read my eyes in the hospital when Alexander was acting up. You knew what was going on, just like I did."

"Yes, I did, but as long as I'm around, he's not going to take over the theatre from you."

"Tell me what happened, and tell me the truth. I'm not that sick."

"All right," I said, "But I don't want my answer churning up in your stomach. It's really nothing."

"I'll be the judge of that."

"Well, I was ready to go on and Alexander said, 'Take the skirt off,' and I wouldn't. So he came over and pulled it off. The snap broke again. I told him I wasn't a stripper, and I wasn't going to be one. I just walked right off stage, got my things, took a bus and here I am. I don't know if I'm fired or not."

"You weren't hired anyway. You're my protege."

About that time, Madam Zurenski came upstairs and said, "I want to talk to you, Judyenne."

"No, you don't!" Baba countered. "If you're going to talk to her, you're going to talk to me, too."

"Alexander said, as long as *he* is running the theatre, the girls have to do what he says; this is a strip joint," Madam Zurenski reported.

"It's not a strip joint," Baba came back, "It's a burlesque theatre. We have professional dancers and a higher class clientele."

"You know what I mean," replied Madam Zurenski.

"No, we aren't the average joint," Baba defended, pausing for a second. "He won't be in charge for long. I own over half of the Bijou, and *I* make the rules!"

Madam Zurenski said, "Yes, as long as you're alive. Keep going like this and he'll get it."

"Well, I'm going to do as the doctor says," Baba said. "I'm taking Judyenne, and we're going to Palm Springs, have mud baths and eat fruit and vegetables. I'll be better in no time. Then, when I return, I'm taking over."

I had no idea Baba owned controlling interest in the Bijou.

I had heard about these fabulous hotels and beauty spas in Palm Springs. 'And now I'll really see them,' I thought, 'Of course I don't like hot weather, but there are "swamp coolers."' "Swamp coolers" were early attempts at having air conditioners, but only with air blowing through dripping water within smaller units in a window.

XVII - Palm Springs Trip

1939

Three days later we left for Palm Springs, the doctor telling Baba, "Take it easy and relax. When you come back we'll do more x-rays."

And Madam Zurenski said, "Don't worry about the room. It'll be here when you get back."

The suitcases were packed. Maria had come up and helped. Frank had to get some of Baba's clothes from her home, which I found out was in Beverly Hills. I also learned she had another home in Pasadena.

I had a really neat pair of white slacks, a cute tie top in real silk, shorts, a good-looking swim suit and other outfits. I packed the big patent leather hatbox and was ready to go.

Madam Zurenski looked at me and asked, "That's all you're taking?"

"Sure."

"If she needs anything, we can get it there, " Baba offered.

I took Baba down on the elevator, and Frank got us into the car. You could fly to Palm Springs, but Baba didn't like planes. Baba was just thrilled to be in her own car. Anybody would have loved to be chauffeured to Palm Springs in that beautiful Packard. First they stopped at the Pasadena house, where the live-in couple, the Mac Millians, took me around. We rested there for an hour, but Baba said, "I feel fine. I could ride all night."

We went from there to San Bernadino and stayed overnight. Baba got each of us our own room in a motel that had a restaurant, where we had dinner. Boy, we were really living it up. I looked at the menu — and the prices! I thought, 'All I better order is a shrimp cocktail. It's less than a dinner!' "I'll have a shrimp cocktail."

"That's not enough to eat," Baba countered.

Frank warned her, no fried food, only mashed potatoes, but hold the gravy. She had chicken soup and mashed potatoes on the side. She asked the waiter to put cream peas on top. She wanted ice cream with chocolate topping, but Frank talked her into strawberries.

They were having a fit that I was only eating the cocktail.

"I don't want to eat in front of Baba," I replied.

Baba said, "It's not fair." Then, pointing to the menu, she said to the waiter, "Judyenne will have this big fruit salad and two bran muffins."

We each had a muffin. Then I saw one thing on the menu that I really would have liked. For a ritzy place like this, they had chicken fried steak with mashed potatoes and country gravy. Yummy!

Entering Palm Springs, I felt like I was in the Sahara.

I thought, 'I wouldn't be surprised if I saw a camel caravan of desert nomads riding toward us. Maybe I'm in Egypt.'

The houses had that California look, yet not just Spanish, but Moroccan architecture. We drove by the El Mirador Hotel. Baba had made reservations at the Dunes. We all had individual rooms again. Baba also wanted to spend some time at La Quinta Resort, fifteen miles away.

The next day we went to a spa where they gave you mud baths and facial packs. They put us into a big tub full of warm mud. I'd never had a massage before, either. I wasn't going to have a man rub my back, so Baba got a woman masseuse; and she thought that was so funny!

Then there were the pools. It was gorgeous there. I must have swum twenty laps in one pool.

Baba wanted to take a ride up to a new resort with bungalows. We stayed in Palm Springs another week, then rented one of the bungalows for a week. It was the same service as a hotel.

I had a one-piece bathing suit that was a robin's egg blue satin spandex, and it really fit.

Baba took me to this wonderful beauty salon, where we had the works. Baba and I had another facial with ground-up rose petals, pineapple and ground almonds, like a mask. When I got home, I copied that formula* and even added a few other things, including coconut milk. We had our nails done, pedicures, too.

During the pedicure, when the man was massaging my feet and legs, I wondered, 'How far is he going to go?'

When he got above the calf of my leg, I was getting a little uncomfortable. When he got up to my knee, I said, "I don't think I need to be massaged any further."

The masseuse came to Baba's room. She massaged a person's foot in such a way in different areas for the healing effect, even to get rid of migraines. She was telling me all the parts of the foot, in reflexology, that could help the body.

"Do Baba's foot; she's got ulcers, " I then suggested.

She did, and Baba said that it soothed her.

That evening I said good night to Baba and thanked her for bringing me.

"Anything you want, order it and charge it to my room number," Baba said.

On my pillow was a chocolate truffle, wow! Then they brought in a bottle of champagne. I thought, 'I'll bet they gave Baba one, and she can't have that stuff. I'm sure Frank would tell her.'

---

*Body and face washes and body packs in the Appendix.

I called the office and said, "I don't drink alcohol, but I would like some Ginger Ale. The lady on the switchboard said she'd take care of it. Sure enough, there was a knock on the door. A waiter exchanged what he called a club soda drink for the champagne, then set down a fluted glass and left.

I was so excited I didn't think I could sleep. Oh boy, would I love to stay in a place like that again some day!

I pulled the covers back, got into my nightgown and rolled into those sheets. They were percale, but felt like satin. I slept like a baby. The next morning, before showering, I noticed all the things on the counter — the large vanity with two sinks and a huge mirror. There was a big bottle of cologne with a ribbon on it and different shaped, colored and scented soaps, one rose, one peach and one strawberry. I thought they were almost too nice to use. I decided to use the peach and take the others home, not knowing they would replace these every day! The rugs on the floor were so thick that my toes disappeared in them. I had never seen anything like this before. I took a shower; and when I got done, I danced around the room in the towel, watching my reflection in the mirror, thoroughly happy.

I put on the white pants, silk top and open toe sandals, then went next door and knocked on the door.

Baba said, "Come in," just like she knew who it was.

I had a poached egg on toast in Baba's room, and we all had a baked apple peach cobbler! Baba wanted coffee so bad, but Frank said "No," so she ordered hot milk with cinnamon and sugar.

"Today, you can do anything you wish," Baba told me. "I'm going to sit by the pool. But first, I want to talk to you about Alexander. You know, Alexander thinks he owns the place, but he doesn't. I own fifty-five percent. My dad left it that way on purpose because sometimes Alexander gets carried away. Alexander may think he owns the burlesque; but I've got the papers that prove what's what, so he cannot hurt you as long as I'm here."

We moved to the bungalows for four days then back to the resort again, and Baba was starting to feel good.

We stayed two more weeks, then Baba said, "I don't need two *months* off."

"Don't you think you should follow the doctor's advice?" I countered. "You were terribly ill."

"You're always thinking of me."

"I don't know, Baba, but I'm worried about you and me. I have to do something to support myself."

"No, no, you're taking care of me, Judyenne. I'd have to hire someone anyway, and I need you."

"Frank's here."

"Yes," she said, "But he's got to fly back to check on Alexander, see what he's up to and come back. I can't be left alone. I've hired you. That's it! I don't like being alone anymore. I just feel better when you're here. So this is a permanent job."

I did whatever I could — brought pillows out to put under her head, got her shawl from the dresser. It was from China, long and slinky. She said it used to go over her baby grand piano. It had long fringe that was pink with ivory and was hand-tied. The shawl background had roses on ivory. I loved it.

I put the shawl over her and I said, "There, now you're the Queen of Sheba."

"Yeah, that's what I am beginning to feel like," she joked.

At the end of the three weeks she announced, "We're going back, but we'll stay a while at the Pasadena house."

XVIII - Return from Palm Springs

1939

Baba, Frank and I managed to get back from Palm Springs to Pasadena, and the doctor's office was our destination before going to Madam Zurenski's.

I thought, 'Without Alexander knowing we are here,' as we didn't tell him.

Doctor Goldstein said she was a bit better, but he still wasn't happy.

Later, Baba was on the phone constantly. She called department stores and specialty shops. Soon trucks delivered a seemingly endless stream of shoes, dresses and gowns. She wanted me to try them on to see how they fit. She was back to the promotion of Baby Judyenne. She was going to show me off, using some of the finest outfits.

"I know how to work this," she said. "I'm going to do this first, then take over the theatre."

She had a fitter from one of the major department stores come to the house, and I had to try on the clothes. One was a Princess style formal I loved. I wore silk stockings with a seam up the back that had to be straight — nylons didn't exist.

It was endless hours for fittings standing on a footstool, walking and posing in the gowns.

About 5:30 Baba said, "Okay, everybody, quit and go home. Baby Judyenne and I, we're leaving."

She called Frank. He came over and Baba said, "Get ready. We're going out for Chinese." And away we went to Cathay Gardens.

When we walked in, there were the familiar high-backed booths with half moon carvings and high arches at the entrances with a curtain of pretty glass beads that made the meal more intimate. The same man was there who talked to the girls and me when we'd pick up Chinese pork noodles. We knew his name was John Paul.

He looked at me, then he said, "Oh, hello again!"

"Oh, you know him?" Baba inquired.

"Not really, but I've seen him here before when Dimples and I or the other dancers came in to eat."

We had a wonderful meal and Frank drove us back home. We listened to the news on the radio, and Baba gave invitations to Frank to deliver to VIP's.

It was late. I made her some hot milk toast with cinnamon and sugar. It always seemed to settle her stomach. She had eaten shrimp, and a lot of it.

The next morning Baba said, "It's very difficult to break into the movies, you know, as an extra. There are so many beautiful girls in town. We need a way to get you face to face with these VIP's, and I have a plan. I know some good cinematographers and the right people. I'm inviting them here, and you'll be modeling some of these clothes. We'll be taking moving shots with different types of lighting. Then, when that's done, we will do some other still shots. I want to make a little production of this."

The photographers were absolutely marvelous. I think they had known her over the years; and possibly she was calling in some heavy markers, so they came. There were dimming spots, the soft lights with diffusers. She had been teaching me how to model clothes for months. She had me walking with a book on my head until I was starting to think they looked more normal than my hats! If I could absorb knowledge with a book on my head, I'd be a genius. These famous photographers took shots of me by the fireplace, the French doors, sitting on a leopard rug and posing in those beautiful formals.

All went well. A florist placed flowers and plants, and other people were rearranging the living room. The marble floors were being polished. There was a Turkish Rug placed in front of the fireplace, so I asked Baba, "What are we going to do now?"

"I'm throwing a private party to show you off. Only a few directors and agents. You watch, we'll get something moving."

This was to happen the following day. The night before, we put on mudpacks; then, in the morning, I had the bubble bath of all bubble baths, with glycerin, rose water and buttermilk. A couple of maids came over. There was liquor being delivered. It was a busy place. I was hours getting my hair prepared and makeup on. She called to have Dimples come over and a beauty operator. Baba decided I'd wear this gorgeous fuchsia rose dress with silver sequins and spaghetti straps. She had sent invitations to the chosen few, and it was really a cocktail party between four and six p.m. People started arriving, and I was excited.

As I peeked from the den awaiting my cue, I noticed our old standby, Ivan Kahn, was there, also Charlie Feldman, a fellow she knew who handled contracts, Bill Gossit and Adolphe Menjou. I don't know if it was a wise thing, but she had called in Joe Schenk. Many of them didn't like working with each other. The guests were all men. My job was to show myself, on cue from her, such as, "Judyenne, would you go to my desk and bring my notebook and pen."

She did it on purpose so that I'd have to walk kind of slinky right in front of the men. Two maids went around serving the guests cocktails and hors d'oeuvres. She was telling them of her plan to introduce me to the Hollywood power players. She wanted their personal opinion on ways to help mold

Judyenne into a star. They were all talking *about* me, but not *to* me. I was also supposed to be sitting with my legs crossed, showing my ankles in those beautiful high heels. I did all those maneuvers and answered their questions. That was my private party showing. I felt like I was a piece of property being shown off, and I guess that's what it was. To me, the highlight of the affair was meeting Adolphe Menjou. I really liked him — he was so European.

It was after 6 p.m. when I had to say goodbye, shake their hands and thank each for coming. After they left Baba said, "You did wonderful. Did you see how they looked at you?"

Baba was still excited herself over our "cocktail party" and what benefits would be coming from it, but she was still drinking. The problem was, where was she getting the liquor? So I said to myself, 'I need to investigate.'

I went into her upstairs bathroom and noticed the toilet handle wouldn't go down. I took the lid off, only to see a bottle of vodka standing in the tank, which kept the chain from going up. I removed the bottle and fixed the chain. Then I wondered, 'What to do with the vodka?'

I put it behind the rolls of toilet paper in the cupboard. Now Baba's secret hideaway was revealed, but I couldn't tell on her. I decided to wait and see.

The next morning after a late breakfast-brunch Baba announced her plans to get back to the theatre. But first stopping at a photographic studio, she came out with a large container. Frank put it in the car for her. Then we were off to the theatre with the big portfolios. She was laying pictures from them out on a table in the theatre. There were some of the special shots taken of me by Bill, a cameraman at one of the movie studios. Her idea was to put them up outside the theatre for promotion.

At about the same time, in came Alexi with a frown; and he huffed, "What are you bringing those in here for?"

Baba said, "I want to show Judyenne off. I think now she could be one of our headliners."

"Well, she isn't going to work here unless she strips, like everybody else."

Then the argument really erupted. They started walking to the makeup room, arguing all the way. Frank was following her and got the portfolios. The arguing continued toward her office. Baba said to Alexander, "When we were kids you were just stupid noise, but now you've grown into a crude jerk!"

I said to Buddy, the old stage-door security man, "She's too ill for this. He always yells at her."

Buddy answered, "Don't worry, she can stand up to anybody."

"I know, but she's been ill."

So I marched back to her office, where the door was ajar; and I heard Baba say, "That's what you think, *I* own controlling interest."

"But the doctor hasn't said you can work! Until he does, I'm in charge!"

Baba said again, in Russian, "When we were kids, you were just a *bolvan*, but now you've grown into a *mudak*!"*

After more choice words, I stuck my nose into the fray. I felt a responsibility to Baba when he started getting into her face so close, nose to nose. I thought, 'That's it!'

So I walked in the door and said, "Your sister deserves your respect, not your bullying. You're certainly not a gentleman. So stop it!"

He laughed, "Who said I was a gentleman? This is a business. She doesn't know how to run it."

"She's been doing very well for a long time before you ever came!"

"You can't talk to that thick-headed jerk!" Baba fumed.

Frank then came in and asked, "Are you in trouble, Baba?"

"Not yet," Baba said. "But I'm late for my appointment, so let's go."

Turning to Alexi, Baba said, "Don't you ever think you're going to take advantage of me or take my theatre, because it isn't going to happen."

She was taking fast strides toward the front door with me in tow and Frank bringing up the rear.

We reached the car and left for her doctor's appointment. The doctor did more tests and sent her to the hospital for what was to be an overnight stay. He said that then he would make his decision. Frank took me back to Madam Zurenski's house.

I returned to my room; and Madam Zurenski followed, showing me a big new birdcage she had bought. Later she led me down the hall to the study. She was continuing to talk to me and looked very serious.

She said, "You know, I've wanted to talk to you about my cousin Baba. She's sicker than we think. The family doesn't think she should be running that theatre."

She continued, "She has cirrhosis of the liver. Furthermore, Frank says she is drinking behind your back and his. This has to stop, or Baba won't live long. Alexander is a very strict manager. If Baba's drinking can't be controlled, she's going to have to be put into a special hospital."

"I can help Baba stop drinking."

"You really can't. She's improved since you've been around, there's no doubt about it, but the family in New York is going to go by whatever the doctor says, this time."

This was quite a blow to me; and I thought 'If we continue with her hot milk, cinnamon and sugar, she'd get better.'

Madam Zurenski said, "Let me look at your palm."

---

*The author has predicted that bolvan (stupid noise) and mudak (crude jerk) will become pop cultural words, starting on the West Coast.

"Sure, which one?"

"Let me see both of them. You're left-handed?"

"Yes."

She studied both hands, frowned and said, "You've had many hardships."

'How can she tell that?' I wondered.

Motioning to a mahogany end table with a brass Chinese lamp, she said, "Put your hand under this light. This is your life line, and all these different lines tell something about you."

I'd heard about palmistry, so I asked, "And you can tell about me by looking at my hand?"

"Yes."

"I could tell a lot about you in a tea cup," I told her.

She raised her head and said in surprise, "What?"

"I can tell tea fortunes. I've been telling them since I was a little girl."

She laughed; and, with a slight question in her voice, asked, "You really can?"

"Sure. You want some tea? I'll show you."

Madam Zurenski called Maria, who made the tea that she requested. Maria brought the teapot, cups, spoons and cookies. I loved the cookies.

Madam Zurenski said, "These are cookies that my mother used to make in the old country."

"They taste like the *anise springerle* cookies my Grandma and Grandpa made.

"Yes, there's anise in them."

"They're really good. Would you give me your recipe?"

"Of course."

"I've collected recipes since I was just eight years old," I boasted.

We enjoyed the tea, and when Madam Zurenski's cup was about finished I said, "Sip all the tea out of your cup."

She did.

"Now turn your cup upside down, point the handle toward your face and turn it to the right three times. Make a wish, but don't tell me your wish."

She did that. I saw a lot in that cup. I told her different things that were in the cup, then said, "Your wish will come true. A tea leaf's on the cup's rim." Pointing, I added, "See three little leaves right there?"

"Yes."

"You're going to take a long trip."

"Judyenne, this is very interesting, because we're having parties where we're going to need some fortunetellers, Tarot Card readers, and in your case, someone who can read tea leaves. Would you like to do that?"

"Oh, yes, I'd like to." I didn't think there was anything wrong with reading tea leaves.

"There's something about you, Judyenne," she said. "This gives me some new possibilities to work on."

"Are you getting Baba tomorrow?" I asked.

"We'll see her in the hospital, see how the new tests come out. In the meantime, we're going to visit her now. You can stay here and answer the phones."

I wasn't making any money now, as I wasn't at the theatre. Alexi was in charge; and Baba was in the hospital, so I had not heard any good news and my situation seemed tenuous, at best.

At dinner, Carlos made a sort of a sweet and sour chicken that was kind of Chinese.

Finally Madam Zurenski came back, but without Baba.

She walked in and said, "Well, we've had a big day. I want to talk to you about Baba. There is evidence that her liver condition is worse. She's getting weaker all the time."

"I did notice that," I said, with a cold chill going down my back.

Three days later they brought Baba back and took her through Madam Zurenski's wing to an elevator. She was too weak for the stairs, and she was in a wheelchair. They put her in the same room across from mine. I went into her room and exclaimed, "Oh, Baba, I'm so glad you're back!"

"I'm all right, I'm all right. I'm just a little weak. I guess I have a few more problems besides ulcers. But I'll be right across the hall from you."

I was really getting scared now, because the money that was coming in from when I danced had stopped.

I stayed while Baba ate. She was having a little trouble swallowing, so I asked Maria, "Don't you have one of those back supporters that looks like a little chair?"

"Madam Zurenski does." Away she went and got it, and I put the backrest behind Baba.

When she finished eating, I said, "Do you think Alexi would let me dance, like you did, if I ask him?"

Looking somber for a moment, Baba said, "I don't think so. But I'm trying to get that letter from the doctor. When I do, *we'll* run the theatre."

"I'm so proud of you."

"Why?"

"You can adapt to anything, no matter what happens. You have a smile, and you're always thinking of me."

I waited 'till she was asleep, then went downstairs and Maria reheated my dinner.

Once again, Madam Zurenski caught me before I could go upstairs. She sat next to me as the table was cleared, then asked, “Would you like some ice cream with pineapple topping or strawberry?”

“I like both.”

“Maria, get her both.”

Maria was surprised because Madam Zurenski didn’t eat things like that. Then Madam Zurenski said, “The doctor’s report isn’t that good. Baba’s not going back to the theatre.”

I felt like someone had hit me in the head!

“Never?”

“She won’t be able to operate it right now, but maybe in six months to a year. Remember Baba is near sixty years old and very ill, Judyenne.”

“But, Madam Zurenski,” I said, “What can I do for Baba? What can I do to earn a living?”

“The pictures Baba had taken of you are being distributed to some important agents. We’ll see what happens. I cannot take Baba’s place, Judyenne. I have my work. I don’t think you should be near Alexi. What Baba was doing was giving you the training you needed. I do think it increased the house, too. More money was taken in when you were there. But Alexi won’t change his mind. He said, ‘Frankly, I’ve been worried about how old Judyenne is.’”

Madam Zurenski continued, “Baba told me Mister Kahn said the same thing to her. I’d like to talk to someone in your family.”

I had run away from home to marry John Moran Severette. My family, what would they say?

She handed me twenty dollars; then said, “Baba told me to give this to you. You still don’t owe any rent. You’re paid up. I want to talk to you more about the fortune telling later.”

I went upstairs thinking, ‘I suddenly have a home, temporarily. I don’t have a job. Baba couldn’t handle me any longer. I was her protégé. Am I still her protege?’

I really felt like crying.

‘I must wait until the next turn in the road, as Uncle Al taught me,’ I thought to myself. ‘I just may need to go into the tea fortune business. But most of all, I should pray for Baba to get well.’ And I did, as tears ran down my cheeks.

XIX - Judyenne's Gift

1939

Reading tea fortunes was exactly what I was going to have to be doing, but what was I going to tell Madam Zurenski about myself and who my family was? One can only cover up so much. The truth would come out when they looked at my birth certificate or talked to my parents. I was eighteen now. But not the twenty-one needed to sign contracts back then. 'That same numerical sum is back to haunt me again,' I thought. It had been a roadblock with John Moran Severette. I sat on the edge of my bed and looked at the clock.

'It'll be seven o'clock pretty soon,' I said to myself. 'Well, I can tell her I'm eighteen. Maybe I could give her Aunt Grace's phone number. She would verify my birthday.'

It was almost seven p.m., and I had to meet Madam Zurenski then.

'Gee, this is such a paradise. I wonder if I'm going to be able to stay or not?' I was thinking. Grandpa came from Europe and had hard times, yet made himself a million dollars. Madam Jean Marie Severette had many odds against her, yet became successful. There must be an answer for me. Remember what Grandma Latimer said, 'There's always an answer. You never give up. Giving up denies you success. A Latimer never gives up.'

So, fortified with those words, I walked through the French doors, where I heard her call, "Judyenne."

"Yes?"

"Would you please come into the study?"

I almost ran to the study. She was at the table under the big chandelier. The room was elegant and stately. It made me feel safe.

I thought, 'That's what I need, I need to feel safe.'

She said, "Sit down. I'm going to have Maria bring some tea."

I must have looked a little surprised because she said, "No, no, I'm not going to ask you to read my fortune."

The tea was served with some more of those tiny cookies.*

We were talking, and she asked, "Do you think you could tell *anybody's* fortune?"

"Oh, yes," I answered. "I'd have no trouble doing that. My Uncle Al used to bring his girlfriends to me for a tea fortune. I even set up a card table in the garage telling tea fortunes."

---

*Russian Tea Cookie recipe in the Appendix.

She laughed and asked, "You did what?"

"Kids in the neighborhood wanted their fortunes told; their mothers, too. I had a tea set, so I told their fortunes. Our neighbor, Jeanne, a French woman whose cat had a broken leg I fixed, wanted me to read her husband's fortune. He was a very sick man. He had been in World War I and had trouble breathing because of mustard gas. Sometimes she would ask me to just talk to him. He married her in France. His one joy in life was jigsaw puzzles. When he got stuck, she'd call me. It was always nice because she always gave me homemade fudge. I told his fortunes many times."

Madam Zurenski got a big kick out of my telling about my "professional" work. Then she said, "I'm going to call Maria and Frank, and I'll have Maria bring more cups. I want you to tell their fortunes."

"Sure."

First I did Maria. I saw that Maria also had a string of tea leaves going around like a road in hers. I knew Maria would be taking a trip like Madam Zurenski's. I told her she was going on a long journey. I showed her three tea leaves and said, "It will be in three weeks."

She looked real excited. "How did you know that? We're leaving in three weeks for the Philippines to see my mama. My sister had a baby!"

I guess Madam Zurenski was pretty impressed.

Next Frank came in. He turned his teacup around three times. I looked at the cup. First I noticed that the leaf was not on the very edge of the cup, but was under the edge. I saw another trail of leaves, also a square shape of leaves, an L shape and two dots. "You're also leaving. You'll be gone, maybe two months. I see many changes."

He spoke up and asked, "How soon will I be leaving?"

"These two little dots say you will leave within two weeks," I replied.

Everyone was silent for a few seconds after I finished. I had begun to think about it, too. Would that mean he would be going somewhere with Baba? It was starting to make me scared. "There's a good part here, too," I continued. "You're going to get some kind of award. I don't know if it's a medal or money."

"What about my wish?" he asked.

"No, your wish tea leaf is down on the lower edge of the rim," I answered. "Only part of your wish will come true."

"Oh, well, I guess that's better than none," he allowed.

After they all left, Madam Zurenski was just sitting there studying me. She had watched closely while I was doing the readings. Now she said, "You're pretty good at this. How did you know all that?"

"The tea leaves say so," I replied. "It shows the trip, the house, the people and time."

"But it's incredible!" she exclaimed. "Do you have other feelings when you say those things?"

I said, "In the fortune I told Frank about an award and that half of his wish would come true. The award appeared in my mind. I didn't find that part in the tea cup."

"That's amazing," she praised. "You know, Judyenne, you're psychic."

I asked, "What do you mean, psychic?"

She said, "You read people."

"Oh, I've been doing that since I was a little girl. But I don't like to, because sometimes there are bad things I see."

"Well," she said, "It's really a gift."

"I told a lady once, and she said telling fortunes was against God's will."

Madam Zurenski said, "No, that couldn't be. Perhaps Tarot Cards could be. I think it's perfectly all right to read someone's horoscope, that is, their astrology by the stars. We plant our gardens by the moon. I'm very careful what I say to people, because I don't want to hurt people and I don't want to offend God. I think you feel the same way."

"Yes," I agreed. "If I see too many bad things, I just won't read the fortune anymore. I would just warn them to be careful in the car, or not take a trip that day and handle it like that."

"I have to be much more careful," she said, "Because I can't advise people about their money holdings and property. I did that for a while, but I realized I could be making a terrible mistake. Even though I thought I was right, I could have been wrong."

For the first time I felt really close to Madam Zurenski, but I still felt very alone. "I don't know ... I really should start going around to the studios."

"Wait 'till your pictures make the rounds. Something will break."

I hoped it would be pretty soon. I didn't know when the rent was due.

"You know," she said, "I have something to show you. I want you to have something to hang on to." She got up to leave. "I'm going into my inner room. You know, there is a wing off the study in the hall."

"Yes."

"I have a large room where my clientele come to have their fortunes told; but I'm really a psychic, not just an ordinary fortuneteller. In a way, I think I am a family counselor at times, without a degree; but for me experience was my best instructor. My dear young girl, you do, too! As young as you are. Come with me," she added, beckoning.

We walked down the hall to this room. It was locked, so she unlocked it and we walked through into the foyer.

"I want you to close your eyes, take my hand and walk forward with me."

'Why do I have to close my eyes?' I wondered.

I closed my eyes. I was a little edgy about walking into a room with my eyes closed, but I did.

"I want you to see the room as the lights go on."

We walked into the room, and I heard the click of the switch. Then, "Open your eyes," she said all of a sudden.

I opened my eyes, and the whole room was absolutely magnificent. It looked like pictures of King Tut's Tomb or an eighteenth century palace. There were tapestries on the walls, a huge Persian rug on the floor, a magnificent marble fireplace; and the entire ceiling had hundreds of tiny little lights that looked like the stars on a cloudless night. The ceiling itself looked like it was solid gold that had been enameled with huge painted roses and many bright colors that came from the other kinds of flowers — all of these on a gold background populated by a multitude of tiny bright stars. It was like looking up into a colorful starry heaven. I was really awestruck. Next, what caught my eye was this magnificent teakwood table. It was huge and oriental in appearance. The legs were over a foot in diameter and the table was hand carved from top to bottom with many scenes composed of people, animals and plants. The feet themselves ended in the form of a wild animal's feet with claws. On top of this octagon-shaped table there was a base with a crystal ball on it that was a little larger than a bowling ball. She pushed a button; then she stood by the table, and the inside of this crystal lit up. The light was coming from underneath.

"Come over here and look into the crystal ball."

Now I was getting worried. I didn't know anything about crystal balls, and this was beginning to sound like magic.

I walked a couple of steps and asked, "What do you want?"

"I just want you to look into the crystal ball. Come on, come over here, close to me," she implored.

I did, but hesitantly. Then I looked into it. I didn't see anything except the beautiful crystal.

"Close your eyes, then open them again and look into the crystal ball."

I did; and I still didn't see anything, so it made me a bit nervous. I remember people telling me, as a child, about fortunetellers with crystal balls; and it kind of frightened me.

"Put your hands on the crystal ball, one on each side."

I looked and I could have sworn I saw Baba's face, so I looked away quickly.

"What did you see?"

"I just thought I saw Baba."

"You did because you were thinking of her, weren't you?"

"Yes." Well, this was getting to be too much, so I said, "Madam Zurenski, I don't know if I want to fool around with magic or anything like that."

"This isn't magic. No, Judyenne, this isn't magic. It's nothing evil. If you have the gift of sensing other people's feelings as intensely as you do, even if you closed your eyes, you would see their face."

Looking around the room, the centerpiece was this table. On the other side, near huge antique couches, there were large tulip-shaped lamps. Uncle Richard had a lamp like that. He called it Art Deco. Then she pushed another button and a huge crystal chandelier that had been hardly noticeable, lit. She could dim it with another button. As she did that, the refracted reflections all over the surfaces of the room were absolutely thrilling.

I asked her about the lion's feet on the legs of the table, or whatever animal they represented. Each foot had a crystal ball underneath. She said the table came from Europe and had been in their family over two hundred years. She said they took the legs off, wrapped the top and shipped it in a large wooden crate by ship.

Then she said, "Come over here."

She had a little chair for herself sitting by the crystal and pulled one out for me.

"I think I have a plan. I don't want you to be discouraged. No one knows what the future brings at this time. But I think we should try and wait it out. We should try to give the studios and the agents a little time. If you will go to this function we are having to raise funds and read tea leaves in a tent, I will pay you a dollar an hour. We should be there about six hours. So you should be able to make six dollars."

It sounded great to me.

"I have an idea that I could train you with the crystal or in palmistry, and you could still use it in addition to reading tea leaves."

I wasn't too sure about this, because I still felt it might be against God's will, so I said, "Well, I don't know about the crystal. I think that reading a crystal still might be against God, but I think tea leaves are Okay, because Aunt Ada did it, and that helped her survive."

It was beginning to get late in the evening. Madam Zurenski graciously allowed for my thinking which had been shaped by my family background, and said, "I need you to think about this, and I really need to know the name and phone number of your parents. Are they alive?"

"Yes, but I haven't seen them in a while."

She looked me straight in the face and asked, "You're a runaway, aren't you?" I thought I would fall through the floor! I didn't have to say anything. She was reading me.

"Yes, but I actually left home to get married to a man I knew who was a sailor. He was going on a submarine. We were going to get married in Mexico, because my parents wouldn't give me permission. When he never showed up, I had this screen test coupon I won in a hair and beauty contest. I sold my watch, a Christmas gift from John, my fiancee, and made it to Hollywood. But I haven't really made it here at all. I've had a couple of small extra parts and scenes riding horseback in a couple of Westerns. I thought if Baba was going to train me at the burlesque, possibly someone might see me; and I'd get into the movies."

Smiling, Madam Zurenski said, "Well, we're going to do our best to get you your break. Better go check on Baba. We'll talk more tomorrow."

It was the beginning of a whole new adventure for me.

I covered Tootsie up in his beautiful new cage, then went to bed. But I thought I'd better go back to check on Baba again, so I tip-toed up to her bed. Baba opened her eyes. I took her hand and held it saying, "Oh, Baba, please get well."

"I'm trying," she said and patted my hand. "Would you pray for me?"

I always had Baba in my nightly prayers, but I had never openly prayed for her while holding her hand. I held her one hand in my hands and she closed her eyes. I bowed my head and said, "Dear Jesus Christ, Dear God of the Universe, Bless Baba and please help Baba to get well. I think you sent her to me, I really do."

Baba opened her eyes. She was crying. "Please God, keep her safe, amen," I ended.

"The priest used to pray for the Orthodox Congregation," Baba said. "But no one ever prayed for me personally."

"Well, we can pray that you'll get better, and we must trust in God. I have a small book of Psalms I brought from home. Let's study Psalms."

"I would love to hear the Psalms. Let's start in the morning."

"I'll read one of the Psalms every morning and night," I agreed.

She patted my hand. I just wanted to hug her. I did and kissed her on the forehead. She clung to my hand and held it up to her face. For someone who had lived a rather hard life, she was so tender and thoughtful of other people.

"Good night," I said, and tip-toed out of her room.

I slept well that night, for the first time in a while, and I felt good about everything when I got up in the morning. The breakfast tray wasn't up yet, so I helped Baba out of bed and into the bathroom. Then I helped her back to a sitting position in bed.

The doctor had suggested that Baba use a wheelchair. However, we had Baba do a little exercise, walking, while accompanied by Maria and me when at home.

"You are truly a joy to me," she praised.

I told her I'd come back when her tray was brought up. I showered and dressed. When I heard Carlos with her tray, I took my little book of Psalms back to her room and read the 23rd Psalm. I didn't know if I was praying right, nor was I attending church, so I wasn't sure God would even listen to me, but I felt better; and so did Baba. Then I went downstairs for breakfast.

Madam Zurenski said, "I'm going shopping, and I've got some ideas. We'll talk on my return."

I thought I heard a car outside, so I peeked out and saw one. Doctor Goldstein's nurse, to whom I had talked several times, was walking toward the front door! Carlos led her to Baba's room, and I followed. "The doctor wants me to check on Baba every other day," she said. Then she took Baba's blood pressure and left in about thirty-five minutes.

After she left Baba said, "She listened to my heart rate and took my blood pressure."

"I could take your pulse," I offered.

"I don't need an R.N. if I have you."

"I'll be your second nurse."

"That's a good idea."

I left the room. There wasn't much to do, so I went back to my room to put more things away and make my bed.

"I guess I'd better think about my tea leaf business," I told Tootsie aloud. I thought about how I could make money reading tea leaves. I pondered how I could ask God to forgive me if I was doing something wrong. 'Clients! I would have clients like Madam Zurenski does!'

Ada used to put a little scarf around her head. She meant it to look like a turban; so I experimented, wrapping scarves around my head.

It wasn't long before I heard a car pull up and the doors slam. Madam Zurenski came in, so I walked downstairs.

She said, "Come on into the inner room. I think this plan will work. Tomorrow we're having this big convention. We're going to put you in one tent, just for the reading of tea leaves. We'll give you a dollar an hour, like I said. You'll get your lunch and dinner, too."

"Oh, that's even better!" I exclaimed.

"There will be a lot of people telling fortunes: card, palm fortunes, crystal ball readings and sand readings."

It all sounded exciting to me. She said she was going to dress me as a Gypsy. It was to be held on the carnival grounds. The tents would be arranged lining both sides of a sort of a midway entrance to a convention of professional astrologers and palmists.

Madam Zurenski asked, "What is the scarf for?"

"I've been playing with this scarf to make me a turban."

Madam Zurenski burst out laughing and said, "I have the costume right here. We have to give you a name."

"My name is Judyenne."

"No, no, we need a different name for this ... you'll be Madam Zelda."

"Madam?" I questioned. "That's for an older person!"

"Don't worry, we can make you look eighty years old with makeup," and she laughed again. "We'll just call you Zelda, then."

The whole day I felt just giddy. I tried on the costume she had brought me, and I had five bracelets on each arm. The dress was really quite pretty. "This is like being in the movies," I said to Madam Zurenski.

"Yes, it is. You're a natural."

The next day we all got into the car and away we went. Carlos took us, and Frank stayed with Baba. I read about two tea fortunes an hour.

That night, after the patrons left, we mingled with all the fortuntellers. One was from Turkey, and some were from Europe. One said he was a Hindu Mystic. It finally ended about nine thirty, and we drove back home. I ran upstairs to show Baba my costume. I twirled around so that the skirt flew out. Its little coins sewn on the hem clinked together when it moved.

"Look, Baba, I made six dollars! I can give you your twenty back."

"You keep that. Just hide it; don't spend it." There was an air of urgency in her voice.

"I won't spend it."

Madam Zurenski came in and said to Baba and me, "Judyenne was just wonderful, playing Zelda. She played Zelda perfect. I think Judyenne is going to do wonders, or should I say, *Zelda* is going to do wonders."

"No," Baba said, "our Baby Judyenne is going to do wonders."

They both laughed; then Madam Zurenski said, "We'll be going to another fortunetellers home in a couple of days; and I'd like you to come, too, Judyenne. She wants a tea leaf reader. We'll be telling fortunes there. She has some clientele who would like to have their tea leaves read. I have to run now, but I'll be back soon."

That began my career of tea leaf reading in California. Madam Zurenski said I had to split the money in Los Angeles with the fortuneteller there, because I was using part of her space in the tent, so I made fifty cents an hour, or half. They said I was practicing, but I didn't have to buy my lunch.

Every morning and every night I read Baba a Psalm.

Returning at six, Madam Zurenski said, "I guess we'll go back to the Chinese Restaurant. I know Mister Chang."

That's where Baba, the dancers and I always ate.

"Yes," Madam Zurenski said, "He's a wonderful man. I often buy things from China through him. He owns a Chinese Antique import business in San Franciso."

"Oh," I said.

"I want to talk to him anyway so we can 'kill two birds'," Madam Zurenski said. "We can have dinner, too."

As we walked in, John Paul was there in the opposite booth, eating. He introduced Alfred Benavides to us as his store manager. We sat down in our booth, and Madam Zurenski ordered shrimp and pork noodles. That was a treat for me.

She seemed so happy, not as reserved. She excused herself from the table, then John Paul parted the beads in his booth. "Where is your friend Dimples?" he asked.

"I don't know. I don't work in the theatre anymore."

"I come here every day for lunch," he said.

I knew — I'd seen him many times before.

Madam Zurenski then came back, and she gave them a funny look. "I don't know about those two characters," she huffed.

I said, "The tall one always eats lunch here. I saw him when I was here with Baba and Dimples."

"You don't want to take up with strangers," she continued. "You don't know who he is!"

"I don't, but Dimples knows him, so I figured he couldn't be all bad."

We finished our meal, and the waitress brought our fortune cookies.

Mine said, "Much good fortune is in your future."

Hers read, "You will make a safe journey."

We finished our tea and Mister Chang followed us out with a box. Another Chinese gentleman was carrying a large case, and both had Chinese lettering on them. They put these in the back of her car.

When we got home, Madam Zurenski had Carlos carry the boxes to the kitchen. I loved that box with all the Chinese writing, so I asked if I could have it when she was done with it.

"Yes, actually there's a bamboo case inside. You can have the box right away. We'll be using the bamboo case to store canisters."

"What is it?"

"It's tea."

"Oh."

She took the bamboo basket out of the box.

"You must drink a lot of tea," I said.

"We didn't before, but now we will. We're going to start doing tea readings right here, so you might as well start with quality tea if you're going to have quality readings."

Madam Zurenski got me four clients, as she called them, the first week. I don't know what she charged them, but I got a dollar each.

She said, "You don't have to rush, but see if you can do two an hour."

Isn't it interesting that I started reading tea leaves for fun as a little girl and now found myself employed, telling tea fortunes in California? Yet, not my real goal in Hollywood.

Madam Zurenski said, "You'll be making more money soon if the "Rex" stays off shore in Santa Monica."

"With the cake routine?"

"Yes," she answered; then added, "Be sure and leave your door open and check on Baba."

"I will. Anyway," I continued, "I haven't read her nightly Psalm yet."

She looked at me strangely and asked, "Read what?"

"I'm reading her one of the Psalms before she goes to sleep," I replied, "And one in the morning."

"Psalms?" she questioned.

"Yes, from the Bible."

"Oh, don't forget you've got three readings at Madam Olga's tomorrow. It's important that you make a good impression on her. She has a big following, and you can always count on work there." Madam Zurenski then said, "More good news ... we have three tea leaf reading clients for Saturday afternoon for you to do here beginning at three."

"Where am I going to do the readings?"

"We're fixing the library for you," she answered; then said, "Good night, dear," and she left.

"Oh, thank you for all you're doing; I do appreciate it."

"I know."

I went to Baba's room and told her, "Baba, I know it's late, but I have a lot of good news. I have a chance to do the cake dance routine, and I have tea leaf readings at Madam Olga's."

"Olga?"

"Do you know her?" I asked.

"Oh, yes," she said with some disgust in her voice, "But I don't think she's above board in her work."

"I didn't like her either," I said, "But Madam Zurenski said we have to appease her. And guess what? Madam Zurenski is going to put me in the Library to do tea leaf readings."

"Oh, that's wonderful," Baba said. Her face just lit up at the news.

I opened the Book of Psalms to Chapter Seven and read, "Oh LORD God, in thee I do put my trust. Save me from those that persecute me ..."

I read all seventeen verses, and Baba smiled, then said, "Tomorrow will you make me some milk toast?"

"Sure I will, but I'm going to be gone a while tomorrow."

"Who's driving you tomorrow?"

"Madam Zurenski said Frank would drive us. They'll drop me off, then get me later. Don't worry; we'll read the Psalms when I get back."

She took my hand and hugged it against her cheek, saying, "I just have so much faith in you."

"No," I said, "It's the other way around. I have so much faith in you."

Kissing her on the forehead goodnight, I left the room, leaving our doors ajar.

At 8:30 that morning it was time to shower and check on Baba. I helped her to the bathroom; and she seemed to be leaning heavily on me, so I asked, "Do you feel all right?"

"I do and I don't," she replied, "But I can hardly walk."

Again she was leaning against me heavily; and I didn't know if I'd get her to the bathroom, but I did.

"Call me when you want me. Maybe we should call the nurse."

"She'll be here at eleven."

"Oh, good."

Maria came up with the tray; and I picked out another Psalm, which I read. We had a difficult time helping Baba sit up. Then I guess Maria reported it to Madam Zurenski, because she came up.

She said, "You can take pulse, can't you?"

"Sure," I answered.

Baba had a watch with a large face, so I took Baba's wrist. Her pulse was 60. Madam Zurenski asked if Baba might have a fever. Maria got a thermometer. I shook it down. When she took it out, it read one degree over normal.

Madam Zurenski said, "I'm going to call the doctor."

Baba could hardly eat, but wanted milk toast. I walked downstairs and asked Maria if I could fix Baba some milk toast. Maria knocked on the study door and asked Madam Zurenski if I could make Baba milk toast, since she didn't like the eggs.

She said, "Of course."

I did and took it to Baba. When Madam Zurenski came upstairs later, she said, "I think we'll put you back in the Gypsy costume."

"I didn't think we had that costume any longer."

"Oh, yes we do," she said. "I bought one. I *think* you're going to have a lot of use for it. If so, you can buy it from me."

The nurse did come and check Baba's pulse, and it was very irregular. The nurse wondered if her erratic pulse was from the medicine. She called the doctor who said he'd come over.

We were leaving for Madam Olga's. I had my costume on, and they left me at Olga's. She had a very nice, old red brick house. It had a large porch with an awning. She had me in a den off the living room that had a wall of bay windows. There were long, beige curtains with fringe and a cute little table with two small chairs. Knotted beaded cords hung across the archway.

Tea leaf reading is more involved than many know. You have to figure out what they think, then say what will help them, and avoid anything upsetting. This all along with designs in the cup whose meanings have been handed down generation to generation.

My first client was in her fifties. I poured the tea and went through the usual ritual. Into the session she said, "You're right. I had been planning to visit my daughter." That was the first thing I had said: "You have a relative you're going to see, and she's your daughter." The trip I saw in the cup. The relative I had a hunch. I told her of two dates not to go out, even for shopping. They were the seventeenth and thirtieth. She marked these down on a little calendar; then asked, "How did you know these dates?"

"I counted these little leaves on this cup. See," I said, pointing to the cup.

"How do you get that high of a number?"

"Just mathematics; multiply the leaves."

"Isn't that something," she said. "You're a very bright girl; it must be a gift!"

The lady was very pleased.

I think Olga was timing me.

This old frame opens the door to the Photo Album

Clues to the Contest. See Book 2

The Clues

The "Harriett Victoria" doll, the gold ring, the book, the stickpin, the pearls, the pen knife, Lady Marian evening cap, the baby ring, the Key, the silver sugar shell spoon, the frog leg fork, the old coffee mill, silver creamer, and sugar bowl.

Clues in each of six (6) books for a prize and surprise finale!

Figure 23 Uncle Richard, debonnaire, was a Rudolph Valentino Stand-In.

Figure 24 Aunt Florence, Uncle Robert & Aunt Grace

Figure 25 Figure 3 Me at the fountain

Figure 26 Grandma Hanna and Uncle Richard driving

Figure 27Great Grandma Nana Marie Swinderlein, 1897 Dresden

Figure 28 My doll buggy, 1926

Figure 29 Children and me, ready for school

Figure 30 My beautiful Great Aunt Anna Marie in Paris

Figure 30A Aunt Kate and Uncle Fred in Saginaw, 1889

Figure 31 Walter and Clara at farm in Sebewaing, Michigan, 1916

Figure 32 Grandmother's Indian sweet grass basket and her favorite teacup, 1925

Figure 32A Alexei Chapachinkoff

Figure 32B Me – Lily

Figure 33 Little French princess and coral beads given to my mother in Cassel, Germany, when visiting Madame Swinderlein, about 1896

XX - Aunt Florence's Telephone Call

septiembre de 1939

I finished the readings at Madam Olga's. Frank was to pick me up after Madam Zurenski talked to Baba's doctor; so I was sitting waiting, when Madam Olga spoke to me in a rather friendly manner. "You did very well."

"I tried. I don't know about my second reading."

"Oh, don't mind her," she said. "I know her. I read her palms, too. She was checking to see if your reading was different than mine. When she came in to pay me, she said that you were 'very enlightening'. You're doing just fine. You're beginning to read your customers. You tell what they want and need to hear. I'm amazed how you described that cup to the other lady. I want you to do my tea fortune."

I said, "I'd be glad to," and I did.

When I was finished reading her teacup, Olga said, "I'm surprised at how accurate your reading was."

Madam Olga seemed nicer than I'd thought.

She said, "You're very worried. May I take a guess? With Baba ill, you're worried about Mister Kahn?"

"Yes, Mister Kahn has been fighting me about getting my birth certificate."

"It isn't just that. The studios always like to have the signature of a husband or guardian if you're under twenty-one."

"I don't need a guardian. I'm already eighteen."

"That doesn't make any difference. There are new rules in the studios now. They have to be careful. Paramount is clamping down, so is MGM. Much of our clientele are stars and directors. There are some directors who won't start a movie without talking to us, so we hear things."

"Maybe if I call my mother or my aunt."

"Which one would get the most upset?" she asked.

"Mother cries the most. Aunt Florence gets mad."

"Call Aunt Florence."

"Could I? I've got three dollars."

"Sure. I'll time you."

I phoned Aunt Florence. "Hello? Who is it?"

"It's Lily. I'm calling because I thought you might be worried about me. I didn't want you to worry."

There was a silence from the other end.

"I also wanted to find out if you or Mother Clara had heard from John Moran Severette."

There was more silence.

"Yes, I heard by the grapevine, though, that he was to marry some other girl."

I caught my breath, thinking, 'A Navy nurse, maybe.' It was like a knife in my heart.

"Oh, no! It couldn't be true, it couldn't be," I stammered. "He loves me! He said so. I know he does."

"Well, you ran away."

"I ran away because John told me he'd meet me and marry me in Mexico."

"Do *what*?" she screamed.

"That was why I ran away, because Mother and Dad wouldn't let me marry John."

"Well, that was a foolish thing to do," she yelled. "Now you're in a mess. Nobody wants you home."

"I want to stay in Hollywood. All I need is one of you to sign a contract. I got a chance for starlet training at the studio. I'd be in the movies!"

"Your mother and father won't sign it," she declared.

"Well, would you and Uncle Roy sign?"

"Uncle Roy can't be involved. People would find out about you."

"Would you sign?" I asked.

"No," she huffed, "It's foolish!"

"But I won't be able to get into the studio without someone twenty-one signing, or a husband. Why are you so mad?"

"After all the years of suffering, raising you ... food, clothing, school, music lessons, this is the thanks we get!"

"Aunt Florence, all I wanted to do was marry John Moran Severette. But John never showed up. He was to write to me. I wrote him, but his letter never came! I'm sorry you're upset."

Aunt Florence was just furious. "You're sorry! You're *sorry*? That's all you can say! You've got some nerve calling after running off like a trollop. That's the gratitude I get. Your real father bought you fur coats every year until the day he died."

I was so surprised! I wondered if she realized what she had said?

"I tried to keep you in the station of life which you enjoyed. I was so ashamed and suffered so, having you. You're just an ungrateful and spoiled girl who failed in her marriage plans."

I thought, 'Who's failed in her marriage plans? W. C. Worthington dumped her when he got her pregnant with me. He married a socialite instead. At least, I'm still a virgin!'

I quickly said, "I don't see what a fur coat has to do with what we're talking about. If I get into the studios, you'll be proud of me."

"Proud? Another tramp in the movies? That's a joke!"

"You always thought so much of Jean Harlow and Clara Bow. In fact, you said you looked like Clara Bow," I added.

"You should apologize to your mother on your knees. Walter almost had a heart attack!"

"Well, I didn't know you felt this way."

There was a stony silence, so I said, "I guess I'd better say goodbye."

I heard a click in the receiver. I didn't want to cry, though tears were streaming down my cheeks. The words echoing in my mind were, "*He* was to marry some other girl."

"Now you're more upset than before the call," Olga said.

"What's the use. They never understand."

"What's happened with your family?"

"They think show business is a dirty business. When I begged to go to college, it was too expensive. All I needed was to know how to cook, clean and marry a decent man. When I found a decent man I loved who asked permission to marry me, they said "NO."

"They wouldn't let you marry? That's terrible."

I was surprised I was telling her these inner secrets that I hadn't told anybody else. Maybe I wasn't as close to Olga as Madam Zurenski and Baba, but all of a sudden I poured out my story to her.

"What you need is a rich husband over twenty-one," she suggested.

"Do you think that would work?"

"Sure," she said, "Why don't you talk to Big Al? He knows everybody."

"But I don't want to marry just anybody. I wanted to marry John Moran Severette."

"Well, it looks to me, honey, like you've missed out on him."

I wouldn't talk to Big Al. I wasn't positive what his connections were; but I had a pretty good idea, so I only said, "I'll think about it."

I would be leaving for Santa Monica, as Frank was to pick me up; so I went back to the bathroom and splashed cold water on my face, then redid my makeup.

I thought, "Maybe Olga is right. I'd better look for a husband over twenty-one. Maybe I can make a business deal with him. All I need is someone who will sign the contract."

Frank was waiting for me as Olga handed me two dollars. Frank said he took Madam Zurenski home early because she had a movie client for an urgent reading.

"Oh, a movie star?" I asked.

"Perhaps," Frank said, "But we don't ask."

"Maybe she'll introduce me."

"No, I don't think so, Judyenne. These contacts of Madame Zurenski's are confidential. Those in the movies don't want their public to know they see astrologers or psychics."

Frank and I drove home; and once at the Santa Monica house I dashed upstairs to see how Baba was, tell her about my three clients and that I made two dollars.

"Two! You should have made six," Baba said. "That cheapskate!"

"Don't worry, Baba, I'm getting experience. Olga said I was very good, and I'm building my ability to read people."

"Maybe so, but I know she's charging five dollars a reading."

"Gee, I should get two dollars."

"Judyenne, when's your birthday?" Baba asked.

I was almost tongue-tied. "It's June sixth, but I'm more Aquarius than Gemini, why?"

"That's almost four months ago. Why didn't you tell me? Why, it's October first!"

She grabbed her bell, ringing loudly; and Maria came running.

"What is it, Madam?"

"Get Ta Ta."

"Madam Zurenski's with a special client. She will soon finish. I'll tell her," she said, leaving.

Baba turned to me and said, "You have to have a birthday party! We're going to have a party. Why didn't I ask you sooner? What brought it to my mind was Ivan Kahn called. He's all upset. You haven't got a birth certificate. Now, Baby, you have to level with me."

"What do you want to know?"

"I need to know your birth date. How old were you in June?"

"Oh, I was nineteen."

"So you're nineteen."

"Yes."

"That poses a problem. Maybe I could be your guardian. Apparently Mister Kahn's tried to reach your mother."

"What!"

"Well, you gave him your name and where you came from. It was pandemonium in the office, because your mother became hysterical and said she would sue the studio."

"Oh, no! She always gets excited like that! We'd better call back and tell him. My aunt's just like her. They both get upset easily."

"We'll take it up with Ta Ta," Baba said, then asked me what kind of cake I liked.

I thought, 'How different this is from my last birthday!'

Madam Zurenski came upstairs. I had gone into my room. I was heartsick about the news concerning John, Aunt Florence and her attitude..

'If I could get into the movies, I could really be somebody,' I was thinking. 'Then maybe they'd be proud of me. I just can't seem to please them. When I baked a big cake or made a nice dinner, they seemed pleased. The only ones who ever agreed with me were Grandpa Weigmann, Grandma Latimer and Uncle Al. They were always proud of me.'

'When she'd yell, even Uncle Roy would say, "That's enough Florence. You don't have to talk that way to her!"'

Madam Zurenski was in Baba's room, and I heard Baba insisting on a big birthday party.

"You can't stress yourself, Baba," she said. "We'll have a very quiet little dinner and a cake. That's all, no excitement."

I went to Baba's room and told her Madam Zurenski was right. "I'll even bake the cake."

"No, you can't!" Baba ordered.

Madam Zurenski said, "I'll handle it, Baba; you tell me what you want. Judyenne, this is going to be our surprise for you."

"I can make the cake and save money," I said.

"We want to do this for you," Madam Zurenski said more forcefully.

On Sunday Carlos outdid himself, I have to admit.

Baba said, "Get into any pretty dress you want and come downstairs at four. You'll be the star of the evening."

Baba was brought down stairs a little before four. "Tonight," she said, "I'm going to taste a little of everything!"

They had beautiful candelabras on the table and a white damask tablecloth with napkins in silver rings. It was really quite posh; carnations encircled a bowl full of fruit, Carlos brought out a huge standing crown rib roast and there were dollops of whipped cream on a gourmet fruit salad! A big cake was wheeled out on a tea wagon and put on the table when dinner was over. It was a yellow cake with custard filled layers over almond butter frosting similar to a Martha Washington cake. Then it had a top of fine chopped coconut. It looked like a big, fluffy marshmallow. I was thrilled with all this and then being seated by Carlos.

"How different from a year and a half ago," I thought. "These people treating me like one of their own."

There were a few speeches made by Madam Zurenski, Frank, then Baba; and everybody raised their crystal glasses of chilled white grape juice.

Madam Zurenski said, "To Judyenne, who has made Baba so very happy, a happy birthday!"

"To Judyenne, a happy birthday!" everybody chimed in.

The cake had nineteen candles on the top. I blew them out after making a wish. Maria came in and helped me cut the cake. Oh, it was so wonderful! The warmth of these friends was light-years away from the German picnics where I sat alone, the hours in the coal bin, the stinging words: "Go back where you came from!"

The table was cleared, then came the presents. Baba said her gift was something from her heart. She said she had it from when she had once been an actress in Europe. Baba's gift was a blue oblong-shaped satin glove box. Inside there were her white leather elbow length gloves, with white pearl buttons that buttoned up the side. They must have cost a fortune and were absolutely beautiful.

"Oh, Baba, they're wonderful!"

"I wanted you to have something of mine that you could keep forever."

"I will keep them forever!" I vowed. That just touched my heart. Fighting back tears, I said, "I'll call it my treasure box."

Madam Zurenski gave me a beautiful card on top of a box of candy. I opened the card and there was a fifty dollar bill in it and a note. The note said, "Thank you for making Baba so happy." She added, "And bringing all of us a little joy each day."

Frank had a big box. I opened it up; and it was a huge teddy bear similar to my Steiff teddy bear, only five times bigger. Frank said, "I know you have your own bear, but I thought you needed a bigger one to keep you both company."

I thought that was such a sweet thing to say. I think he got the idea from a day when we were walking by this toy store enroute to the Chinese Restaurant. I had made a remark about the big bear in the window.

In came Carlos and Maria. She did elaborate crochet work and she gave me a beautiful pineapple pattern table centerpiece.

It was a wonderful birthday!

When it was time to get up, we got Baba in her wheelchair, onto the elevator and took her upstairs. I thanked and hugged everybody, letting them know how grateful I was.

Madam Zurenski said there'd be more readings on Monday afternoon, the next day.

I went upstairs, got ready for bed, put on my robe, fed Tootsie and covered him up. Then I went to Baba's room.

Madam Zurenski came upstairs.

"We all just want you to know, we do care about you," she said. "Sometimes life can be very cruel. It isn't quite so bad when you have someone who's there waiting in the wings."

I understood that so well, "waiting in the wings," whether it's on stage or anywhere else. If there's someone there for you, that's what counts.

Monday, just before I was ready to tell tea leaf fortunes, the phone rang downstairs; and Madam Zurenski called me. She said it was Ivan Kahn, and he was extremely upset. I went down, and she gave me the phone.

"I want you to call your mother. Tell her to stop her threats. You're over eighteen. We can't go any further. We've got to have a birth certificate. Will you get one?"

"Yes, I will."

I handed the phone to Madam Zurenski. She said a few words and hung up.

She just said, "Don't worry about it. We can get a birth certificate. I'll talk to you later."

The following day after breakfast, I went upstairs to see Baba, and she asked, "Did you try your gloves on?"

"No, I put them away."

"I think you should try them on."

"Oh, I will; I'll go right now."

I got the box out of the dresser drawer, opened it up and took out the gloves. As I started putting my fingers into the left-hand glove, they wouldn't go in. I looked inside the glove, thinking there was tissue paper in the way. It was a hundred dollar bill! I grabbed the other glove really fast to see if there was something in it. There was another hundred dollars! Hooray, I was wealthy! This meant I had two hundred plus the fifty. I ran into Baba's room, jumping up and down.

"Oh, Baba, we're rich!"

"So, you found your surprise."

"Yes, yes! I've never, ever, seen a hundred dollar bill before, I don't think."

Laughing, Baba said, "You hang on to that. You never know what's going to happen in life."

It was good advice. I took the money out, and the gloves fitted perfectly. They looked beautiful. She just thought that was fantastic. "They fit you! A perfect fit!"

"Now, all we have to do is go to an opera," she joked.

Time was marching on, and Madam Zurenski said she would get my birth certificate.

I asked Madam Zurenski, "Why do you think Mister Kahn hasn't called?"

"They get awful itchy at the studio. Things are changing. There are a lot of new ethical codes. You can't say things you used to say; you have to be more covered up. They're afraid of parents, lawsuits, negative publicity."

I pondered her explanation. The phone rang as I returned to my room.

Madam Zurenski called upstairs, "Judyenne, they want you back on board the ship again. Baba won't be able to go with you this time; and she said you shouldn't go alone, so Dimples will be there. We're also thinking of sending Frank with you."

'Well,' I said to myself, 'If Frank is there, I'll be all right.'

XXI - Halloween Aboard the "Rex"

Octubre de 1939

After I read Psalm 86, "Bow down thine ear, O LORD ..." to Baba, she said, "It's three days to Halloween."

"That's right."

"You won't be here Halloween."

"I won't?"

"No, they want you on the "Rex" again for the cake routine, except the colors will be orange and black. You girls will be dressed as cats with big tails. I wish I could be there."

"Oh, I wish you could, too. I'll try to bring you a table favor or balloon or something."

Frank came with Dimples to pick me up. Our lead dancer was showing some pictures of the costumes we'd wear. As we left Madam Zurenski said, "Now, Dimples, I don't want you discussing any of Baba's gigs with Alexi. It's none of his business!"

"Oh, I won't."

"Frank can take you and Judyenne for the costume fitting tomorrow. Judyenne, you and Dimples can go for Chinese when Frank returns."

I kissed Baba, went downstairs and away we drove to Madam Olga's.

I finished my tea leaf readings, and Olga had just finished reading Dimples fortune, so, handing me three dollars for my readings Olga said, "Frank's here; you'd better go over for Chinese."

Arriving at Cathay Gardens, I saw John Paul Jamison, the tall, lanky fellow, in a back booth with Alfred Benevidas and another man he introduced as Bill Rivers. They all looked like they were two sheets to the wind, but they had ordered "the menu" for three and at least ate well.

John Paul said, "Why don't you join us?"

"Sorry, no, we're discussing business," Dimples replied.

We took the booth across the aisle.

Just minutes later, who is standing behind our waiter, but John Paul, who said, "I want to give you my business card so you can reach me if you ever need any help or want someone to talk to."

I saw that the city was Phoenix.

"But this says 'Phoenix, Arizona'?"

"I'm here temporarily. On the back is my local number. Alfred works for me and Bill is in a training program."

"What kind?"

"Store management in one of our stores."

"What kind of store?"

"We operate clothing stores."

'Wow,' I thought, 'This guy must be rich!'

He said, "Goodbye," and I waved.

I put his card in my purse. Frank paid the bill and I left the tip, then we went to Santa Monica.

Later I learned that Frank was not only a close friend who came to America with Baba, but he was also an assistant in her other business interests besides the burley.

Baba called me into her room where she was eating the Chinese food we brought back and asked me to look at some of the sketches of the costumes we'd wear on the "Rex". Madam Zurenski was eating on the run, but they were making big money at this fortune telling. Some of their clients paid her twenty-five to even a hundred dollars. I started thinking of my dollar a customer I received; but they were professionals, I told myself. They said I was a psychic. I didn't really think that. I just called them my "hunches." Grandpa told me many times that I had "intuition."

We picked up the costumes at the costume shop, but we didn't go to the Bijou to practice. We went over to a friend of Baba's who owned a dance studio. Dance marathon contests were held there, as well as dime dances where you bought tickets to dance. Frank took Dimples, Elizabeth and me there to practice in our costumes. They showed me the steps. There was a good-looking fellow there who had beautiful curly blond hair. He was our choreographer and worked with some of the studios. Taking my hand, he said, "You can call me Danny," and guided me on the steps.

He guided me back and forth, correcting my mistakes very slowly until I got it. Then he had me go through it with Dimples and Elizabeth for about two hours. He said that, for one of the numbers, four other dancers would join us. They were outlining the steps and blocking positions. It was practice, practice. Danny told Frank it wouldn't hurt if I had private lessons.

Danny took my hand several times and said, "Count in your mind your steps, Judyenne. Every step is a part of you." He was very kind and knew my fears about making a mistake.

Weeks earlier I had made some of Grandma Latimer's date balls, giving some to Baba, Madam Zurenski and Frank, who had wolfed them down. Olga asked me for the recipe. She put hers in a crock and sprinkled a sweet dessert wine over them to age. She sent homemade treats to key power players in L.A. I remember she sent a big box of them to Benjamin Segal in Holmby Hills.

The last day at the dance studio I made a batch of the date balls for Danny and the girls at practice. I was serving them when Big Al sauntered into the studio.

Walking toward me, he asked, "Are those the famous date balls? Don't I get one?"

"Yes, of course, Big Al."

I got one and reached out to hand it to him. He clasped my hand and the date ball, eating it from my hand as I tried to pull away. I ended up not only personally feeding him, but his lips grazed the palm of my hand before he released it.*

We left after this for the gambling ship. I understood that the mini-cake and costumes went by barge. We'd take the water taxi early, boarding the "Rex" at three o'clock.

The fishnet cat costumes fit our bodies tightly, with a cap at the neck snug to our heads and two cat's ears sticking up on both sides. There was a long, stuffed, satin tail that swished around on the floor. The only thing not covered was your face, and under the net we had only a G-string and stickons in orange satin.

On the "Rex" there was a large ballroom and dining room, then the stage and another deck. That deck was all glassed over, as that was the gambling area. We were told to get into the cat costumes because we would be parading around the gambling deck first.

All the decorations were in orange, black and white, with ghosts dangling, plus orange and black balloons with glitter. Goblins and skeletons hung from the rigging around the stage.

We were taken up into the gambling area, and we walked around the gaming machines swishing our tails for the patrons' diversion and a fun time. We were introduced at this time as "The Kittens, a Special Act for the 'Rex'."

"If you would just brush up against the male customers and flutter your eyelashes, it will help advertise the routine," we were told. "Don't neglect the women. Tell them how pretty they are and how you admire their dresses," Danny said with a wink.

After working the tables, we went backstage to prepare to do the cat dance when the lights dimmed and four dancers joined us.

I thought, 'Oh, No, how am I going to keep up with these girls?'

Our netting was black, but theirs was silver and they were gorgeous. They were cats, too, complete with tails. This dance went off perfectly. I didn't forget a step. This was all new for me. I hadn't done any great dancing and never a show like this.

---

*Recipe for Lady Harriet Latimer-Jackson's Parisian Sweet Holiday Treats in Appendix.

The applause was wonderful. I began to realize what Dimples and Maria had said: "The applause — it gets in your blood. The excitement — you just can't believe. But it's addicting."

Backstage we were told we had a stateroom. We had another show coming up, another intermission, then the finale for the evening, the cake dance. All I had to do, really, was pop out of the cake, then a simple routine, deep bows backing up as the curtain fell and more goblins and pumpkin shapes dangled.

Danny handed Dimples a key. "Just leave the door unlocked. Nobody will bother you down there. You can rest between shows."

There were other acts like jugglers and comedians, even a fellow swallowing swords — strange for a ritzy place like this. He was somebody famous from New York and Europe.

The girls took our makeup cases to the stateroom. It was like a suite. This would compare with a cruise line. So, we sort of collapsed there. Precision dancing makes you appreciate a rest. Danny said if we needed anything, call the steward.

Dimples ordered Vodka Collins, Elizabeth a Gin and Tonic, and I a Gingerale with a cherry. They teased me about it.

We had a couple of hours before the next show. I had lost track of Frank. I last saw him heading for the gambling deck. We were fixing our hair, checking makeup and costumes, then Dimples and Elizabeth said they were going back to the gambling deck. They said they were looking for somebody and would be back soon. I was rubbing the calves of my legs, as I didn't want to get a charley horse.

I thought, 'I'll just put this robe on.' It was satin, smooth and comfortable. I felt much better with my shoes and tights off. I'd get charley horses in my left leg sometimes, so I continued rubbing my leg. I could feel a knot-like sore spot.

The door opened without a knock. I had only seen him once at his birthday party. It was Tony Conera.

"Congratulations on your dance, Judyenne, you're really good. I talked to Danny. He said you're a fast learner."

"Oh, well, I'm trying."

I felt a little uncomfortable. I'd heard he owned the ship. He said the "Rex" was his. He had *connections*, if you know what I mean — often seen with Big Al. I thought, 'I wish he'd leave.'

"I'll be getting into my costume soon," I said. "I was just trying to massage a sore spot in my leg."

He kneeled down and grabbed by left leg, saying, "I can fix it."

I didn't like this, but he seemed to be helping. "Oh, it's really all right. I can massage that sore spot."

"Not like me, I'm experienced at getting knots out of girls' legs."

I thought, 'I'll bet you are!' "I must get ready, Mister Conera."

"You've got time."

'Thank God, I'm not on the chaise lounge!' I was thinking.

"Why don't you lay down and rest. I could put some pillows under your leg."

"No thanks, I really have to go back on the floor."

"Not if I don't want you to," he said.

"Mister Conera, I need to get my costume on."

I stood up. He put his arm around my waist and pulled me close to him.

"Mister Conera! *Please!* I must get my costume on!"

"All right, I'll let you go this time," he said, "I just wanted to compliment you. If that leg continues to hurt, I've got other things that will ease that muscle. Just learn to relax, honey."

He finally left, after squeezing me with those steel arms of his.

"Oh, thank you, God!" I said out loud.

I got into my cat costume fast and almost ran into Elizabeth as I was going out the door.

Elizabeth said, "I've located my friend."

"We've another show to do."

"Oh, that's more than an hour," she said as she whisked past.

I walked toward the tables to join Dimples. The flower girl handing out corsages approached us. "Would you please help give these flowers out to the ladies? I'll never make it before the show starts."

"Of course we will," Dimples answered.

These were real flowers, and we went around the tables giving beautiful corsages to all the ladies while the men supposedly examined our cat tails.

The music started again for dancing, and we saw Frank walking over. "If you want to eat, better order something light."

"I don't like to eat before dancing," I said.

"Did you see anybody after the girls left?" he asked.

"No, not really, but Mister Conera came in," I replied.

"What did he want?"

"He wanted to compliment me on the dance routine," I fibbed. "Danny told him I had picked up the steps and was a fast learner."

"What else did he do?"

"Nothing. He saw me rubbing my leg and offered to help. He massaged the muscles in my calf. It *did* help. I felt a bit uneasy, but it's his boat. I didn't want to get him mad. I told him I had to get into my costume right away. I made that up."

Frank said, "If that ever happens again, remember, call me or the steward. I'm here to protect you."

"I'll remember. I will."

"Tony can be persistent. He thinks he's God's gift to women."

"I hope Tony doesn't come back," I said.

"Okay, I'll be going, but be careful."

I didn't want Frank to have words with Tony.

When we got summoned back stage, Danny said, "I wanted to alert you. There'll be balloons that will be released between 11:55 and 12:00 while you're on stage. Don't be alarmed because there will be a skeleton released to a drum roll as your cake routine finishes. Get ready for the next cat dance, then your finale, the cake routine. Dancers, don't forget, put your legs up before show time and rest."

Danny gave two quick hand claps, "Okay, that's it, people."

I went to the stateroom to get ready for the cat dance. I fixed my eyelashes and redid my makeup.

Dimples came in all excited about Elizabeth, who had a multimillionaire with a big yacht on the hook. "She met him in Vegas," Dimples said. "She met him because Baba had contracts to supply dancers in Las Vegas."

"I never knew that."

I had discovered that Baba was more important than I thought. She rarely spoke of herself. Was it modesty, or was it the cultural secrecy of a Russian Gypsy?

There was a knock on the stateroom door. The steward had a huge box for me that looked like a flower box. Opening it, the card said, "Tony." I didn't have time to really look at it and set it on the table, taking the flowers out. I put them in the bathroom sink in a couple of inches of water. "Is this Tony Conera?" I wondered. "Well, it must be." There was a box of candy along with the flowers, too.

Elizabeth was late for the dance, but she did make it.

We did the other cat routine with the four regular dancers from the ship, and I was proud of myself. I could tell by the sound of the music where my feet should be. I remembered Danny, "Mentally think and count." I remembered what Baba always said, "Pick one person and dance for that one person." Finishing our act, we received tremendous applause; then we headed back to relax.

Elizabeth and Dimples were looking at the flowers as we entered our stateroom. Dimples asked, "Where did you get the flowers? The card says 'Tony.' Conera?"

Elizabeth looked very surprised, saying, "Tony Conera!"

Dimples exclaimed, "Oh, no! Judyenne! He's a fast worker."

"What do you mean by that?"

"He'll have you in bed so fast you won't have time to draw a breath!"

"Oh, no, he won't, and he better not try!"

"You don't know how this guy works?" Dimples warned. "He sleeps with all the dancers."

"This girl isn't sleeping with him, and she's a dancer — or trying to be one," I said.

Dimples and Elizabeth were bent over laughing. Elizabeth said, "You'll be doing more than dancing with Tony." They were giggling.

"He doesn't like to lose, honey," Elizabeth cautioned.

"Well, I'm not his personal property."

Dimples said, "Well, be careful."

It was minutes before our cue. I felt excitement in the air as I peeked from behind the wings. Orange and black glitter was on the balloons. We did our Naughty Girl Cake Dance, and actually it was easier than the large original dance. They had two real skeletons, like you'd see in a hospital, that fell from the overhead ropes. They looked real to me. Later I found out they *were* real! When they dropped, the crowd roared.

Many people who were gambling came down to see this particular cake routine, and it was a full house. With the cake sides opening, our act was beautifully done. We were basically nude under a stretch lace except for silver and black metallic patches glued on our nipples and a little black G-string. Hearing the drum roll, we dashed back to our cake and posed in the center as the curtain came down, then the bow, returning for the second bow amid much applause.

Danny walked up and said, "You remember that guy who was pulling on your tail before?"

"Yes."

"Well, stay away, he's dangerous. He's Bugsie Seigel's driver."

"Thanks, Danny, I'll stay clear of him."

"You're so young, I don't want anything to happen to you." He put his hand on my shoulder like a big brother.

"I've been in this business a long time, and guys like him think you're just property to use. You're too nice a girl for that, Judyenne. I'm a choreographer for another studio, but I have a dance studio, too." Then he said, "Come on with me," and led me to where his jacket was hung up.

He took a business card from the pocket. "If you ever have a problem, call me."

At the same time a male dancer came up, and they walked toward the exit holding hands. I figured they were together. People called them "queers," but I saw nothing queer about Danny; he was a wonderful person and very kind to me.

I went to our room to change from my costume to a formal and beautiful spike heels and wait for Frank. Dimples and Elizabeth weren't there yet. I changed my makeup and hair. Twenty minutes went by, and the girls hadn't showed up. I remembered the flowers and the candy, but I didn't want anything to do with Tony, other than work.

I thought, 'Maybe I should give the candy back, but I'm afraid of offending him.'

I decided to give it to Baba. That settled, I put it in the hatbox, but I didn't know what to do with the flowers.

About that time I heard a knock at the door and a steward said, "I'm to take you four staterooms down from here."

"Why?"

"Change of plans. You're supposed to meet the girls there."

"Oh, all right."

I left everything else, but grabbed a little evening bag and followed him. He opened the door. I walked in. I didn't see anybody there; but then, from an adjoining room, came Tony Conera. I thought I would die! Quickly, I said, "Oh, I must be in the wrong state room. I was supposed to meet the girls here."

"You're supposed to meet me here," he said.

"Well, I have to go. Frank is coming after me."

"We'll have a private party. I've got champagne, Judyenne, don't go."

"No! Furthermore, I don't drink! Or fool around. I must go!"

"I'll take you home later."

"Mister Conera, you know I work for Madam Zurenski and Baba, and I must get back."

"You have to go this soon? I've given Frank a message that the dancers are being detained at least an hour."

"You did what?"

"We've got a little time together," he answered, then started moving in fast. I remembered what Elizabeth said. He had me on that bed and my dress almost off my body in about forty seconds. I was wriggling, hitting, screaming and trying to get away.

He had my little G-string torn off of me, while pressing his body upon mine. 'What is this man going to do to me?' I thought in panic. I could feel his breath on my face, the rotten smell of half-digested booze as he exhaled.

I remember hooking my right leg around his left ankle and pulling as hard as I could to get him off balance. I succeeded, but by this time, I was literally nude. He was going crazy with passion. I was a virgin, nineteen and terrified with fear. I'd heard women could get diseases. With a guy crazy like this, I didn't know what all he was going to do.

I remembered what Grandmother Weigmann's housekeeper always said, "All a man ever wants is to put his poker up your chimney." Those words flashed through my mind in seconds.

I looked him right in the eyes and yelled, "You're not putting your poker up my chimney, Tony Conera, you dirty-minded rat!"

I became wild. I don't know how I did it, but I flipped him off the edge of the bed with my leg. He hit his head and face as he crashed against the wall. He seemed dazed. It appeared he had the air knocked out of his lungs. I don't know what possessed me, but instead of running out the door, I grabbed two good-sized pictures, framed under glass, off the wall and sailed them at him. They both sliced through the air, spinning; and the second one hit him on the neck. That seemed to stun him momentarily. I pulled down my dress, found my evening bag and my shoes and then I said, "If you dare come near me, I'll scream and I'll call Big Al!"

He seemed to have gotten his breath and revived, because he laughed like crazy even with the blood on his bow tie and running down the left side of his nose. He was starting to get up; then he said, "So you wanna fight?"

I was shaking the doorknob with both hands, trying to get the lock open, holding those high spike heeled shoes in my hands. As he approached, my fingers grasped the shoes like weapons, one in each hand with the high spike heels pointed right at Tony Conera's eyes. I yelled, "Not one step closer! You think I'm kidding?"

"No, I don't think you're kidding," he said. "I like playful kitty cats."

At that point I spun around, fairly ripped the door open and flew through the doorway, running like crazy. I heard him call, "I'll see ya soon, little kitty," laughing like the devil!

I ran like a gazelle down the hall to our stateroom. Once inside, I slammed the stateroom door and locked it. The girls were there. When they saw me they both started talking at once. "What happened?" "Judyenne!"

"I got a message that I was to go to a different cabin where I was to meet you." By this time I had broken down crying. I was realizing how close I had come to being raped. Elizabeth started laughing, and I got mad. "This is nothing to laugh at, Elizabeth. I just want you girls to know that I'm a virgin and proud of it! What's a joke to you is serious to me!"

Dimples said, "I *thought* you were a virgin."

"I never met one," Elizabeth said.

I was crying and hopping mad, but the only consoling I got was from Dimples, who put her arm around me.

"Come on now, let's calm down. We'll tell Frank. Do you want a cola?"

"Maybe a root beer," I answered. "I'm going to shower and change."

Dimples said to Elizabeth, "You stay here. Don't you dare unlock that door for anybody but me! I'll knock three, then two. I'm going to find Frank," and she left, locking the door after her. Fifteen minutes later she came back with Frank and knocked the code. I opened the door. I had just gotten a fast shower and dressed again. I told him what had happened. He looked wild-eyed.

Frank said, "Okay, get your stuff!"

I grabbed my things and left with Frank and Dimples. I was still furious with Conera and Elizabeth. Boarding the water taxi, Frank patted me on the back and said, "Don't worry, I'll straighten this out."

His face was grim, his eyes enraged. "It's OK, kid, I'll take care of everything."

I said, "I don't know what to do with the flowers."

Grabbing the flowers, Frank said, "I'll take care of them," and flung them overboard into the Pacific ocean. But I had the candy for Baba.

I was still so shaken I couldn't remember getting out of the water taxi or walking to the car.

As Frank started to pull out, Dimples said, "She hasn't eaten anything. I think she needs something hot."

"You're right," Frank said, "And I know where we can go. It's small, and we'll not be noticed. They even have your favorite."

"How do you know my favorite?"

"I heard you telling Baba you like chicken fried steak with mashed potatoes and gravy."

"If she eats that, she'll die," Dimples said.

"Oh, no," I piped up. "Not if they have chicken fried steak and mashed potatoes with gravy, I won't."

"I think she's feeling better already," Dimples ventured. "You probably like creamed corn, too, I suppose?"

"Yes," I replied. "I put that on my mashed potatoes."

Frank just roared with laughter, and it helped break the tension.

Frank said, "We can go there and probably get a private dining room."

"Why private?" I asked.

"Be just to ourselves 'till this cools off," he responded. "I'll see what it looks like."

There were a lot of people in the place when we arrived, even as late as it was. Frank walked over to the owner and shook hands. As the owner beckoned to us to join them, Frank said, "Sid is giving us a private room."

Frank told the waiter what we all wanted as we entered. It was after one a.m., and I would be eating chicken fried steak, mashed potatoes, gravy and creamed corn!

Later Frank said, "I never saw anyone eat so fast."

"It tastes so good. Anyway, I've hardly eaten. I eat little when we have a show." Sid joined us after the main course and treated us to his homemade lemon meringue pie, yum!

He told Frank we could go out the back door to the alley. Frank took a look, then started to get the car, saying, "You two wait right here."

In a couple of minutes we saw headlights shine down the alley. Seconds later, Frank pulled up and we got in the car. "Don't say anything to Baba or Madam Zurenski," he cautioned. "We'll talk about it tomorrow. It's late, and I need to get Dimples to her place."

Frank even carried my things upstairs, then we went into Baba's room. She was still awake. "Tell me all about it ... what happened?" she asked straightaway. "Frank, what was she like?"

"She was wonderful. She did everything perfect."

People like Frank don't make a habit of bragging about you, so when he gave you a compliment, you earned it.

Baba said, "I waited up for you."

I didn't see Madam Zurenski anywhere. I ran back to the hatbox, got the box of candy and returned to Baba's room. "Look at the Halloween present I got for you."

The candy worked out just perfectly. I didn't know Baba would smoke cigarettes while she ate half of one chocolate layer, but she needed some "happiness."

"Happy Halloween," I said. "Do you know what I just had to eat?"

"No."

I told her and she laughed and laughed.

"Yes, you're like I am; we know what's healthy, but eat things that aren't sometimes."

The candy was an extra large box with three tiers of assorted candies. It must have cost the rat a "real chunk." I never told her where it came from. It made me feel a little avenged to misdirect his gift.

After telling Baba all about the skeletons coming down from the rigging, the flittering balloons and our double act, her eyes revealed her excitement. I could see, though, she was getting tired.

Frank left, then I kissed her forehead and said, "We'll do Psalms tomorrow."

As I returned to my room to cover Tootsie and dress for bed, I, too, was excited, not only for our show, but thinking about how I might outsmart Tony.

'Surely he knew I meant business, even though he laughed at me.'

I got into bed and drifted off, picturing Baba's eyes as Frank said, "She did everything perfect."

I felt the warm morning sun peeking through the curtains on my face; and I thought to myself, 'That was the most exciting Halloween I ever had!'

XXII - Baba's Prayer

noviembre de 1939

**"Царь п бог пажадуйста
прощай ммой
Я оставд ю ребёйока
Я оченъ прощу вас что
Я оправдюся ещё раэ
амеиь "**

Baba fled Russia in 1925.

Baba prayed, "Almighty God, please forgive me, I left my baby. I pray to You, that I may be well again." Baba said to herself, in after-thought in English, 'And thank You, God, for sending me another daughter, Judyenne,' "Amen."

It was another trip to the doctor's office, more medicine, and now the knowledge that Baba had cirrhosis of the liver. She really didn't look bad, just seemed so weak.

The doctor told Madam Zurenski that Baba would have to be in the hospital for a few days. Both Frank and I asked the doctor in the hall outside Baba's room why more tests were needed. He took us to a conference room, and Baba demanded I go with them. Baba remained in a wheel chair in the inner office.

He said, "Really, with her condition there isn't a cure, but we can ease pain, reduce swelling and extend her life somewhat. A long life of heavy drinking caused other liver problems, heart trouble, too. I think we can keep her around a while."

I just about collapsed when he said this! "What do you mean 'keep her around'?"

"Judyenne, she should live a year, possibly two."

I thought, 'God, how do they know this? What a terrible thing to say!' "You can't let Baba die," I said, my voice rising in pitch, "You can't, she's like a mother to me."

"I'll do what I can, Judyenne."

Frank looked stunned. Madam Zurenski looked serious in thought.

We walked back to Baba's room. I squeezed her hand and kissed her on the forehead; then said, "I'll see you every day, Baba."

The doctor said, "I'm sure her new medicine will help."

Baba clung to my hand. Then Madam Zurenski and I left first. Frank stayed a few minutes; I saw him kiss her cheek, and he was talking to her.

A few minutes later Frank drove Madam Zurenski and me back home to Santa Monica.

The next morning Madam Zurenski had me meet her by the pool, where we brought our coffee and a slice of apple streusel coffee cake, as appeasement to me, I'm sure. I was so devastated over the news of Baba's health.

"My cousin has more serious health problems than all of us believed. We're not quite sure what to do, Judyenne."

"What do you mean, not sure? We'll just take care of her and get her well again, won't we?"

"It depends. We've sent Baba's current medical reports to our doctor in New York. She might get better care there."

"But then she would be away from me!"

"Of course, but we must give her the best care. Then if she improves she could return."

"I can't lose my Baba!"

Madam Zurenski got up and put her arm around my shoulder. "Now don't get worried and upset, Judyenne. I just wanted to let you know some of the thoughts the family has. Baba seemed to improve when she had you around. That's actually why I had you come here."

"We're going to get Baba better and just go on as before, aren't we? I know Baba made several contacts at the studios. We planned to go there."

"Yes, but we can't bother Baba now. I'll do some checking for you myself."

"Should I find a regular job?" I asked.

"Technically, Judyenne, you've got a job here. You'll be taking care of Baba if she comes home. I'll get you a few readings here besides at Olga's. We can get you lots of work."

Frank and I went to visit Baba again, and she was so happy to see us.

Frank said, "We're going to Olga's. Judyenne has some readings."

With a serious look Baba said, "Don't you go out with Olga."

"No, I won't. Dimples and I might go for Chinese. That's all."

"Oh, that's nice, but don't go anywhere alone with these people unless you talk to Frank or me. They read for people like Tony. For your career, you must be careful who you're seen with."

"Oh, I promise I'll be careful." I kissed Baba, and we left.

Frank dropped me off at Olga's.

I said, "Hi, Olga. How many readings do I have?"

"Oh, several, but I want to talk to you in the parlor first." In the parlor Olga said, "This is an astrology chart. I want to show you this hand chart showing pictures of hands. Study these. Practice it on Baba or Frank."

"But that's palmistry. I'm not a palmist," I protested.

"You'd probably be the best palmist on earth."

"Why?"

"How do you read tea leaves?" she asked.

"The shapes, size and positions all have a meaning. Ada taught me."

"It's the same thing. You study the different lines, these tell you how to read anyone's palm."

"I know, but isn't that like fortune telling, or like astrology? I'm afraid. It might make God mad at me."

"Of course not. The lines are on your hand," Olga argued.

"That's true, but it seems like witchcraft."

"No, it's as ancient as time itself. Reading palms has been written down for hundreds of years."

I listened to her, but I wasn't totally convinced. She told me to go upstairs and study the charts in my room that I sometimes used when there. My readings started in an hour.

Olga said, "If you want anything to drink or eat out of the refrigerator, you can help yourself at this time."

"Could I fix some tea?"

"Sure."

I made tea and took it upstairs with the charts. I could see that this was not going to be done in one day. There was a lot to study.

Olga called, "You'd better get down here, because you have a client coming up the walkway. She's early!"

I whipped on my gypsy costume.

The lady came in, hung up her fur coat and sat down at my cute corner table. This lady looked important. I poured her tea. She looked worried sick, so I looked into the cup. There was definitely something for her to worry about! Ada always told me not to say too much if the leaves clumped. It could mean death.

"I don't want to worry you," I began.

With that, she opened her handbag, took out a handkerchief, wiped tears from her eyes and laid her hand on the table. I felt really bad.

I patted her hand and said, "It will be all right, honest. Just have faith."

"There's a lot of illness in my family."

"Yes, I know. There's more than one person, and you may lose one of them. You've been expecting this. Life goes on. Your trees in California are all green most all year; but where I come from, the leaves turn red, orange and yellow. Soon they fall, but the tree grows new leaves. That means life goes on."

"You're right. I forgot about the trees and colored leaves. I'm from New York. It makes me think maybe I should do a little traveling when all this is over."

"I think you should."

She was getting happy again.

Olga came out and helped her with her coat. She paid Olga, and then she turned to me. "Here's a dollar just for you."

"Oh, thank you."

The lady left, and Olga called me into her parlor. "Why did you tell her someone was going to die?" she asked.

"I just said, you're going to lose someone. Not die."

"Well, she was crying."

"I know, but she was smiling afterwards."

"I don't allow tipping, so that's your pay."

I did my other readings and gathered up my charts from Olga. Frank picked me up and we drove back to Madam Zurenski's. As I was walking upstairs, she said, "Let me see what those are?"

"These are for palmists. Olga wants me to study," I said.

"Why? You're doing fine with tea readings."

"I know, and I don't think I'd be good at palmistry."

She looked at me and said, "Oh, yes you would. You'd be very good at it, Judyenne. I'll be late — I'm going to a party this evening with some old friends, but I'll talk to you later. If there's something you want, ring for Maria."

"Oh, thank you, Madam Zurenski, and have a good time."

Later I called Maria and asked her what she had left over. I was going to sit on the terrace. Maria brought a cold roast beef sandwich with two beefsteak tomatoes sliced on top of butter lettuce and a choice of Roquefort or thousand island. I said, "Put a dab of each!"

Two days later we learned that Baba was coming home, and she did return. Oh, I was so happy!

Later, taking Baba downstairs to the pool, she said, "We must plan Thanksgiving." She loved looking at the pool. Then she asked, "Should we go to the Ambassador?"

"I know what I'd like to do."

"What?"

"I'd like to fix you one of my homemade turkey dinners with mashed potatoes, gravy and Grandpa's stuffing. My stuffing that my grandfather made is the best turkey stuffing in the world."

"I don't want you to go to all that work," she said.

"I've always wanted to make you a dinner."

"It would be kind of nice to have a real homemade Thanksgiving dinner. I'll talk to Ta Ta. What did you say you were going to fix?"

"It's a surprise," I answered.

"But, your famous turkey stuffing!"

"That's right. It's wonderful! I even put a chopped oyster and chopped walnuts in it, extra! Besides the usual ingredients, I cook the gizzards, liver, hearts and everything. I use half of that broth in the dressing and the remainder in the gravy."

"That sounds marvelous!"

"Oh, that's only part of it. I use extra sage, thyme, leeks, chopped green onion, currents, half of a chopped apple."

She really got a kick out of all this. "Hmmm, nuts, too."

"Oh, yes, like I said, I sauté a big oyster in butter, chopped, and throw that in," I continued. "Yes, and two tablespoons of chopped walnuts."

"An oyster?" she mused.

"Yes, and more!"

Baba said, "That's what I would really like, but I want Carlos and Maria to help."

"Okay, but I want to be in charge of the dinner."

"Okay, then at Christmas we can go to the Ambassador and have dessert here. You're always telling me about your luscious plum puddings and pies."

"All right, if you'll let me fix Thanksgiving dinner," I insisted.

The next day some of the lab reports came in, and I heard Madam Zurenski talking to Frank in the living room. I came down the stairway, but didn't want to interrupt, so I hesitated a minute, then came on down. "Did you have any readings for me today?" I asked.

They stopped talking. Then Madam Zurenski said, "There'll probably be two. If these don't turn out, maybe you'd like to go to Olga's. Did you study your palm charts?"

"Yes, but there's a lot to remember."

I went out on the terrace. I wished I could have heard what those reports were.

Returning to the terrace, Madam Zurenski said, as if reading my mind about the new medical reports, "Judyenne, I want to talk to you about the medical reports on Baba. We have to send them to our doctors in New York."

Days went by with the usual readings, both at Madam Zurenski's house and Olga's. Then one day when I returned to Olga's she said, "I have two ladies to read soon, but I want to see how much study you've done on the charts."

"I only tried it on Maria, but I didn't seem to be doing so well. However, I could tell a lot about Maria by just talking to her. I must have hit the jackpot.

When I mentioned what I thought I saw, her eyes lit up. She was jumping up and down, all excited."

"I'm thinking you could do palms *and* tea readings, but you'll have to practice. Soon it will all come to you, just like when you were taught tea leaves. You didn't learn that in one week."

"No," I admitted.

When the last lady left, Olga said, "I have a gentleman who wants a tea reading."

"A gentleman? I've never — well, yes — I did tell Uncle Al, Uncle Ernie and Dad's. Of course, I've done Frank's."

"He will be here in thirty minutes. I'd put on more makeup. And here's a different pair of earrings for you."

They were big, double gold rings, really pretty.

"Tonight, when you go home, take these little coins," she added.

"Coins? Like on the original costume?"

"These coins have holes in the top. I want you to sew them onto your gypsy dress hem."

"Oh, I will. They make a cute tinkling sound. I've had them on the other costumes."

Olga gave me bracelets for each arm, and then I hurried upstairs to get ready and heard a door close.

Soon Olga called, "Zelda?"

I hurried down; and here was a tall, handsome, very well dressed, blonde man.

First I asked him, "Have you ever had a tea fortune before?"

"Only palm readings, but I've heard how well you do with tea fortunes."

"I try."

He turned the cup three times and made a wish.

I thought, "He looks very familiar to me."

Later I found out that he was a producer friend of Baba and Olga's.

I said, "I see you're going on a plane trip, and you are the pilot."

Now this time, I was getting this from the sensations in my head. I saw a trip in the cup, though. He was cute and had beautiful dark eyes and long eyelashes a woman would have killed for; but he was restless, tapping one finger on the table.

I finished his reading; and he thanked me, slipping a five-dollar bill under the cup! I slipped it out quickly, as he turned to leave!

"She's a very bright gypsy," he said to Olga before leaving.

Later, Olga said, "He's very important in Hollywood, and you did a good job. He liked you. Oh yes, there's another gentleman, Victor, a client of mine who wants a tea reading."

A medium tall, rather suave fellow came in, sat down and asked, "Have you ever read palms?"

"Sometimes, but I'm much better with tea leaves."

"I just wondered."

He made his wish. I saw canines in my mind, so I asked, "How many dogs do you have?"

"Isn't that funny you would ask me? How many do you think I have?"

"I see three in the cup."

"I'll be darned! I *do* have three dogs!"

I finally finished, and he seemed extremely pleased. "Zelda, you're a *dream*." Then he turned to Olga and asked, "Where did you find this girl?"

As they chatted, he said, "And so she's a real gypsy from the East?"

When he had left, I looked at Olga and huffed, "I'm not a gypsy."

"Oh, go along with me, they love it. Remember, I know my way around in this business. Be sure you sew the coins on. I want you to look like a gypsy."

I left with Frank to go back to Madam Zurenski's. Arriving as dinner was served, Baba said, "Sit by me."

We continued talking about recipes. Baba seemed a lot better and happier, I thought.

Later upstairs, Baba said, "I think we should have an early Thanksgiving."

"Why?"

"Oh, I can't wait to taste Grandpa's stuffing," she answered.

"How soon?"

"Oh, the fourteenth or fifteenth."

"Sure, we could have it early, but it's your surprise dinner."

She was excited just like a little kid, I swear. Sometimes, when she was very sick, I felt like the mama and she the child.

"If you fix Thanksgiving dinner, I'm taking you to the Ambassador at Christmas," Baba repeated.

"Oh, that's wonderful!"

Madam Zurenski walked in and hearing this, said, "I'd better call for reservations now, or we'll never get into that place."

The next morning I read Psalms 14 and 25 to make up the days we missed.

Then I went down for breakfast and took my coffee outside. Maria came towards me.

"Judyenne?"

"Yes?"

"Would you like to pick out the turkey with me?"

"Oh, yes, I know exactly what I want to buy!"

"We're having an early Thanksgiving, you know," Maria said.

"Yes, but I don't know why, though," I replied.

"I don't know either, but that's what Baba and Madam Zurenski want."

I said, "We'd start the turkey very early in the morning. Eating late isn't good, especially for Baba. In case Baba can't eat pumpkin pie," I said, "I'd make two apples, one crust and one streusel top, pumpkin, and one custard. I know custard pie, she could eat."

"Yes, custard pie, I agree," replied Maria.

Their kitchen was almost like a restaurant kitchen. They had everything, and this time *I was* in charge, so I outdid myself. I baked pies the evening before. We fixed the bookings so that there were no readings that night or the next day.

Maria and I went to a special butcher shop for fresh turkey. I was in seventh heaven! I made Grandpa's wonderful dressing that I always make. It was a real old fashioned Thanksgiving dinner, with this gorgeous golden brown turkey on a shining silver platter, center stage on a damask table cloth with napkins in silver rings. Two triple candelabras yielded a warm glow at the table as we dined on lovely ornate Havilland. Their best sterling and crystal was used. The pies and Grandpa's dressing especially were a hit. Carlos made a giant shrimp salad with forty large jumbo shrimp around the edge.

I'd made a corn casserole they'd never had before. Carlos even wanted the recipe. We all made a toast with sparkling white grape juice.

Even Carlos said, "This is the best stuffed turkey I've ever eaten. What a meal!" They all joined in. Baba was so happy with me and my cooking! It was a true family dinner party, amid this luscious service, the lit candles and the big chandelier above making its crystal glimmer — just unbelievable!

I never had another Thanksgiving quite like that. Baba held her glass up for a toast. "To Judyenne, who's brought us all such joy and happiness."

Then I made a toast: "To Baba, to Madam Zurenski and to Frank, to all of you who have made me very happy and given me a second home, may God Bless all of us, each and every one."

We wheeled Baba out on the verandah, and the brilliant orange sun was already touching the water as we started watching the sunset.

Everyone retired early, the end of a perfect day.

The next day I came home from Olga's and ran upstairs to see Baba. She was propped up on her bed writing a letter. I was amazed to see it wasn't in English.

I asked her, "Is that Hungarian, Russian, or what?"

"It's Russian. A lot of things are happening in Europe. We have four younger family members we need to bring here. There are two girls. You could teach them English."

"I'd like that. Are they my age?"

"Just about. I wish I felt better. We've so much to do."

"Baba, we just haven't been praying enough."

"I didn't realize what a religious girl you are."

"I don't know if I'm religious or not; I rarely go to church, but I always pray when I'm unhappy or afraid. I've had a lot of practice in that department."

Baba said, "Maybe you should say a prayer like you've done before."

So I did, and this time Baba bowed her head and repeated after me. I thought that was really something, because when I completed my prayer, she said a prayer in Russian.

Baba prayed, "*Tsar e bog pazhalusta prashai mnoy. Ya astavlio ryebyonka. Ya ochen prashu vas chto ya apravliosya yeeshcho ras. Amyen.*"

I will never forget her praying in her native tongue the first time.

Three days later, Baba went back into the hospital, staying overnight for tests. Frank brought her back the next morning. About that time, Madam Zurenski entered the room, and we were all drinking tea. She said, "Judyenne, the family thinks that we should send Baba back to New York for consultation with the family doctors. We feel it's urgent. We plan to leave in three days."

I was just stunned. Baba didn't say anything!

I said, "You're coming back, aren't you, Baba?"

"Of course, dear, I'm coming back. Probably in a month. Not over six weeks, the doctor said. I didn't want to worry you. That's why I wanted Thanksgiving earlier, so you could make those wonderful pies and delicious foods you wanted me to eat."

I thought, 'Now I don't have a job. Where do I go? And dear Baba — she'll be so far away!'

The night before I found out that Frank and Madam Zurenski were going with Baba. They didn't like flying and were going on the newest most modern train, the *Santa Fe Chief* — real class. As the luggage was being put into the motor car, I began to realize the enormous change coming into my life. I felt like somebody was pulling a rug out from under me. Worst of all, my dear Baba, my best friend in the world, was leaving!

I thought, 'Well, I'll have Carlos and Maria and Olga until Baba gets back. I guess I can hang on six weeks!'

They were getting into the car, and Madam Zurenski was pushing Baba in the wheel chair. I ran and caught up to the wheelchair. Baba slipped a scarf-wrapped book of *Omar Khayyam* into my hand, then held my hand. There was a knot in the scarf. "Now you hang onto this, and when I get back, we'll put a new stone in it. I've had it since my 20's."

Tears were running down my face.

Madam Zurenski said, "We have to hurry, Judyenne. You'll be staying here, but I'll call you from New York in a few days as to what's happening."

I didn't think about where they were going in New York. I hugged Baba and kissed her on the forehead. She kissed me back. I could see she was fighting back tears, then she said, "Always remember you've made me very happy."

"You've made me happy, too. Oh, Baba, I'll pray for you every day, every day, Baba. You're all like my second family."

I could see it was even affecting Frank, who hugged me, as did Madam Zurenski.

'Guess I'll have to be "Zelda", reading fortunes from now on,' I thought.

Almost reading my mind, Madam Zurenski said, "You'll be doing readings as Zelda at Olga's. If she wants you to pretend to be a gypsy, don't worry about it. And don't go anywhere alone, now."

"No, no, I promise."

The doors closed, and the car started out the driveway. I held the French door open and continued to wave my hand as the car backed out. I finally ran down the drive, still waving until the car was out of view. Then I broke down crying as I ran in the house and up the stairs.

I put the little book on the bed, untied the knot in the scarf, and out fell a ring. It was a little gold ring with two raised heart designs. One had an emerald, but another was missing it. Then I remembered that she said, "We'll put a new stone in it." That's what she meant. I leafed through *Omar Khayyam.* As I did, I realized there was something in between the pages! I looked inside. In three different places, there was a one hundred dollar bill! She was trying to protect me. I was so upset, but the money, the ring, the book and her scarf smelling like English Lavender and rose oil, her favorite scents, were wonderful.

As I turned the pages, the third to last page, I saw a note in an unsteady hand, "Dear Judyenne- show this to Olga to tell Madame Zurensky, you are to have the Crowned Heart Pendent, in case I'm not home for Christmas. Keep it close to you. I'll be there. With love, Baba" I'd keep that scarf forever, and *Omar Khayyam*, too. I love that book, "... and the moving finger wrote ..."

Figure 34 Ring, missing stone, from Baba.

I put the scarf under my pillow when I went to bed, tears still running down my face, thinking, "Well, if going was the best for Baba, she belongs with the best hospital, doctors and her family."

Days went by.

I went to Olga's. It was prearranged that Carlos would drive me.

I hadn't realized, I guess, until they weren't there, how much Baba, Madam Zurenski and Frank meant to me.

The next day at Olga's I asked, "Do you know what part of Russia Baba came from?"

Staring at me for a second, she said, "Who said they were from Russia?"

"Baba told me."

"Oh, I'm not sure."

"I thought she said Minsk. I just wondered where that is."

"I've got an atlas. I have relatives there," she offered.

"You have relatives there? I think I do, too. My Aunt Grace talked about several relatives with Russian Hungarian in the bloodline. Some lived in Minsk and some in Moscow. All I know is I have three sets of parents."

"You have three sets of parents?"

"I have my real mother, I knew my real dad, I have my step-dad and birth mother, then I have my foster parents who adopted me."

"That would get confusing."

"Wouldn't it be funny if my Russian relatives were from the same town as Baba's Russian relatives?"

"Why don't you just ask your family?"

"Because they don't tell me anything."

"That's strange. If I had a daughter, I'd tell her," Olga replied.

Several days had passed, and no word. Olga said that maybe we could use the big crystal at Madam Zurenski's. She could look to see about my relatives and Baba's health.

"Gee, wouldn't that be something, but I still think it's kind of evil."

"Why?" she asked.

"It just bothers me."

"Maybe we could get an answer on your family."

"Well, maybe, for that purpose."

She looked at my Gypsy dress. "Did you sew your coins on? Oh yes, you did. Good girl," she answered herself after looking.

"Could I call Dimples?" I asked.

"Yes, just pay for the phone call."

"It's not a long distance call."

"Everybody has to pay me a nickel. There's a little dish there."

I did, and I left a message for Dimples.

Dimples called back and said, "I'm going to have a very busy weekend."

"Could you meet me at Cathay Gardens?"

"Yes, but I can't stay too long. Buy me dinner?"

"A bowl of pork noodles."

I asked Olga if I could go.

"Oh, all right, there's no readings tonight, anyway."

I told Dimples "Okay," and hung up, then said to Olga, "I won't be gone long."

"Just so you're not over one hour. Well, maybe an hour and a half."

I thought, "Boy, I will have to eat fast."

"Olga, you can't start timing 'till I get there. Give me ten minutes," I said.

"All right, but be quick. I don't want to be alone. Sofie's away tonight."

Sofie was a nice older lady, usually there, who cleaned.

I ran to Cathay Gardens. Walking into the restaurant, I saw a hand wave between the clinking curtain of beaded glass strands. It was Dimples. She ordered pork noodles and wanted shrimp, too.

Finally I surrendered, saying, "I guess I can go ninety-nine cents for jumbo shrimp."

I told her how upset I was about Baba, now with relatives in New York; and how I wondered if I might be related to Baba's Russian family in Minsk. I said, "You know, she just has to get better. Do you ever pray?"

"Not much."

"Well," I said, "I think we should pray for Baba. She's done a lot for you as well as me."

"You're right, Judyenne."

"Give me your hand," I said, and we both bowed our heads as I prayed.

It seems funny, but it wasn't. It was very serious, because we both loved Baba. I don't know what the waiter thought when he brought the shrimp. He saw us with heads bowed over pork noodles when he poked his head through the beaded curtains. He had a strange look on his face. We were praying for Baba's health and to come home for Christmas. I thought of John Moran Severette, my foster mother, Clara, Florence, my real mother, her husband, Roy, Grandma and Grandpa.

We completed our prayer and ate.

Dimples said, "I think you should look for a rich husband."

"Olga said that, but you just don't go picking up a man asking if he's rich."

"This guy that comes here and talks to you, John Paul?"

"But he's like a big brother."

"They own a store."

"Yes, I heard him say that. He does have a 1937 Olds, but I don't know. It would have to be a business arrangement."

"What do you mean?" Dimples asked.

"I couldn't sleep with him just because I married him."

"Why not?"

"I can't. I'm waiting for John Moran Severette."

Dimples said, "If he's ever coming back! The postman did tell me that servicemen's mail is often waylaid, maybe months!"

"I'm pretty sure he's a pharmacist on board a submarine at sea."

"There's submarines down at Long Beach," Dimples said.

"How would we know what submarine he was on?"

"I don't know."

"Can't you ask your boyfriend?"

"Good idea."

"I promised Olga I'd be back, so I'll have to go," I finally said.

Dimples said, "I'm leaving for Las Vegas soon."

"Please call before you leave," I said as I took my last bite.

"I will, Judyenne, but you should come, too! Howard Hughes is taking Elizabeth to Vegas. There's a new hotel casino opening. The town's going to boom."

"I promised Baba I wouldn't leave. I have to stay and work at Olga's 'till she returns," I said as I got up from the table and left the tip. "I must wait for Baba."

I didn't have to stay overnight, because Olga didn't have any late readings. So Carlos picked me up at 9:30 p.m., going back to Madam Zurenski's.

On Sunday, the next morning, I didn't have any readings, either. Near lunch time, Maria was in the dining room and I asked, "Can I make myself a sandwich?"

"Yes, sliced roast beef is on the top shelf of the refrigerator. You just help yourself. We're off for the day. All you have to do is answer the phone and take messages. If anybody asks, say everyone is away for a week."

"That means that Madam Zurenski is coming back in a week?"

"No, no, I was just told to say that."

"Oh, I will too, then."

I made myself a big sandwich, then went back upstairs to feed Tootsie, telling him about Baba leaving and that she would be back in six weeks.

About six-thirty the phone rang, and it was Madam Zurenski.

"Judyenne, I wanted to keep my promise. Tests here show her liver condition is far more serious than we were told. They need more tests. We won't know more for another week. I'll call you in a week or ten days. Are you still working at Olga's?"

"Yes."

"Is she training you in palmistry?"

"She's trying, but I don't like it."

"You have to practice, practice, practice. Get ahold of Maria and practice on her."

"I will when she comes back."

"Oh, that's right, she's not there today."

"Yes, I told her she had relatives coming when I read her tea cup."

"That's right; she'll be bringing them over."

"Yes."

"I'm glad you're there. Are you taking messages?" Madam Zurenski asked.

"Yes, there are two." I got the little book out and gave them to her.

"Okay. Baba sends her love. They're putting her on some new medicines. Don't worry now, I have to go."

"Goodbye. Tell Baba I love her."

"I will. We know how much you care."

XXIII - Baba Dies

el quinto de diciembre de 1939

I was busy with clients at Olga's, but my hints for a raise from one dollar to two a reading went on deaf ears. Olga was fairly nice, about ten years younger but not as kind as Baba, and she acted somewhat like an aunt. She was shrewd and wary. Like Baba and Madam Zurenski, she had fled Russia.

I had hidden the money that Baba gave me for my nest egg. The regular Thanksgiving was near, so I asked Olga where she was going for Thanksgiving.

"I guess I'll go to a restaurant."

"I was thinking of just going to Cathay Gardens," I said. "I love their prawns and plum sauce. I guess we should save our money for Christmas, too; because when Baba returns, we're going to the Ambassador."

"Shrimp is only ninety-nine cents at Cathay Gardens," replied Olga.

I said, "Want to come with me? You love shrimp."

"Sure," she said.

"I think that's a good idea. Let's call Dimples. She'd like to go," I added.

Dimples said, "I have a date for eight o'clock, but I'll be free between two and six."

Turning, I asked Olga, "Three o'clock all right?"

"I don't like to eat late, so that's fine. Why don't you call that fellow who has the clothing store?" Olga asked.

"He's probably in Arizona."

Olga said, "Then let's ask Sophie; she never gets to go out." Olga called her, and Sophie said to pick her up.

Thursday arrived. Yes, we had two noon readings; then we both got out of our Gypsy costumes, redid our makeup and left to get Sophie. About an hour later we parked in the rear of Cathay Gardens. You had to be brave to enter the rear kitchen door amid flying cleavers, as we did!

Dimples was waving her arm and pointing to the right of her. John Paul was there with his friend, Bill Rivers, and he said, "I took a chance you might be here."

"I love shrimp. I had a real turkey dinner two weeks ago, but now I just crave shrimp."

"Why don't you join us?" Olga suggested.

Dimples looked at me and gave me the open eyes sign.

So, the guys moved to our booth. Bill Rivers decided that he'd sit between Olga and Dimples. That left me sitting next to John Paul, with Sophie on the end.

Bill Rivers then said, "Isn't it funny, but John Paul thought you'd be here."

Olga said, "J.P., I told Judyenne she ought to call you, as she said she has your business card."

I thought I would die!

"Well, she works for me part time as Zelda, you know," Olga went on. "Her stage name is really Judyenne."

"Yes," John Paul said. "I heard that."

Dimples had filled the men in on part of my life story before we got there. The menus were given out, and there was a holiday mood. Our teacups were decorated in gold. We ordered a dinner for six, and John Paul ordered the ninety-nine cent shrimp cocktails for each person.

I thought, "Wow, he's spending a fortune." We were all given ivory chopsticks. I couldn't handle chopsticks, and neither could Dimples; but Olga, Sophie, John Paul and Bill Rivers used them like they were born in the Orient.

Pretty soon, Olga started the conversation again. "I just don't know what poor Judyenne is going to do. Her mother has given the studio so much trouble that Mister Kahn is all upset. Her mother's threatened to sue the studio. Poor Judyenne, she should be in the movies. Why'd her mother do this?" As she spoke, she turned toward John Paul.

Dimples chimed in, "Not only her mother, but her aunt, who's really her mother, also called the studios."

"What seems to be the problem?" John Paul asked.

No one wanted to say too much, but Olga looked at me and flashed her eyes.

I said, "Well, I ran away from home at eighteen. I'm nineteen now, but not legal age to sign contracts. The studio requires someone twenty-one or over to sign, and my family won't help."

Olga said, "Judyenne needs a guardian or parent. It's something about insurance. If Judyenne had gotten married to some responsible person over twenty-one, it wouldn't have made a doggone bit of difference! She needs a husband who can sign the papers and be responsible for her."

I felt my cheeks redden. I was very embarrassed, but I said, "Oh, it would have to be a business arrangement. I don't want a husband for anything other than to be able to get into the studios, so he can sign the contract. Maybe then Mother and Aunt Florence would stop causing the studios trouble."

John Paul said, "I thought Florence was your mother?"

"I know it's confusing," I replied. "All right; the ones I call my mother and dad are my adoptive parents. My Aunt Florence is my birth mother — I call her

Aunt Florence and her husband is Uncle Roy. She married Roy Levant, who would be my stepfather. Oh, but I know who my *real* father is."

"That's a lot of parents!" John Paul said.

No one said a word for a few seconds after that. Some of them were very surprised by the explanation, trying to digest it all. I hadn't told anyone that much up 'till then.

"I'm pretty upset, too, because Baba is so ill and so far away. I'm staying part time at Madam Zurenski's and at Olga's. They all have helped me so much," I continued. "I don't know how much longer I can go on reading tea fortunes. If only the studios knew I wasn't a threat!"

John Paul then spoke up. "Well, no wonder. Olga's right; you need a husband, a protector."

Then I saw Olga's eyes flash toward me.

He continued, "One who can speak for you at the studios. Because, once you're married, your parents can't do anything about it. It would be you and your husband who would make the decisions."

I thought Olga would choke on her food. She kept looking down, tapping on the table edge and shaking her head, "No, no." Pretending to choke, she asked John Paul for more water as he had not touched his glass. I guess she was afraid I was going to tell him that I was waiting for John Moran Severette. After that part of the conversation had coasted to a rocky halt, Olga got John Paul to talk to her. He was telling her about the men's clothing store and the haberdashery business in general. He also said, "You know, we're going to get into the war in Europe."

Olga said, "I have relatives in Europe, in Vienna, St. Petersburg and Helsinki. They want to get out. I'm very worried, too, but it's hard to get your passports renewed or get travel visas."

Sophie and Bill just listened.

Dimples chimed in, "I'm going to Las Vegas, and I want Judyenne to go, too."

John Paul said, "If Judyenne has a chance to get into the studios, I think she should try and do that. I've been to Las Vegas, and it's not a place for a young girl like Judyenne."

Soon the dinner was over.

As we opened up our cookie fortunes, Olga said to the group, "Why don't you come up to my place, and Judyenne can make us some sundaes?"

I said, "It won't be like Sanders hot fudge." Then I turned to John Paul and Bill Rivers and added, "My Grandpa Weigmann helped develop theirs. I love hot fudge sundaes!"

Olga said, "No, not like your grandpa's, but it'll be a sundae, and I have real whipping cream."

"Sounds good! On to Olga's!" John Paul exclaimed. I went with Olga and Sophie. Dimples went with John Paul and Bill Rivers. I put chocolate topping over the ice cream in big tulip glasses with whipped cream and a maraschino cherry over that. It looked pretty fancy. Sophie and I served.

John Paul had picked up the tab at the restaurant! Everybody tried to go Dutch treat, but he insisted! That kind of added fuel to Olga, because she was sure he must have money. The more we got to see him, the more we realized he was quite a bit older than I was, but this was not a love match. The men excused themselves and started to leave, then offered Dimples a ride home. Olga hugged them goodbye, and away they went. She was getting really chummy with John Paul.

Once inside, Olga said, "See, didn't I tell you? This is a *catch* right here. He likes you."

"Olga, I told you, I'm in love with John Moran Severette."

"It's a different kind of love."

"What do you mean?"

"Well, someone with similar interests, hobbies and that kind."

"Well, it's not my kind of love. I want someone to love me, and I want sparks to fly; also someone who will spend his life with me. This is like loving a stranger!"

"No, no, you'd learn to love him."

"Well, I want to go to bed with a man I love and keep him there for a couple of hours!"

Olga just roared. "How do you know what to do to keep a man there for a couple of hours?"

"I've read books, but Dimples and Maria also told me plenty."

"Well," Olga said, "I know what I would do. If I saw John Moran Severette, I'd tell him, he's a damn fool! A lovely girl like you abandoned! I don't know why you even waste your time thinking about him! I've been around a lot, Judyenne, and if he really cared for you, he'd have found you by now."

Well, I didn't want to believe that. I still believed that John loved me and was going to try to find me, but I didn't tell Olga that again.

Olga then took me back to Madam Zurenski's, dropped me off in the driveway and left, saying, "We must go to Cathay Gardens again soon."

As I entered the door, Maria was standing there, screaming, "A phone call from the hospital!"

I grabbed the phone. It was Madam Zurenski's voice, but I couldn't make much out of what she was screaming while she was crying. Then I heard Frank's voice.

He said, "Now, Judyenne," and he must have turned to Madam Zurenski, as he said, "Ta Ta, you have to stop this hysteria. Now, Judyenne, everything is being done here that can be done. They say Baba is much worse. If they can get the kidneys to start working, she has a fighting chance. We will keep you informed. We're not going to leave her bedside. We'll call you again tomorrow."

Crying as I spoke, I wailed, "I wish you people would pray once in a while." I was beginning to get very angry as I said, "I *know* what it is. It's all this fortune telling, that's why God is cursing us."

I really started to cry then.

"Calm down," Frank counseled. "It has nothing to do with the fortune telling. It's her health condition."

Of course I started feeling guilty because I was studying palmistry. I wondered if maybe *I* caused Baba to get sick. They all did fortune telling. Was this a warning?

I said, "This is what it is. It's a warning, and you'd better tell Madam Zurenski — she might be the next one to get sick. This is just terrible, you're all taking my Baba away!"

"No, no, you don't realize it, but you brought more happiness into Baba's life in the year that you've been with us than all the years since she came to the U.S. all put together. Please don't think that. Now, you go do your praying like you said you're going to do. Don't say too much to Maria. Just say that Baba is getting worse, and we'll call you tomorrow."

"Why don't you give me a phone number?"

"I have to go, they're calling me," Frank ended and he hung up.

Well, I don't know what I did. Maria stood there, and she could hear me cry, scream and yell all at once. She must have called Carlos; because he was coming through the dining room toward the living room, looking almost as bad as I did. Maria had her hands up to her face and praying out loud. Carlos looked wild-eyed, and both were praying out loud in Spanish.

"Tell us, tell us, what's happening, what's happening," Carlos demanded.

I told them about the whole conversation, then said, "Madam Zurenski was all hysterical, too. They told me that Baba's condition had turned worse because of something to do with how the liver was starting to affect the kidneys. The strange part of it is, why they won't tell me where the hospital is or the phone number?"

I was beyond distraught. Maria started to cry and threw her arms around me. Carlos was walking the floor. Then he stopped, and looking at me, he said, "We're going to go to our church."

"You're going to go now?" I questioned.

"Yes, yes, *now*. You want to come to our church?"

"Well, sure. Let me get my lace head scarf."

"Come on then."

So we went quickly out the driveway and down the highway. It was a big, stately Catholic church, and the door was open. We lit candles and knelt down. An older priest came out, and I heard him talking to Carlos and Maria in Spanish. then he spoke to me in English. He said that he knew what was happening. Carlos, Maria and I were crying all at once. The priest asked us all to come with him into his study. He prayed with us and said he knew Baba. The whole thing was becoming unreal to me — as if I were watching a movie about someone else. Here I was in a church I had never been in before, Maria and Carlos praying in Spanish, I in English. The priest reminded me of a grandpa. He said special prayers for Baba, and that made us all feel better. As we left, he told us to come back any time. He patted Maria and me on the shoulder saying, "God will take care of her." Tears ran down my cheeks, even on the scarf tied under my chin.

When we arrived home I went to my room, grabbed Baba's scarf off my head and started crying and praying again. I asked God, "How could you do this to Baba? I love Baba. We all do. She's not bad! So she drank. Is that a reason to kill her?"

I was mad at God. I thought, with all the praying I did, He ought to save Baba. But after a few minutes, I thought, 'I better not stay mad at God.'

I covered up Tootsie after I told the bird all about it. I had the two bears and the scarf on the bed, then I finally curled up and went to sleep.

In the morning, still no phone call; and we all looked bleary-eyed.

I said, "You don't have to fix my breakfast; I can make it myself."

I walked into the kitchen and asked Carlos if I could make my own breakfast. "All right, if you want to. I think we should just remain calm and continue to pray," he added.

I scrambled eggs, craving a good Mexican tamale, and made do with the eggs rolled in a tortilla and Pico de Gallo relish. Fixing breakfast calmed me down some. Maria brought me coffee. This time Carlos and Maria came into the dining room together, and Carlos said, "We think that the family's on Long Island."

"Well, I think we should call every hospital there," I suggested.

Then Carlos said, "I think Olga knows where they live."

"That's it. Oh, dear God, we didn't call Olga!" I took another swallow of coffee; then ran to the phone.

"I'm going to call her. Let's see what she has to say."

I called Olga. She was also very upset. Yes, Madam Zurenski had called her. Then she said, "I think we should cancel all our readings today. This is an emergency. I think I should come over there. Put Carlos on the phone."

They talked a while. She didn't like to drive that much, so she asked Carlos to come and get her.

About a half-hour later they walked in, Olga saying, "I just can't believe it. They haven't called! I'm going to call Frank and Ta Ta."

She did, and when she hung up, she said, "I talked to Frank, but there's no new news. They're returning to the hospital."

It was just hours, but it seemed like days. I must have drunk two pounds of coffee. Then I walked out to the pool, thinking, 'This is such a shame, and everybody here has all this money. I haven't thought much about rich people having tragedies, but they do.'

We gathered on the veranda overlooking the pool and drank coffee without saying a word. For some reason they all raided the sweet pickle jar. They were too upset to realize that a week earlier I had added a cinnamon stick and two tablespoons of brown sugar to make it better, and all of a sudden it didn't matter to me. I grabbed a couple of sweet pickles, too, pondering the tragic events unfolding.

Olga finally said, "How things can change so quickly. It's so hard to believe that this happening, happen ...ing ..."

I stopped her before she could finish. "That's the word. Everything has happened so fast."

Olga called New York again, but there was no change.

I said, "Would you give me the number?"

She said, "Judyenne, I'm not allowed to give out their number. I would if I could. Olga turned to Maria. I'll stay over. I should be here. Maybe I'll have to fly to New York, I don't know."

I said, "Well, maybe I can go, too. I should see Baba."

"We'll see."

We spent the whole day and evening waiting. Olga suggested making soup, so I opened three cans of Campbell's tomato soup. I added a can of stewed tomatoes and one and a half cans of milk and one and a half cans of water, a pinch of baking soda and a teaspoon of sugar.*

Maria said, "Oh, no, you can't make canned soup!"

I said, "You watch me! It'll be good soup."

I served it with oyster crackers, and even Carlos said it tasted good. After eating I begged Olga, "Please call back."

"No, they're busy; they're doing everything they can. Our duty is to remain calm and stay by the telephone."

The phone finally did ring, and it was Frank. He said, "There's no change. We're getting a couple of cots, and we're going to lie down. She has a big room. We're beat. I suggest you fellows go to bed early."

---

*Lily's canned tomato soup in Appendix.

We did, but it was a restless night.

The next day, no more word and now we were entering the third day. I just didn't even want to pray anymore.

I thought, 'It isn't working. I'm so sincere, and I have so much faith in God. *Why?*'

Well, I can only say that on the 5th day of December we got a call from Frank. His voice inflection was shaky, and he was hoarse.

He said to Olga, "She's slipping into a coma, the kidneys have shut down and the doctor said she's dying. There's nothing we can do."

Olga was repeating it. Maria called Carlos, who came running. We were all standing around, listening.

As Olga put the phone to my ear, Frank said to me, "Just try and remember this, Judyenne. You have brought so much joy and happiness to Baba. Don't blame yourself, don't blame God, and don't blame anybody. I just wanted to tell you, that before Baba went into a coma, she said, 'Tell Judyenne I love her. She's my lost child and my little girl. She is my little girl.'"

Tears of happiness and sorrow came down my cheeks! I had actually known a mother who really loved me! Even though I couldn't have a real mother who loved me, God had given me Baba. How I thanked God that day and every day since. I have lit a candle for Baba every Christmas since that day and had an ornament on the Christmas tree every year for my dear Baba Rose.

Frank went on, "You just can't imagine what this has meant to her just to have you near her for almost a year. Baba had a smile on her face as she said, 'Tell Judyenne I love her.' I was holding her hand. Remember, I loved her, too."

Well, that broke me up completely, and I started crying uncontrollably.

He said, "Please don't cry. If at all, you should cry for joy, because you've made her so happy. She didn't even want to drink any more. She began to realize the things that you talked to her about and to pray. We hadn't heard her talk about the Orthodox faith since we left Mother Russia, and here in the hospital she's prayed in Russian."

"Yes, she did that with me."

"This hasn't happened in twenty some years."

He said he would call back.

"Can I fly there, can I come there?" I asked.

"I don't think we're going to have any big funeral. We're going to have just immediate family. I'll get back to you and give you all the facts."

He wanted to talk to Olga, so I gave the phone back. I was just sobbing and walking across the room, back and forth. Maria, Carlos and I were really basket cases; and I thought, 'I don't know if I can pray anymore. He's taking away my best friend. Yet I must. I know He also gave me Baba, for a while, a real mother.'

Three hours later, we got a call. Olga picked up the phone, and it was Frank. He said, "She's gone."

To this day, I just don't know why God took her away. I thought she was improving, but I guess it was my perception being controlled by my own wishes and my fear of losing her.

Olga hung up the phone as she turned away. She had a numb look on her face and tired, glassy eyes. She was crying. She said, "I think what we should do, Judyenne ... I think we should have a memorial service."

I said, "I don't even have a picture."

"I have pictures. We'll take care of it; we'll see that you have Baba's picture and some of her personal things."

Olga gave me a little hug, which was unusual for her.

"Don't worry, Judyenne, I'll take over now."

That was the plan. She and Carlos left, and Maria and I were all alone. It was like a dream — a bad dream. All I know is that we were in Madam Zurenski's car. Carlos was driving. It was two days later. Most of what transpired during that period is still sort of foggy. Olga had a private memorial service for Baba, mostly close friends. Sophie, Irena, Dimples, Maria and eight dancers, cinematographers, stage people, Buddy, Carlos and Maria, Olga and I. A Russian Orthodox priest said a few prayers. They had a picture of Baba with roses all around the picture. I remember taking a rose, as we all filed out. Olga picked up the picture, and she handed it to me.

I thought, 'This is in memory of my Baba Rose.'

This was worse than when I ran away from home, worse than when John Moran Severette let me down by not showing up in El Paso to marry me, as terrible as when Uncle Al got killed and Grandma Latimer Jackson died.

When we got back home, I just went to my room. I wasn't going to read any more fortunes. I had this in my mind anyway, as I was always taught that fortune telling was against God's will. I never thought tealeaf fortunes were. But I knew I'd never study palms ever again. I must say, Olga really went beyond herself to be kind. I hate to think of December 5th, any December 5th of any year.

It was about seven o'clock at night, and the house was so lonesome. I don't know what made me do it, but I got my purse, pulled the card out that had John Paul's number on it and called him. I told him where I was and the terrible news that Baba died. I told him about the memorial service.

I said, "You once told me that if I needed someone to talk to, that I could call your number."

He said, "I just got in, but something told me that I better come home early; and I did. Give me the address. I'll come and get you, and we can just drive around. Maybe we could get a milk shake. It does help to talk. I'm so very sorry. What color is the house?"

I gave him the address. "You won't miss it. It's a great big Spanish type mansion. I'll put the porch light on."

I got dressed and tried to put on some makeup. As I cried, the mascara ran down my face. Anyway, I tried to look human. He was there pretty fast, but I was ready to go when the car pulled up. I opened the door and walked outside. I had called back to Maria to tell her I'd be going out with a friend of Olga's, John Paul, and I wouldn't be late.

I jumped into John Paul's car and we drove off. First we drove all around Santa Monica on the road that outlined the edge of the ocean. Then we drove back into Los Angeles — just drove and talked.

I said, "I don't know what I am going to do. I feel that the fortune telling might have contributed to why she died."

"No, I don't think God would do that," he replied. "Anyway, didn't you tell me you just read teacups? I can't see how that would be bad."

"Well, I never thought so either, but Olga was teaching me palmistry. I don't know about palmistry. All of them are fortune tellers, you know."

"I don't know. I just don't know if that's bad or not. I think they just did it, more to give people a hobby. They didn't look like fortune tellers. How could Madam Zurenski have this gorgeous property if she were bad? As far as that goes, Olga wouldn't be able to have her place, either. No, I don't think that's it," John Paul went on. "I have a friend who drinks; and he says, when the liver goes, then it affects all the organs. There's not much you can do about it. You shouldn't blame yourself in any way."

"Frank said she called me her little girl." I started to cry.

"Don't cry, Judyenne. I think you should always think of that part. That she thought you were her little girl, and in a way you sort of were a substitute for her little girl. I think if she had to die, she died at peace. She died happy that she had you for a short while. Think how terrible it would have been if you'd never met her and she never had your friendship."

Well, I began to feel better. "I guess that's right, but I don't want to tell any more fortunes."

"When are you going back to Olga's?"

"I don't know if I'm ever going back to Olga's."

"I don't know. She seems like a nice lady. Why don't you think about it? I could pick you and Olga up tomorrow if you go there. We could all have a Chinese dinner. We can all talk this over. Anyway, I think I'd better take you home. You're such a young girl, you shouldn't be out this late."

I laughed and said, "It's not that late."

He told me about the city and that there was a Chinatown here, as well. "I've got a lot of things going for me in Arizona. We've got Arizona's Governor Osborn who won another term in Arizona. Maybe you can come over and spend a few days; and if you want, you can bring Olga. I bet you could do a lot to help Governor Osborn. He has aides, and some of them are getting paid."

"I know, but then I wouldn't be near the studios."

"If they're all afraid of your mother, or aunt anyway, maybe it's a good idea to get away for about six months, then come back. If you came to Arizona you would have an excellent chance to work for Governor Osborn. You've got acting ability, and you meet the public well. I bet we could get you on the radio; you could do some radio interviews. They pay good money."

He took me home, and I was a little happier because I didn't feel quite so alone now. Maria was happy to see me come home. She asked John Paul and me to have some hot muffins. It was 10:30 at night, and I was hungry, too. Boy, could Carlos make muffins! We had some of the best muffins, hot out of the oven, and more coffee in no time. After eating, John Paul left, and I thanked him again.

I talked to Tootsie while I got undressed and got in bed. I got back up and took the scarf and my teddy bears off the dresser. When I still couldn't sleep, I got up again and got Baba's picture. I put Baba's picture, face down, under my two pillows, and I finally went to sleep.

The next day I felt much better, and Maria and Carlos seemed to be calming down, too. I knew I must go on. We all prayed several times a day. That really helped.

The next day John Paul called, saying, "If you don't want to disturb Carlos, I'll pick you up and take you to Olga's. I've already called her, and she said it would be all right."

"Well, all right, if you don't mind."

"No, no. Olga suggested that I pick you up about eleven o'clock and meet her at her house." So we picked Olga up and drove to Cathay Gardens.

We found a rear booth. John Paul was telling her about Governor Osborn.

Olga said, "I don't know if she should leave Hollywood."

"It might do her good to get away," J.P. argued.

I turned to Olga and said, "I'm not going to study palms any more. I won't ever do it, because I feel too guilty. I might do tea readings. Even Grandma Latimer read tea leaves, and she was like a saint!"

I could read Olga, and her little wheels were turning in her head, too. Then she finally said, "I feel responsible for Judyenne, and I just don't want her driving with you over to Arizona alone."

"You can go with us," he offered.

"I can't leave my business. Is there anybody, a reference, to phone?"

"I could give you Governor Osborn's assistant. You could find out anything you wanted to know."

She said, "If I called him and everything checks out, well, we might consider it. Judyenne is very young and inexperienced in most of life, no matter how she talks. I have a responsibility to Baba."

When we got back to Olga's, we weren't there twenty minutes when the phone rang, and it was Madam Zurenski.

Olga said, "Judyenne is here," and she handed me the receiver.

Madam Zurenski said, "You should move your things over to Olga's. I won't be home for several months. I'm going to give everybody a vacation. I just think you will be better off where I know there's someone there near you. You can continue to study your palmistry."

"I'm not studying palms any more, Madam Zurenski. I think that's maybe why I'm being punished and why Baba died."

"No, honey, it had nothing to do with that."

"I don't know. I'm still trying to get in the movies."

"I think you should stay with Olga. Well, do your tea readings, then."

I said, "Okay, I'll think about it. I could do some radio work for this man who is Governor of Arizona. John Paul said they are looking for somebody to do his radio spots. Maybe I could do that and get more experience. Then if I go back to the studios in a month or two, I can show them what I've done."

"That is true, but I still think you should study palmistry or do your tea readings and stay in California. We'll talk about it later. You know, Tootsie was Baba's bird, but she never had time to take care of him and couldn't keep him down at the theatre. So, she gave him to me, but I want you to have Tootsie."

"Oh, I can have Tootsie? Oh, that is just *so* wonderful!" Then I thought, "She must understand how I miss Baba. I always assumed it was her bird."

Madame Zurenski said, "We have some things we want to give you. I'll have them sent over to Olga's. We're going to close the Pasadena house. I'll write to you in care of Olga."

We hung up, and I felt like I was almost being pushed out of her house. In that next hour, there was a frenzy of things to do. I told John Paul everything, and Olga was talking to him, too. Olga said, "Maybe it would be better if you didn't do the palm studying for a while. Maybe you should just stay with your tea leaves and work here. I'll call Carlos. You go over there tonight, and I'll have Carlos help you get your things together in the morning."

Then she turned to John Paul. "Could you help? We have two carloads of Baba's things for Judyenne."

"Sure, I'll help."

The next day, the birdcage, the cage holder, clothes and the things they gave me turned out to be many times what I expected. There was the beautiful chaise lounge, lamps, dishes, all her linens and much more. The furniture was carried over by a pickup truck.

Before we left Baba's old house there was a real estate man putting up a "For Sale" sign outside. It said "Pasadena Realty", and seemed to look so final to me. I stared at that sign, and I knew for sure I would never see Baba again.

Some of Baba's gorgeous robes and lingerie that were never used were given to me. Olga said, "Baba had things packed in these closets she never used, beautiful things. I want you to have all of this. Some of the jewelry we're keeping for the family, but you can go take all of her costume jewelry, and I'll pick out some of the gemstones for you. You'll have a lot of her things, because that's what she'd want."

We were now moving the things out of both houses, Santa Monica and Pasadena. Olga said something about Alexi staying in New York; that he had transferred ownership of the burley house.

I said, "He doesn't own the burlesque any more?"

"No, he's out of it. They have changed the name."

He was the administrator of Baba's estate; and I thought, 'Boy, what a no-good he was!' Well, that happens in families.

Olga gave me the two gorgeous furs. One mink full length and a white fox. I loved them, holding them close to me, but it was a day with poignant memories. She also handed me a little box with an envelope and a one hundred dollar bill.

The closing of another chapter, but the beginning of a new one. "Another turn in the road," Uncle Al would say. "Latimers never give up," Grandma always said. 'Yes, they're right,' I murmured to myself. 'I must go on.'

XXIV - After Baba's Death

diciembre de 1939

We were busy going in and out of Olga's kitchen, unloading the car; and John Paul had just taken a lot of things upstairs that we had brought from Baba's Pasadena house. Olga had given these things to me, on instructions from Madam Zurenski. The maids, the butler, the chauffeur, needed their wages for two weeks, with the exception of Carlos and Maria, who would stay on at the big home in Santa Monica. But the house in Pasadena was to be sold. Baba's other home was already in Alexi's name, so that took care of that.

I knew that I had to go back to the Russian Orthodox church one more time. I had Grandma Latimer's chantilly black lace scarf my Aunt Grace had put on my head at Grandma Latimer's funeral when I was ten. Aunt Grace had put a rose in my hand to drop on the casket. I didn't get a chance to do this for Baba, but I could go to the church and wear Grandma Latimer's scarf while I prayed.

I ran upstairs, got the scarf and brought it down. I met John Paul as he came downstairs and said, "I want you to take me to church."

He looked kind of strange and said, "Now?"

"Right now, before we do anything else," I demanded. "I have to do it!"

Then I walked into the kitchen and said, "Olga, I want to go to church. I won't be gone over thirty, forty minutes, tops."

"Church?"

"Yes, I want to talk to that priest just for a minute. And you know what we forgot to do?"

"What?"

"We forgot to light a candle."

"My dear, if it's upsetting you this much, you go. I have phone calls to make, appointments to rearrange for my readings. But, please be back in one hour. We have much to do. Judyenne, I know how you feel, and I know that Baba would be very pleased. She couldn't have asked for a better daughter to equal her own whom she missed all her life. You just walked into her life. Baba said to me that your coming through that stage door and over those cold concrete floors of that theatre was the better memory of what she lost in the old country. She said, 'When I saw that child, that beautiful girl, I knew I was going to have a chance to raise a daughter.'"

Even John Paul heard that, but I couldn't understand why he didn't cry, because Olga and I were. Olga was wiping tears from her eyes after this tender revelation, and I again realized Baba's love for me.

John Paul said, "Well, let's go! How do you know the church is open?"

I said, "I don't, but I think they are. Gees, John Paul!" I tried to compose myself. Then I finally went on. "I think they're like a Catholic church."

Of course, in those days the doors were open. We rushed out of the house. He thought he knew where it was; but we finally found it, parked and walked up the steps.

He said, "Oh, I'm not a Catholic."

"You don't have to be Catholic to go into the church. Besides, this is Russian Orthodox."

I don't want to go in. I'll wait right here."

"You don't want to go in?"

He said, "The only church I ever went in was on Christmas with my mother. That was a Methodist church."

"Well, what's the difference? We're all praying to the same God, aren't we?"

"Maybe so, but I'll wait out here."

I walked in and followed the same procedure that we did in the Catholic church. I knelt and said a few prayers. Then I saw a whole rack of candles up at one end, and only a couple of older ladies sat in the back. So I lit a candle, then I knelt again. I didn't know what to say. I wasn't sure how Russians prayed. I thought I'd start with three Hail Marys while I was continuing to wonder what I was going to say. I couldn't remember the Beatitudes, but said the Lord's Prayer and the Twenty-third Psalm.

I said, "God, Jesus Christ, dear Virgin Mary, dear Mother, please save Baba by your grace. She didn't get a chance to raise either daughter, her own or me. So help her to do something that she loves, in heaven. She couldn't be anywhere else. You couldn't put her in a bad place, just because she drank. A lot of the showgirls would be broke, and she gave them an extra dollar. I know one of them, Dimples. When the heels came off of their shoes, she'd take them down to the shoemaker to fix them. She always had extra money or a book of food tickets. If the girls were down on their luck, they got a ticket and went into the restaurant where Neil, who owned the place, redeemed it for a meal. How could you put her anywhere but heaven?"

I had the chantilly black lace scarf over my head as I prayed. Then I felt a tap on my shoulder. For a fleeting second I was kind of frightened, because I had felt the same kind of tapping on my shoulder several times when Big Al came up behind me. I looked up, and I was relieved to see it was the priest. I liked Big Al, but I was afraid of him.

The priest said, "Do you need some help? Are you in trouble?"

I said, “No, I’m here because my best friend in the world died. Baba died.”

“Oh, yes, we know. I’m so sorry. I’ll say some special prayers if it will help you.”

I said, “Oh, yes, it would.”

“Things will be all right, and if you need anything, come back here.”

“Oh, thank you, Father, so much.”

I knelt down, said another prayer, then stood up and walked back out. There John Paul stood.

We got into the car and went back to Olga’s.

XXV - Contract Marriage

el dozavo de diciembre de 1939

So much of my life had changed. John Paul was emptying the car out, but it wasn't late when Olga motioned to me to come into the kitchen. I joined her in the kitchen, and she said, "I think you should marry him. If we could get you a legal guardian for contracts, that's what you need. You can't sign contracts, and the studios are really leery of your parents and your Aunt Florence. That's what Ivan told me. You know, I do readings for producers and directors. Two of them told me this. They knew who you were. I think you're missing the boat. If John Moran Severette was really serious, he would never have left you in El Paso! Even if he was shipped out, he would have reached you somehow!"

I guess the shock of Baba's death really made me see that Olga was telling me the truth. John Moran Severette had literally abandoned me. My first feelings in El Paso, as I left, were that *I* was abandoning *him*. Here I go again. Why must I always feel I'm to blame?"

I looked at her and said, "As long as he'll marry me like in a contract."

She said, "I've talked to him. I've told him that you're sort of pining over puppy love, due to some fellow in Michigan, who's in the Navy or something. That he left you stranded in El Paso and broke your heart. I told him that what you needed was a good husband with a business mind who would just take care of you and help you handle the studio demands and contracts. This happens lots in Hollywood. Even stars marry where there is no love. They just need a business manager. You can think about this. He said, 'I really feel sorry for her.' I think you should marry him right away."

Well, Olga was a mover, I tell you.

John Paul came back with some other packages, and Olga turned to me, saying, "I guess I'll go on like Madam Zurenski told me, at five dollars a week for your rent. If you're not living here, it's only going to be two fifty a week to store your things." Olga had a mind for money, that was for sure!

"What do you think, John Paul?" she asked. "Come on in the kitchen; I've got the coffee percolator on."

We had brought some more of Carlos' fantastic muffins, which he had loaded us up with; so she put the muffins out with butter and jam, and we all sat around her kitchen table.

She said, "I told Judyenne about many stars and starlets having managers. They have men they marry in order to sign legal contracts. A lot of them are strictly agents and managers. But Judyenne needs a business manager. I told her that you said you felt sorry for her, and you wanted to help her get a chance at being in the movies. How would you two kids like to get married today?"

Figure 35 Governor Sidney P. Osborn, a good governor, nice family, 1939-1940

I said, "I don't think I could get married in one day."

He said, "If we were in Arizona today, we could be married by the 12th."

"You could?" Olga asked.

I turned to him and said, "You understand this would be just like being my agent, my manager. You will bring me back here so we can go to all the studios?"

He said, "Sure, I would, and if there's nothing right away, we can go back and you could help me with administrative duties for the newly elected Governor Osborn."

Well, it all sounded really good, as I wanted to move on. If they had paid me a hundred dollars a cup, I couldn't have read even one tea fortune that day.

Olga said, "Now wait a minute. Now, let's see." Then she got on the phone and called Sophie. She, too, came from Russia with Irena, at the same time as Baba. They referred to her as "Babakovitch". I thought it interesting that my family's name way back was Chapachinkoff and they lived in Moscow and Minsk. Irena agreed to come with Sophie to help Olga.

Olga said, "I'm going to do it. I'll see that you get married. I will have done my duty. We can get Judyenne in the movies and get you working for the Governor."

Olga said to Irena, "Come on, we're going to pack a suitcase, and I'm going with them."

Within an hour we were in the car. John Paul was very nice, but later on I learned that he wasn't always a man of his word. However, in this case, he was. We got into the car and headed out of Los Angeles. A sign went by that said, "Phoenix 376 miles."

John Paul made a second phone call to the Benavidas', about 30 miles from Phoenix, while we stretched our legs and got coffee. Then we all got back in the car.

He said, "We're going over to Alfred and Ruthie Benavidas', some friends of mine. They can be very helpful."

"He has a wife?" I asked.

He said, "Yes, yes, he was in the training program for the clothing store. I'm just trying to think where to take everybody. We can get a motel, but I want all of us to go over to Ruthie and Alfred's first."

John Paul turned into the drive and pulled up to the rear entrance by the Benavidas' kitchen. They were both waiting, and we all smelled the enticing aroma of Alfred's homemade bean soup as we got out and walked up to the door. John Paul introduced Olga and me to Ruthie — Alfred I already knew. They invited us in and told us to have some of Alfred's soup if we were hungry. We all sat around the table in the kitchen and got acquainted while we ate his wonderful soup.

Olga said, "J.P. and Judyenne want to get married as soon as possible, and J.P. says you could probably help."

"Yes, I have a friend, a justice of the peace, who can help with the papers," Alfred replied.

Ruthie said, "I could help, too. It would be fun; and between all of us, we can get you two married." Then turning to John Paul, she said, "We think it's just wonderful."

Alfred had it all organized: "If we hurry we can meet the justice of the peace. I phoned him. He can get your marriage license tonight. If we hurry, it's only in Scottsdale, a few miles from here. And we can get your health certificate from Dr. Horace Green. I already called him. He said he'd wait until midnight."

John Paul said, "I told you Ruthie and Alfred could help."

So away we went, this time in Alfred's car, enroute to get the license and health certificate. Both Alfred and Ruthie treated us like they had known us for years.

As we drove, John Paul said, "I've been telling Judyenne about Governor Osborn's need for people to help him."

"Yes, tomorrow we can all go down and introduce you to the other people working at election headquarters, Judyenne," Albert agreed.

The next day, Alfred, Ruthie, John Paul, Olga and I went down to the campaign headquarters, where John Paul introduced me to the staff working there while he showed me around.

We did a little sight-seeing around Phoenix. I saw some of the tallest saguaro cacti I ever saw. I said to Ruthie, "They look like sentinels or really an army protecting the desert." "Yes," Alfred said, "You're right, the Indians think so, too." We then picked up the health certificate, and Alfred took us to eat at the famous *Westward Ho!* hotel.

There was a beautiful Southwestern atmosphere, wonderful food, amid Spanish string music. There were many real well-dressed cowboys! It was a lovely evening. I just wished John Moran Severette was next to me. 'Why hadn't he tried to find me?' I thought, but quickly came back to the present as the music to the peppy strains of "La Cucaracha" filled the room.

We went back to Alfred and Ruthie's to discuss last minute wedding plans. Ruthie put Olga and me in a charming guest room with maple twin beds and curtains with blue lilac flower designs. It was cozy. John Paul they put in their son's room. Their son was all grown up and lived out of state, but he still kept his room.

All in all, it had been a very successful day.

The following day we went back to the Governor's headquarters. Of course, John Paul wanted us to meet Governor Osborn, who invited us to meet his wife later, as well as Dick Harless.

Ruthie said, "We've got to hurry, we've got to hurry; we can't stay here too much longer." Then she got a phone book and started to look for churches, asking, "Do you want to have your wedding at the courthouse or in a church?"

I was just stunned. Here I'm thinking about politics one minute, and the next I'm getting married! "When I marry, I want it to be in a church."

Ruthie said, "We'll have to call several churches. You might get in, though."

We called two, but they had too many weddings scheduled; then we hit it lucky when we called the Presbyterian church and talked to the secretary.

She said, "Is this a big wedding party?"

Ruthie said, "No, no, this is just the bride, groom and three or four friends, that's all."

"Oh," she said, "We won't have any trouble. Just come in to the little church chapel office, the side door. Did you want music? We can get you in today, and we have an organist, too. He will be practicing tomorrow, as well."

We thought that was just great, free music.

"If you need witnesses," she continued, "I can be a witness or the organist could."

I had forgotten that we could have Alfred, Ruthie or Olga, for that matter; but Olga was supposed to be my maid of honor, Ruthie my bridesmaid, and Alfred would be Paul's best man. They thought that was great. I didn't know much about weddings, mostly what I had seen in the movies. Mother Clara did help put on the reception for Ada's daughter when she got married, and I helped with that when I was twelve.

But I hadn't really been prepared for this type of thing when it came to myself being the bride. Anyway, she said to be there by one thirty that afternoon. She gave the phone to the minister, who said to come in the side door by the garden. He described how to get to the church, how the service would be done, and so on. When we got there, we walked in through a pretty flower garden to a side door leading to the study just off the chapel. We went through into the study. The minister was sitting there with some papers for us to fill out.

We could hear the organist in the chapel starting to play. I think he must have been notified that it was us. He was also playing several pieces that would be appropriate wedding music, but not the wedding march. He played "I Love You Truly" several times and later did play this during the wedding. I thought that was kind of nice. He played several beautiful hymns, and he seemed to be going from one to another in a medley. I was getting teary-eyed, but not from anything amorous. There was no love here, and for me it was just a business deal that I had to get out of the way. I noticed that Olga almost seemed relieved. She had a big smile on her face.

'Maybe these people are just trying to get me out of their hair,' I thought.

As I looked at her and listened to the music, I thought, 'This is not the marriage I had hoped for. This was not John Moran Severette who was soon to stand next to me. The man that I really still love is not here. This is just an arrangement!'

I kept fighting back tears that were still trying to form, but I thought, 'No, this is just a business deal. You have to get in the movies.'

We all got assembled in front of the pulpit, in the main chapel; and the organist was playing the same tunes again. I had a dress that had been my mother's. The bottom was a beautiful crepe with a princess design that flared out and the bodice was in velvet with a very deep throat. I had a beautiful diamond clip, one of the things of Grandma's I brought with me in my hat box. The pin was a 1900 design. It was a black dress.

My mother was very tiny, as was I. I weighed 108 pounds and was 5'3". The dress was quite flattering. You could twirl in this dress and the skirt would just go all over the place. I thought I looked pretty nice, but it wasn't what I wanted. There was no beautiful trailing bridal train coming down the church aisle as I would march. This was not that kind of a wedding. I was just standing there in front of the pulpit with a rather curious minister who, by the look in his eye, seemed to be wondering what I was doing marrying a man nineteen years older than myself? He didn't say anything at that moment, and I don't know what I would have said had he asked me something. Olga pulled me back out of my thoughts, saying, "Excuse me, but this is your wedding."

The secretary came around the corner and asked, "Do you have flowers?"

"No, I don't."

She said, "Oh, we have a whole garden full. I'll run and get some."

Olga pulled me closer to her, getting something out of her purse. She put it on top of my head. It was an adorable veil with a hatpin in the back that held it on my hair.

I thought, 'It's a kind of a strange shape, almost an oval.' It was black lace.

It went over half of my face and down the back of my neck and was tapered down to the center of my back. Actually, it looked like a Spanish Manta. The secretary came rushing back with a little bouquet. She whipped a ribbon out from somewhere and had it tied in a bow on some of the pretty desert flowers and rosebuds I saw while walking into the church. She took a little rose bud and stuck it in the top of my hair underneath that hatpin. By this time, the minister had got our attention by clearing his throat and said, "I guess we're about ready."

There was not another person in the church now, other than the organist at the organ, the secretary, Olga, Alfred and Ruthie Benavidas, myself and John Paul. Reverend Rowell C. Laporta was standing in front of us, starting to read the vows. I don't even know what he said. I wasn't even listening. All I know is that when I was supposed to speak, I opened my mouth and uttered whatever I was supposed to. The ones watching the wedding were more emotionally involved than the two it was all about.

I thought, 'I'm already acting. All I have to do is get to Hollywood and get signed up, but I would hope the part has more depth to it than this!'

On the other hand, it *was* serious, as this *was* God's house.

No one had thought about the ring. Alfred Benavidas had to grab his wedding band off and give it to Paul to put on my finger when the minister asked for a ring. That provided a little levity. After the ceremony I gave him back his ring. The papers were all signed, and we left. I guess the marriage license was sent to the county clerk and re-mailed. I know they had Alfred and Ruthie's address.

That's really the way it all happened — that quick, kind of improvised and convenient.

I thought, '"As convenient as a tangerine is to peel," as Baba used to say.'

In a short time it was all over. If I had known that those few minutes and those few words that were spoken were just the beginning of suffering; the effects reverberated for years and years. Had I known a quarter of what was going to happen to me from this "casual arrangement," I would have run out the chapel door and on up the road until I got back to Michigan! We sometimes enter dark storms and great peril in our incidental play at life. Sometimes we pay big prices for a folly that went unrecognized. On the other hand, these things have a way of evolving into new possibilities.

I am sure the minister didn't understand what all this was about, of course, but he said, "I now pronounce you man and wife." We took the same side door outdoors where we had entered, making our way through the garden toward the car.

I suddenly became aware of a very strong wind that seemed to be a forerunner of a storm. I was running across the courtyard with a borrowed veil flying in the air and a hand-picked bouquet of flowers held tightly in my hand as we rushed back to where the car was waiting.

As I got into the car, I turned to Olga and said, "I don't feel married. I wonder what a girl is supposed to feel like when she just gets married?"

"But this is just an arranged whim marriage," Olga reminded me.

'An arranged whim marriage,' I thought.

As I had run through the courtyard garden, it seemed strange, indeed, almost surreal, ducking my head under the roof and into the car. I found myself sitting down, finally shielded from the strong breeze that seemed to be frantically trying to warn a young girl of impending doom.

I peeked into the rear view mirror from the back seat to see what I looked like. It was almost unreal, because I was surprised. It was a beautiful veil. The little rose looked just adorable where it sat. Somehow or another, I kind of looked like a bride.

This was an innocent arrangement on my part that they had helped me weave that day, to get to where I was trying to go. Yet the reason didn't match the magnitude of the event's consequences. Weeks later I began to think it might not have been as innocent from the standpoint of Olga's knowledge or from John Paul's viewpoint. But I wasn't thinking this back then, not that day. I so wanted to be in the movies to prove to them, to both mothers, and to John Moran Severette, that I was worthy.

XXVI - Mexican Wedding Party

el dozavo de diciembre de 1939

Soon we arrived at Alfred and Ruthie's house; and when we came through the door, I think half of the Mexican village was there. A Mexican band was playing loud, beautiful music. There was a Marimba, (and I love Marimbas), Spanish guitars and violins. Also people, wall to wall, from the living room and dining room, spewing out through the doors into that huge patio he built. Flowers, lawn chairs and people surrounded the patio on the grass.

In winter the Arizona Diller oranges and tangerines were ripe and the weather mild, so the scent of orange and tangerine blossoms filled the air. They had arranged this quickly. Alfred had his contacts and was always the one to accomplish things. He had called all of his friends to have them there when we returned. I guess maybe he thought that I loved John Paul and that John Paul loved me. Later he found out this was some kind of an arranged marriage.

He said to me, with a twinkle in his eye, "That's what you think."

I really didn't grasp the meaning of that, either, but the party was fun. They had tequila in every kind of drink. I had my own little drink without tequila. I was just as excited and having as much fun as they were. The music was great, as was the food. There were trays of every kind of Mexican dish one could think of: tamales, tortillas, tostados, enchiladas, just piles of grated cheese, chopped lettuce and tomatoes to make your own. Such good food — it was unbelievable, and the salsa, "to die for."

And there were avocados. I love them. I thought, 'If I could afford it, I'd buy an avocado ranch — well, a small one, maybe.'

Everybody was dancing; and it took a real crowd to fill that patio, which was probably over five hundred square feet. Alfred said he had poured the concrete himself. They put a big cardboard sign up, reading "Mexican Hat Dance." It was a contest for who could do the best Mexican Hat Dance. First two men came out carrying a huge Mexican sombrero. They put it over Paul's and my head. They laughed, spoke in Spanish and winked at us. They put the sombrero on the patio. Everyone moved back, and the music fired up.

Alfred said, "We're going to show you how to do the Mexican Hat Dance. John Paul, do you want to learn the Mexican Hat Dance?"

"No, no," he said.

John Paul was not a very good dancer. Actually, I think he was embarrassed. When the music started, one of the Mexican ladies and her husband did the Mexican Hat Dance, where you go in and out of the rim of the hat while you're dancing. It takes a little dexterity to do it. Then Alfred got in and told me to get on the other side of the hat. We danced all around the hat. Actually, it was a lot of fun, but you really had to watch your footing.

These people were so happy, it felt good; although I was not happy about being married. I was just happy that maybe I was on my way, at last, to becoming a movie star. Soon somebody started up a Rhumba, and everybody was going around in circles to the Rhumba. I love the Rhumba. Really, I guess, for the first time in months I started to feel a little happy. Maybe things weren't quite as bad as I thought.

This is what happened on December 12, 1939.

The next day, we would be heading back with Olga to California. However, John Paul had to touch base with the so-called store that we thought he owned.

He said to one of the people in the store, "I have to take these people back to California," but he didn't introduce me at all. Then he said, "We're going to have our sale starting in ten days, so I'll be back before Christmas."

I thought about that. 'Well, he's coming back before Christmas? I've got to get to the studios.' I had to let the studios know I had a guardian husband manager.

XXVII - Back to the Business of Fortunes

diciembre de 1939

The next day Olga and I repacked our suitcases, getting ready for our return trip.

I really loved Arizona, including that short visit to the *Westward Ho!* hotel where I met Governor Osborn in his suite of rooms. I was introduced to his wife, who was in a wheelchair at that time. He was a second term governor. It was all very exciting for me. In the area of the *Westward Ho!* cowboys still walked about wearing chaps and cowboy hats, authentic Arizona, as they were the real thing. It was kind of romantic, like in a Zane Grey story. I loved Zane Grey books and collected them, or started to. It seemed far more real to me in Arizona than Hollywood.

As we left town, we stopped at several Indian stores, and it kind of reminded me of the Indians I had met as a small child when I used to play with the Chippewas. I bought a little Oiya for two and a half dollars and two Zuni pots for nine dollars. I loved the work of the Indians. Today that Oiya and the Zuni pots would be worth hundreds.

John Paul had to roll up the big sombrero and tie a ribbon around it to get it into the car. We sure looked like a group of happy tourists on our way back to Olga's house.

Before we left Alfred and Ruthie's I remembered that in my suitcase I had Baba's scarf and the little ring. I didn't know why I didn't think to take it to use at the wedding.

I remembered that Alfred said that his grandfather had a town named after him in Mexico, called "Benavidas." I said, Alfred, was your grandpa, or great grandpa, an official?"

"Yes," he said, "He was, *sí.*"

"Well," I said, "I have this ring of Baba's, and I could use that for a wedding ring. On your great-grandpa's behalf, and on behalf of Baba, would you put her ring on my finger, where I took yours off that you loaned me?"

He said, "Of course," and he did.

I turned the little ring around so you couldn't see the stone and said, "This is for Baba."

We had a really nice lunch, yes, tamales! Spanish rice and refried beans. Yum! Then a fast trip to Los Angeles and Olga's house. Boy, I was really glad to get there. Olga came up the steps two at a time. She said, "Where will I put John Paul to sleep?"

I said, "Well, he won't sleep in my bed!"

"I have to charge him extra, then," she said.

I just glared at her, then said, "After all, this marriage is supposed to be a business arrangement. Anyway, he's like a big brother to me."

John Paul had just arrived at the top of the stairs, and I'm sure he heard some of what we said.

Coming to my door, she turned and said, "John Paul, I can give you the back bedroom."

There was embarrassment evident on his face when he looked at me in the doorway. I said, "Remember our agreement, John Paul."

Turning to Olga, he asked, "Do you want me to pay the same as Judyenne pays?"

"That'll be fine," she answered.

He pulled out five dollars and gave it to her for a week's rent.

Changing the subject, Olga said, "You know, people really like Judyenne. It wasn't just the tea readings; they like to be with her because she really cares about people."

John Paul said, "Yes, she does. I know that. I've watched her do readings and listened to her."

"I have a feeling that when I prove I'm married, Mister Kahn will give me a chance," I ventured; and the next afternoon I went to just about every studio. John Paul went with me.

There was nothing. I didn't get to see Mr. Kahn, but I left my message with Dee Dee, Mr. Kahn's secretary — I had a husband who could sign contracts.

If you go from place to place for seven hours with a portfolio under your arm, you get pretty tired. At least I had a car and driver. Finally, the day was nearing the end; no luck, no nothing, and I was really getting disgusted.

After eating a quick corned beef sandwich with a big dill pickle at Herman's Deli, we drove back to Olga's.

When we got there, she looked a little bit strange and said, "There's a fellow named Tiny, and he said it's urgent."

I just didn't know who it was, either.

"He'll be coming for a reading," Olga went on.

"I blame myself for Baba's death with doing tea fortunes," I muttered.

"Oh, don't be foolish, Judyenne. You had nothing to do with that, but maybe we should have tried harder to help her stop drinking."

That's when John Paul "chirped up" and said, "Nobody had anything to do with it. The fact was, she drank, and it caused her sickness. You made her very happy." Then he turned to Olga and said, "Somebody must have been telling this young girl ... " Then he stopped suddenly and looked kind of foolish for a couple of seconds. "I mean, this young woman, my wife, some one has been telling her bad things about herself. I don't understand it, Judyenne; you're a beautiful person and a lovely girl, so why do you feel that way?"

Olga said, "I think everybody in her life has put her down, John Paul. It hasn't been a happy one." Then she turned to me and said, "Every person on earth has an important place. God just made it that way."

I was more than surprised by her first time ever reference to a "divine power."

She said, "Everyone is a part of a puzzle."

"I guess you're right," I agreed somberly. I said, "I didn't come here to be a tea leaf reader; I came here to try to get into the movies."

John Paul said, "Go ahead with your readings, and I'll just read the L.A. paper."

My client did arrive, and he was not tiny. He was a huge, heavy-set strong man who looked more like a wrestler. Olga put a much heavier side chair in place where he was to sit; then he sat down.

"Oh," he said, "Dimples told me that you might have an answer to some of my questions. I have some offers, and I don't know which one to take."

As his "bear paw" of a man's hand clasped the delicate English teacup, he looked embarrassed, then asked, "You can read this?"

Pouring one half cup of tea, I asked him to drink it 'till all gone, turn the cup upside down, turn it around three times clockwise and make a wish. Then I would pick up the cup and tell him what the tea leaves said.

I already knew he wanted an answer to a change in his life, so I said, "I don't know what to call you. Do I call you Tiny?"

"Yes, call me Tiny." Then he asked, "And you're Zelda, the gypsy?"

"Yes," I said, "And your wish is going to come true."

His eyes lit up. He was squeezing his hands. I was so glad he wasn't holding that English teacup. It was one of my favorites of Olga's.

I said, "Yes, I see you leaving for the East Coast. You are in some kind of show business?"

"Well, not exactly," he said.

I said, "You have a wonderful career opportunity."

He looked happy at hearing this; and he said, "So I am going East? That's what I wanted to know."

"Yes, you will," I replied.

"Will I be happy there?" he asked.

I turned his cup, then answered, "Yes, very happy. It's far more peaceful than where you are now. Aren't you planning to get another car?" I saw little dots like a road.

He said, "I've been thinking that maybe I should get a car here." "You should," I said, "And there's a young lady in the cup." His face lit up. "That's good news."

We talked about relatives he wanted to visit, and that concluded the visit. He got up to leave, took my hand and patted it with his big paws, then left a big tip. I grabbed it from underneath that cup.

He turned around to Olga as he left and said, "I'll see Zelda again before I leave."

Olga said, "You're leaving?"

He said, "Yes, that's what I wanted to know. I'm going to the East Coast. Your gypsy, Zelda, said so."

I found out later that, yes, he was a wrestler; and yes, he did very well out there.

Olga was going to be working late, but there were no more readings for me, so I suggested we go out to eat.

John Paul wanted to get pork noodles and see a movie. He had been waiting over an hour and a half. We called up to John Paul, then Olga nodded to me and said, "I'll pay my own way this time."

We went to Cathay Gardens again. I really felt at home there.

It was the 16th. I couldn't believe that I wasn't getting any calls from Ivan Kahn. In fact, no one who knew me when Baba was alive was calling at all.

"People seemed so interested in me then, and now they're not," I said to Olga.

She said, "I think it's because Baba's gone. You know, a lot of these people owed Baba favors, and they were trying to pay her back. Now it's like the "loans" were all paid off, but you should hang in there. Other people might help you in the future, too. Who knows? Like Big Al."

I said, "I guess you're right, but getting into show business via Big Al doesn't mean that much to me if I have to sleep with somebody to do it. The heck with it!"

After some thought I said, "I wonder why Madam Zurenski hasn't called back? She was going to call Mr. Kahn and call us back."

Olga said, "Well, you know, they had an awful lot to do after Baba died. There was a lot of real estate she had and financial dealings, so I guess they're just busy."

We were at Cathay Gardens again. When we finished eating, we walked out to the car and returned to Olga's. "Don't forget you have a reading soon," Olga said. So I quickly got the gypsy costume on and went to my little table. Whom did I see walk in but Big Al and another man I had never seen before. They talked to Olga a second and then Big Al came over to the chair.

"Hello, Big Al," I greeted him.

He said, "You're getting quite a reputation," putting his face close to mine.

"I hope it's good," as I tried to move back.

"Yes, there's never anything bad said about you. What you tell people comes true."

"It's not always a hundred percent, but sometimes I get lucky."

He said, "Let's see how lucky you can get with me."

"Ummm," I said as I began the reading, "You are having trouble with three partners. I suggest you be careful! If I were you, I would see if your partners and yourself could discuss the problems together. If each of you would give a little ... if each of you gave a quarter, you would solve your problem. So far, you have been very lucky, but the advice in the cup is true. Don't go into any dark alleys. Don't argue with these partners. I see a phone call from a long distance. I see a very long trip."

"I'll be! You can see all of that in that little cup?"

I looked him straight in the eyes and replied, "You'd be surprised what I can see in this tea cup."

Big Al fascinated me, but at the same time I was afraid of him. I liked him, but the reason I didn't want anything to do with him was, I knew what business he was in. Big Al's eyes were beautiful, round and dark. He looked through me when our eyes met. He seemed to work a spell, in reaching inside a woman mentally, so she felt a warm, dangerous feeling that was alluring rather than repelling. He leaned toward me when he stood up. I could feel, just in an instant, the intrigue, the sexual power. I could feel the electricity of his being, as he leaned against me and grabbed my hand.

I thought, 'He can't hurt me in here!'

There was a bill in his hand, which he crushed into the palm of my hand, then closed my fingers over it and patted my hand. I peeked into my hand, and it was a fifty dollar bill! So, he wanted something? People might think so, but that was not what he was thinking. The fifty dollars would have been an insult to him if he thought it was seen in that way.

He finally said, "Judyenne, soon you'll know how much I care about you."

He was always making remarks like that to me. His eyes peering into mine were demanding, yet childlike, eager, yet tender. I knew why women would swoon over him.

"Big Al, you know I appreciate all you've said and done, but you know I'm only interested in a movie career."

His body again leaned against me; and our eyes did meet, almost touching faces.

"I'll be back," he whispered. "You know I'll be back."

Olga was coming around the corner, nearly stopping as she saw us. Then this little guy started to walk toward me. I thought he was going to follow Big Al, but Big Al went back into the parlor.

This little fellow came sauntering into the room. I wondered if this was another reading.

"Can I have a reading? Big Al said so."

Olga looked at me and said, "Judyenne, I didn't know about this, and I'm sorry. But would you do it for Big Al?"

I thought to myself, "I have to!"

The little man, Vincent, sat down. He said he was just visiting from a recent trip to the East Coast.

"Oh," I said, "What part of the East Coast?"

He stared at me and wouldn't answer my question. He drank his tea, turned his cup upside down and did what I told him. I noticed his hands were shaking and were a mottled pink and white. He looked sick and terrified.

I asked, "Do you have stomach trouble? Because I feel you should see a doctor."

He cringed and tightened his hands into a little knot.

I said, "I see something that shows that you are ill; you have a bad stomach, but you have been putting off seeing a doctor."

"I have. I hate doctors," he huffed.

"You know what you should do?"

"No," he answered.

"You should go home and get some hot milk in a cup, put a little bit of cinnamon, a little ginger and a little sugar or honey in it. Stir it up and drink it."

He said, "Oh, God, the ginger would kill me."

"No, no," I said. "A sixteenth of a teaspoon of ginger, one fourth teaspoon of cinnamon, one fourth of a teaspoon of sugar or honey in the hot milk. Stir it up and drink it."

"Well, what'll that do?" he asked.

"It'll help soothe your stomach. My grandma gave it to me, and it helps."

"It's worth a try." Then he watched intently as I looked at the cup some more. He had beady little eyes.

"And I think you should see your doctor. You don't belong in a hot climate," I continued. "You need to be where it's cooler. Maybe you ought to go to Boston." I saw danger in his cup. "Yes," I went on, "I'd leave as soon as possible."

He looked startled, then said, "Yeah, I do like cooler weather. I think I'd like that."

"Yes, you would," I agreed.

"When did you say is best to go?"

"Yesterday would be better, but go quickly," I replied. "Go tonight."

I didn't know at the time that he was one of the partners. I didn't know, also, that he was in a lot of trouble with the Mob. Later I heard he did go to Boston and did go to Maine. He asked me about his love life. I really started reading leaves now, and finally said, "According to the cup, this leaf's you and that one is the girl you left behind."

"If she cared about me, she'd have called," he grumbled.

I said, "No, no. She does, but she's waiting for you to call. She's right here in the cup." I pointed to a short stem.

"Yeah?"

I said, "She's not happy."

"How do you know?" he asked skeptically.

I said, "That's what it says. You know how you can read a deck of cards, don't you?"

"Yes."

"Then your cards tell you things just like the tea leaves tell me things in the cup."

"Oh, I've got you," he said. Then asked, "Do you think I should call her?"

I said, "Yes, I would phone her quickly."

His face lit up, almost a smile on his face; then he said, "I feel much better."

Later, Olga confirmed that he was one of those three partners of Big Al. He seemed very happy as he pushed his chair back. As he did so, he shoved five bucks into my hand, escaping Olga's vigilance. Then he went over and paid Olga.

Olga said, "Boy, you outdid yourself. Big Al sat back there with me, and he and Vincent said you hit the nail right on the head. You can't know for sure if you're right, but you get hunches, and honey, you really know how to talk."

"It's what the cup says, or it's my inner feelings," I replied.

She said, "If your inner feelings ever say anything about the stock market, honey, tell me!"

Many years later Olof Jonsson, the famous psychic, told me that people had said the same thing to him. He was asked to pick a winning number of casinos and the first place horse at the track. He said that he always told them he would rather not do anything like that. I wouldn't tell them anything of that nature that I saw in a teacup, either. Of course, I am not a psychic, although I have keen insight.

XXVIII - Shrimp Cocktail

diciembre de 1939

The movie, "The Buccaneer" was playing, and John Paul and I wanted to see Fredric March, the star. First we went to the Brown Derby, not to go in, but to watch for stars. Walking towards the Brown Derby, a hand was laid on my shoulder and one on John Paul's.

We both turned around and there was Big Al. It scared me, but John Paul turned ashen gray. I thought he was going to faint.

I asked, "What are you doing here, Big Al?"

John Paul stood stiff.

"What are *you* doing here?" Big Al asked back.

"I was just showing John Paul the Hollywood sights, hoping to see a star."

"Oh," he said, looking John Paul over from head to toe like a hunter. I had never seen John Paul look so stressed.

"Is he that friend of Olga's?" Big Al asked.

John Paul turned his head to me as if to solicit an answer.

"Yes, he's visiting Olga."

"Do you want to come in my car?" he asked. "I can take you where the stars are, and I'd love to talk to you. We can go dancing later."

Big Al had that persuasiveness, like, you were afraid to say "No." I looked at John Paul, but he still had no help for distractions, so I explained, "Olga is waiting for us to get back. Not tonight, Big Al."

Big Al slipped his arm in mine and said, "But come with me a minute."

He appeared to forget John Paul. We walked briskly about fifteen feet to his car. The motor was going, the driver inside. I felt uncomfortable. As Big Al talked, he kept leading me closer to the car. The rear door was open. I didn't like this. I was just too close to that vehicle.

"Sit down here, Judyenne." We both did.

"Now listen, I want to talk to you, Judyenne. This is serious. Baba is gone and nobody else can help you, but I can. I don't take 'No' easily. I want to be your friend because I care for you, Judyenne, more than a friend. I can get you into the studios. I can make you a star. You can't get everything for nothing, like from Baba, Olga and Madam Zurenski."

"But I didn't. I paid rent at Madam Zurenski's. I'm paying rent at Olga's. I tried to help Baba."

"I know. We all know what you did. Now, I want you to call me."

He put his hand on mine.

"Please, Judyenne, I know you like me. I can feel it. You're just afraid of me, but you have no reason to be." He handed me a card. "Here's my card and phone number. Call me Saturday."

"Why Saturday?"

"I want to introduce you to some very important people. I have this business trip to Monterey. You mentioned you'd love to go up there, so maybe you could go with me?" he added.

"That's a long way from here."

"We can stay overnight. The Inn is gorgeous."

"I can't stay overnight with you, Big Al."

"I'll get you your own room. I get all my girls a separate room, adjoining mine, of course." He kind of smiled. "Oh, come on, Judyenne. I'm just teasing you. I'm not going to hurt you."

"Well, Big Al, I can't do that."

"Why not?"

"I don't think you understand me. I don't stay out all night," I explained.

"I don't know why. A lot of girls want to."

"Maybe so, Big Al, but I came to Hollywood for one reason, to get in the movies. I didn't think I had to spend the night with someone to get in the movies. I'm not promiscuous."

He had this big grin on his face, and was staring straight down into my eyes.

I thought, 'Boy, I guess I'm in over my head!'

He was tall, had dark hair and was suave like a tall George Raft and a Valentino. Big Al was a very handsome man, and he knew it. That night he was wearing his narrow black mustache over a mischievous smile. I really wanted to like him, but there was another feeling that I had to be wary.

"Well, look, Big Al."

"Call me Al."

"Al, I may have a casting call. And I just don't sleep around. I just don't do that."

He grabbed my hand and pulled me closer, "You don't know what you do to me. I'm falling in love with you, Judyenne. It's not like other girls. You're special."

I thought to myself, 'Boy, I'd hear guys in high school say things like that, and I'd leave!'

I looked him straight in the eyes. "Don't you understand, Al? I'm not getting involved. I want to get into the movies. If I can't, I'm leaving. It's too hot here! I'd rather be in Maine raising blueberries, or Michigan picking up Petoskey stones."

He said, "What's that?"

"They're stones that are fossils from ocean coral that lived before the dinosaurs and now wash up around the city of Petoskey, Michigan, as well as the rest of the Great Lakes shore line," I explained.

"Oh. You don't explain things like my other girls do, either — all that knowledge," Big Al confessed.

"No, I suppose not. Look, Al, I'll call you later," I said. "I must get back."

"Are you calling Saturday?" he asked.

"I could be on a set Saturday. If I get a casting call, I'm gone."

He said, "Call any time Saturday."

Pulling away, I said, "I'll try. OK? Goodnight, Al."

"Don't go with this John Paul guy! You understand?"

"Yes, No, I won't."

I got out of the car, and he did too, following me a short distance.

"Remember now, I always know what you're doing, Judyenne; and I'll pick you up. Don't forget your promises. And don't forget Christmas! I've got plans for us!"

His hand tightened around my waist, and he drew me closer. He brushed my hair with his lips in a kind of a kiss.

Big Al looked at John Paul. John Paul stood there aghast and silent, watching.

Al turned and was walking over to his car.

John Paul whispered, "Let's get out of here; my God, he's a *gangster*, Judyenne!"

"Of course, he's a gangster! Gee, Paul; everyone knows that there's mob money invested in some of the Hollywood studios."

We both got into the car fast; and John Paul yanked the keys out of his pocket, but had trouble getting the car started.

"Damn, of all the times!" he grumbled.

A second later the engine turned over and the car shot out into the street.

I said, "Let's go back to Olga's. Forget the movies!" Then I thought, 'Big Al is serious!' I was now starting to get really scared.

Paul was zig-zagging through the streets like a crazy man. He was going down one street and up another. I remembered in Big Al's attempt to persuade me to go up to the Inn, he kept saying, "I'll buy you lots of shrimp." I thought about what Benjamin had asked that day on the "Rex". Baba's reply to his question didn't seem so funny now! I realized that Big Al had to work under Benjamin. Then Big Al had said, "You know how you like shrimp."

As we were dodging down side streets I said, "I need a cup of coffee!"

"Should we go to a coffee shop?" he asked, still nervous.

"No, we'll get some at Olga's."

Parking in the rear, we rushed inside; and Olga asked, "What is wrong with you?"

I said, "I'm petrified."

"What are you afraid of?"

"Big Al grabbed me right off the side of the street, almost in plain sight of the Brown Derby."

"He did what! What did he want?" Olga said.

"What do you think he wants? He's been chasing me for a long time." I answered.

"Well," John Paul said, "You do wonderful tea readings, but ... ."

"Of course, but he doesn't want tea fortunes, he wants me!"

John Paul's face was ashen; and he muttered, "You mean he's hassled you before?"

"Yes."

Forty minutes after our arrival, as we were drinking our coffee, there was a knock on Olga's front door. The sign on the door was marked "Closed."

Olga said, "I'll get it."

She opened the little slotted window in the door and peeked through.

She said, "My God, it's a courier of some kind. He's got two big boxes with bows on top, in his hands."

Olga opened the door.

The young man said, "It's packed in ice, so you better hurry up and eat. I hope you enjoy it."

He returned to a 1939 black Lincoln as Olga quickly locked the door.

I thought, 'What's he doing in a car like that?' Then it hit me — Big Al!

The deliveryman looked more like a bellhop. Olga brought the two large boxes into the kitchen and opened them up. There were two beautiful cut glass crystal bowls full of shrimp nestled in separate bowls of crushed ice, lemon slices and shrimp sauce.

The card read: "We're going to my Uncle's first. Our priest will be there."

I thought Olga was going to choke to death on her coffee when she read the note.

John Paul read the note and exclaimed, "He's serious, Judyenne! How will you get out of this?"

Here we were, three terrified people eating the shrimp and *loving* every mouthful. Then John Paul mumbled, "You're gonna have to hide out!"

XXIX - Shopping in Mexico

diciembre de 1939

The phrase, "Remember your promises," was still on my mind. Thoughts of the Brown Derby and Big Al had returned. Big Al was showing up everywhere, it seemed.

Sophie and Irena joined us to hear about Al's demands.

"I wish I could get out of here for a couple of days," I said.

Olga said, "I've got Christmas shopping to do. Want to come along?"

"Oh, yes, but where are you going?" I asked.

She looked at John Paul. "Would you like to go to Mexico?"

"Sure, I'm familiar with Mexico. I go to Nogales when I'm in Arizona, so I'd like to go."

"Have you been to Tiajuana?" Olga asked J.P.

"Yes, a couple of years back."

"How about it? I don't want to drive. Do you want to take us?"

"That's fine with me."

Irena wasn't a bit interested.

Sophie said, "I'm afraid of Mexico."

"Well, let's us three go then," Olga suggested.

She handed the appointment book to Sophie, saying, "If there's any of my readings come in, tell them I need a couple of days off to do my Christmas shopping."

Olga looked at the book. "I've got two tomorrow, but not Judyenne. Sophie, could you do these two?"

"Yes, I'll do them."

I looked in surprise. I didn't know Sophie did readings. 'Wow,' I thought, 'Are all these folks related?' Oh yes, they were, all of them, and fortune tellers, too. "When do you want to go?" I asked.

"If we started early, say six, we could leave at seven in the morning," Olga replied.

John Paul said, "I could be up at five."

I thought, 'Oh, no, another early morning riser! And I'm a night person.'

Olga said, "Look, six is early enough. We'll get up at six. We can eat on the road."

"I need coffee and toast," I said.

"All right, all right," said Olga. "A roll, then leave." I really think that now Olga also was worried about Big Al.

I said, "Well, if I'm going to wake up early, I have to get to bed."

When six came, I really knew it. I had set two alarm clocks, Olga's and my travel alarm! One was for five thirty, the other five forty-five. Then I was showered, dressed and even beat Olga to the kitchen, where everybody grabbed coffee. Olga had those hard rolls with the soft insides from a bakery an old Greek man had in L.A. I cut them in half with a steak knife and dunked them in coffee, as did Olga and John Paul.

We left at exactly seven a.m., and it was a happy trip. In San Diego we stopped for gas. Then, when we got to the border, I didn't have any I.D.; but I had the little piece of paper from the minister showing we were married. I didn't have a birth certificate nor a driver's license, but I wasn't aware of this as a problem until we got there. The border guard stared at me and asked, "Where were you born?"

"Michigan."

He looked at John Paul.

"Where were you born?"

I sure didn't know where John Paul was born!

"West Virginia."

The man looked at Olga. "Where were you born?"

"Russia."

"Have you got your naturalization papers?"

She did, and Paul had his driver's license from Arizona. The only thing I had was that piece of paper, and I showed him that.

John Paul spoke up and said, "This is my wife."

Olga picked up on this and added, "Yes, I'm shopping for the honeymooners."

The man then lightened up and let us through. John Paul drove into Tiajuana and parked. We went in all the little shops as we walked along. I went nuts over the pottery piggy banks, the jewelry and colorful blankets.

"I know where to get the good leather goods," Olga offered.

Of course John Paul knew Mexican goods and bargains, and he could speak some Spanish. Every time I picked something up, he started arguing about the price and got it cheaper. They did beautiful copper work with inlaid silver and mother of pearl like the bracelet I got for three dollars and a half. I purchased a darling cross, also a rosary of ivory, which I put on.

We left Tijuana because Olga wanted to go to Ensenada for the duty free shops there. Olga knew quality. She was European and years ago traveled in affluent circles.

Arriving in Ensenada, we rented two adjoining units there at a motel on the waterfront. Olga and I stayed in a unit with queen-size beds, splitting the cost.

"We should share the unit with J.P. and save money," she suggested.

I said, "We just can't start something like this. How much do we really know about him?"

Olga and I laid all our packages down in the motel; then went to John Paul's unit to see if he wanted to shop some more after we ate, which he did.

Checking all the darling shops and looking at all the wares along the street, we came upon a lady making those big tortillas; and John Paul wanted me to taste one hot off the griddle. She put refried beans, chopped onions, tomatoes, salsa and cheese on mine. John Paul and Olga had one, too. Eating these delicious concoctions, we continued walking around town. I bought one of those full skirts with all the bright colors and a fancy embroidered low-cut blouse. We went back to the motel room where Olga and I changed into these beautiful Mexican clothes. We were having a ball shopping in native dress. John Paul had gotten himself a black sombrero with little red ball fringe around the edges.

Olga said, "We should get one, too," so we went back and each got one. We felt like *The Three Musketeers*. John Paul was funny, and we were having a good time. This was really easing the pressure of Big Al. We decided to go in a beautiful restaurant overlooking the water.

"This is a nice place," John Paul said.

In spite of having eaten three tostados, in we went. All that walking on sidewalks and cobblestones had built up our appetites. While we were in the restaurant Olga and John Paul had Margaritas. It was hot; and I thought the big wide glasses, the rims with salt on them and all that crushed ice looked so inviting.

I asked the bartender, "Couldn't I have one without the tequila?" He looked at me like I was crazy, but said, "*Sí.*"

I didn't know he also said something about a drop or two of vermouth. A Mariachi band was playing, and they were singing. I loved the Mexicans, and I loved their food. We were having the combination plate, which included enchiladas, tamales, frijoles, tostados, Spanish rice and lots of salsa. We took tostados topped with beans, chopped tomatoes and cheese and wrapped them up to take to our room.

We even bought a donkey piñata. I bought a hammered tin serving tray with Mexican designs and tall blue glass goblets. Olga was as excited about the shopping as I was.

I thought, 'I'll get a tooled leather purse for Mother, Aunt Florence, Aunt Grace and myself.' I was ready to open a store — with such bargains. I thought I'd sell them for double back home. I had my rosary, four bracelets on both arms and rings on every finger. At those prices, I still had never touched Baba's money.

We wanted to do a little more shopping; and there was a nightclub down the street with Mexican music playing, so Olga said, "Let's go there!"

There were people squatting down on the sidewalk in front of these restaurants and more stores selling their merchandise as we walked by. One Mexican woman showed us some beautiful jewelry. She had two little children next to her and a baby in her lap, but she didn't look a heck of a lot older than I was. I bought some things from her, hoping it would help her and the kids. Little did I know that I could have been looking in a mirror!

Olga was pushing us through the door of the place with all the live music pouring out. It was just full of people dancing. John Paul led us over to a table. We were full already, but he wanted us to see the dancers. People were pitching Centavos at these professional dancers, and that brought back some memories.

I had my usual drink without the alcohol. The second set of dancers started, and we watched a few minutes. It was sort of a contest. We, too, pitched centavos at these wonderful dancers.

When we started to leave, it was so crowded we had to squeeze through people to move. As I threaded my way toward the door, I suddenly felt a hand press into my shoulder. I turned around, and there was Big Al looking down at me with a big grin on his face. His other hand was on Olga's shoulder. Olga had turned and looked at the same instant. Her eyes widened with fear! Paul was ahead with his back to us.

Al said, "For Heaven's sake, I thought you'd be out on the casting call."

I thought, 'Oh, No!'

Olga said, "I needed her to go Christmas shopping with me. I'm afraid to come down here alone. There was no phone call, but I expect one tomorrow." Her mind was sharp.

"Are you spending another day?" Al asked.

"Oh, we're not sure," Olga replied.

We hadn't checked out, as a late check-out was possible. Did this ever change our minds fast! You can believe that two people were thinking the same thing in a millisecond.

Olga finally said, "We've got to finish our Christmas shopping."

"If I knew that you girls wanted to come, I would have brought you. Judyenne, why didn't you say something?"

Olga said, "She didn't know. I only asked her last evening."

Well, that took me off the hook. John Paul was by the doorway, but he still didn't see Big Al.

"Don't forget to call me," Big Al said.

"I will, soon as I can."

Big Al remained there as we nearly ran up to John Paul.

Olga grabbed hold of his arm, whispering, "We're not spending another night here! Hurry, let's get out of here!"

"Why?"

"Because, I wouldn't want to end up in my own box for Christmas, that's why! We were just talking to Big Al!"

"Big Al, here?"

"Yes, yes," I nearly screamed. "Hurry, let's get back to the motel."

I thought John Paul's knees were going to buckle. We hurried back to our rooms and rushed to get our things in the car. John Paul said, "If there's going to be driving at night, to save time let's leave in our holiday clothes that we've got on."

We decided that we'd leave soon while the leaving was good!

XXX - Kidnapped!

diciembre de 1939

The late afternoon was hot but a breeze from the bay was cool. We were rushing. We went back to check our rooms. Most of the suitcases were in the car. I carried some of my purchases out. John Paul had put his things in the car and had gone back into his room. Olga had put most of her things in the car and was trying to get her clothes into her suitcase. I was wearing my Mexican skirt and that beautiful embroidered Mexican blouse.

I took my hatbox out to the car and was bending over the car trunk with it in my hand when a hand suddenly was on my shoulder — Big Al again. I didn't hear a car drive up. I couldn't believe I didn't hear it! This, after all, was a motel parking lot with cars in and out easily heard. Big Al had me in that car so fast I almost left one shoe out in the gravel. I didn't have a chance to scream. I had my new Mexican purse over my shoulder because I had transferred everything into this new one.

He pushed me into the car, got in, slammed the door and the driver popped the clutch. I was in the back seat of this black car in about three and a half seconds, and it was driving fast. The driver gunned it so fast that I could hear gravel landing that the tires threw out. Big Al was next to me, still holding on with the iron grip that had snatched me. I had nothing else, just my skirt, top, one shoe; and the other one I was pulling on. And my purse and jewelry, of course.

The car was heading to the commercial fishing boat pier. It stopped, and he pulled me out on the pier, with his arm locked in mine. He led me down the pier and onto a big fishing boat. Two crewmen and Big Al got me into this fishing boat. I stumbled and almost fell when I was dragged over the side. It was scary. I mean, I was petrified. The crew looked Mexican, but two spoke Italian. Who was going to hear me yell "Help"? I didn't even know the word *"socorro"* then! I saw several of the crew were not Mexicans. They looked Italian; and that didn't calm me at all, as perhaps they were Big Al's "boys."

I was literally pushed and pulled down into the cabin below. This was a pretty good sized boat. It was a fishing vessel, but the cabin was clean. There was a galley and a little head. I looked at it real fast because I knew boats. I was trying to figure out how I was going to get out of there. He shoved me up against a bunk and almost pushed me backwards. This man was incredibly strong.

He finally said, “You know, I could make you mine right now, but I don’t like doing those things to girls unless they want me back.”

Well, this would scare anybody. I wasn’t stupid, but there were a lot of things I didn’t know about men. My heart was pounding so hard I was afraid I was going to have a heart attack. He pulled the purse off of my shoulder and pushed me back some more. I started to fall backward on the bunk that was shaped like a ship hull, coming up to meet me. As I landed I was surprised it was comfortable. I felt the boat slowly rocking in response to the ocean. Seconds seemed compressed into minutes.

A loud boat whistle pierced my ears; and I snapped back into reality, thinking, ‘NOW what do I do! Supposing they take me out to sea. They could throw me overboard! They could do anything!’

He did not rape me, but he could have. There was no way I could have gotten away from him. The little cabin door was locked; I saw somebody up there close the door. He was a passionate man, and he was practically lying on top of me. He was kissing me violently. He was begging me and hinting of things he could do for me.

He said, “I’ll make you want me back. I’m not going to force you, Judyenne. I have never wanted anyone so much in my life. I’m used to getting what I want. Don’t disappoint me. You can’t do that to me. Judyenne, you *can’t*! You know I love you. I’ve given you months to come around. I’m giving you a chance now, Judyenne, to say ‘Yes!’ You know I want you to be mine. You know I want to marry you, Judyenne. Don’t you understand? I want you to marry me!”

I was twisting and pulling away from him. I started to cry. Tears were running down my face.

“Please, Big Al, take me back,” I said between sobs.

I think the tears affected him. It’s hard to explain this. Here, this man is all over me; he still had his clothes on, but it wouldn’t have taken long. And he was sensitive to my tears. He took one hand off of my shoulder, reached for a handkerchief in his pocket and wiped the tears away. Then he kissed both cheeks very tenderly.

He said, “I wasn’t raised to do this to a girl. I have a sister and a mother I love very much. I want you to want me as much as I want you, Judyenne. That’s the only reason. But, I want you to promise me you’ll be mine. But first say ‘Yes.’ You will want me. You will marry me.”

I was so terrified I didn’t know whether I should say “Yes,” or what. I was still crying. I was scared to death. He could see that, as I whispered, “Yes.”

I think what made him almost crazy was my crying. He was still holding me close to him.

I finally said, “Al, I’m a virgin, and you can’t treat me this way!”

It was amazing how Big Al’s face changed. Now there was a look of real concern; and he half sat up, still holding me.

He said, "You've never been with a man before?"

"No, and I thought everybody at the theatre knew that."

"Dimples said something about it, but I didn't believe her. My God, I'm willing to wait for you. I will wait for you, Judyenne; and you're going to want me more than ever. Just keep your word. You've promised to marry me."

All I knew was I was scared almost out of my skin. I couldn't think of anything else, but to get out of there. "Please take me back. Olga will be a nervous wreck."

He was holding my purse; and I said, "Could I please have my purse back?"

He said, "I won't hurt your purse, and I won't hurt you. I'm going to make you feel better than you ever felt in your life. Just set a date for our wedding!"

My stomach started doing flip-flops. I didn't know what all Big Al had in mind, but I heard the girls talking back in the dressing rooms. Not to mention the fact of, how do I tell Big Al I'm already married, even though it is a business arrangement? He might kill me, and maybe Olga and John Paul, too!

He said, "I'm going to take you back, but I want you to do one thing before I release you." Holding me tighter with this iron strong grip, he said, "I want you to kiss me. I don't want to force your lips. I want you to kiss me so that I know you've forgiven me for frightening you."

'Well,' I thought, 'If that's the price I have to pay to get out of here, I'll kiss him.' In a situation like this, fear makes you think faster and move faster. I just lifted my head, tried to move my arms, and he let go of them. I put my arms around his neck and kissed him, with as deep and passionate a kiss as possible; because if he believed me, maybe he'd let me go.

That was amazing to me, kissing this man; because he suddenly became extremely tender, very gentle. He wasn't pushing his body hard against me any longer. He was more relaxed, more like a lover in a movie. He gave me a gentle, sweet, tender, and I would say, loving embrace. I have thought of this many times since then, and I think Big Al truly was in love with me.

I thought that after the kiss was over — and it was a long one — he'd take me back; but he wasn't going to let me go right away. He did continue to kiss my face, my eyes and even the curls along my neck and hanging down my back. Then he said, "I can tell you do forgive me; and if you like that kiss, you don't know what you're in for."

He slowly moved over and stood up.

"You will call me and give me the date. You had said Christmas. There's so much to think about, plans to make. We'll have a big church wedding. Maybe the priest could arrange for us to be married in Sicily. Would you like that?"

"You mean Sicily, like in Italy? Yes," I finally said. "But shouldn't I meet your family? Maybe we should talk to the priest."

"Yes, yes. I have much family there. A mother, great-aunt, uncles. And yes, I'll arrange for our priest to meet us. Of course, my uncle will be there, too. You're mine, Judyenne!" he said. "I'm not waiting much longer! No one else better lay their hands on you!"

When our eyes met I knew this man meant business. Maine looked better all the time! He let me stand up, then he leaned over and kissed my rosary cross. He combed my hair back with his hand and put my shoulder bag back on. He helped me up the ladder. When I got topside, these same two Latin men were staring out to sea. He helped me onto the pier. We walked down the pier past one fishing boat after another. I never knew there was such a big fishing fleet there. When we got to the car, Big Al put me in the back seat and slid in, too. The driver had been sitting in the car all that time; and he never said a word, even when he saw my flushed face reflecting in his mirror. He took us back to the motel.

Once again as the car door opened, Big Al leaned over me and said, "Call me tomorrow night. Let's plan a meeting with my uncle. He already loves you. He said you'll give us beautiful babies and will be a famous star. And we can do this. You will be famous; but you'll be my wife, first." Once again, Big Al's lips brushed my forehead and cheek. He squeezed my hand, and I suddenly had the urge to kiss his cheek. But I was afraid, so afraid.

As we drove up, John Paul was standing in his doorway. Olga was standing outside our motel room, with her hand cupped over her eyes to keep out the setting sun. She was looking toward the car and saw me get out of the car. I ran toward Olga. She had an extremely frightened look on her face. I was shaking all over. Olga ran in after me. John Paul didn't. She not only locked the front door, but also locked the bathroom door.

She said, "My God, what happened, what happened?"

I couldn't talk. A bottle of club soda was sitting on the counter. I poured some in a glass and drank it; then I blurted everything out as we left the bathroom. There was a knock on the door of the outer room, and we both about jumped to the ceiling. Olga walked over, peeking quickly through the little grill in the front door. It was John Paul.

She opened the door. "You about scared us to death! My God, you'll never guess what happened!"

I was telling him and Olga more when John Paul said, "Get in the car, everybody. Get in the car! Get your things! Hurry!"

Figure 36 The rosary that protected me, caused Big Al to set me fee, unharmed.

So we all quickly got into the car. All of our things were already packed, so we left Ensenada and were in Tijuana in record time. We had to stop at the inspection station going back into the United States and show our purchases. I was so ignorant, I didn't know. I had a Mexican blanket I bought which I put over my packages on the floor, and no one paid any duty. Apparently the blanket wasn't high priced enough to pay duty.

I don't think anybody ever drove through San Diego as fast as we did without breaking the speed limits. Anyway, we came tooling into the back of Olga's place. It was late. Quickly we got our things upstairs and went to the kitchen. We must have drunk a gallon of coffee after that. Olga and John Paul were just like me; coffee helped us to relax. By then Sophie had joined us.

"This is really bad, J.P.," Olga began. "If Big Al can't have what he wants, no one else will." At that point Olga turned to me and said, "In this case, you!"

"I've never done anything to make him think I loved him, but I did make promises to get off the fishing boat."

"That has nothing to do with it. You don't have to want him at all. He wants you, and nothing will stop him. I think he's really in love with you, Judyenne; I really do."

"What?"

"Yes, I saw his eyes. He *is* in love with you," Olga said. "He gets this way. He's been married four times! I don't know if he's married now or not, but he's in love with you; and you're in trouble, either way."

Olga continued, saying, "You'll just have to stall. I'll tell him we've got three big special performances all the way through Christmas Day! Anyway, we do, so it's the truth. We'll stall him. Let's say Valentines Day, perfect for a marriage. If that doesn't work, what about a holy day, say Epiphany, January 6th. Tell him your family observed the day."

I piped up, "My Aunt Grace does!"

"Well, there's your answer," Olga said. "I hope it works," she added uneasily.

XXXI - The Don and the Jeweled Belly Dance

diciembre de 1939

The Don said about Judyenne to Big Al, "*Si, Bella, Leggiadra!*"
"Yes, beautiful, lovely!"
Later the Don said about Judyenne's agreeing to marry Big Al,
"De Accordo, si." "By compact agreement, yes."

Olga and I were having a discussion about my going back on the "Rex", and I said, "Olga, I'm afraid. After all that's happened with Big Al and Tony."

"No, no," Olga reassured me, "Nothing will ever happen to you again because I'm going with you. Dimples wants to go, so does Maria. She's back from Vegas."

I still had a foreboding about this. John Paul had gone to work in the clothing store in Phoenix for a few days.

"We can make all kinds of money," Olga reminded me.

She was kind of happy about this, because Madam Zurenski gave her permission to handle the dancing parties that Baba booked. I remember Dimples telling me later that Olga made plenty.

We were going to do a belly dance and a gypsy number. There wasn't too much to the belly dance costume, as far as coverage. It was kind of a G-string, but with teeny little threads of gold sequins and jewels that went over the hips and then up to zig-zag across the bustline, around the neck and back down. Each of us had a different one of these jewels that fitted right into our navels. Mine was an imitation ruby that was on a string of the rhinestones that went around my waist. The rhinestone strips with sequins and beads would dangle and shimmer as they moved with our bodies. The many layers of strung beads hung from my hips like a long skirt of strung jewels. Our headpiece was a sequined headband with jewels hanging down across our foreheads. There was so much glitter and jewels to the costume, we didn't feel nude because certain areas had sequined rosettes.

The gypsy costume was made of a silk chiffon, with coins all around the skirt bottom, accentuated with tiny bells. The ruffled top was so low that the audience could see my bosom. We wore bracelets on each arm.

We took the costumes, props and makeup with us. Olga said a man came to the house and gave her a message that we were to go on the *Rex* off Long Beach.

This didn't sound right, because we thought it would still be at Santa Monica. Olga made a few phone calls and was told to go to Long Beach. That was a bit of a drive for us, since we had two engagements. We had this one on the *Rex*, and we were also to do a private dancing gig at an estate in Beverly Hills. Olga said it was the chance of a lifetime. "I think it's not far from the Guggenheim Estate, and it's a private party for some important studio executives and other V.I.P.'s," she added.

We packed up the car and drove to the pier's private drive. All of us boarded the water taxi, which was a much larger boat then we had usually seen. It was open around the gunwales so we could see in all directions, and it had a canvas top. We were bobbing around, and it was windy. We were all trying to hold our hair back. I wasn't too happy with the choppy seas. No one got sick except Olga, but she put a determined look on her slightly green face. It didn't deter her.

Turning to Olga, "I thought you said they were going to move the ship here, but it's not here?" I questioned.

"What do you mean, it's not here?"

"Well, I don't see the *'Rex.'*"

She looked too, and then she tapped the pilot on the shoulder.

"Where is the *'Rex'?"*

He said, "Right over there. They've moved it a little bit."

How could you lose the *'Rex'*? It was just too big. Suddenly we saw a large motor launch approaching toward our port side. When the operator of the launch came alongside, he yelled to the pilot, "Follow me!"

Our pilot immediately swung around, and away we went in pursuit. Soon we came up to this huge, beautiful yacht that was probably over two hundred and seventy five feet long. The man who was the pilot of the water taxi must have been in their employ, because I think someone else might have argued, turned the water taxi around, or done something to resist.

"It's going to be a private party," Olga chortled with glee in her eyes.

She still didn't suspect anything, but I was a little hesitant. I said, "Are you sure it's for us?"

"Oh, yes," Olga said, but with a slight hesitation in her voice.

We boarded this gorgeous yacht and were taken into the main salon. I still had that feeling in the back of my neck.

The steward said, "Would you ladies follow me? Your cabin is ready."

We followed him. This cabin was a double, two divided cabins with ample room. He had a man helping to carry all the costumes.

As he left, the steward said, "This is a private party; and we're sorry for the change, but the *'Rex'* is being moved back to Santa Monica."

Olga said to me, "Don't worry, it's probably one of those rich millionaires. I told you, some kind of a smoker."

There was a knock on the door; then a very distinguished-looking man took Olga out in the passageway. We heard her talking as we changed into our costumes. She came back in, looking worse than when she was seasick, and said sort of abruptly, "Finish getting into your belly dancing costumes. You'll be performing in the main salon."

"That sounds nice, but is it big enough for three dancers?" I asked.

Dimples, Maria and I would often work at private parties, "smokers," they called them. Maria left Mexico City wanting to be in the movies, but became a wonderful dancer instead.

Olga said, "Don't worry, we're getting fifty bucks apiece."

Knowing Olga, she'd probably get twice that, but it was good money anyway.

"Afterwards, you'll be mingling with the guests."

"In our belly dance costume?" I questioned.

"Oh, well, there's not that many guests."

I thought, 'Not that many guests?'

Olga then called for us to follow her.

The handsome gentleman greeted us again and gushed, "This is so wonderful of you girls to perform for us. This is a private party, and we don't usually have our dancers this close to us, it's just wonderful."

I thought, '*Our dancers*?'

Following him to the stage we noticed there were men seated in a semi-circle. We had to walk behind their chairs in order to get around to the front of this miniature stage. I noticed at once this older gentleman in the very middle who was prominent among the five men on each side of him. A man standing behind him looked almost familiar.

There was a small orchestra, and it turned out that they had our sheet music. The handsome man was the M.C. He announced we were doing the same numbers we had done on the '*Rex*', especially for them.

The music began, and we started our dance. The man who sat in the middle was seated in a big armchair. The others were seated in side chairs. He kept watching me, but at first I thought I was imagining this. 'Oh, it's just me,' I was thinking.

I had to concentrate when doing the belly dance, but I could feel the man's stare. A belly dance takes time, a lot of movement of the hips. I had to practice to do that number a long time, but Maria and Dimples were experts. I was really still learning, but Dimples said later I was very agile and doing a good job.

When the lights came up, the men clapped and clapped, and they seemed elated. I wondered whether this was all of the audience. There were twelve people, including the man behind the central figure, not counting a couple of stewards and the crew. All the M.C. said was, "My name is Harrington." We were told to walk around and talk with the guests. As I walked forward, this Harrington took me by the hand and led me over to this older gentleman who had been watching my every move. I wondered where I had seen him before. He was wearing an expensive burgundy velvet smoking jacket. I also noticed his patent leather shoes and big diamond ring.

'He must be the owner of the yacht,' I thought.

He took my hand and said, "I've wanted to meet you for some time. I know all about you. Your name is Judyenne."

"But who are you?" I said, trying to sound child-like, opening my eyes wide. I felt I could get away with it because I was saying it with a coy smile on my face.

"I'm an uncle of a very dear friend of yours."

I thought, 'I don't know anybody's uncle! Who would it be?'

Then, coming from behind the salon, in walked Big Al! Oh yes, yes, indeed! Big Al moved in, replacing another gentleman behind the uncle! Then he said, "Can I introduce my uncle to you, Judyenne?" And he added, "This is the Don."

I didn't get it at first, because I thought he meant Don, like the first name "Don."

"This is my Uncle Dominic Donatello."

As I smiled and shook his hand he said, "I understand you are making plans to marry my nephew?"

I thought I would die right there!

"Oh," I stammered, "I don't know, Mister Donatello, we haven't known each other that long. But we did discuss it."

The girls were all close by, listening. Olga was standing to my left, looking very surprised. For some reason, Dimples and Maria were keeping clear of us. I was starting to figure it out. I think Harrington told them to stay away.

Directing her words to the Don, Olga finally said, "I don't think I understand. I thought this was a private smoker party we were dancing for."

The Don said, "You are dancing for a private group."

Of course, she knew who Big Al was, and I found out later she knew who this Don was, too.

She said, "I think there's been a mistake, Mister Donatello. We were actually supposed to be on the *'Rex.'*"

"No, you were supposed to be on *my* yacht. I wanted to meet with you, Olga, to see in whose hands our dear Judyenne is. She's very important to us. And I wanted especially to meet Judyenne. You know, when a member of my family cares for someone, we look out for their welfare and keep a close watch over them."

Al walked from behind the Don just a few feet to where I was. The former fellow replaced Big Al. Walking up to me, he put his arms around me as I let his arm slip around my waist, pulling me closer. Then Big Al said, "Isn't she beautiful, Uncle?"

The Don said, "Si, *bella leggiadra! Si, si!* We must plan a wonderful dinner party soon, an engagement party. Si, si. Right, boys?" As the men beside him joined in, "Si, si."

"Yes, maybe if I shower her with flowers, she'll agree to an early marriage," Big Al quipped, squeezing me tighter.

I felt my face flush, but I still let him brush his lips again on my forehead, then said, "I don't think we should discuss wedding plans yet in front of everyone," hoping this would satisfy Big Al and his uncle.

Watching me, Big Al said, "Oh, these gentlemen, they're all my family, so don't feel embarrassed. Now I want to see that belly dance again. Wouldn't you, too, Uncle?"

"Si" and "yes," they all answered after the Don gave his approval.

The Don nodded to the orchestra, and they played the music over as we danced some more. Then we left for our stateroom for a few minutes, reapplied makeup and returned.

As we entered the main salon the Don said, "Judyenne, my dear, come sit with me." The two men who were sitting next to the Don stood up and left, and each of them pulled in another armchair. Big Al took the chair to his right, and I was on the Don's left. Olga sat next to Big Al. Dimples and Maria sat next to Olga. There was always one man standing behind the Don while we were there. Olga had a look that Baba once described as, "the eyes of a fox that had escaped the hunter the first time, but was caught the second time."

The Don turned towards me and said, "Tell me about you! Let me look into your eyes, first. Oh to be young again! I see innocence in your eyes. Yes, you are a good girl, Judyenne." He was staring right into me.

Then he clasped my hand and said, "You will make a wonderful wife for my nephew. All he does is talk about you! You will be a good wife. *Capish? Promessa!* Promise?"

I was stunned and scared! All I could say was, "Yes, yes, I will."

The Don said, "*De accordo, si.*" His eyes were like Big Al's, dark and deeply penetrating. He was smiling and patting my hand. He seemed like a kind man. He certainly looked rich.

There was a lot of food being wheeled out after we finished the second belly dance, and then the Don said, "We thought we'd feed you before you did the gypsy dance."

Olga and I were hungry in spite of the circumstances, though. I was pretty sure of one thing, the Don didn't intend to allow his men to harm us. He had a serious expression on his face, yet he seemed to enjoy our company while he was talking to Olga and me most of the time. Every once in a while, he would turn and talk to Big Al.

He said, "I want to be sure that you understand what it means to be engaged, to marry my nephew. We are a very important and influential family. Once you are betrothed to one of us, you *never* break that vow."

This sent chills down my spine. Yet, what made him say I was *engaged*? One thing I couldn't figure out was why he looked so much like the man I had met at Madam Zurenski's when Big Al was there once. Later I learned they were brothers.

The food served was wonderful. There was caviar and about everything one could think of. We really should have been happy as the food was *delicious*, but we were so darn frightened of our hosts.

Olga loved the caviar. Considering that the Don pointed out that it was Russian *huso* caviar, or better known in America as "Beluga caviar," and that he had specially imported it from the Volga delta, I can understand the enthusiasm she displayed.

Olga kept saying, "This is Russian huso caviar! I had it first when I was a little girl in Russia."

"I hope it's not our last meal!" I whispered in Olga's ear.

But before we danced in other costumes, something else happened. The Don took a beautiful ring with engraving on it from his pocket and handed it to Big Al. I'm pretty sure the engraving was in Italian. Big Al took the ring, and the Don held my hand while Big Al put it on my finger. "An engagement ring?" I wondered.

He said, "This is to remind you ... that *you* belong to my nephew. When you belong to him, you belong to *me* as well and my family." That was the part that scared me, because I knew that once someone got into *that* family, they could never leave. No one ever spoke that whole night when the Don spoke! They stood up when they addressed him. I was really amazed at the courtesy, although I don't know if it was fear or courtesy. After Big Al put the ring on my finger, the Don took Al with one arm and me with the other. Mister Harrington led Olga behind us as we proceeded to the Don's private stateroom, which was like a suite.

After everyone was inside, the Don said, "Dear Judyenne, didn't you promise that you would be engaged to my nephew?"

I answered faintly, "Yes."

"You gave a vow to him, didn't you, Judyenne?"

As I kept thinking and thinking, I remembered hugging and kissing him and telling him I forgave him. I had to. Or I knew I couldn't have gotten off the boat. Did I say "yes" to his demands to marry him?

I kept running it through my mind, 'What did I say? What did I say? I know I gave him a kind of a passionate kiss. I had to let him think I meant it in order to get off the boat!'

The Don was referring to the fishing boat in Ensenada, of course. Reaching his hand to take my other hand, he said, "Big Al kissed your cross you wore."

"Do you remember holding him close to you, as he has described to me? It means only one thing to us, in our family. You *belong* to my nephew. We want you to love him and to be his wife. We'll be making arrangements for the wedding. You'll have the finest wedding, the wedding of your dreams, Judyenne!"

"Much has to be done," he said to me as he lifted my hand to his lips. "I will take my ring and replace it with a three-karat diamond at your engagement party soon. Very soon! Now, show me you really love him."

Big Al raised me from my chair and held me close as I kissed him. We held each other so tightly that I almost felt safe. For a moment I did feel safe. I almost wished I could love him — almost — then the fear returned. I really was shaking by then.

I kept thinking, 'He means soon! If I don't do as they say, will they kidnap me again?'

The Don walked over and hugged me. I liked the Don very much, although the fear was always there.

"Such passion I see in her eyes. Yes, Judyenne, you do care. You love my nephew, I know. Don't you, Judyenne?"

"Yes," I murmured. "Oh, yes, I do, Mister Donatello. I do, Mister Donatello."

He gave me another tight hug and said to Big Al, "You picked a lovely bride." Then he said something in Italian and hugged Big Al.

It was time to dance, and the Don put my arm in Big Al's and led everyone out to where the band was playing. He asked me to dance first. He was a very good dancer and seemed to be having a real good time. What could we expect? With the costume I had, he seemed to enjoy holding me while I was half-naked, but it was a gorgeous costume. After this I danced with Al not once, but twice. The girls were dancing with some of the men. Then the orchestra started playing mood music from the 30's to give us a break for about twenty minutes or so while we went to change. Dimples and Maria weren't nearly as frightened as Olga and I. We were the ones who were scared, but the other girls hadn't been in Mexico at the hands of an insistent Big Al, either.

When we got back to our stateroom Olga said, "This is terrible, Judyenne! You have to understand what these men mean!"

"Yes, I do. I understand *exactly* what they mean."

She said, "The only thing you can do is put the date up, change the date. Tell them you want to get married on Valentine's Day or New Year's Eve, but push the date up! Well, figure out something."

After the girls and I got our gypsy costumes on, the orchestra struck up our opening of the gypsy number. We danced the full gypsy dance to the most beautiful music, and our skirts sailed out like a wind was flowing when we twirled. The music was exciting; and actually, Maria, Dimples and I were enjoying the dancing.

After our bows, a beautiful almond cake with slivered almonds on a large crystal plate was rolled out by the stewards along with a beautiful silver service. The stewards served Maria and Dimples. Surprisingly, the Don's own men were serving the Don, Al, Olga and me.

'Family serving us? Perhaps in the tradition of accepting me as *family*,' I thought.

Afterwards we changed costumes, and Olga cautioned, "Just continue to *agree*. Do nothing else but agree, or you may never get off of this yacht." Then she added, "A couple of times, Judyenne, I felt you led him on to get out of going out with him."

I said, "Yes, I did! I had to! The only other times were when I sat in his car and tonight on this yacht, but I only tried to get away. It was the only thing I could think of."

She said, "I have an idea. I think I should mention something about a Christmas Show, and earliest you can get away for the announcement of your wedding would be New Year's Day or Epiphany, as we said before."

I was actually forcing myself through the routine, but all of us thought we were pretty good that night. We still had the Beverly Hills mansion party ahead of us.

As we were leaving the ship there was a hugging and kissing scene between Al and me, and I had to kiss the Don, too. He was nice. I'm not saying these people were angels, but they had lovely manners in front of me. They were cultured people when they wanted to be. These were not some ruffians with a gun in our ribs. I knew what their reputations were although, as Big Al and his uncle said, they were from a famous Sicilian family.

Olga said, "If you don't let him think you mean it, you're in trouble!"

"Well, I'm in trouble either way. The Don may have actually believed that I wanted to marry his nephew of my own free will. He and I could have both been innocent parties."

"Yeah," she said, "You may be right, but when the dust settles on the *steppes*, it isn't going to make any difference. If you marry him you are in trouble; and if not, you may not even be alive to run!"

I really took that to heart, and I was petrified inside. I really believed then, and still do, that Big Al loved me. I'd be another possession, but I was the one he wanted at that time. I kind of felt guilty. I promised myself to this man in fear, as I did with the Don.

We got taken back on the water taxi. After the water taxi ride she gave us each fifty dollars, big money then. I wondered what she got, but I never did find out.

When we got near the pier, I could see a man standing a little bit to the left of the debarkation area. He was looking all around, and when we got on the pier he came walking over to Olga.

"You're Olga?"

"Yes."

"Our limousine is right over here. I've been waiting. I was told that you were taken to a different ship."

"Yes, that's right. We did our show in plenty of time, but they wanted us to have dinner with them."

"Oh, well, I hope you have a lot of room in your stomachs, because they're having a huge banquet where you're going."

I said, "Oh, no!"

Then she piped up, "Any caviar?"

That Olga and caviar!

"Oh, yes, ma'am," he responded grandly, then put us into the limousine and whisked us away.

I understood that the mansion was the Atwater Kent Estate. Olga said it was a big mansion with ten bedrooms, all private baths and three powder rooms. We had to change completely again, but there was an hour before the show. We just put on our terry cloth robes and tried to unwind.

Olga was sitting in the chair looking at me. Then she said, "Well, *this* is a night to remember!"

"Yes, but it's not over, and I'm the bait!"

Maria and Dimples started to laugh; and Dimples said, "You'll have to go to Vegas with us, yet!"

"That's not any better," I groaned. "I think Dominic has interests there, too."

There weren't that many gambling places in those days. Gambling was in the developmental stage. With the advent of Benjamin Segal's Flamingo in Vegas, the gambling ships soon went out of fashion. That and the fact that the Coast Guard and the Feds caused them trouble.

There was a tap on our door, and a maid came in. She was a sweet little Mexican girl, not much over sixteen years old. She said, "They will be ready for you. You ready to dance?"

I saw her again later as she was peeking from behind a curtain, watching us dance.

We put on new makeup and got into our belly dance costumes. We walked out into a large ballroom with a live band. It was very glamorous. There were about sixteen people filing in from different locations, seating themselves in chairs to watch us. They started to clap as we entered. They should have clapped, as we were really pretty girls. I noticed a lot of champagne and other drinks for the guests as I marched by the French doors where a bouncer stood.

When we finished dancing in the belly dance costumes we went back to put on our gypsy outfits. The gypsy dancing was lively and really fun.

We had done all our routines before they served any food this time. It was also suggested we dance with all the gentleman guests. One man who had too much to drink tried to take the emerald out of my navel before we changed.

Waiters brought out all this wonderful food, tray after tray of magnificent things. I wish I had some today. I guess it's true, what you didn't finish eating yesterday, you'll yearn for tomorrow. I was so excited. I recognized Joan Blondell, Ivan Kahn and Bruce Cabot.

There were small tables situated in the corners, and people started sitting down. The lights went on outside, the curtains were all pulled open and the French doors opened. There was a huge swimming pool outside with fountains spraying up in the air that had colored lighting. It was absolutely beautiful. The host, a very influential man, was late. We didn't know who Mister Perry was, because he never did show up to meet us. I wasn't sure who owned this magnificent mansion.

Looking up, who was coming toward me, but Tony Conera! He was moving right in with a strange look in his eyes. Olga was standing there when he walked up. He said, "I guess I deserve a dance." Then he turned to Olga and added, "I see she's got those high heels on."

"Yes, she has, and you'd better be careful!" Olga joked.

I had to dance with him, and he knew it. All of these men were good dancers and strong leads, like I needed. He kept kissing my ear as we danced; so I said, "Stop it, or Big Al will get you!" Well, he stopped right away then! So I did dance with Tony Conera, not one dance, but two. Several other people came up with whom I danced, as did Dimples and Maria. Shortly after that there was a lot of handshaking and meeting different people. There were some pictures taken with us holding hands. I wish I had the pictures. I had a picture taken of me with Bruce Cabot and Tony Conera.

The party ended, and everybody was in very good spirits as we were escorted out to the limousine. The driver even helped us with the costumes. I couldn't wait to get home to the kitchen table at Olga's. This was just too much for me. It was another one of those times when we had more coffee and sat around the table, tired, but we just had to talk.

I said to Olga, "I just can't dance like this in the area anymore. Everywhere we go it's either Big Al or Tony Conera, and this is not what I came to Hollywood for."

"But you don't understand — these gamblers, these syndicate people — they're part of Hollywood. You're going to meet them no matter where you go. You may meet a lot of other people, and I wouldn't be surprised if the next party isn't up on Holmby Hills."

"Well, isn't that where Benjamin lives?"

"Yes."

"I really don't know about this. Are you sure this is what Madam Zurenski would want me to do?"

"She always had dancers go there to perform."

"Well, not me," I said with finality.

XXXII - Escape to Arizona

el veinte y dos de diciembre de 1939

Paul returned from Arizona; and when he learned of the recent events he said, "My God, we've got to get her out of here! They're going to force her to marry Big Al!"

"That does it, I'm leaving!" I agreed. "Olga, I'll come back, but I think I'd better get away from here for a few weeks. John Paul has to go back to his store again, and I could go live with Alfred and Ruthie for a couple of weeks. Say there's a family emergency. Maybe I can rent a room there. Can't you take all my calls? Here's Benavidas' number, but please, please, don't give it to anybody!"

After John Paul's remark we came back to reality. We drank our coffee and continued making plans, but I felt sad about leaving.

"I have so much stuff," I moaned. "I can't take everything, but I'm going to take some of my Mexican things." I had bought two pairs of long silver earrings I loved; and I knew Ruthie would love them, too. I packed those in for Ruthie. Everything else was stored in my room. I had a key to my room and locked it.

"I don't know what to do about Tootsie," I told Olga. "I've got him setting outside my room. I can't let anything happen to Tootsie."

She said, "Put Tootsie in my room, and I'll take care of him until you get back. When will you be back?"

"I hate to let you down on the Christmas show, Olga, but I almost feel my life is in danger. I'm going to spend Christmas there, for sure; I don't dare stay here. And maybe Big Al will cool off after New Year's."

"I think it's a good idea," Olga agreed. "This is just getting too serious. You know that's kidnapping. What he did was kidnapping!"

I said, "Don't even mention the word. Just don't say anything."

"Well," she agreed, "I wouldn't say anything. I've got a business to run, and I've got to protect my own life." She ran a hand across her neck, simulating a knife cut, then added, "I think you should stay away a while. I think at least three to four weeks! He'll get over this; he'll find some other babe to fall in love with."

"Well, I don't know about that. *Maybe* in a month or five weeks he'd start looking for someone else. But I'm worried about the Don. Now he could be real trouble."

"Oh, why did all this have to happen?" I lamented. "I want to stay, Olga. I know my break will come. I just know it."

Well, both Olga and John Paul said, nearly in unison, "You will, Judyenne, you'll get your movie break, but let this Mafioso cool off."

It was going to be another one of those crazy early mornings. John Paul suggested, "Even if you're not awake, let's just take a shower and change clothes, but let's leave our travel clothes on — just take a nap. Let's leave at 3 a.m.

"Yes, 3 a.m." We put the things I'd need in his car out back. He packed two Mexican blankets, as I did.

We left at three in the morning. I paid Olga in advance and got a receipt for two fifty a week for three weeks. I said again, "Olga, tell everyone my mother is ill — I'm back east."

Thank God for the money Baba gave me. I had my own new suitcase, my hatbox, teddy bear, Baba's ring and Baba's scarf and picture. These were things that meant a lot to me. I had a lot of things they had given me of Baba's except the furniture packed in his car and much more in my room. I hugged Olga goodbye, and she said, "I'll phone you, but stay undercover. I'll miss you, Judyenne," as we hugged again. I started to cry, saying, "I always have to leave someone I love." Olga was crying, too, and hugging John Paul and me again.

John Paul said, "This is a call for action, and we've got to get out of town."

When we drove from Olga's he was afraid to put the headlights on as he backed up in her alley. He drove in the dark all the way down the alley, stopped at the street, looked both ways and made a right turn. He crept down the street three blocks before he put on the headlights. In fact, he made two side street turns in case we were being followed.

He said, "I know a couple of different alternate routes to Phoenix, so it may take longer, but at least we'll get there alive."

It was a scary run, trying to get out of town. By then Big Al could have come straight back and could have been watching the house. Or, he could have had someone else watch her house. All I remember is, it was a fast drive through strange towns. Only dark shadows under moonlight. I felt alone once again, speeding along into the unknown.

John Paul made another turn, saying, "We're going to Elsinore, then to Escondido. Then from there to Ocotillo Wells, Brawley, El Central, then Yuma and Buckeye into Phoenix."

It was a round about route on back roads and through small desert towns of the time. We were on the highway that would become Interstate 8 from San Diego to Yuma for a while, and I asked, "How did you ever know all these roads"

He said, "Both my brothers, Chester and Wilbur, were very sick years ago, so we took them to the desert places, hoping for a cure. They had TB and black lung disease from the coal mines in West Virginia."

I thought to myself, 'Grain by grain, I am learning more about my *business arrangement* husband.'

He said, "We took them to Escondido, Palm Springs, and of course, Phoenix; so I know all these roads."

And that's how we finally ended up, many, many hours later, in Phoenix. In almost twice the time it would have taken by the direct route. There were a few mistakes, and we had to turn around and go back a couple of times. Of course there were stops for gas and the rest room and no stops to eat, except a good Mexican restaurant we found in Brawley. At any rate, when we got to the outskirts of Buckeye, he stopped to get us two tacos and called Alfred Benavidas. John Paul said, "Alfred, I hate to impose, but I need a place for Judyenne to stay for a couple of days. She can pay rent!"

"No, no, you're always welcome and forget the rent!" Alfred replied.

We tried to make ourselves presentable and then continued to drive over to Alfred's house. Well, I sure saw a lot of cactus. They were beautiful silhouetted against a moonlit sky. It was kind of spooky, though, especially when you think somebody could be following you. Every car we saw that looked shiny and new, or any new sports car, caused us to freeze. Every time we saw anything that even looked remotely like one of Big Al's cars we both had icy chills go up our backs. John Paul drove like we were in a race.

At last we arrived at Alfred and Ruthie Benavidas' house; and we pulled right into the driveway up to the back by the garage, which was completely out of sight from the street. Then I just grabbed my purse and went immediately into the back door. There they stood waiting for us, so it really felt safe there.

Ruthie took me to the same guestroom next to their room, the one I had before. it was much larger than the other spare bedroom. It had a cute old-fashioned vanity with a bench and adorable English Chintz curtains. It was a darling room.

Ruthie said, "If you want to stay over night, Paul, it's perfectly fine. I don't know what the problem is, but you can tell us." And, leaning toward me, Ruthie put her arm around me and said, "You can trust us, Judyenne. We can keep secrets, whatever it is. You're safe here."

Tears were in my eyes as I said, "Oh, thank you, Ruthie." I hugged her again and said, "Thank you so much."

"You can take a shower and change, if you want," she offered. "You're probably feeling dusty from all that sand driving through so much desert."

Alfred's son was still away from home, so he took John Paul to his bedroom.

I soon got organized, took a shower, got into my mu mu and later came out to the living room. Alfred had homemade split pea soup; and he called to John Paul and me, "Soup's on."

I swear, the rich aroma of that soup just about pulled us into the dining room. He added pinto beans to his green peas and used ham hocks for the meat and stock. I don't know what all was in there, but there were chillies, some cillantro, lots of garlic and other things. It tasted wonderful. They had coffee and all different kinds of tasty sandwiches, especially thin sliced baked ham. They thought the soup might help us gain strength, and it did.

We just laid it all on the line, told them everything that had happened and why I was there. Alfred's eyes bulged out as big as saucers, and Ruthie was getting mad. "How dare they treat her that way; she's just a child."

Of course I didn't think I was a child. But that's what they thought. John Paul was almost nineteen years older than I was, and Ruthie and Alfred were the same age; so they were quite a bit older. They were a lot of fun, had many hobbies and loads of friends, so I felt safe at last. I really liked the Benavidas'.

I ran back into my room, got the little box of earrings and realized I hadn't gotten anything for Alfred. Anyway, I gave Ruthie the earrings.

Alfred and Ruthie were so understanding of the whole situation, but she finally suggested we all go to bed early and try to solve the problem tomorrow. After my prayers and putting Baba's scarf and my bear on my bed, I slowly fell asleep. It was December 21st, and I was safe — for a while. But that was another date which was burned into my memory, the day we reached safety.

On the morning of the twenty-second it just hadn't dawned on me when I went into the kitchen that there were only three more days 'till Christmas. Alfred was busying himself around the stove, and Ruthie was sitting there with what I thought was a glass of juice with vodka in it, which painfully reminded me of Baba.

Later I found out that she drank a lot more than most people knew, but now she said, "Here, I'll get you some coffee."

I said, "No, no, you sit there, and I'll help myself. You shouldn't wait on me. I should be helping you for letting me stay here."

Alfred said, "No, you don't have to do anything, after what you've been through. You'd better take a day of nothing." He added that he thought I should lay low and not go anywhere for at least twenty-four hours.

"I don't think Big Al could find us here," I said, but not completely convinced.

"Well," he said, "We don't know. John Paul said that you gave that lady you worked for, Olga, our phone number. This Big Al could trace it. He'd have the ability to do that, with all the people he knows. I think we've got to be very careful. I'm going to take my car out of the garage and put yours in. Use my car the next few days. You know what? It's almost Christmas."

"Oh, my Heavens, I'd almost forgotten!" I exclaimed.

"We still have three days 'till Christmas, and the day after tomorrow is John Paul's birthday," Alfred related.

"His birthday's Christmas Eve?" I questioned, greatly surprised.

"Yes," said Alfred.

'Some more information on John Paul,' I thought.

Alfred was a wonderful gardener, and so was Ruthie. There were flowers everywhere in their yard. He grew the tallest Hollyhocks I think I ever saw in my life. He was also as great a cook as Ruthie. Both spoke several languages.

On the twenty-third we sat around the breakfast table eating apple coffeecake Alfred had just made and discussing the dangers in which I found myself. Alfred was afraid Big Al could trace the phone number to get our address. So we did the car thing — put it in the garage and always used Alfred's. John Paul and Alfred both had to go to work during the weekdays. That left Ruthie and me alone, and we felt afraid when the men weren't there. At any rate, Alfred suggested that, whatever we needed, he and John Paul would do the shopping. Ruthie and I planned Christmas Eve and John Paul's birthday. I had Christmas gifts, but nothing for Alfred!

I said, "I may not have enough gifts, so I'd like to make you both a pineapple upside down cake."

"Ruthie and I, we love pineapple upside down cake," Alfred gushed.

"I promise, give me twenty-four hours here to unwind, and I'll make you the biggest upside down cake you ever saw. All I need is a huge iron skillet, pineapple, lots of nuts, preferably walnuts, brown sugar, butter and maraschino cherries, plus the regular ingredients for a cake."

Ruthie said, "We don't need to make another cake, then. Maybe we can use that for John Paul's birthday, and you and I can make some pies for Christmas. We'll just bake up a storm and decorate the place. It will be fun."

"Well, I hate to bother you folks on Christmas," I lamented.

"Oh, no, we want you and John Paul for Christmas dinner; and you can stay as long as you need to," she insisted. Then she added, "John Paul's going to have to go visit his mother. And we have to get something for her. We'll have a busy week or so for sure."

"His mother? I didn't even know his mother lived here. I thought she was in West Virginia," I said, quite surprised.

"You didn't know that she lived in Tempe? Well, I kind of forget how much you don't know," Ruthie apologized.

"Where's Tempe?" I asked.

"Tempe is only about twenty-five miles from here, approximately."

"Well, John Paul and I don't really know much about each other, partly because we've been running like crazy from you know who," I explained.

Ruthie was like me, and so was Alfred in many respects. They had gifts stashed away, and they always had food stored. These people planned ahead. Thank You, God. Of course their store closed at noon on Christmas Eve Day, so that gave us a little breather.

"I'd like to meet his mother, too," I said, "But, considering the security precautions, I wonder."

We talked it all over on Christmas Eve, and Alfred said to me, "You can't go out at all."

I said, "Well, this is awful. I like Christmas."

"You can decorate the tree and the house with Ruthie," he suggested.

Alfred and John Paul got the tree. Normally, if there'd not been all this excitement coupled with fear, they probably would have picked it up days before and Ruthie and I could have gone, too. Anyway, the two men brought in this beautiful eight-foot tree and set it up on its stand, then Alfred put a big sheet under it. Ruthie and I decorated the tree, and Alfred went for the groceries. For a man, he could shop like a female "home-ec major"! He got a huge turkey, lots of ingredients to stuff it and an array of other things. He also cooked very much like I did, as he bought the extra bag of gizzards, extra bag of chicken and turkey livers, and so forth. This made the stuffing and the gravy much richer. Of course, he had a lot of Mexican foods, too. He'd gone to the Mexican bakery and bought a lot of their sweet rolls, so I could see that this was going to be quite a Christmas.

Ruthie said, "We're all alone; and our son is out of the state, not going to be home for Christmas, so we're happy you're both here."

Well, we had the best Christmas Eve. We sang Christmas carols around the tree and still had the pineapple cake for John Paul's birthday. Ruthie and I made a lot of pies, though, for the next day. There were two mince and three apple. And there were three peach pies as Alfred had bought a bushel of peaches some time before in northern California when he was there and canned them.

The turkey was fixed on Christmas Day morning. They played records of Mexican carols in Spanish as well as other music from Mexico. It was really very festive.

Then friends and relatives of Ruthie and Alfred started calling around four on Christmas Day.

This Christmas was very different from other Christmases and the one we had been planning earlier in California. All the dreams of going for Christmas dinner to the Ambassador had been changed. There was no Baba to wish Merry Christmas and no Madam Zurenski. There was no John Moran Severette. No mother, no aunt, no grandma and no grandpa. But, how fortunate it was that John Paul had taken me to the Benavidas'; and what wonderful friends they had turned out to be! I thought, 'You have to be grateful for what you've got.' And I was.

It was a marvelous Christmas Eve, a terrific Christmas Day, and John Paul enjoyed his birthday, too.

The smells of Christmas filled the house, especially the spruce tree scent, pine. We reheated the mince pies to have another piece for each of us as we sat around the Christmas tree.

I said, "I thank God for you both having me here."

Then the phone rang, and Alfred answered it. It was Olga, and she was hysterical! He put me on the phone as Olga screamed, "You must hide! Hide, Judyenne!"

"But, Olga, does he know where I am?" I asked.

"No, no, I won't tell! But he yelled at me that he's coming back. I'm going to Sophie's to calm down. I just want to warn you! He said he's going to find you and they're going to take you to Reno and you will marry him! I'll get in touch later. I've got to go!" The phone clicked.

I repeated this to a transfixed audience, Alfred, Ruthie and John Paul.

"Oh, no," Ruthie moaned. "What will we do?"

Alfred said, "Calm down, calm down; I've got a plan. We must find a safer place for you both, like in the middle of an orange grove; and I know where there is one!"

So, our peaceful Christmas was not so peaceful after all! But still, by eleven p.m. every one went to their room. I was happy just to curl up under the covers. I said a prayer of thanks to God for protecting us, asking blessings on all of us, including Olga; then dozed off to a peaceful sleep.

XXXIII - The Orange Grove

el veinte y cinco de diciembre de 1939

Putting a stack of Mexican ballads and Guy Lombardo records on the RCA, Ruthie said, "We must stop worrying. Music will make us think better." So we thought and thought about my situation, hiding from Big Al. Then Ruthie continued, "It might work. We know an owner of a big orange grove way out on Northern Avenue. He and his wife came to several of our Mexican dances. They have a cute gardener's cottage that their daughter lived in for a while. She's out of town, in college now in New York; and I bet you and John Paul could rent it!"

I said, "I won't have a phone, and I'll get my mail General Delivery. Big Al won't find me."

"Yes, yes," Ruthie said. "It might work." We relaxed as the strains of "It Had To Be You" filled the room.*

Ruthie called them, and surprisingly it was vacant. "What would the rent be?" she asked. "A young lady we know, soon to be working for Governor Osborn, would like to rent it. She needs something reasonable... . Oh, can we see it? ... Thank you, Ginny, we'll be over soon." Hanging up the phone she said, "Judyenne, it's only thirty-five dollars a month, and fifteen for the utilities."

We went to see it. Ruthie introduced me as Mrs. J.P. Jamison. As we looked through, John Paul looked strange; no one mentioned him. He just followed me as we were shown around.

It was an adorable little one-bedroom cottage with French doors, a rocker, a new fold down chintz couch and a darling corner fireplace. The air was filled with the scent of orange blossoms outdoors, and there was a picnic table shaded by fruit laden trees.

"What a perfect place to write," I said, half thinking to myself. "I always write letters, poems, short stories; it helps me to cope. I'm a book lover," I added, speaking to Mrs. Ginny Atkinson, the owner.

"How wonderful, I love to write and paint," she answered.

I thought, 'Thank God! An answer to my prayers! A safe haven!'

We'd move in right away, so I took John Paul aside and said, "You can stay here while we're working for Governor Osborn, but I have the bedroom, you

---

*Lyrics by Gus Kahn, music by Isham Jones. □1924 Bantam Music.

have the couch. We share the rest of the house. Remember, you're like my agent."

"That's fine, Judyenne, I agreed to that."

We paid the rent and utility in advance, leaving a hundred dollars hidden and fifty-five of Baba's money in my purse. Things finally were falling into place. And, besides eating big navel oranges, I was now working on the Governor's committee. Of course his staff continued because there were new appointments in the administration.

The next day Ruthie came over to help organize the cottage and brought me some dishes. She brought emergency bedding, towels, soap, etc. Even a box of tea and tea pot and a pound of coffee. There was a coffee percolator on the stove.

We were sitting on the couch by the fireplace drinking our tea and eating springerle cookies I'd made. Ruthie said, "You know, Judyenne, maybe by summer you'll feel much closer to John Paul and really want to be his wife. In my forty years, I've seen many friendships turn into a love match. We've known him for some time, and I think you two need each other."

"It's something to think about, Ruthie. We'll see. But my main concern is getting into the movies. I love acting, and it was Baba's dream. She believed in me. I must try, and I must be true to Baba's memory. I'd also like to know what happened to John Moran Severette. It's really hard to believe that he just abandoned me. How could he throw away all of our dreams? I'm going to have to hide out here from Big Al, but even *he* won't find *this* place." Now I was talking to myself more than to Ruthie.

"Maybe I should read my teacup," I said as I gazed into the flickering fire and felt the safety of this gardener's cottage.

As the logs crackled, the door opened; and in walked Alfred and John Paul. Alfred, all excited, exclaimed, "You, John Paul and I are going to get a reward for all our work getting Governor Osborn elected."

Bubbling with excitement, Alfred said, "Here's a gift for you, Judyenne. John Paul had it at the business."

"Yes, John Paul added, it's a belated Christmas present."

It was a cute little red plastic radio. "Now you can listen to the news you always want to hear and music, too."

I was elated! "Oh, this is wonderful, thank you so much, John Paul. Just what I wanted!"

Turning to John Paul and me, Alfred said, "You two, I know, will get some post in the government."

John Paul sat down on the couch, looked at me and said, "Judyenne, you won't have to worry about a thing. You won't ever have to worry again."

I looked at Ruthie as John Paul slipped his arm around my shoulder. "Ruthie, maybe some of your ideas could happen."

Ruthie smiled and looked at Alfred, who beamed and winked back.

Figure 37 Sugar bell - hand made by Grandpa Weigmann, won 1st prize at Chicago Chef's convention.

Appendix

Grandpa's Old Fashioned Baked Beans

2 Cups dry beans, soaked overnight, rinsed and drained
1 quart and 1 cup fresh water - Cook 45 minutes, drain and save liquid to add later

Add:
cup fresh water
1 large fresh tomato, chopped
1 large chopped onion
3 green onions, chopped
3 Tablespoons catsup, or more
2 Tablespoons dry mustard
1 Tablespoon salt
1 cup Risling white wine
or 1 cup of malt beer
1/2 cup blackstrap molasses
1/4 cup brown sugar
1/4 cup honey
1/4 cup maple syrup
or 1/8 cup dark Karo syrup
1 full cup salt pork, diced
or two large ham hocks, or both
1 Tablespoon minced celery
1 Tablespoon vinegar
1 Tablespoon Worchester Sauce
1 Tablespoon minced green pepper
1 Tablespoon minced sweet red pepper
1 garlic clove, chopped
1 large can of tomatoes, chopped

Put beans and all ingredients in a large cast iron pot with a lid and cook on low 20 minutes on the stove while a hole, 2 feet wide by 2 feet deep is dug in the yard. Line the hole with rocks and in the bottom build a wood fire and put charcoal on top. Put a heavy grate on top of the fire and transfer the pot from the stove to the grate. A level flat rock may be used in place of the grate. When the fire has burned down to coals, fill in around the sides with stones, but do not smother the fire. Continue with stones and sand until it is banked on the outside and this circular wall is about a foot high. Add more wood or bricketts to fire as beans cook. Continue cooking for about four to five hours. Add reserved liquid as beans cook down. Potatoes and/or corn may be buried around the bottom of the pot to cook during the last hour.

Hattie's Barbecue Sauce

Soak ribs or chops in 1/2 cup buttermilk and 1/2 water (or more, to cover), add and stir in:

1 cup black strap molasses
1 cup honey
1 cup brown sugar
1 cup catsup
1 Tablespoon dry mustard
Bayleaf (or Bayleaves)
Garlic cloves, chopped
2 Tablespoons Balsamic vinegar
1/4 cup apple cider vinegar
1 cup apple juice

Add salt and pepper to taste. Smoke flavor optional. Cover, set in a cold place for five (5) hours, then cook in your usual barbecue facility.

Mother Clara's Marshmallow Melts

12 - crispy crackers, lightly buttered
12 - 1" square pieces of sharp cheddar cheese
12 – marshmallows
12 - 1/4" squares of cheddar
12- Maraschino cherry halves

Place 1" square of cheese on cracker, place 1 marshmallow on top of cheese, put 1/4" square of cheese and cherry on toothpick and drive it through the marshmallow. Leave toothpick in place in marshmallow. Prepare all, place on a cookie sheet, place in a broiler 5 or 6 inches from flame. Keep door open, watch closely for marshmallow to melt and get golden, but not completely melted. Remove to serving tray and serve hot.

Body and Face Wash and Body Pack

Peel one fresh pineapple and one fresh mango. (Reserve fruit for low-calorie drink recipe below.) Soak peelings in 1/2 cup water, pound with pestle, place in blender with juice of 1/2 lemon, sprig of mint, handful of rose petals and/or nasturtiums, and add:

1 teaspoon cinnamon
1 teaspoon ginger
Drops of pure almond oil, optional
1 cup Witch Hazel
1 cup water

Blend well in blender, strain into a fruit jar. Remove pulp from strainer and put in small dish. Take Jar and Dish into bathroom, fill tub with warm water. While tub is filling, massage pulp into all body areas. Wash hair and face with juice. Relax in warm bath with wash cloths on face and neck.

Low Calorie Drink

Put the fruit reserved from the above recipe into blender with juice of 1/2 lemon, 1 pint water, blend well; add a liter of 7-up, Canada dry or Vernor's Ginger Ale. Drink for lunch. Cleanses intestines.

Russian Tea Cookies

Sift 3 cups of pastry flour, use as needed

1 cup butter
1/2 teaspoon baking soda
1 cup granulated white sugar
1/2 teaspoon cream of tartar
2 eggs, well beaten
1/2 teaspoon salt
3/4 cup powdered sugar
1 teaspoon grated lemon peel
1/2 cup half & half or canned milk
1 teaspoon vanilla
2 teaspoons anise flavor

Cream butter and sugar, sift dry ingredients into first cup of flour, add eggs, peel and vanilla, add dry and wet ingredients alternately until a stiff dough is formed. Cover and chill 30 minutes. Roll 1/2 of the dough 1/4" thick and cut with cookie cutter. Place on lightly greased cookie sheet or ungreased non-stick sheet. Sprinkle sugar on top and decorate with 1/2 maraschino cherry. Bake until firm, 350 degrees F. Repeat with other half of the dough.

Lady Harriett Latimer-Jackson's
Parisian Sweet Holiday Treats

1 pound dried figs
1 pound dates
1 pound English walnuts, or
combination of walnut, hazel, almond, cashews
1 pound confectioners' sugar
1 teaspoon brandy or grape juice

Chop nuts fine in meat grinder, or other utensil, remove stones and stems from figs and dates and chop fine in same grinder as nuts. Reserve 1/2 cup of confectioners' sugar to roll sweets in. Mix fruit and nuts on bread board and work sugar in. Roll in balls, and finish coat with reserved sugar. Pack in gift boxes or serve on fancy plate.

Lily's Canned Tomato Soup

3 cans of Campbell's Tomato Soup
1 can of stewed tomatoes
1-1/2 soup cans milk
1-1/2 soup cans water
1 pinch of baking soda (to keep the milk from curdling)
1 teaspoon of sugar

Combine all ingredients in large sauce pan and beat with wire whisk. Heat until hot (do not boil), stirring continuously with whisk. Serves four. Serve with oyster crackers.

About the Author

June Latimer-Jackson was born in Michigan. She published her first poem in the Detroit Free Press at age nine. June wrote a newspaper column, "Around The Hearth", for the *South Arizona Times*, which was advice, thoughts of the day and recipes. She took a crash course in nursing in World War II; served many departing servicemen with coffee and doughnuts at the train station. She has published a cookbook and has written the *Star Eyes*© series of children's books about her wonderful bear. June is working on other stories in various stages of development, including Books II, III, IV, V, and VI, of the *Secret Bloodlines*© series.

She raised six children and is a great grandmother several times over.

The author loves to cook and bake, also enjoys gardening of herbs, vegetables, grape vines, rhubarb, apple and cherry trees. She owned a restaurant by the San Lorenzo River in California, using many recipes of her grandfather, a European chef. She enjoys genealogy and has researched her family tree, traveling through England, Ireland, France, Austria, and Hungary. The colors for the dust jacket of *Secret Bloodlines*© come from the Latimer Coat of Arms and shield, which have a gold cross on a red background. Below the Latimer shield is the River Esk spanned by the Duck Bridge, below Danby Castle, built by some of her distant ancestors, the Latimers and Nevilles, between 1301 and 1330 A.D.

June lives in her home in Northern Michigan, Lilac Cottage, built in 1947 on a mini-farm that includes a few colorful Bantie and Auracana chickens. The property, once a logging camp, is now registered as The Ghost Town of Simons. The settlement of Simons was cut from the virgin white pine when it was founded in 1882. Since the 1920's a forest of maple trees and many wild flowers have re-grown to surround her home and what is left of the town, including the 1883 Simons one-room school house that June hopes to save.

June loves the 30's, 40's, 50's, and 60's music, and adores piano. Her favorite song is "It Had To Be You." She is interested in people, drama, history, medicine, travel, short wave radio, is an avid book reader and loves spy stories. She collects teddy bears, elephant, camel, deer, and moose statues, anything art deco style, teapots, W.W. II memorabilia, old maps, Nancy Drew books, sheet music and books by Gladys Tabor, her pen pal of years ago, and herb books by Gertrude Foster, who also encouraged her to write. Today she spends her time writing with Ki-boy, her American Eskimo dog, and Kittie Bittie, her cat. To learn more about her upcoming semi-monthly newspaper, "The Ghost Town of Simons Epitaph," visit June's website at:

http://www.geocities.com/danbycastle00/index.html

Figure 38 Author, June Latimer-Jackson

June says there is a new trend of returning to "old fashioned values" with a strong desire for responsible individual expression of all women of all nationalities and backgrounds wanting to improve the world around them. For her, some of these beliefs are: marriage is supposed to last and not be a pre-nuptial agreement though she knows sometimes it can't be; marriage is a real partnership, your own corporation; glamour and class are shown by the hint of a figure under a swirling dress, not by showing practically every square inch; being demure is sexy; a mother AND a father in the home are God's plan. June says, "Believing in a God is not old fashioned – it's always in fashion."

She just wishes she could meet every reader of her books, as well as hug every crying soul. She wants you to know she's the friend you haven't met, but whom you'll find in her books.

- —- - •••• • •— —- -• -•• • •-• ••-• ••- •-•• •-• • •-
-•• • •-• •••
T o t h e w o n d e r f u l r e a d e r s

—- ••-• ••• • -•-• •-• • - -••• •-•• —- —- -•• •-•• •• -
• • ••• —-•••
o f S E C R E T B L O O D L I N E S :
-••• —- —- -•- •• —••- - •••• • •••• —- •-•• •-•• -•— •— —
- —- -••
B O O K I , T h e H o l l y w o o d

-•— • •- •-• ••• —-••• •• - •••• •- -• -•- -•— —- ••- •-
•-•-

Y e a r s : I t h a n k y o u .

-•— —- ••- •— •• •-•• •-•• •-•• —- •••- • -••• —- —- -•-
•• ••
Y o u w i l l l o v e B o o k I I

•-•-•-
.

••• • • -•— —- ••- - •••• • -• •-•-•-
S e e y o u t h e n .

••• •• -• -•-• • •-• • •-•• -•— -••—
S i n c e r e l y ,

•—- ••- -• • •-•• ••- -•-• •• •-•• •-•• • •-•• •- - ••
— • •-• -••••-
J u n e L u c i l l e L a t i m e r —
•—- •- -•-• -•- ••• —- -• •-•-•-
J a c k s o n .

A Morse Code Message